Paula Guran is the senior editor for Prime Books. She edits the annual Year's Best Dark Fantasy and Horror anthology series. Guran has also edited around thirty other anthologies as well as numerous novels and single-author collections. She edited the Juno fantasy imprint from its small press inception through to its incarnation as an imprint of Pocket Books. The recipient of two Bram Stoker awards, Guran has been nominated twice for the World Fantasy Award. She lives in Akron, Ohio.

D1082310

Recent Mammoth titles

The Mammoth Book of Cthulhu

Edited by Paula Guran

ROBINSON   RUNNING PRESS
PHILADELPHIA · LONDON

ROBINSON

First published in Great Britain in 2016 by Robinson

Copyright © Paula Guran, 2016 (unless otherwise stated)

The moral right of the authors has been asserted.

A CIP catalogue record for this book
is available from the British Library.

ISBN 978-1-47212-003-8 (paperback)

Typeset in Whitman by Hewer Text UK Ltd, Edinburgh
Printed and bound in Great Britain by CPI Group (UK) Ltd, Croydon CR0 4YY
Papers used by Robinson are from well-managed forests and other sustainable sources

MIX
Paper from
responsible sources
FSC
www.fsc.org   FSC® C104740

Robinson
is an imprint of
Little, Brown Book Group
Carmelite House
50 Victoria Embankment
London EC4Y 0DZ

An Hachette UK Company
www.hachette.co.uk

www.littlebrown.co.uk

First published in the United States in 2016 by Running Press Book Publishers,
A Member of the Perseus Books Group

Books published by Running Press are available at special discounts for bulk
purchases in the United States by corporations, institutions and other organizations.
For more information, please contact the Special Markets Department at the
Perseus Books Group, 2300 Chestnut Street, Suite 200, Philadelphia, PA 19103,
or call (800) 810-4145, ext. 5000, or email special.markets@perseusbooks.com.

US ISBN: 978-0-7624-5620-8
US Library of Congress Control Number: 2015945284

9 8 7 6 5 4 3 2 1
Digit on the right indicates the number of this printing

Running Press Book Publishers
2300 Chestnut Street
Philadelphia, PA 19103-4371

Visit us on the web!
www.runningpress.com

Contents

Introduction: Who, What, When, Where, Why . . .
Paula Guran

___

CTHULHU WHO?

This anthology has little to do specifically with Cthulhu and everything to do with "new Lovecraftian fiction." But Cthulhu and the "Cthulhu Mythos" (more properly the "Lovecraft Mythos") has become a brand name recognizable far beyond genre in every facet of popular culture: mainstream literature, gaming, television, film, art, music; even crochet patterns, clothing, jewelry, toys, children's books, and endless other tentacled products . . . so one does what one can to sell books!

But, to answer the question posed . . . H. P. Lovecraft invented Cthulhu in 1926. The entity makes his first appearance in Lovecraft's short story, "The Call of Cthulhu," published in the pulp magazine *Weird Tales* in 1928. A small bas-relief of the creature is described in the story as:

> "[A]sort of monster, or symbol representing a monster, of a form which only a diseased fancy could conceive. If I say that my somewhat extravagant imagination yielded simultaneous pictures of an octopus, a dragon, and a human caricature, I shall not be unfaithful to the spirit of the thing. A pulpy, tentacled head surmounted a grotesque and scaly body with rudimentary wings; but it was the general outline of the whole which made it most shockingly frightful."

"Dead Cthulhu waits dreaming," immured underwater in the "nightmare corpse-city of R'lyeh . . . built in measureless eons behind history" by the Great Old Ones, "vast, loathsome shapes that seeped down from the dark stars" to Earth. Cthulhu is a priest to these ancient aliens, but is also worshipped as a deity by some humans as are the loathsome invaders from space. Such devotion is based in superstitious ignorance, age-old familial ties, the promise of power, or the need to hedge their human bet: the Old Ones are supposed to return (or perhaps arise) someday . . . and that will be the end of humanity as a whole.

Since the name Cthulhu was, according to Lovecraft, "invented by beings whose vocal organs were not like man's . . . hence could never be uttered perfectly by human throats," and the author himself provided several varying pronunciations, there's no "right" way to pronounce the name.

Cthulhu is, really, a symbol of "the vast unknowable cosmos in which all human history and aspirations are as nothing." [S. T. Joshi, *The Rise and Fall of the Cthulhu Mythos*]. And this is an important concept in the fiction of H. P. Lovecraft.

LOVECRAFT WHO?

[Note: Much of the following is self-plagiarized
from previous introductory essays.]

H. P. Lovecraft was, according to Fritz Leiber, "the Copernicus of the horror story," and can be credited with at least being *a* father of weird fiction, if not its only sire.

Born in 1890, Howard Phillips Lovecraft was little known to the general public while alive and never saw a book of his work professionally published.

His father, probably a victim of untreated syphilis, went mad before his son reached the age of three. The elder Lovecraft died in an insane asylum in 1898. (It is highly doubtful that Lovecraft was aware of his father's disease.)

Young Howard was raised by his mother; two of her sisters; and his maternal grandfather, a successful Providence, Rhode Island, businessman. His controlling mother smothered him with maternal affection, while also inflicting devastating emotional cruelty.

Sickly (probably due more to psychological factors than physical ailments) and precocious, Lovecraft read the *Arabian Nights* and *Grimm's Fairy Tales* at an early age, then developed an intense interest in ancient Greece and Rome. His grandfather often entertained him with tales in the gothic mode and Lovecraft started writing around the age of six or seven.

Lovecraft started school in 1889, but attended erratically due to his supposed ill health. After his grandfather's death in 1904, the family – already financially challenged – was even less well off. Lovecraft and his mother moved to a far less comfortable domicile and the adolescent Howard no longer had access to his grandfather's extensive library. He attended a public high school, but a physical and mental breakdown kept him from graduating.

He became reclusive, rarely venturing out during the day; at night, he walked the streets of Providence, drinking in its atmosphere.

He read, studied astronomy, and, in his early twenties, began writing poetry, essays, short stories, and eventually longer works. He also began reading Jules Verne, H. G. Wells, and pulp magazines like *The Argosy*, *The Cavalier*, and *All-Story Magazine*.

Lovecraft became involved in amateur writing and publishing, a salvation of sorts. Lovecraft himself wrote: "In 1914, when the kindly hand of amateurdom was first extended to me, I was as close to the state of vegetation as any animal well can be . . ."

His story, "The Alchemist" (written in 1908 when he was eighteen), was published in *United Amateur* in 1916. Other stories soon appeared in other amateur publications.

Lovecraft's mother suffered a nervous breakdown in 1919 and was admitted to the same hospital in which her husband had died. Her death, in 1921, was the result of a bungled gall bladder operation.

"The Horror at Martin's Beach" was published in the November 1923 issue of *Weird Tales*, which became a regular market for his stories. He also began writing letters at an astoundingly prolific pace to a continuously broadening group of correspondents.

Shortly thereafter, Lovecraft met Sonia Haft Greene – a Russian Jew seven years his senior – at a writers' convention. They married in 1924. As *The Encyclopedia of Fantasy*, edited by John Clute and John Grant, puts it, " . . . the marriage lasted only until 1926, breaking up largely because HPL disliked sex; the fact that she was Jewish and he was prone to anti-Semitic rants cannot have helped." After two years of married life in New York City (which he abhorred and where he became an even more intolerant racist) he returned to his beloved Providence.

In the next decade, he traveled widely around the eastern seaboard, wrote what is considered to be his finest fiction, and continued his immense – estimated at 100,000 letters – correspondence through which he often nurtured young writers.

Outside of letters and essays, his complete works eventually totaled fifty-odd short stories, four short novels, about two dozen collaborations or ghost-written pieces, and countless poems. Lovecraft never really managed to make a living. Most of his small livelihood came from re-writing or ghostwriting for others. He died, alone and broke, of intestinal cancer on 15 March 1937, and was buried at Swan Point Cemetery in Providence. Forty years later a stone was erected to mark the spot by his admirers. It reads: "I am Providence."

Why Lovecraft?

Lovecraft's literary significance today can be at least partially credited to this network with other contemporary writers. Letter writing was the "social media" of his time, and he was a master of it. Although he seldom met those who became members of the "Lovecraft Circle" in person, he knew them well – just as, these days, we have friends we know only through the Internet.

H. P. Lovecraft was probably the first author to create what we would now term an open-source fictional universe that any writer could make use of. Other authors, with Lovecraft's blessing, began superficially referencing his dabblers in the arcane, mentioning his unhallowed imaginary New England towns and their strange citizens, writing of cosmic horror, alluding to his godlike ancient extraterrestrials with strange names, and citing his fictional forbidden books of the occult (primarily the Necronomicon of the mad Arab Abdul Alhazred): the Lovecraft Mythos – or, rather, anti-mythology – was born.

There were certainly "better" writers of science fiction and fantasy of roughly the same era – like Algernon Blackwood, Clark Ashton Smith, Fritz Leiber, and Olaf Stapledon – whose work may be influential, but is now mostly ignored by the general public. Lovecraft's survival, current popularity, and the subgenre of "Lovecraftian fiction" is due in great part to his willingness to share his creations. His concepts were interesting, attracted other writers, and ultimately other artists.

Lovecraft's universe was fluid: the "Great Old Ones" and other elements merely serving his theme of the irrelevance of humanity to the cosmic horrors that exist in the universe. As S. T. Joshi wrote: "Lovecraft's imaginary cosmogony was never a static system but rather a sort of aesthetic construct that remained ever adaptable to its creator's developing personality and altering interests . . . there was never a rigid system that might be posthumously appropriated . . . the essence of the mythos lies not in a pantheon of imaginary deities nor in a cobwebby collection of forgotten tomes, but rather in a certain convincing cosmic attitude."

Lovecraft never used the term "Cthulhu Mythos" himself. (He was known to refer to his "mythos" as the Arkham Cycle – named for the main fictional town in his world – or, flippantly, as Yog-Sothothery – after Yog-Sothoth, a cosmic entity of his invention made only of "congeries of iridescent globes.") The term "Cthulhu Mythos" was probably invented by August Derleth or Clark Ashton Smith after Lovecraft's death. They and others also added their own flourishes and inventions to the mythology, sometimes muddling things with non-Lovecraftian concepts and attempts at categorization.

Derleth misused Lovecraft's name to promote his own work, and tried to change Lovecraft's universe into one that included hope and a struggle between good and evil. This accommodated Derleth's Christian worldview, but was at odds with Lovecraft's depiction of a bleak, amoral universe. However, to his credit, Derleth – with Donald Wandrei – also founded Arkham House expressly to publish Lovecraft's work and to bring it to the attention of the public. Without it, Lovecraft may never have had a legacy.

Authors like Robert Bloch (now best known as the author of *Psycho*), Robert E. Howard (creator of Conan the Barbarian), and younger writers such as Henry Kuttner, Fritz Leiber, and Ramsey Campbell all romped within the Lovecraftian milieu and added elements to it. Later writers with no direct connection to Lovecraft joined in as well.

LOVECRAFTIAN WHAT?

Lovecraft's best works were atmospheric tales that, to quote Stefan Dziemianowicz, "strove to express a horror rooted in humanity's limited understanding of the universe and humankind's arrogant over-confidence in its significance in the cosmic scheme." Lovecraft felt such stories conveyed "the fundamental premise that common human laws and interests and emotions have no validity or significance in the cosmos-at-large."

S.T. Joshi identifies four broad components of the Lovecraft Mythos:

- A fictional New England topography. (This eventually became a richly complex, historically grounded – if fictional – region.)
- A growing library of "forbidden" books and manuscripts. (Rare tomes or texts holding secrets too dangerous to know.)
- A diverse array of extraterrestrial "gods" or entities. (Often symbols of the "unknowability or an infinite cosmos, or sometimes the inexorable forces of chaos and entropy.")
- A sense of cosmicism. (The universe is indifferent, chaotic, and humans are utterly meaningless nonentities within it.)

A fifth element – a scholarly protagonist or narrator – is not unique to Lovecraft, but is another identifiable motif.

Although Lovecraft occasionally attempted to emulate writers of supernatural fiction, his truly influential work differed fundamentally from such earlier fiction.

In his introduction to *At the Mountains of Madness: The Definitive Edition*, China Miéville points out: "Traditionally genre horror is concerned with the irruption of dreadful forces into a comforting status quo – one which the protagonist scrambles to preserve. By contrast, Lovecraft's horror is not one of intrusion but of realization. The world has always been implacably bleak; the horror lies in us acknowledging the fact."

"Lovecraft's stories were noticeably devoid of vampires, were-wolves, ghosts, and other traditional supernatural monsters appearing in the work of his pulp contemporaries," noted Stefan Dziemianowicz in a *Publishers Weekly* article. "Though written in a somewhat mannered gothic style and prose empurpled with words like 'eldritch' and 'squamous,' his atmospheric tales strove to express a horror rooted in humanity's limited understanding of the universe and humankind's arrogant overconfidence in its significance in the cosmic scheme."

When: Merely a Man of His Times?

We also must acknowledge how H. P. Lovecraft's personal beliefs tie in to his work. Lovecraft – as evidenced in his fiction, poetry, essays, and letters – was racist, xenophobic, and anti-Semitic. He may not have hated women (misogyny), but he does seem to have feared them (gyno-phobia). His abhorrence of sexuality and physicality went beyond the Puritanical.

The author's prejudices have often been brushed aside as "typical" for a man of his era. Yes, Lovecraft lived an age when racism was more overt and racial segregation was the law, but Lovecraft's prejudice seems, at the very least, somewhat more pronounced than many of his contemporaries.

To again quote Miéville (from published correspondence):

> [The]depth and viciousness of Lovecraft's racism is known to
> me . . . It goes further, in my opinion, than "merely" being a
> racist – I follow Michel Houellebecq (in this and in no other
> arena!) [Note: Houellebecq is the author of *H. P. Lovecraft:
> Against the World, Against Life*, 2005]in thinking that Lovecraft's
> oeuvre, his work itself, is inspired by and deeply structured
> with race hatred. As Houellebecq said, it is racism itself that
> raises in Lovecraft a "poetic trance." He was a bilious anti-Sem-
> ite (though one who married a Jew, because, if you please, he
> granted that she was "assimilated"), and if you read stories like
> "The Horror at Red Hook," the bile you will see towards people
> of color, of all kinds (with particular sneering contempt for
> African-Americans unless they were suitably Polite and there-
> fore were patricianly granted the soubriquet "Negro") and the
> mixed communities of New York and, above all . . . "miscege-
> nation" are extended and toxic.

Bigotry is part of Lovecraft's fiction. Miscegenation, racial impurity, ethnic xenophobia, "mental, moral and physical degeneration" due to inbreeding, interbreeding with non-human creatures – spawn of degenerate women who consorted with the abhorrent – these were all integral to the fiction Lovecraft produced. Yes, we must consider the context: Lovecraft lived during what was probably the nadir of race relations and height of white supremacy in the US. But whether these were prevalent views of his day is beside the point: H. P. Lovecraft *chose* to make them horrors to be feared in his fiction, to alarm and distress the primarily male, supposedly "superior" possessors of light-skinned Nordic genes. One must assume Lovecraft never considered anyone else as a potential reader.

Just because we recognize Lovecraft's racism does not mean we must deny his influence or reject his work, but we must acknowledge and condemn his bigotry. In fact, to be cognizant of his prejudices is necessary to understand his fiction.

Elizabeth Bear – an author who has written a number of New Lovecraftian gems and feels Lovecraft's views are "revolting" – reminds us: "Authors are read, beloved, and remembered, not for what they do wrong, but for what they do right, and what Lovecraft does right is so incredibly effective. He's a master of mood, of sweeping blasted vistas of despair and the bone-soaking cold of space. He has at his command a worldview that the average human being, drunk on our own species-wide egocentrism, finds compelling for its sheer contrariness."

WHAT: NEW LOVECRAFTIAN

What I term "New Lovecraftian" fiction seldom attempts (although it does occasionally) to emulate Lovecraft's writing style – a style that's faults are, admittedly, many. Written with a fresh appreciation of Lovecraft's universe, its writers do not imitate; they reimagine, re-energize, renew, re-set, respond to, and make Lovecraftian concepts relevant for today.

New Lovecraftian fiction sometimes simply has fun with what are now well-established genre themes. Authors often intentionally subvert Lovecraft's bigotry while still paying tribute to his imagination. New Lovecraftians frequently take Lovecraft's view of fragile humans alone in a vast uncaring cosmos where neither a good god nor an evil devil exist, let alone are concerned with them, and devise highly effective modern fiction. But there are other themes to choose from as well.

You'll find a variety of Lovecraftian inspiration here. But you need not take that from me: each story in *The Mammoth Book of Cthulhu* is prefaced with an authorial explanation of their tale's Lovecraftian inspiration.

Where Can You Find This Stuff?

Here, of course. But elsewhere, too. (I've compiled two volumes of reprints of twenty-first-century New Lovecraftian fiction myself.) There are so many fine examples of both fairly recent short stories and novels, they are far too numerous to mention . . . both with and without "Cthulhu" in the title.

> While my chosen form of story-writing is obviously a special and perhaps a narrow one, it is none the less a persistent and permanent type of expression, as old as literature itself. There will always be a small percentage of persons who feel a burning curiosity about unknown outer space, and a burning desire to escape from the prison-house of the known and the real into those enchanted lands of incredible adventure and infinite possibilities which dreams open up to us, and which things like deep woods, fantastic urban towers, and flaming sunsets momentarily suggest.
>
> – H. P. Lovecraft, "Notes on Writing Weird Fiction" (1937)

Persistently,
Paula Guran
Summer Solstice 2015

"If we pare back Lovecraft's stories," notes **Lisa L. Hannett**, "pruning the dense prose, tossing out the objectionable elements, what we're left with are the tantalizing bits: the sea and the stars, the greatest heights and depths of this world of ours. 'In Syllables of Elder Seas' explores our tiny, cramped place within the cosmos, and our inability to ever really get out. And on each page – of this piece, and also Lovecraft's fiction more broadly – there's the sense that HPL himself is hunkered down beside us, pressed small by the weight of so many limitations."

Hannett has had over sixty short stories appear in venues including *Clarkesworld*, *Fantasy*, *Weird Tales*, *Apex*, *The Year's Best Australian Fantasy and Horror*, and *Imaginarium: Best Canadian Speculative Writing*. She has won four Aurealis Awards, including Best Collection for her first book, *Bluegrass Symphony*, which was also nominated for a World Fantasy Award. Her first novel, *Lament for the Afterlife*, was published by CZP in 2015.

In Syllables of Elder Seas
Lisa L. Hannett

———

To pass the wet hours crammed in his bottle, Aitch counts cylinders.

Tonight, only those he can actually see get tallied: not the darkened hurricane lamp dangling on its chain, not the perforated lid screwed tight on his jar. With some effort Aitch can tilt his head back, turn it side to side, but down is impossible with bent knees wedged under his chin. No points for his short thighs, his shorter shins, his cramped toes. He looks forward, left, right. Starts with what's closest. An easy ten: thin shadow fingers lifted out of the brine. Bobbing on the breath-rippled solution is another: a sealed, thumb-length leather tube, strung from a cord around his neck. Aitch worries the pouch in his cold grip, its familiar *squish* comforting. The caul that had helmeted him at birth is preserved inside – to protect him, Mother had promised, from drowning.

To the left of his container, moonglow floats in from the room's ocean-side porthole – the round window itself too high to view – illuminating a bank of bookcases lining the curved walls. On the floor, six glass vessels are now limned silver-blue: replicas in everything but size, perfect cylinders with threaded brass caps. Each slightly bigger than its predecessor, the largest slightly smaller than the one in which Aitch is currently squeezed. Seven in all.

Seven he's counted a hundred, hundred times.

Seven months, or more, in each – he's sure, he remembers – and he's seven years old, at least.

The eighth will no doubt be coming soon, the rate he's growing.

On the shelves, a regiment of forty-six candles are snuffed, stiff wax digits raised against shushing lips. He double-checks the number, though he played this game yesterday, and the day before that; the amount hasn't changed since. The Aunts are frugal with supplies, stingy with any light but the one beacon they shine every night out to sea.

Sometimes Aitch adds that bright beam to his total.

Always, he includes the lighthouse.

He fidgets, as much as possible, a squirming heave in his guts, imagining the view from the Aunts' lantern room above. The sheer drop from storm panes to ocean. The rocks below, jagged fangs primed to impale. The water's maw stretching wide, frothing and lashing. Basalt waves gnawing the headland. Salt talons steadily gouging the cliffs, grabbing, yanking . . .

It's hungry, he remembers saying, staring at the roiling expanse between the lighthouse and reef. Unblinking. Soon after, the Aunts stopped bringing him upstairs. *It wants to swallow us.*

Don't be ridiculous, they'd answered, referring to charts on a counter girding the great spinning lamp, marking currents and tides. Eyes filled with stars and swells, ever vigilant. *It's bland as milk out there. Linen-smooth sailing. Every seafarer's delight.*

Aitch didn't think so, but the Aunts still hush him whenever he mentions it. They see calm where he sees squalls. Fair winds instead of hurricanes. Sweet gulls in place of carrion crows. When he's unbottled and playing in his small chamber, they say he's *at work*. Now his tools are scattered on the bare wood floor, next to the washstand: four sticks of brown Conté and nine violet pastels to replace the set he's scribbled to stubs. These are *toys*, he tells them, not *tools*.

It's like they're not even listening.

When he draws his dreams, the Aunts interpret squares from his circles. Arrows and directions from houses. Submarines, they say, not the intended sharks. Chevrons and triangles and rampant squiggles – the language is his, he knows its true meaning, but the Aunts read into it whatever they want.

Quietly, Aitch wonders when Mother and Father will come to collect him.

Soon, the Aunts once assured him. *Soon enough.*

So many cylinders later, he has stopped asking.

Behind him, the door opens. Weird shadows stretch across the floor; yellow light catches in Aitch's bottle, blinding. Bright semi-circles precede two identical women, tall and black as wicks. They totter in tight-buttoned boots, lanterns balanced on dull pewter salvers. Stovepipe hats erect on slicked heads. Ankle-length skirts binding legs close, blouses buttoned to the jaw. Aitch squints and blinks, following their progression. At a little table beside the narrow cot he rarely sleeps in, they stop and set down their trays.

"What a treat we have for you," says the one on the left. Seventy? Seventy-one? Aitch has lost count, as he does every night at this point. Perhaps she's cylinder seventy-two?

"A real treat," agrees maybe-seventy-three. She retrieves a canteen from the bedside, pulls the cork, then thunks it down on Aitch's lid. A few seconds later, a long straw scrapes through a puncture overhead;

the Aunt pushes it, scratching his temple and cheek, down to his mouth. He drinks greedily, though the tea is weak and tastes of mud.

"Can I come out now?" Aitch asks, already knowing the answer. It hasn't been long enough, they'll say, only a few days. "Please?"

"Be good."

"A few minor aches now for an eternity of joy."

Through the holes, the women slip eight, nine, ten tiny pellets (eighty-one? eighty-two? eighty-four?) and wait for Aitch to consume them. The things bloat almost instantly. Yesterday, it was bloodworm capsules. The day before, it was kelp and compressed carrot. Other times, squid meal. Chaff and shrimp. The Aunts' idea of delicious.

Despite himself, Aitch submerges as far as he can and begins to eat the sodden pills. Mid-chew, he presses his face to the glass. Distorts his features. Bugs his eyes. Squashes his nose until snot oozes. Scrunches his brow. Splays hands beside his cheeks and stretches his tongue until it hurts. Gobbets tumble from his mouth, plopping into the brine. If he is hideous, he thinks, the Aunts will no doubt see beauty. Maybe he'll even earn a laugh, or a smile.

The Aunts watch and wait, and do not laugh.

They never tell him he's special, the way he's sure, he *remembers*, Mother and Father did. They never give him red wine in etched crystal goblets. They never bundle him into handsome four-in-hands, never let jolly horses clip-clop him along to the mayor's very own private *soirées*. They never dress him in long satin robes, robes that match theirs, robes that shimmer like precious gems under starlight. They never sing nor dance around him on the shoreline. They never tell him tales, drunk on midnight and comets, of frolicking in a May Eve sea.

Now that Mother and Father are many months and many train rides away, Aitch recalls them through the green-tinted glass of his container. Features warped, wide-set eyes with no lids, pinprick nostrils, drooped and toothless mouths . . . Not quite what they had been, what they are. But he still feels the gentle trace of Mother's fingertip along his caul scars. The feathered breeze of her breath as she kissed the stripes and ridges along his hairline, the raised dots beside his ears. The salmon-sharp tang of her skin.

We won't be long after you, Father had said, obviously using the Aunts' definition of *soon*.

What skies were above when you were born, Mother had said, voice thick with pride. Such old constellations! Such perfect alignments.

Draping the lucky talisman over his head, she'd promised he wouldn't drown.

You are so special, she'd said, then sent him away. You are so special, Aitch.

No, he thinks, chill water splashing as he shakes, realigning his thoughts. *No*, she didn't call him by letter. That's his guardians' method of address. Aitch. The initial a reflection of distance, a refusal of intimacy. No names, they'd said. They were the Aunts; he was barely a fragment of himself, a snippet of prayer uttered in syllables, sputters and remote stops. Nonsense jumbled together, he thinks. Nonsense kept apart.

Aitch had been complete with Mother and Father. He had made sense.

He's sure he remembers what that was like.

Underwater, Aitch's heart beats loud, a deep thrum-thrumming to accompany the chanting.

Satisfied that he'd eaten, the Aunts had withdrawn measuring tapes from their skirt pockets, held them up against the tank. Muttering, they'd made notes, given instructions, the routine now stale as the stench of his fish breath. *Stretch*, stretch *child, extend that spine*; Aitch had straightened until crown scraped lid, cropped blond hair poking through perforations. *Lower those shoulders. Expose that neck. Show us those hands. Turn* – painfully – *this way and that*.

Once they'd finished, pencils and implements and lamps and stern heels retreated. Within minutes, the air in Aitch's quarters thickens with a familiar hypnotic drone. Unintelligible words repeat from above and, it seems, from below. The endless chorus building, echoing, spinning out of the lighthouse while he weeps, cramped and shivering. Marinating in dark noise.

He begins to nod. Skull clunks against glass; he wilts forward, then clunks back again. Cold leaches, lulls. Dreams beckon him down, down, further down. Ancient fishhook voices snag Aitch's untethered, inner-most self and jerk it from his fragile, prune-skinned shell. They haul so quickly he can't resist the vertiginous *whoosh*. Bubbles scream past his ears; he plummets into a realm of coral-toothed beasts, razor-edged fins, pearl-eyed hunters that track by vibration, by liquid scent. Powerless, he is zipped around streets paved with sailors' bones. Weed-strewn build-ings, barnacled castles, fossilized carcasses. Down, down into caverns crawling with neon cilia, through steam-spewing pipes, along an eel-path, a sculpin-trench, a giant isopod ravine. Further down, the canyon gaping before him, night after night, seemingly boundless, and yet pressure builds as he draws closer, lung-crushing, bone-breaking pressure, he can't swim, he can't move, he is confined in infinite space, he is suppressed, held under, *release me*, suffocating, he needs to *break free* . . .

The bottle rattles as Aitch jolts awake. Pulse choking, whole body trembling. Runny nose dangerously close to the brine.

I won't drown, he thinks, necklace seized in fist, head cocked. The chant is still tumbling from verse to verse, the Aunts' voices fervent but steady. Lately, they've kept him jarred for longer and longer, until he is grey and blue, the pinkie between his legs completely retracted. Not a peachy little boy anymore, not a good boy. A salamander. A jelly-limbed axolotl. A creature designed to crawl.

He waits, listens.

The song's crescendo is hours off yet.

Plenty of time, Aitch thinks, feeling numbly overhead for the hole he's worked at for months, the one widened with leather-sheathed determination. *There.* He grins, shoves his baby finger up, wriggles it through to the first knuckle, hooks, and *pushes*.

Metal screeches against glass as, slowly, the jar's lid turns.

*   *   *

He's learned not to climb too soon after flopping onto the floor.

It takes some maneuvering, just sliding out, placing the lid silently; then the monumental effort of getting up. Bending at the waist. Trying not to slip, water sluicing down his arms, his naked gooseflesh. Waiting for the blood to rush, the spots in his vision to clear. The pins and needles in his rump, legs, and feet to stop stabbing. The burning ache in his joints to ease. A puddle dries around him as Aitch stretches tip to toe, luxuriating in the sensation of being *long*.

Time, however, is short.

When it's safe – raw feeling returned, limbs pliable, balance more or less restored – he creeps across the room to collect his crayons and a sheaf of blank paper. He stops frequently to catch his breath. To listen. Through the roar and hiss of nausea, he hears the Aunts singing, their rhythms redoubled in the wind outside.

He can't scamper the way he did years ago, but follows the same route up the bookshelves now as then. There's no ladder, though the cases are more than twenty feet high. No matter. Aitch is small, a flimsy wool boy, shrunken and felted from too much time in the water. The mahogany boards are sturdy enough.

At this height, dust blankets every surface. He could feel, but hadn't quite realized, how long he'd been bottled. Chalk and pastel powder shows through the thick layer of grey. Sticks of color await Aitch's touch. Around his secret drawing place, beneath the moonlit porthole, favorite volumes are splayed, spines cracked, pages well-thumbed. On hands and knees, he shuffles from the top of one case to the next, careful not to knock any books to the floor. He tries not to, can't help but, look down. From here, his glass prison looks so tiny.

Halfway around the room, he stops below the round window. Steels his nerve and peers *out*.

Chimneys dominate the landscape, near and far. Cold scratches point skywards from village rooftops, leading his eye to the refinery's smokestacks, a dozen or more thick pillars spewing clouds of ink between the stars. Closer, to the right, a breakwater describes the harbor. Aitch drops his gaze quickly, avoids taking in the reef, the ever-churning sea.

Don't be frightened, the Aunts told him, long ago, when they used to promenade through the fish markets on the wharves, Aitch by their side, harnessed and leashed.

Born liquid-breathing, as you were, one began.

Encauled, interrupted her sister.

Shrouded in brine, the first went on, *inhaling the most profound essence of life—*

A natural water-baby—

You should feel, said the Aunt – and Aitch remembers the moment stretching then, as he'd stopped on the rough jetty, the splinters in his bare soles forgotten, chest swelling with pride and hope and the memory of love, of Mother calling him *special*, believing, suddenly, that the Aunts thought so, too, that they wanted him, that he *was* special – but they weren't looking at him at all. As she'd continued, the Aunt's gaze was unfixed, irises full of the deeps. *You should feel—*

An affinity, supplied the double.

Gratitude, said the other Aunt firmly. *To be forever submerged, to be reunited* . . . A shimmer in her eyes then, a ripple of emotion as she'd turned, Aitch finally in her sights. Was it reverence in the quivering cast of her features? Jealousy? Disappointment?

Not admiration, Aitch had known, certain as the stone in his guts.

Not love.

Be thankful, she'd said, breaking the spell. *Soon you'll always be in your element.*

That's where Nick Pierce's family moors their dory, the Aunts had said that day, playing tour guide on the wharves. Perched on his bookshelf inside the lighthouse, Aitch now draws absent-mindedly: the vista before him, the ghostly one superimposed in his memory, the landscape risen in dreams. *That's Luelly's tackle and bait stall*, the Aunts had said, pointing to an open-sided booth, boards reeking of worms and fresh paint. *That's the last of Marsh's fleet. Over there is Southwick's berth.* The old seafarer himself had sat on a low stool, shucking shells into a pail. The sails on his brigantine had been tightly furled, flags limp on its masts. The haul more than half unloaded.

The *scritch-scritching* of pastels on paper intensifies; thoughts are channeled into images and signs, filling sheet after sheet.

Southwick had given him an oyster. The sailor had smiled at the face Aitch pulled when the slimy glob slid down his throat. Great black beard like a puff of steam, heaving as he laughed. Aitch renders it in charcoal smears and swirls.

He tries to write the captain's name, but the letters come out all wrong, curves and crosses misaligning. After countless hours sneak-reading the Aunts' books, Aitch has developed a strong sense for words . . . but, lately, they won't stick in his head. On paper they're moth-eaten, bad as initials.

Pictures arrive clear and fast.

Some he replicates, based on those tucked away in the Aunts' library: pen-and-ink sketches of submarines, volcanoes, whales; etchings of distant islands, stone-carved idols, long-lost tribes; full-color anatomies, endless species of fish, barbed lures. Others he cannot explain. Images and lyrics appear full-formed in the darkness, as though projected into his mind. Urgently, he records strange hieroglyphs. Maps to as-yet-uncharted provinces. Constellations and moons never seen.

Tonight, he can hardly keep up with the onslaught. It's been too long since he's climbed, since he's *played*; the pages practically fill themselves. Tidal waves and ships. Tunnels and caverns. Darkness scribbled in, claustrophobic, with bright sinuous streaks slithering towards the margins . . . Aitch draws and draws, arm aching and smudged to the elbow. Before one picture drifts off the ledge, floating to the floor, he has already begun the next.

He does not notice the quiet, until it is broken.

Key against iron, the bolt shunts. Hinges squeal as the door opens. Two sets of heels *click-clack* into the room. The Aunts skirt around the lidless jar, stepping over small puddles, mouths thin lines of disapproval. *How can it have gotten so late*, Aitch wonders, resisting an urge to look outside, to search for sunrise. Dropping pencil and paper, he freezes, vainly hoping to blend into the shadows. Below, the Aunts sigh, nostrils flared. They bend and retrieve the discarded drawings, each gathering a sizable stack. At first they afford the things little attention – but as the moonlight strikes the topmost illustrations, their glances linger. Studying the hurried doodles, they communicate with nods and clicks of the tongue. They flick through the papers. Quick, quicker.

Just when Aitch begins to feel the tension in his belly ease – they've overlooked him, surely – the Aunts cock their heads and squint at his roost. Brows furrowed in concentration, not anger.

"Aitch," the one on the left begins. "You are—"

A gift, Father had said.

So special, said Mother.

"—not designed for heights. You are not a bird. Come now, child. Continue your work down here."

Stomach churning, the boy lowers his supplies, reacquaints his feet with the ground. Booty in hand, the Aunts turn their backs.

"Goodnight," he whispers as they retreat, bolting the door behind them.

The sun winks through the ocean-side porthole long before the boy stretches out on the cot, finally sure they've forgotten to bottle him.

Freedom survives line by line, page by page.

A week's worth of sketches keeps Aitch occupied, earning him seaweed soups and a flat bed. First thing in the morning, his palms are mottled: brown and purple and navy. While he slept, the Aunts had visited his room – he's sure, he remembers – and observed his slumber. They put sticks of chalk in his grasp, then watched figures and symbols appear, channeled directly from dream to paper. Clucks, glottal approval, whenever he gave his drowsy hands free rein. On his breakfast trays, new reams arrive.

He wants to make the Aunts happy.

He wants to be dry.

So he draws, even after the nightmares have stopped.

From the shelf-top vantage, looking out over the village, Aitch lets loose his imagination. A raging ocean – yes, the Aunts appreciated those pastel-flecked swells. Bizarre golden treasure, twinkling on the reef; they'd almost smiled at that one. Misshapen creatures emerging from the deeps, gills fluttering in dank air, webbed fingers flapping. Hordes of spine-crested mermaids crossing the pebbled shore. Tentacled men bent on ascending the lighthouse. Oh, how the chanting had soared, the evening he'd produced that lurid vision!

Next day, the seas are calm as the Aunts have always pretended. The waters are clear and barren. Activity on the wharves is sedate. Finding little inspiration outside, Aitch scours the library's collection of artwork. Displacing the cylinders he lately hasn't needed to count, he copies imprints of fire-fueled airships soaring past the sun. Pyramids inscribed with illegible messages. Vines strangling strongholds. Crumbling ruins.

There's no release in making these copies. No butterflies in his belly. No urgency. For a while, he abandons the crayons and simply reads.

Around dusk, the Aunts deliver a jug of metal-tinged water, a bowl of spirulina flakes, and a shrimp cake. One changes the chamber pot, the other the sheets. Toying with his pendant, Aitch stands with his back pressed to the farthest bookcase, as the latest batch of drawings is swept up and inspected.

A frown on the left. Expression neutral on the right.

"Have you napped this afternoon?"

Aitch shakes his head.

The Aunts exchange glances.

"So you've been sleeping well these past nights?"

"Yes, Aunt. Extremely well, thank you."

Another unreadable interchange.

"Indeed."

Unsure how to respond, Aitch shrinks under the tight-lipped scrutiny. Instinctively he inches away, stopping short as he collides with the largest empty jar. Glass resonates as it strikes the neighboring bottle; a solemn church bell summoning dawdlers inside. Aitch swallows hard, *willing* the sound to ebb.

Shhhhh, he silently pleads. *Don't remind them*. His back is only now beginning to truly unkink, his ankles and hips barely straightening . . .

"I have been very good," he says aloud, voice breaking.

"Indeed," says the left, unconvinced.

"Indeed," repeats the right, taking the latest sketches and her sister by the arm. "We expect no less, Aitch."

As if to reassure, *this* Aunt leaves a lantern – and the door unlocked behind her.

The Aunts aren't impressed with the juvenile horrors Aitch has created. The haunted house with its gambrel roof, widow's walk, broken panes of stained glass. Their hands twitch, ready to scrunch the bone-filled pits seething with rats. They sneer at the Arctic tundra made by crushing white chalk over a dark ground. If they were prone to laughter, they would have guffawed at the giant penguin.

The Aunts do not laugh.

"You were right," says one.

With the slightest nod, the other acknowledges her sister's deferral. "Like attracts like, blood calls to blood, element to element. The message is meaningless if not spoken fluently, *fluidly*."

"Agreed," comes the reply. "His strength is undeniably liquid."

Immediately, she reaches into the front pouch of an apron cinched around her gaunt waist. She pulls out a rag and a sloshing cylinder.

Against his will, Aitch feels the count starting anew.

One: the vial in their hands. Two: the Aunt dousing the cloth. Three: the Aunt pinning him with eyes, with hands, with nails. Two: the Aunt grabbing . . . Three: the Aunt holding . . .

"No," he cries, attempting to wriggle free, thrashing. Arms throbbing in their brutal grip. Legs quivering. Piss dribbling. Backed against the seventh jar, he whips his head from side to side until it is trapped.

Fingers gouge his cheeks, piercing flesh, *turning* his face. "No," Aitch moans, pulse hot and throbbing. Tears stinging.

Cold wetness smothers him silent, fabric pinched around his nose, palmed against his mouth. Aitch tries to hold his breath, tastes bile. Scentless fumes seep between his lips, infiltrate his nostrils. His body sags against the gaping bottle.

"Mother," he sobs, falling into the black nothingness of defeat.

He rouses in near-darkness. Chin on knees, feet twisted numb, joints screaming. Breath hollow in his ears, waves splashing. The slow rhythm of strange verses intoned. Inside the jar, the air is close, humid, and reeks of glue. Overhead, all the tiny stars in Aitch's sky have been plugged, the metal lid sealed to its tracks. Through the glass, he sees the room blearily. Moonlight streaming. Bookshelves. No cot now, no table, no chamber pot. No *tools*. The door thrown wide, taunting.

No escape but into sleep.

"I'm a good boy," he mumbles, the Aunts pulling him on his harness and leash, yanking him off the wharf, plunging into the water. Their spindle-fins clawing, clamping, dragging him down, down, further down. Diving, songs bubbling from their gills. Descending at a strangling pace. Flippers kicking, kicking for the ocean floor.

Release me, Aitch thinks, the silent cry echoed from the abyss stretching for miles below. *Release me—*

Busy singing, the Aunts don't hear him. They don't listen – he knows, he's sure – they never have. They don't believe he will stay if not forced.

The time has come, they seem to chant, alighting on the chasm's precipice. Clouds of silt stir as they land, lifeless grit caught by the current, tossed out over the void. *The time has come*, they demand, but the words are crooned with a lullaby cadence, mesmerizing and slow. *Wake*, they say, leading Aitch to the precipice, slicing at his neck until it bleeds. Holding fast, binding him in long ropes of dead-man's bootlaces. *Wake*, they repeat, floating the boy-bundle over the edge, pushing *down* as serpentine shadows writhe *up*.

Release me—

Aitch flails, spasms shaking his body so ferociously the bottle quakes. He throws his head violently back, forward, back, smashing it again and again to rid it of the voice – that soul-rending voice! – still slicing through his sleep-fevered mind, still pulsating through his heart.

Release me—

The jar pitches as he pounds his spine against its walls, as he huffs and grunts, using shoulders and arms and ribs and skull, his only weapons, his only *tools*. Thrashing and rocking, building momentum, leaning into it, *tipping*. An audible crack as glass meets floorboards, but it's merely a weakening, not a break, not a shatter. Brine sloshes and for a moment he's submerged, he's back in the nightmare, he's drowning. As Aitch gasps, sputters, sucks in salty gutfuls, instinct takes over. He contorts his torso, flexes, and flips. Mother's talisman finds its way into his mouth; teeth clenched, he concentrates, holds his breath. Focuses on rotating, revolving, building up speed. Rolling, the bottle radiates great corkscrews of sound, faster and faster, like a fisherman's copper coin spinning on the docks. Faster and faster across the planks, light refracting, a dizzying kaleidoscope of water. Faster and faster, until it smashes to a stop.

Candles topple from the bookshelf; wax cylinders crash onto glass, encouraging the jar's new split to widen. Bracing with his forearms, the boy *heaves*. A high-pitched whine as the structure around him weakens, pinging as it cracks. With a sharp squeal, the container shatters. The water level and jagged shards fall, slicing and stinging. Aitch weeps as blood courses into his limbs – and out of them.

Lurching onto all fours, he grinds the pads of his fingers into the bottle's wreckage until the red trickle becomes a steady flow. Without pencil or paper, he has no other means by which to record the vibrant images flooding his vision, the instructions, the dark mariner's pleas. The Aunts will want to know every foreign word, every primeval beat. He smears every note, every glyph, every incoherent medley, until his head is light, his hands raw.

Taking a step back, Aitch considers what he's made.

This work.

This message.

The Aunts are going to love it, he thinks. Hope and pride turn him toward the door, take him by the hand. Whispering *the Aunts are going to love you*, they lead him into the corridor, push him at the spiral stairs. Convince him to go and get them.

Alone outside the lighthouse's lantern room, Aitch's hands throb while his nerve shudders and dies.

Gas flames burn low within caged sconces, barely illuminating the narrow hallway. The ceiling is shadow-cloaked, held aloft by cobwebs and century-old beams. Darkness runs its fingers along Aitch's bare back, tickling the nape of his neck. It ushers him across the short landing at the top of the stairs. He'd been so brave below, an artist drunk on revelation. Now he hesitates, facing a set of double doors that rattle as though desperate to break away from the jambs. Light pulsates out of two small circular windows centered at head-height, harsh yellow-white beams piercing the corridor, then fading. In the strange between-glow, Aitch feels exposed. He's not brave at all. Not special. Just a barefoot boy in his smallclothes, dripping blood and fear.

Up here the chant is chilling, louder than ever, underscored by a wild howl.

On tiptoe, Aitch approaches. He peers through the left-hand opening, flinching each time the lantern turns its glaring irises his way. Inside the round chamber is strobed, observed in snatches. Polished timber counters ringing the central lamp, strewn with parchments, maps, rulers and compasses. Leather volumes stacked on a trestle table, on ledges, on the floor. Dozens of specimen jars, labeled and lidded. A hard bench on the right, a pillow and grey wool blanket folded at one end. Too many cylinders for Aitch to count: telescopes on tripods; brass spyglasses; plinths topped with crude wooden idols; fat pillar candles, flames full and guttering. All around, from floor to vaulted ceiling, Aitch's drawings are pasted in indecipherable patterns on the grand windows. The pages whip and curl in the gale; now black holes in the night, now constellations.

To the left, the room's easternmost glass is missing; its salt-rimed casement admits a fierce wailing. Framed in the gap, the Aunts sway. Starkly illuminated for a few blinding seconds, then silhouetted against the waning moon. Hair unbound, long tendrils undulating, storm-tossed. Aitch gasps, glimpsing the robes fluttering from their shoulders like wings. He's sure, he *remembers*, the silken sheen of that fabric, the way it shimmers on a starlit May-Eve . . .

"Mother?" he whispers, though he knows she's not there. Not now, not ever. The lamp spins and Aitch blinks a second too late. When sight returns, the Aunts have shifted position; they're performing an irregular dance, their song changed to suit, lyrics guttural as a seal's bark. As they step back, the bottom ledge of the window is revealed: a plank juts like a parched tongue from the lighthouse's side. A hemp rope is firmly fastened around the board's outermost end. Spilling into the chamber, it forms an immense snake-nest on the floor, spooling and coiling, eventually attached to the vessel lying at the Aunts' feet.

Unlike its precursors, the eighth jar is not cylindrical, nor is it pure glass.

Six-sided, it is not flat-bottomed but pointed and arrow-tipped. Its facets are smooth and oblong, smoked mirrors chased with lead; each pane absorbs more light than it reflects. Aitch whimpers. He has seen its like before in the Aunts' books – but not on this scale, not for this purpose.

It is a fishing plummet.

And he is to be the weight.

It's an hour, at best, before the Aunts cease their invocations and find Aitch gone.

The sea is in turmoil as he flees. Legs pumping, he prays they didn't hear the slap of his feet on the lighthouse stairs. The screech of the ground-level door opening, the thundering clang of it swinging shut. Breakers crash against the headland, spray soaking the pebbled path to the wharves, washing away the crimson trail spattered behind him. He looks down, always down, unsure which is more frightening: the ocean roaring, wild and vicious, or the roiling, boundless cloud-sea. The light-house, forever watching.

No matter how far he runs, Aitch feels the Aunts' glare from above. At first their song keeps pace with his flight, but soon it outruns him. Picked up by many voices, the strange chorus is repeated, reverberating from reef to village and back. It surrounds Aitch as he sprints, urging him on, to break free—

I have, he wants to scream, but foul air burns his lungs, reeking of clams and grave-soil and rot. *You are not a bird*, he hears the Aunts say, clicking their tongues. *You are not built for flying, but for swimming* . . .

Whistling on the docks, a scattering of oil lamps flare to life. It is early yet for fishing, Aitch thinks, but takes some comfort in the men's presence. The assured way they handle both oars and fire, rowing out to join their mates on the reef. Taking only their nets. Wearing flippers.

I'll sail with them, Aitch thinks. *They'll take me away, back to the train, back to Mother* . . .

"Help," he breathes, dashing past stalls battened for the night. Too quiet, he tries again. Pitches his voice to out-sing the Aunts. "Help me!"

Clunking across weathered boards, he aims for the one berth he clearly remembers. An old sea-dog, an oyster, a puff-of-steam beard. "Captain Southwark," he cries, startling a sharp-beaked carrion crow. The brig is moored midway down the jetty, a small fleet of rowboats ready at its stern. Under a tarp at the foot of its gangplank, a grizzled guard snoozes in a whiskey fug. Aitch thunders past him, halfway up the footbridge. Safety, he's sure, awaits him on this ship. Fair passage, wind-bellied sails. The swiftest – the only – way home. "Captain—"

"Muffle it, swain. That screech of yers is fit to wake the dead. And far as I know, I en't there yet."

Aitch stops. Turns. Slowly descends and approaches the man emerging from under the mold-spotted canvas. "Captain Southwark?"

"Heard ye the first time, mate." The old man stands and belches, then reaches up under his sweater to scratch his big belly. Plugging one nostril at a time, he leans over the railing and snorts into the water. Ablutions done, he pinches the bridge of his nose and speaks into his cupped hand. "What ye hollering for?"

For a minute, Aitch jibbers about tentacles and boy-weighted plummets and voices rising from the deeps. "The Aunts—"

"Always does things too fancy," Southwark says. Clapping Aitch on the shoulder, his gaze drops to the talisman hanging round the boy's neck. Thick, callused fingers inspect the leather pouch, then pat it gently against Aitch's chest. "It's their way or no way . . . Ye ken me, don't ye?"

Aitch nods, relieved.

"Told them, didn't I, to keep it simple. But those women . . ." Southwark pauses, slants an eyebrow. "They's got a different take on *simple*, don't they just?"

Aitch's cheeks tighten and twitch, caught somewhere between a sob and a smile. "Can you take me home? Please?"

"'Bout time someone did."

Grinning now, really grinning, Aitch makes for the brigantine, but again the captain stops him short. "Crew's reveling," he explains, steering the boy toward the last rowboat, guiding him under the railing and over the gunwale. "I'll take care of yer me own self, won't I."

"Hurry," Aitch says.

For a man of his bulk, Southwark is light on his feet. The dory hardly rocks as he boards; despite the choppy water, his stroke is smooth, their progress swift. Within moments the shoreline has fallen away, the wharves, the gold-littered reef. Southwark tilts his cap at the shadows chanting there, then puckers the billows around his mouth and begins trilling, picking up their funereal beat.

An icicle forms at the base of Aitch's heart, stabs into his stomach. "I don't know the direction," he says, leaving bloody palm-prints on the crossbench. He looks back at the headland as the boat shoots past the breakwater. The lighthouse searches, searches, but he's gone. He's out of reach. Turning back to the old man he asks, "Is it far?"

Southwark glances up at the moon, gauging distance by the few visible stars.

"Fathoms," he replies, locking oars.

Pouncing.

With practiced ease, he pins Aitch with one hand, grabs the anchor with the other. A flick of the wrist and the sink-rope whirrs round the boy's ankles. "This business don't have to be hard, son," he says, upending Aitch easily as emptying a pail of chum. Throwing him overboard. Aiming the weight at his surfacing head, tossing it. "See?"

Fluid hymns sing Aitch down, down, further down.

Limbs numb, ankles bent out of shape, arms waving ten little cylinders in front of his face. He grabs the leather tube strung around his neck, tears it open, *wrings*. His caul oozes out, unfurls, and is swept away by strong undercurrents.

Mother, he quails, voiceless. *I'm drowning.*

Tessellations spark around him as he exhales. Neon alphabets, pink and purple and green. Luminescent pictograms of algae. Jellyfish punctuation, bright tremulous sentences felt as fin-flutters. Paragraphs sketched in krill, tiny oxygen explosions. Entire stories swimming in syllables of elder seas.

All ushering him down towards – what? He can't say.

All communicating things he can't understand.

Aitch is not special.

He's just a half-finished thought, sinking into the abyss. He's an initial, merely one of the first. Many others – he's sure, he *foresees* – will be thrown in as bait after him. On and on, until – when?

Soon, the Aunts would say, meaning, possibly, forever.

Meaning, We don't know either.

At last, Aitch inhales.

A tentacle emerges from the darkness, latches on. Squeezes him for dear life.

Caitlín R. Kiernan has been quoted as feeling "too many people are obsessed with Lovecraft's monsters, tentacles and polyps and shoggoths . . . I think they're missing the point. At least, they're missing the part that has played the greatest influence on me, and those elements would be the importance of atmosphere, the found manuscript as a narrative device, and his appreciation of what paleontologists and geologists call deep time. Deep time is critical to his cosmicism, the existential shock a reader brings away from his stories. Our smallness and insignificance in the universe at large. In all possible universes. Within the concept of infinity. No one and nothing cares for us. No one's watching out for us. To me, that's Lovecraft."

With "The Peddler's Tale, Or, Isobel's Revenge," Kiernan uses oral storytelling rather than a discovered palimpsest for a story told (in the fabled city Ulthar) of Lovecraft's vast Underworld, a universe as indifferent to humankind as the rest of the cold, remorseless cosmos.

Kiernan is a two-time recipient of both the World Fantasy and Bram Stoker awards. Her recent novels include *The Red Tree* and *The Drowning Girl: A Memoir*, and, to date, her short stories have been collected in fourteen volumes, including *Tales of Pain and Wonder, A is for Alien, The Ammonite Violin & Others,* and the World Fantasy Award-winning *The Ape's Wife and Other Stories*. The most recent collections are *Beneath an Oil Dark Sea: The Best of Caitlín R. Kiernan (Volume 2)* (Subterranean Press) and *Houses Under the Sea: Mythos Tales* (Centipede Press). She also wrote *Alabaster*, an award-winning, three-volume graphic novel for Dark Horse Comics. She recently wrote her first screenplay and is currently working on her next novel, *Interstate Love Song*.

The Peddler's Tale
or
Isobel's Revenge
Caitlín R. Kiernan

"If you are very sure that's the story you wish to hear," said the peddler, the seller of notions and oddments, to the tow-headed girl child who called her Aunty. They were not related, by blood nor marriage, but very many people in Ulthar called the peddler Aunt or Aunty or the like. Few people living knew her right name or her history. Most felt it impolite to ask, and she never volunteered the information.

"You should be certain, and then be *certain* you're certain, before I begin. I've come a long, long way. And tomorrow I leave the city and will not soon return. So, be *sure* this is the tale you wish to hear."

"Aunty, I *am* very certain," said the girl impatiently, and the other two children – both boys – agreed. "I have no doubt whatsoever."

"Well, then," said the old woman who wasn't her aunt. She sat back in her chair and lit her pipe, then squinted through gray smoke at the youngsters who'd arranged themselves on the floor between her and the crackling hearth fire. Also, there were five cats, none of whom seemed the least bit interested in peddlers' yarns.

She took a deep pull on her pipe, then began.

"You've all heard the name of the King of Bones, and you've heard the tales of how he came to power. And of his Queen, his twin sister, Isobel."

The children nodded eagerly. And the peddler paused, because she knew that the making of beginnings is, as many have noted, a matter not to be undertaken lightly. And, too, the girl had requested of her a very grim tale, which made the beginning that much more delicate an undertaking. The old woman watched her audience, and they watched her right back. She was well versed at hiding exhaustion, disguising an aching back and sore feet behind a pleasant demeanor, not letting on how her weary sinews wished for the rare luxury of a soft mattress. Duty before rest. This tale was the price of her night's lodging and board, and she was a woman who paid her debts.

Shortly after dawn, the peddler had led the strong draught pony that pulled her wagon over the ancient stone bridge spanning the River Skai, that wild path of meltwater gurgling down from the glaciers girdling Mount Lerion and flowing northwards towards the Cerenarian Sea. She'd lingered a while on the bridge, admiring the early autumn sunrise, the clean smell of the river, and the view to the east. This was always a welcome sight, the cottages and farms speckling the hills beyond the bridge. Behind her lay Nir and Hatheg, neither of which had proven as profitable as she'd hoped. With so many merchants and craftsmen – and it seemed there were more every year – few in the villages and cities had use for a traveling tinker and a seller of oddments and notions, a peddler of medicinals and salves, a woman up to almost any menial job for a few coins. She'd become an anachronism, but at so advanced an age it was hardly practical to seek some other more lucrative trade.

Out beyond the farmland, just visible in a gauzy mist starting to burn away beneath the new day, she had been able to discern the suburbs of Ulthar. She was born in the town and hoped to spend her last years there, fate willing. She did not ever think *gods willing*, as she had long since learned the folly and dangers of placing one's hope in the hands of gods and things that fancy themselves gods.

"Isobel and Isaac, the earthborn ghouls," said the girl, prompting the peddler to continue.

"Yes, well," said the peddler. "But they were not true and proper ghouls, only mongrels, birthed of a mostly human mother. They were fair, some even say beautiful to behold, their skin white as milk, their eyes clear and blue as sapphires. Their Ghūl heritage barely showed, excepting in their appetites and ruthlessness. Still, they wished to *rule* as ghouls. By the procurement of a powerful, terrible artifact, they raised an army and threw down the rightful King and Queen of Bones and Rags, and—"

"The Qqi d'Tashiva and Qqi Ashz'sara," the tow-headed girl interrupted. "And the artifact is the Basalt Madonna – Qqi d'Evai Mubadieb – and, Aunty, I've heard—"

The old woman raised an eyebrow and scowled, silencing the girl.

"Now, which of us is telling this tale?" she asked. "And, besides, I'd not guess your ma and pa would think so highly of your palavering in the corpse tongue."

One of the cats, a fat tabby tom, leapt into the peddler's lap, stretched, then curled up for a nap. She stroked its head. In her wanderings far and wide from the cobblestone streets of radiant Ulthar, the cats were, perhaps, what she missed above all else. For an age, the citizens of the city had been forbidden to harm any cat for any reason, upon pain of death or banishment. There were not many laws of man she counted wise and unquestionably just, but that surely was one of the few.

"Yes. Those were the titles that the Snow twins took for themselves when all the forces of Thok had fallen before them and the fire they wielded, after even the city of the gugs and the vaults of Zin lay at their feet, after even the great flocks of night gaunts had surrendered. In the days that followed the war, when I was only a very small girl myself, there was fear even here that Isaac Snow might not be content to rule the shadows of the Lower Dream Lands, that he might have greater ambitions and rise up against the world of men.

"You know, of course, no such thing happened. We'd not be sitting here, me telling you this story, if matters had gone that way. We were, all of us, fortunate, for many are the generals who'd believed the might of the twins was so awful that none could ever stand against it. It is written that the Snows were content to remain below, and that they still – to this day – rule over and enslave the creatures of the Lower Dream Lands."

"But—" began the tow-headed girl, and this time the peddler interrupts *her*.

"But, child, though this is what most count as the truth, there are those who whisper a secret history of the Ghūl Wars. And if this *other* account is to be believed – and I warrant there are a few priests and scholars who will swear that it is so – the twins were never of one mind. Indeed, it is said that Isaac greatly feared his sister, for the same prophecy that had foretold their victory also spoke of the birth of a daughter to them."

"He feared his own child?" asked the boy seated to the tow-headed girl's right.

"He did."

"But why?" the boy asked.

"If you'll kindly stop asking questions, I was, as it happens, coming to that."

The peddler chewed the stem of her pipe a moment and stroked the tabby tom's head. It purred, and she briefly considered changing horses in the middle of this stream and *insisting* they hear some other tale, one not populated with ghouls, half ghouls, and moldering necropoleis, and not a tale of war and the horrors of war. Likely, if she continued, it would end in nightmares for her and the children both. The plains of Pnath and the peaks of Thok might lie far away, and the battles in question long ago, but neither space nor time, she knew, could be depended upon to hold phantoms at bay.

Still, this was the tale they'd asked for, and this was the tale she'd promised, and the peddler was not a woman to go back on her word.

"The prophecy," she continued, "had been passed down since the ghouls were defeated by the Djinn and cast out of the wastes of the Arabian deserts into the Lower Dream Lands, so thrice a million years before the first city of humankind was built. It foretold that someday a daughter would be born to half-ghoul twins, half-*modab* albino twins, and this daughter would grow to be a savior, a messiah, who'd be more powerful by far than even her terrible parents. She would, so said the prophecy, lead the Ghûl through the Enchanted Wood and up the seven hundred steps to the Gates of Deeper Slumber and through the gates into the Waking World. Once above, the mighty Djinn would find their doom by the same hellish weapon her mother and father had wielded in Thok. But . . ."

And here the peddler paused for effect and puffed at her pipe a moment. The air in the room had gone as taut as a harp string, and the three children leaned very slightly forward.

"But?" whispered the tow-headed girl.

"But," continued the peddler, smoke leaking from her nostrils, "the rise of the ghouls would also be the downfall of the father of their champion. Because first, or so went the prophecy, the daughter would have to murder the father and claim both thrones for herself. She would spare her mother, but never again would there be a king and a queen in Thok. Those immemorial titles would vanish into memory and then pass from all recollection.

"The King of Bones and Rags, he did believe the prophecy, for, after all, had it not foretold of his and his sister's birth and their coming to the Underworld and of their ascension? Sure it had, and if that portion of it was not false then how could he *not* fear those passages that had yet to be realized? Sure he was terrified, because even so great a monster as he may fear his own undoing at the hands of such unfathomable mysteries as soothsaying. And, what's more, he soon learned that Isobel Siany Snow – for that was her earthborn name in full, given by their mother Hera – that Queen Isobel was already pregnant. That she had become so shortly before the war began, when she and he were hardly more than storm clouds gathering on the horizon."

And here the peddler departed briefly from her simple narrative, for the bare bones of a tale are a dull affair and should be dressed appropriately in the attire of atmosphere and the garb of mood. Too easily might this story become a dry recitation of *perhaps it was, and so they say,* and *might have been.* So, with words she deftly painted images of the perpetual twilight that lay over the dreaded Vale of Pnath, where gigantic bholes burrowed through unplumbed strata of gnawed bones heaped into the wide valley. She told of towering forests of phosphorescent fungi that pressed in all about the borders of that land in the shadow of the ragged peaks of Thok, mountains so lofty they reached almost to the rocky, stalactite-festooned ceiling of the Lower Dream Lands. It was the ghouls, she explained, who'd made Pnath a plain of dry ribs and broken skulls, for they'd spent untold years tossing the leavings of their unspeakable feasts over the cliffs into the abyss below. In those lands, the peddler assured them, every breath of air was redolent of death and rot. For it was the *realm* of the grave. It was the abode of nightmares beyond reckoning.

"Oh, and the ghasts," she nodded. "I shouldn't neglect to mention them. Terrible, vile, creeping beasts with a bite so venomous none can survive it. The gugs, the architects of Zin, hunted them, and probably hunt them still. But the gugs fear them as well."

Now the eyes of the children were wide, and occasionally they glanced over their shoulders towards the fire or upwards at the autumn night pressing against the windows of the room.

"Oh, but I *have* strayed terribly, haven't I," said the peddler, and she frowned and knitted her brows, feigning mild exasperation with herself. "Must be the wind brushing around the eaves of the house making my mind wander so."

"Aunty, we don't mind," the tow-headed girl whispered, and the other children nodded in unison.

"That's all well and good, but, we'll be here until cock's crow if I keep nattering on that way. Where was I?"

"Isobel was already pregnant," said the boy who'd spoken before.

"Yes. Yes, that was it. Isobel, the Queen of Bones and Rags, was pregnant by her brother, and when Isaac Glyndwr Snow learned this he feared it would be the death of him. Everything was unfolding precisely as the prophecy had promised. For the first time ever he grew distant from his sister and withdrew from her, becoming ever more secretive, spending long hours alone or in the company of his concubines. He took to drink and to chasing the Dragon, trying to smother his worries in the embrace of opium. As Isobel's belly swelled, *his* scheming, anxious mind swelled with plots and designs by which he might prevent the fulfillment of the prophecy and cheat his own undoing.

"He would kill his sister. Yes. That's exactly what he *had* to do. Even though he truly did love Isobel, and even though he knew full well he'd never, ever, *ever* love another woman, he had to do murder against her. Because, you see, he loved himself far more. Still, the King of Bones also understood that he must take care to proceed with the utmost caution. For though it was true there was no end of ghouls so fanatically loyal to him they'd gladly turn assassin even against their queen, it was also true he had enemies. The inhabitants of Thok were, by and large, a conquered, broken lot, and many were the ghouls who despised the twins and named them usurpers and conspired in secret, drawing plots against the Crown. Isaac Snow's advisors warned him even the fires of the Basalt Madonna might not save him should there be open revolt. For before, he and Isobel had possessed the element of surprise. They'd never have that advantage again.

"Worse, there were rumors that some among the dissidents had begun making sacrifices to – well, I'll not say *that* name here, but I mean the dæmon sultan who serves the blind, insane chaos at the center of the universe. No one ought *ever* speak that name."

The children looked disappointed, and the tow-headed girl muttered to herself.

"Anyway, the King of Bones had made up his mind," continued the peddler, "and nothing could dissuade him from the cold and heartless resolve of his decision. He would see Isobel dead, and he chose the method, and he chose the hour. It was with an especial shame that he cowardly set another to the task. At first he'd intended to do the deed himself, which only seemed right and good to his twisted ideas of right and good. But his advisors convinced him it was much more prudent to *order* her death by another's hand. Then, afterwards, he could have the killer tried and publicly executed, and there would be fewer questions about the queen's sad fate. If it were discovered that the Qqi d'Tashiva had murdered the mother of the child who would deliver all Ghūl-kind and lead them to victory against the Djinn—"

"There'd have been a terrible count of angry ghouls," the tow-headed girl said.

The peddler nodded, not bothering to complain about yet another interruption.

"Indeed. It's no small thing to destroy the hope of an entire people, even if the people are so foul a bunch as the ghouls."

One of the children yawned, and the peddler asked, "Should I stop here? It's getting late, after all, and you three by rights should be in your beds."

"No, Aunty, please," said the tow-headed girl, and she thumped the boy who'd yawned smartly on the back of his head. "We're not tired, not at all. Please, do go on."

"Please," murmured the boy who'd yawned, who was now busy rubbing his head.

"Very well then," said the peddler, and she set her pipe aside, for it had gone out partway through her description of the Lower Dream Lands. "So, the king commanded that his sister die, and he chose the ghoul who would cut her throat while she slept. He told none but those closest to him, a handful whom he trusted and believed were beyond any act of treachery. But he was mistaken. The Qqi Ashz'sara was every bit as wicked and distrustful and perfidious as her brother, and she'd taken precautions. She'd placed a spy, a ghoul named Sorrow, within her brother's inner circle. Sorrow was as noble a ghoul as a ghoul may be, which is to say not particularly, but he was in love with his queen, and Isobel did not doubt that he would gladly perish to protect her, should it come to that."

"That's a very strange name," said the tow-headed girl.

"He was a ghoul," replied the peddler. "Would you expect he'd be named George or Juan Carlos or maybe Aziz? His name was Sorrow, a name he'd found on a gravestone stolen from a cemetery in the World Above and brought into the World Below."

"But you said," cut in the boy who'd yawned, "that the Djinn had banished the Ghūl to—"

"—as a whole, yes. I said that, and they did. However, always have there been those few who braved the wrath of the Djinn, hiding among women and men of the Waking World, infesting catacombs and cemeteries."

"Oh," said the boy, clearly confused.

"As I was saying," the peddler began again, "Isobel Snow trusted this one ghoul to bring her word of her brother's doings, and as soon as Sorrow learned of the plot to murder the queen, he scampered back to her with the news."

"Scampered?" asked the tow-headed girl.

"Yes. Scampered. Ghouls do that. They lope and they creep and they scamper. And as the latter is the more expedient means of getting about, Sorrow *scampered* back to Isobel to warn her she and her unborn child were in very terrible danger. Isobel listened, not desiring to believe it was true, but also never supposing that it wasn't. The twins were, as is generally the case with twins, two peas from the same ripe pod, and she admitted to Sorrow that in her brother's place she likely would have made the same decision. Sorrow advised her that she had two options. She could try and make a stand, possibly rallying the very ghouls who would see the King and Queen both deposed, currying their favor with promises that she would abdicate and by pointing out that she was, after all, the mother of the prophesied messiah. Or she could run."

"I'd have run," said the boy who'd yawned.

"But you're a poltroon," replied the boy on the tow-headed girl's right. "You always run from a fight."

"Yes, well, have you never heard that discretion is the better part of valor? The greater wisdom lies in knowing when the odds are not in your favor, and Isobel Snow knew the odds were not in hers. So she dispatched Sorrow to enlist the aid of another earthborn ghoul, one who had once been a man of the Waking World, a man named Richard Pickman. In the century since Pickman had arrived in Thok, he'd risen to a station of some prominence among the ghouls, and during the Ghūl War he'd fought against the Snows. Afterwards, he'd gone into hiding, but Sorrow knew his whereabouts, and he knew also that Pickman possessed the influence to arrange the queen's hasty escape, and that for the right price he would help."

"But wasn't he afraid?" asked the tow-headed girl.

"Undoubtedly, but he didn't believe the prophecy and was convinced that the coming of the albino twins was no more than a coincidence. He was of the opinion that the two were grifters and humbugs who'd seen a chance to exploit ignorance and superstition, and they'd seized it. He certainly did not believe that the infant who'd be born of their union would be the ghouls' deliverance. In fact, Richard Pickman doubted that there ever had *been* a war with the Djinn. He was a heretic of the first order, an unbeliever through and through. It wasn't that he was sympathetic to Isobel's plight. No. More that he was convinced that as long as her child lived, Isaac Snow would be weakened by his fear of their offspring. And, too, Pickman conjured that the brother's confidence would be weakened if he failed to murder his sister. Neither of the Snows were accustomed to failure.

"They were extremely arrogant," said the boy who'd yawned. He rubbed at his eyes and petted a ginger kitten that was curled on the floor near him.

"Sure he was," nodded the peddler, "and more than words ever can convey. It did not cross his mind that his plot would be foiled, once he set it in motion. They say that the first thing he felt upon receiving the news that one of his confidants, a ghoul named Sorrow – and *not* George or Juan Carlos or maybe Aziz – had lain in wait for the King's butcher and gotten the upper hand, the very first expression Isaac Snow's face showed that night was not rage, but amazement that he could possibly have failed."

"Serves him right," says the tow-headed girl.

The peddler shrugged. "Perhaps, if one excuses Isobel her own crimes and makes of her a hero merely because she'd fallen out of favor with her brother. Regardless, after the assassin was slain, Pickman, Sorrow, and several other ghouls led her from the palace and out of Thok, down narrow mountain trails and across the bhole-haunted Vale of Pnath. At last they gained the vaults of ruined Zin, that haunted city of the gugs, and went straightaway to a mighty central tower, the tallest among twice a hundred towers so tall no one could, from the ground, ever hope to glimpse the tops of those spires. They pushed open its enormous doors, which bore the sigil of Koth – a dreadful, awful bas-relief neither Isobel Snow nor Sorrow dared gaze upon – and I should tell you, children, that the history of that tower is a shuddersome tale in its own right, one all but lost to antiquity."

"Maybe you'll tell it next time," said the boy on the tow-headed girl's left.

"Maybe," replied the peddler. "We shall see. Anyhow, beyond that forbidding entryway was a stair that wound up and up and up . . . and *up* . . . to a massive trapdoor carved of slick black stone. It is said two hard days' climbing were necessary to at last reach the top of those stairs and that the strength of all the ghouls present was only *barely* enough to lift open that trapdoor. But open it they did, and so it was that Isobel Snow, Queen of Bones and Rags, Qqi Ashz'sara, slipped through her brother's icy fingers and fled to the Upper Dream Lands. Of the ghouls, only Sorrow went with her, the others turning back with Richard Pickman, who, as I've said, hoped her escape would be the beginning of the end for Isaac Snow's reign. Pickman had instructed Sorrow to lead the Queen in Exile through the Enchanted Wood to the River Xari, where a barge would be waiting to bear them down to the port city of Jaren, from whence they could book safe passage across the shimmering sea to Serannian. Sure, even Isaac Snow would never be half so bold as to venture so many leagues from the Underworld, much less attempt to breach the high walls of the island kingdom of Serannian."

"The people of Serannian let them enter?" the tow-headed girl asked skeptically. "A ghoul and an albino half-ghoul?"

"You'd not think so, would you? But, see, the lords of Serannian were kindly," answered the peddler. "And as I have told you, there were generals and leaders of men who'd learned of the Snows' discovery of the long lost Qqi d'Evai Mubadieb and of the strife that followed, and how they feared the twins might not be content to rule the Lower Dream Lands. So they saw the arrival of Isobel Snow and news of the division between king and queen as a good omen, indeed. Moreover, there is a thing I have not yet revealed, probably the most important part of the tale, the pivot on which turns its plot."

Each of the three children sat up a little straighter at that, for how could anything be more important than the ghoul queen's flight?

"When Isobel Snow departed the peaks of Thok and the palaces of the royal necropolis, she took with her the Basalt Madonna."

There was a collective gasp from the peddler's audience, and she felt the smallest rind of satisfaction at that. If she had to tell this story, at least the gravity of it was not being lost on the listeners, and at least she knew she was not slipping in her skill as a spinner of yarns. She wanted to rekindle her pipe, but this was no place to interrupt herself. She was getting very near the end.

"But if she had the weapon, why did she not turn it against her brother?" asked the boy on the tow-headed girl's right.

"I don't know," said the peddler. "No one knows, no one now living. Perhaps she didn't fully comprehend how, or possibly she was unable to use the Madonna without him. It may have required the two of them together. Or perhaps she simply loved Isaac too much to destroy him."

"Or she was afraid," whispered the boy who'd yawned.

"Or that," said the peddler. "Whatever the reason, she didn't use it against him. She carried it away with her, and by the time Isaac Snow discovered this she was far beyond his reach. When she arrived at Serannian she and Sorrow were arrested and taken to the Council of Lords to whom she told her story and to whom she revealed the Qqi d'Evai Mubadieb. She asked for sanctuary, and it was granted. And this even though she refused to surrender the Basalt Madonna to the men and women of that city on the sea. So, it was there her daughter was born, whom she named Elspeth Isa Snow. There in the shining bustle and safety of Serannian it was that Elspeth grew to be a woman, a strong and fiercely intelligent woman, I should add. Indeed, in the spring of her nineteenth year she was offered a seat on the Council, which she accepted. That same year her mother succumbed to a disease of the blood that had plagued her and her brother since birth, and—"

"Aunty, you didn't mention that before," interrupted the tow-headed girl.

"It wasn't important before. Now it is. Anyway, when Elspeth Snow's mother died the Basalt Madonna passed into her keeping."

"And what happened to Sorrow?" the girl asked.

"Oh, he was still there. He was, in fact, ever Elspeth's dearest friend and confidant. She being one-quarter ghoul herself found his company comforting. But . . . this is not the end of the tale. There's more."

"It *sounds* like the end," said the boy who'd yawned.

"Very *much* like the end," said the tow-headed girl.

"Well, if you wish," said the peddler, "I can stop here. I am tired, and I—"

"No, no, please," said the boy on the girl's right. "Tell the rest. If there is more, then you cannot stop here."

"And why is that?" the peddler asked him.

"My da says that an unfinished tale in an indecent thing."

Somewhere in the house a door creaked open and was pulled shut just a little too roughly, and all three of the children started at the noise. The cat in the old woman's lap opened one eye and looked well and profoundly annoyed at having been awakened.

"So," said the peddler, who had not jumped at the slamming door, "your da believes that stories have endings, which means he must also believe they have beginnings. Do you believe that, child?"

The boy looked somewhat baffled at her question.

"Well . . . do they not?" he asked her.

"I don't think so," she told him. "Then again, I am only a poor peddler who sells oddments and notions and fixes broken wagon wheels and heals warts but . . . no, I do not believe so. Priests and learned scholars may disagree – though I daresay some of them may not. But I would ask you, did our story truly begin when the Snow twins waged their war and conquered Thok and Pnath and all the Lower Dream Lands, or was the beginning when they found the Qqi d'Evai Mubadieb in the Waking World, the World Above, where it had been hidden in a cavern known as Khoshilat Maqandeli, deep in the Arabian wastes? But no, more likely we'd have to say the beginning was earlier, the night the twins consummated their incestuous love on an altar they'd fashioned to honor Shub-Niggurath, the All Mother and consort of the Not-to-Be-Named."

The peddler paused a moment, quietly admonishing herself for having been careless and spoken the name of one of the Great Old Ones, and worse, for having spoken it to three children. She picked up her cold pipe and set the stem between her yellow teeth, chewing at it a moment before continuing.

"Might be," she said, "or might be, instead, the story began when they were born to Alma Shaharrazad Snow, who went by Hera. Or the night she was led by *her* mother into a ghoul warren in an earthly city known as Boston to be bedded by a ghoul. Or perhaps it all started much farther back, when the Snows and the Tillinghasts and the Cabots – all the members of that clan – entered into a pact with the ghouls whereby they'd be given riches and power in exchange for bearing half-caste children. Or much farther back still, when the Ghūl foolishly went to war against their ancient enemies, the Djinn. Or—"

"I think we get the idea," said the tow-headed girl.

"Good," said the peddler, and she managed a ghost of smile. "Good, for I think that is a very important lesson."

"So . . . what happened next?" the boy who'd yawned asked. He was now very much awake.

"Well, Elspeth Snow didn't only grow to be a brilliant woman and a leader of Serannian. She also studied military strategy and became proficient with a sword and a bow and with rifles, too. And she studied the mysteries of the Basalt Madonna as well. She'd learned much of the history of the race of ghouls from Sorrow, who never did come to feel at home in the world of men and longed always to return to Thok. Too much sun. The daughter of Isaac and Isobel Snow loved the old ghoul, and she wished always that he *could* return, and, for that matter, that she might have a chance to see for herself the lands her mother had once ruled, however briefly. She even desired, they say, to look upon the face of her father. She hated him for the strife he'd caused her mother and Sorrow, but some bit of her also wanted to love him as her mother had. In the end, I cannot say what single thing it was led Elspeth to become a soldier, but become a soldier she did. More than a soldier, she became a captain of the Serannian guard, and, by her thirtieth birthday, she'd risen to the highest rank.

"And it was then that she gathered an army from the people of Serannian to march against the despotic Qqi d'Tashiva and end his tyranny. Also women and men from Cydathria did she rally to her cause, and from Thran Kled, and the tribes of the Stony Desert and Oonai and even the fearsome shi'earya of the faraway hills of Implan. She took up the weapon her mother and father had used to crush the Old Kingdom of the Ghūl, and on a midsummer's night she led her army down into Zin and across the Vale of Pnath. There she was joined by another army, rebel ghoul soldiers who followed Richard Pickman, the earthborn ghoul and once-man. Pickman had become an outspoken foe of the King of Bones and Rags and had long since fled Thok to avoid the gallows. The night gaunts and what remained of the race of gugs also followed her when she rode out to meet her father's army in the abyss below the mountains. The battle was brief, for Elspeth Snow chose to unleash the fires roiling inside the Madonna. When she was done, her field of victory was a scorched plain where stone had been melted to slag, and of the bones of her enemies not even ash remained."

The tow-headed girl stopped chewing her lower lip long enough to ask, "And what of the King? Did she slay her father?"

"Ah, what of the King. This is where our tale begins to fray, for none seem certain precisely what became of him. Sure, some *do* say that Elspeth slew her father outright. Others claim that he survived and was taken prisoner and locked in the catacombs deep below the throne room where he'd once ruled. Some would have us believe that he was banished simply and unceremoniously to the World Above to live always among human men and women, stripped of all his power. There is, however, another account of his fate and, I believe, one that more likely is nearer the truth of the matter."

"And what *is* that?" asked the boy who'd yawned, but who was now wide awake and who, the peddler suspected, might not sleep at all that night.

"There is a story I heard the one time I ventured as far as Sinara – I dislike traveling through the Garden Lands, but that one time I did, and, by the way, it is said that soldiers of Sinara were also among those who joined with Elspeth – there is a story I heard there from a very old woman who once had been a priestess in a temple of the Elder Ones. Before that, she'd been a pirate and a smuggler, and before that – well, as I said, she was very old. She'd lived a long and strange life and knew many peculiar tales.

"We sat together in the back of a tavern on the banks of the River Xari, a tavern that served the wharves and all the shady, disreputable sorts one finds dockside, and she told me another version of the fate of Isaac Glyndwr Snow. She said, between fits of coughing and long drinks of whisky – for she was ill and did, I learned, soon after we spoke succumb to her tubercular sickness – that Elspeth took pity on him, for, at the last she saw before her a father. Sure now, children, I grant this is the oddest of all the twists and turns of my story, but often the course of history is many times odder than any fable or fairy tale."

The peddler closed her eyes, taking care here to say only that part fit for the ears of youngsters and, too, only that part she would not in days to come find herself ruing having said. When she opened her eyes, the hearth fire seemed much brighter than it had before, and it ringed the three children like a halo.

"C'mon then," said the boy on the tow-headed girl's right side. "Aunty, what was it the woman in the tavern told you?"

The girl glared at him. "Don't be rude, or she might decide not to say."

"I ought not," said the peddler. Her voice was rubbed thin by the telling of so long a tale, and it sounded to her ears weak and worn thin. "Sure, I should keep it between me, myself, and I. And the cats, of course, for cats know all, or so proclaim the wizened priests and priestesses of Ulthar."

"Please," said the girl. "We'll tell no one else. I swear. It will be our secret."

"It has been my experience," replied the peddler, "that children are not especially good at keeping secrets." She laughed quietly and chewed at the stem of her pipe. "But I will tell you all I know, which is, I have no doubt, not as much by half as you three would wish to hear." The peddler shifted in the chair, and her back popped loudly.

"The sickly woman in Sinara claimed that her own father had stood with Elspeth Snow in the Battle of the Vale of Pnath, and that he had ridden with her after the defeat of the King of Bones and Rags, down winding, perilous canyon roads to witness the sundering of the onyx gates of the royal city of Amaakin'šarr. There he watched as the Twilight's Wrath – this is the sobriquet Isobel had been given by her troops – confronted her father on the torch-lined steps of the palace. His guards bowed before her, praying she would spare their lives. But the Qqi d'Tashiva drew his sword against her and stood his ground. In the decades since his sister's escape he'd known only loneliness and regret, not one single hour of joy, and what was the loss of his life when he'd already lost the kingdom he'd hoarded at the cost of his only love?

"'Father,' said Isobel Snow to him, 'will you not now cast aside your folly and old misdeeds? Will you not put down your blade that I will not have to cause you further harm than already I have?'

"The King of Bones and Rags, he sneered hatefully and advanced towards her, blue eyes blazing, his sword glinting in the light of the flickering torches. There was naught remaining in him but bitterness and rage. 'Do not call *me* Father, whore, for you are your mother's bitch and none of mine. Now, come down off your horse and face me.'

"Elspeth Snow, Twilight's Wrath, the Maiden of Serannian – for she was called that, as well – did not dismount, as she desperately did not wish to slay the man who'd sired her, no matter his crimes against her mother and against the ghouls and all of the denizens of the Underworld. In her heart, she knew mercy, which Isobel had taught her, having learned it herself from the actions of Pickman and Sorrow. Did they not have fair cause to slay her, rather than aid in her escape? Sure. She had been half the author of their pain and the subjugation of their race. But even the black hearts of ghouls may feel pity.

"'No, Father,' said Elspeth. 'I have brought too much death this day, and your blood will not also stain my hands. I shall not be the despoiler you have become. That will not be your legacy to me.'

"'Thief,' he growled. 'Coward and thief, usurper and witch. You come to take my lands from me, but have not the courage to test your mettle against the rightful Qqi d'Tashiva. No whelp of mine would flinch from her final duty, cur.'

"At that, one of Elspeth's lieutenants drew an arrow from his quiver and nocked it, taking aim at Isaac Snow. But she was quick, and she stayed the man's hand. Again, her father cursed her as a coward."

"She should have killed him," said the boy who'd yawned.

"Of a certain," agreed the tow-headed girl.

"That may be. In the years to come, said the woman in the tavern in Sinara, Elspeth would sometimes doubt her choice that day, and sometimes she would wish him dead. But the fact, as this woman would have it, is that she did not kill him, nor did she permit any other to bring him harm. She declared that any who dared touch him would suffer a judgment far worse than death."

"Then what did she do?" asked the boy on the tow-headed girl's right.

"What she did do, child, was bestow upon him a gift."

All three children stared back at her now in stark disbelief.

"No," said the girl.

"Yes," replied the peddler, "if the woman who had been a priestess in a temple of the Elder Ones, and before that a pirate and a smuggler, if she is to be trusted. Though, of course, it may be she was a liar or mistaken or mad, and sure, you may choose to believe or not."

"Then . . . what did she do?" asked the boy who'd yawned. "I mean, what manner of gift did she give such a wicked man?"

At that the peddler smiled and slowly shook her head. "The woman in the tavern did not say, because she did not know. Her father had never told her, not specifically, but said only that it was a gift that lifted from the shoulders of Isaac Snow all his bitterness and insanity, all of his fury and grief. Elspeth's gift, said the woman in the tavern, restored to him that which he'd held so dear, though *how* this was accomplished we do not know. But he was changed – and changed utterly. Afterwards, Elspeth ordered him escorted to the seven hundred steps and up, up, up . . . and *up* . . . to the Gates of Deeper Slumber, where he was sent back to the Waking World to live out the remainder of his days and where he may yet dwell, for none in the Dream Lands have knowledge of what became of him. We can say only, by *this* version of the truth, that he passed beyond the ken of the world."

"That isn't a very good ending," frowned the tow-headed girl.

"It most assuredly isn't," said the boy who'd yawned.

"Not at all," added the boy on the girl's right side.

The peddler tilted her head, and she said sternly, "Do you imagine this is the way of tales, the way of the world, that it is somehow beholden to come with satisfying conclusions? If, indeed, it comes with any conclusions at all?"

The children didn't answer the question. The boy who'd yawned peered over his shoulder at the fire, which was beginning to burn down. The tow-headed girl stared down at her bare feet. And the boy on her right picked at a loose thread in his trousers. Only the girl spoke. She asked the old woman, "Aunty, did Elspeth Snow become the new Queen of Bones and Rags?"

"No, child, she did not. She had no taste for power, though the temptation must have weighed heavily on her soul. Elspeth entrusted Richard Pickman and his compatriots with the future of Thok and with the task of rebuilding Amaakin'šarr. She forsook what remained of the prophecy, vowing never again to be a soldier, and she rode away from Thok and back to the Upper Dream Lands. She took with her the Basalt Madonna, which, I have heard, she carried far across the Middle Ocean and even beyond the Eastern Desert and Irem, City of Pillars. It could not be destroyed, and she dared not entrust it to the hands of any being so mighty *they* could have undone the Qqi d'Evai Mubadieb. But she did hide it, and she hid it well. Some say she cast it over the edge of the world, though, personally, I think that is likely an exaggeration."

"And what became of her after that?" asked the girl, not looking up from her feet.

"Some say that she returned at last to Serannian, where she died many years ago. And others say she went to Celephaïs, and still others that, by wielding the Madonna she'd become undying and was permitted a place among the Old Ones in the shining city of Kadath. But these are all rumors, and no more to be trusted than ever rumors should be," and with that, the peddler drew a deep breath and said that she'd told all she could tell in a night.

There were questions from the children, but she did not answer them. She sent the three away to their beds, and then went to the garret room she'd been provided for the night – in exchange for a story. Several of the cats followed her, including the tabby tom, and they stood sentry at the top of the stairs. However, despite her great exhaustion, the peddler did not immediately seek sleep. Rather, she opened the shutters of the garret's single small window, and there in Ulthar, she undressed before the brilliant eye of the moon and before all the icy, innumerable stars that speckle an early autumn evening sky. The night regarded her with perfect indifference, and she regarded it with awe. And the peddler, the seller of notions and oddments, the nameless old woman who wandered the cities on the plains below Mount Lerion, she recalled her mother, and a kindly ghoul named Sorrow, and the last face her father had worn. And she told herself a truer tale than she'd told the children.

"As early as my boyhood and teenage years," writes **Brian Hodge**, "before I'd even discovered H. P. Lovecraft, wide open spaces and rural ruins and desolate roads struck me as eerie locales, haunted by their pasts and potentially harboring newer menaces. Terrible things can unfold, slowly, where few human eyes are around to witness them, and landscapes have long memories.

"I come from farmers who plowed the earth, from miners who crawled inside it. I grew up a town kid, but when visiting grandparents, my playgrounds were fields and woodlands. My relationship to remote places has always been that of a heathen, allowing for the possibility of heathen gods.

"So, when I first read works such as 'The Dunwich Horror' and 'The Colour Out of Space' they had, despite their alien monstrosities, the kind of immediate familiarity that comes with seeing your worst suspicions confirmed.

"To me, 'Lovecraftian' is more than a stew of ingredients – start with these trappings, sprinkle in these settings, season with references to this deity or that grimoire – although you'll find a few familiar flavors in 'It's All the Same Road In the End.'

"I also regard 'Lovecraftian' as a way of looking at the earth and the night skies that engulf it. It's a sense of memory and process; a recognition of the vast antiquity of the soil underfoot and the waters that carve it. It's a realization that the molecules in your body may have traveled billions of years to get here, and more may be on the way, in a myriad of forms, and that the ground they land on will, in time, yield to whatever proves best equipped to colonize or conquer it.

"And who's to say the earliest emissaries aren't already living at the end of a very long road."

Brian Hodge is one of those people who always has to be making something. So far, he's made ten novels, and is working on three more, as well as 120 shorter works and five full-length collections. Recent and forthcoming works include *In the Negative Spaces* and *The Weight of the Dead*, both standalone novellas; *Worlds of Hurt*, an omnibus edition of the first four works in his Misbegotten mythos; an updated edition of *Dark Advent*, his early post-apocalyptic epic; and his next collection, *The Immaculate Void*. Hodge lives in Colorado, where he also likes to make music and photographs; loves everything about organic gardening except the thieving squirrels; and trains in Krav Maga and kickboxing, which are useless against the squirrels.

It's All the Same Road in the End
Brian Hodge

———

The roads all looked the same again, along with the dried-up little towns they led to. They'd all looked the same again for the last couple of years, the way they had at the beginning.

Funny thing – there was a stretch in the middle when they hadn't. Two or three years when Clarence and Young Will's eyes had grown keen enough to pick up on the subtle differences that, say, set Slokum apart from Brownsville. Here, the peculiarities of a water tower, with the look of an alien tripod; there, the way a string of six low hills undulated across the horizon like the humps of a primordial serpent.

But now they'd let the distinctions slip away. From place to place, it wasn't that different after all. They'd seen it all before and forgotten where. Everything was the same again.

This was how things hid in open daylight, beneath the vast skies, out here in the plains of western Kansas. There was no need for mountain hollows or fern-thick forests or secret caves tucked into seaside coves. The things that wanted to stay hidden would camouflage themselves as one more piece of the monotony and endless repetition.

The worst thing Clarence could think of was that he and his brother were now a part of it too. That the land was digesting them so slowly they didn't even realize it.

Five days into this trip, the latest of many, all the Brothers Pine had to show for it was another gallon of gas traded for another dusty road-side hamlet that, until this moment, was just a name along a blue line on the most detailed map they'd been able to buy. Gilead, this time. Sometimes there wasn't even enough town to land on the map.

Another stop, another chance for the truth. More or less, it always went this way:

They started with a feed-and-seed store a block away from a grain elevator. From the moment they stepped in, they drew looks from the old man on one side of the counter and the farmer on the other. No hostility, just curiosity, and why not – both men probably knew every face within ten or twenty miles. But the pair of brothers was a disruption, their arrival like the stroke of a bell that made the farmer aware of time again, and all he had left to do in the day. He made his goodbye and his exit, out to an old workhorse of a pickup truck with a bed full of fifty-pound bags.

"Help you?" Already the old seed man sounded puzzled. They often sounded puzzled.

Small talk first. Sure is hot today. Sure is. Looks like you could use some rain. Sure could. Could always use more rain.

It was better when they were old. The elders were the ones with the longest memories, and a need to hang onto the stories of the things that had happened around them, especially the things that shouldn't have. They remembered events that younger people – Clarence and Young Will's peers, especially – never knew, or never had time for.

Even Will Senior had known that, way back when.

"This may seem like a funny question," Young Will said. He was the one feeling talkative today. Just as well. He had the friendlier face, oval and open and guileless, and the taller stature that commanded attention. He looked as if he should still be in college, shooting hoops and resolute about never breaking the rules. "But have you ever heard anything about a man named Willard Chambers? This would go back quite a few years."

Then he produced the picture, the first one, black and white in a thousand grainy shades of gray. It had a vintage look, a vintage feel, showing a square-faced, wavy haired man who cracked a grin both impish and wise as he gestured with a cigarette pinched between his thumb and forefinger. Did men in the prime of their lives even look like this anymore? Clarence had never seen one.

The old man dipped into memory's well and came up empty. "Can't say any of it rings a bell. Should it? What did he do?"

"He disappeared."

"Sorry to hear that." The old man's sympathy was genuine and matter-of-fact. You didn't get to be this old without a long acquaintance with loss. "When?"

"A little over fifty years ago."

"Mercy. That *is* a spell." From behind black-framed glasses sturdy enough to take a punch, the old man peered at the photo again, maybe looking for something familiar. "Did he come from around here? Have kin around here?"

"No sir, he didn't."

He took one more look at the photo, then gave them a fresh appraisal, seeing the connection in Clarence, maybe. He had inherited the square features, if not the freewheeling demeanor. He had the knitted eyebrows of a born worrier.

"Are *you* kin to him?"

"He was our grandfather," Clarence said.

The old man seemed to understand their need without having to know anything more. "A thing like that never does scab over, does it?"

Next came the second photo, along with a grainy enlargement of just its subject. "I know there's not much to go on with these, but is there anything here that looks familiar? The place, or who this might've been?"

This time the old man took the photos for himself. People did that a lot. They seemed unable to leave them on a counter. They had to pick them up, had to stare as if to prove to themselves they were real. Not that there was anything, on first inspection, that appeared false, or even out of the ordinary. Perception demanded time. People noticed the wrongness of it in subtle ways they couldn't identify, as if something fifty years behind this moment had left hidden hooks in the image, to hold their attention until they truly *saw*, and then forced their hand to thrust the photos back.

"No," the old man said. "But wherever this is, I think if I'd come across it once, I would've known to make sure I never went back."

Will nodded and slipped the photos into their folder again, the way he'd been conceding defeat for years.

"Did she have something to do with him disappearing?" the man asked. "That *is* a woman there, isn't it?"

No matter how many times they'd heard the question, there was still no easy answer.

"As far as we know," Will said, and left it at that.

Clarence stepped forward. "One last thing. Could we trouble you to listen to a recording? If you've ever heard anything like this, or about something like it?"

The old fellow was game, and slipped on the compact pair of foam-padded earphones Clarence gave him. They were downstream of an old Walkman cassette player, a clunky and outmoded thing to be toting around these days. But Will Senior had lived as an analog man in an analog world, and had made the original recording onto tape. For no reason Clarence could prove, it would've seemed wrong to digitize it for convenience; reducing it to a file would erase some ineffable quality in it that might be preserved by dubbing it to a newer tape.

He pressed PLAY.

The seed man listened privately in the baked stillness of the day, nothing but the chirring of insects outside and the chirping of birds that would eat them if they could. As went the photos, so went the tape, a slow-burn reaction that creased the old man's face with gradual repulsion. The recording went for a little over three minutes, but he had the earphones stripped away in two.

Clarence pressed STOP.

"Is that supposed to be a song?" the old man asked.

"I guess so. We don't know what else to call it."

"Call it quits, why don't you? Sounds like that aren't supposed to come out of folks' throats. No sir." The old man reached up to rub the back of his neck, bristly with gray stubble and as creased as a tortoise's skin. "The closest thing I ever heard to it . . . I come from a long line of Swedes. The women used to have a cattle call song they brung over. You don't hear it anymore. It was an eerie-sounding thing, if you heard it at some distance. But you could still tell it was a woman's voice. But what you've got there . . ." He shook his head, then regarded them with an uneasy fusion of suspicion and worry. "You seem like nice boys. Why would you want to go looking for anything to do with that?"

"You said it yourself," Young Will told him. "It's a scab thing."

They were both named for dead men, grandfathers they'd never met. Men who had died when their parents were still youngsters. For all Clarence knew, it was the first thing their mother and father discovered they had in common.

The carrying on of someone's name was apparently supposed to be an honor, and perhaps it was, but many were the times Clarence wondered if their parents had ever stopped to consider the obvious: the bigger the trophy, the heavier it was to lug around.

Clarence and Willard . . . neither quite felt like a twenty-first-century name.

As Clarence was the firstborn, Dad had gotten first crack at him, saddling him with the moniker of a man who'd succumbed in his thirties to the black lung he'd carried up out of a West Virginia coal mine. His end had come hard and early, but at least it was certain. There was no room for doubt in it, only sorrow and blame.

Six years later, with their sister Dina in between, it was Mom's turn to christen her third child as if he were an avatar of the man who'd vanished around the time she'd been hitting puberty, and the recycled name an invitation for her father to return from whatever void had swallowed him.

The legacy of Willard Chambers was a more complicated thing for a namesake to live up to. He was restless, a roamer, but not without reason. Clarence was grown before he'd ever heard the term *song-catcher*, but that's exactly what the man was.

The inability of Will Senior to carry a tune was matched only by his reverence for those who could. He had an appreciation of history, and must have known by then that he'd lived it himself. He'd come through the Second World War, three years in the Pacific, fighting toward Japan one fierce island at a time, and seeing close up the fragility of everything that lived and breathed.

Songs, too. Songs were living things and could be killed by far less than bullets and fire. All it took was for them to stop being heard. He was a city dweller who had served alongside Okie farmboys and gangly fellows from Appalachian hollers. They brought with them songs he'd never heard on the radio. Obsessed as they were with life and death and the acts that bridged the two – murders and drownings and love gone wrong – they may have appealed to him for their stark understanding that he might not see tomorrow either.

But he had. Three years in the Pacific, and he suffered no worse than a case of paddy foot.

At some point, home again, he'd learned of the Lomaxes – John the father and Alan the son – and realized he'd found a calling. These were men who traveled the country in search of songs whose roots lay deep in the earth of crops and graves: rural blues, cowboy ballads, folk tunes from plains and mountains, prison work songs, and anything else that was a jubilant or despairing cry from the heart of a marginalized life. Will Senior bought the same tape recorder that Alan Lomax was using at the time – a compact, battery-powered reel-to-reel called a

Nagra – and took it on the road whenever he could. Which amounted to as much as four or five months out of the year.

For reasons that likely went back to wartime, Willard had taken a special interest in the region known during the Great Depression as the Dust Bowl . . . an arid wasteland whose great dark eye overlapped western Kansas and eastern Colorado, a slice of New Mexico, and the panhandles of Texas and Oklahoma. He had it in his head that songs from there were most vulnerable, since so many who would've sung them had been scattered by the same winds that carried away the topsoil, leaving them mostly in the care of those who'd been too sick or old to move. He saw it as a race against time.

From everything Clarence and Will had heard about him, Willard Chambers wasn't a man you needed to worry about. He knew nearly everything there was to know about taking care of himself. His family just missed him, deeply, with the resentful ache that comes from being forced to share a man with an obsession, and counting the days until he and his '59 Chevy would be home again.

His eighth run west became his last. Neither he nor the Chevy made it back, or were ever seen again.

At least his gear – the Nagra and a Leica camera from his war years – had found its way home eventually.

Even that had taken months.

They made it through five more towns north of Gilead, then it was the long ride south, back to the motel they'd been using for home base. Clarence took the wheel and Will took the map, looking over what tomorrow might bring. More of the same, that was obvious, only the route would change.

"One day," Clarence said, "every town in the western half of this map is going to have a red dot next to it. Have you ever thought about what then?"

"For you and me, you mean?"

"For Mom. If she even makes it to then. Except she probably won't."

"You mean just lie to her? Tell her we found something even though we didn't?"

"If it gives her some peace, finally, would that be so bad?"

"I see what you did there," Will said. "The next square you advance to after that is, okay, now that we've established lying as an acceptable option, why not lie to her now and save ourselves all that future trouble."

"I never said that."

"It was coming. Don't tell me it wasn't," Will said. "I keep telling you that you can bail any time you want. This doesn't have to be a two-man project. It never did."

Maybe not, but to Clarence it had always felt that way. No argument that he wasn't superstitious was as persuasive as the conviction that as soon as he let Will do this on his own, their mom would mourn a vanished son, too.

It had begun when his brother was nineteen, a college sophomore who'd enjoyed just one year of Daytona Beach debauchery before deciding he'd rather spend spring break in Kansas. Mother's Day was coming in a few weeks, and his idealistic kid brother could think of no better gift to give theirs than the answers she'd craved for decades.

Just like that, huh? Sure. Why not.

You didn't let an earnestly headstrong nineteen-year-old do something like this on his own. No telling who he might run into, and his 4.0 grade average didn't mean he couldn't be stupid when smart mattered most. Elderly Klansmen and their ilk still protected killings half a century old, and there was an uneasy sense they weren't dealing with anything quite so prosaic here.

That first year, Clarence had been counting on the enormity of the task to discourage him, and had never been so wrong about anything in his life. Spring breaks turned into career-era vacations, one year became six, and whatever happened to Will Senior remained as much a mystery as ever. And Clarence still couldn't shake the feeling that, without him, his brother would meet his own bad end.

More than once, he thought of the man in the photo, the grandfather who was two decades younger than their father was now, and wanted to hear it from the man's tobacco-seared lips: Would he even want this for them?

Go on, live your own lives and quit trying to reconstruct mine, he imagined Will Senior telling them. *Have that kid you keep telling your wife you'll get around to.*

Just like that, huh?

What is it, son, you think you've got to wait until after you get me figured out before you do it? You think you'll be doing the same thing to your kids that I did to mine by coming out here to the world's breadbasket?

Something like that.

In that case, maybe you need to get clearer on your priorities.

Easy for you to say, old man. I'm the one you left cleaning up your fifty-year-old mess.

Willard never had a comeback to that one. He never even tried.

As they drove, the sun sank low, lower, the plains and the gentle hills thickening with shadows that reached for their car from the west. Everywhere you looked, it was nothing but wheat and the road that ran through it like a path through a forest. He pointed to the last remnants of some lost homestead, an ancient barn whose bones had bent, the entire structure weathered to a silvery gray, sagging in on itself and leaning like a cripple as if to wait for the good strong breeze that would finally end its struggle.

"I keep thinking I'd like to come back here with a truck one day and tear one of these down," he said. "For the wood."

Back in his real life, he and his wife owned a frame shop. One of these wrecks could give birth to a lot of frames. It appealed, that whole life cycle thing about new life springing from decay.

"Rustic never goes out of style," he said.

Will looked up from the map, reoriented to where they were and what he was talking about, and shook his head. "I think they should stay standing."

"They're barely standing as it is. That's kind of the point."

His brother went dreamy, pensive. "They're like monuments to some other time. You just want to knock them down and rip them apart? For what, somebody's wall?"

"Is there any reason wood rot and fungus should get first dibs?"

"You recognize the irony, I hope. You tear down a perfectly picturesque *real* barn to saw it apart and nail it around a picture of one. That's always seemed like a special kind of hubris to me."

"Also known as recycling," Clarence said. "I thought you were big on that."

Will grumbled and went back to the map, and Clarence took the exchange as one for his win column. His brother's problem? It was as if the weight of his name had infected him with nostalgia for an era he'd never experienced and could never have tolerated. He didn't have the stomach for it. Farms, at a glance, may have looked as if they were bursting with life, but ultimately they all led to something's death.

And whatever rotted out here would rot alone.

It was the same the next day, and the day after that, and it was easy to imagine that Kansas was Purgatory in disguise. They'd actually died in a car crash in Missouri, and their sins would keep them on an endless road for decades of penance, except Will was going to move on a lot sooner than Clarence would.

Shortly after dusk, they returned for their final night in the latest motel they'd been using as home base. The strategy had emerged during their first trip. Rather than checking into a new place to sleep each night, they opted to settle for a few days at some central crossroads, from which they could branch out in any of several directions.

Sometimes you had to cling to whatever illusion of stability you could.

As Clarence showered off the August road sweat, Will got on the phone with their mother to tell her of the day's journey – the places they'd stopped, the people they'd spoken to – and what tomorrow would bring. What made him the perfect son made him a perfectly terrible brother. It wasn't just from out here that he called home every day. He called home 365 days a year. There was no keeping up with that. You'd think he would run out of new things to say, but he always found more.

He's the daughter they always hoped I'd be, Dina had whispered in Clarence's ear last Christmas, after just enough wine, and neither of them could stop snickering.

"Say hi to Mom," Will ordered, and pushed the phone at him while he was still toweling off from the shower.

Clarence took it and dug to find a few topics that Will wouldn't have covered already, and it was okay, it really was. He reminded himself there would come a day when he wouldn't have this chance and would regret every awkward moment he'd been less than enthusiastic about taking the phone. Myelofibrosis, it was called; a bone-marrow defect. There was no coming back from it. She had two years left, if she was lucky, just long enough to trick himself into thinking it wasn't really going to happen, that grieving was still decades in the future.

Then they swapped places, and while Will took his turn in the shower, Clarence cracked open his laptop to see if their latest ads had drawn any responses. Craigslist, local classifieds, weekly shoppers . . . for years they'd been sprinkling such outlets with some variation of the following:

> *Family seeking information on the disappearance of amateur musicologist Willard Chambers, of Charleston, West Virginia. Vanished somewhere in western Kansas in July 1963. He is believed to have gone missing while trying to locate an old woman who was at that time living alone in a remote area, and reputed to have a unique style of singing regarded as "unearthly."*

They would accompany it with his picture when they could. Sometimes they'd run the other one, too, the last photo of Will Senior's life, but it was always too small and indistinct to reveal the details that, with a hardcopy print, made people stop and stare with a rising pall of dread. But at least it showed the oddities of the setting surrounding that strange, stark figure, and maybe that was all someone would need.

Responses? Mostly a lot of nothing. The little that did come in, he could weed through it quickly and flush it with impunity. They could always count on well-meaning people who wanted to help but didn't know anything, and trolls eager to waste everyone's time.

But then there was today. There was always the chance of something like today.

I'm not near old enough to have met your grandfather, so I can't help you there. But when I was little, I'd go visit my Nana Ingrid and she used to scare me into obeying her with talk of an old lady she knew about when she was young. Everybody used to keep away and just let her be. The old lady, I mean. This would've been around a place called Biggsby. I don't know if it's even on the maps anymore, or if it ever was. The nearest place of any size at all is Ulysses, and that's not much. I should know, that's where I am.

What made me think of this is the singing part. Gran said they'd hear her singing sometimes, nights mostly. She used to know this type of song called a cattle call and said it was kinda like that, only she couldn't imagine it bringing the cows in. She said a voice like that would be more like to scare them away.

There's more, but I don't know what's important to you and what's not, and I'm not much for long emails even to people I know. But I love to talk!

He dashed off a reply, then looked up Ulysses on the map and poked his head into the steam of the bathroom to tell Will that, come morning, they would be going south instead.

They met her at a barbecue place in Ulysses, her suggestion. It smelled of hickory smoke and fryer oil, and they got there first by twenty minutes because she was fifteen late. Clarence knew she was the one the moment she walked in. She wore boots with shorts, carried a handbag big enough to brain a horse, and moved with precisely the kind of energy he'd expect out of someone who says "But I love to talk!"

She sized them up instantly, too. "Hi, I'm Paulette," she said. "Paulette, Johnetta, and Raylene . . . can you tell our dad had his heart set on boys instead of girls?" She slammed the handbag into one of the two vacant chairs at their table and herself in the other. "You're buying, right?"

She shot up then and went for the counter to order for all of them, insisting she knew what was best, and best avoided. Paulette was both stocky and shapely, like a six-foot woman squashed down to a compact five-four, and Clarence eyed his brother as he watched her go. Not again.

"Already?" Clarence said. "Not three dozen words out of her and you're already there?"

Will scowled as if he resented the interruption. Somewhere along the miles and years he'd picked up a fixation that he was going to meet the love of his life out here on the plains. Some Kansas farmgirl, all about family, whose commitment would be as certain and uncomplicated as the sunrise over the wheat. Did they even exist anymore, if they ever had?

"You don't match. I've seen couples who match. They don't look a thing like you and her."

Will balled up a napkin in his fist. "Maybe I should handle this while you go back to the motel and take your anti-asshole pills."

As they waited for their food, Paulette wanted to know all about them. If they were still from West Virginia, and what it was like there, and when she found out Will was now living in Boston, wanted to know what that was like, too. When she learned he was a cloud architect, she made a joke about castles in the sky, and Clarence could see him turn that much more into putty. She wanted to know what their parents were like, and when she learned they had a sister, wanted to know which of them Dina was more alike, and what came out of that was a surprise, because each of them had always assumed he was the one, a revelation that made Paulette laugh.

"I figure you're safe," she finally said, "because that ad of yours, that's just not the kind of story someone would make up to draw somebody out on her own. So break 'em out, let's see these pictures of yours."

They laid out Will Senior's portrait first.

"That version you had on Craigslist doesn't do him justice," she said. "Grandpa was kind of a hunk, wasn't he?"

"And here's the one we don't know where it was taken," Clarence said. "But it was the final shot on his camera. It was a twenty-four-shot roll of film, and the last eighteen were never even exposed."

Paulette stared a long time, the way people always did. It slowed her down. She forgot her jittery habit of every few seconds pushing her sun-streaked hair back from her face, behind her ears.

"Well," she said at last, "this looks about like what I would've imagined from those old stories Nana Ingrid would tell to scare me into minding her."

Black and white in a thousand grainy shades of gray, the last photo on the roll of 35mm film in Willard's Leica appeared to have been shot up a slight incline, a wide dirt path bordered by two ragged rows of stout sticks, as long as spears and nearly as straight. They'd either been branches or saplings, cut and stripped, then jammed into the earth like a loose palisade wall. In all their searching, the purpose of this remained a mystery. Beyond these sticks, and through them, in the middle distance, was a glimpse of what he assumed was a farmhouse, and a pair of trees in summer bloom.

But in the foreground, she stood. She stood on a ladder of shadows that the low sun of morning or evening threw from one row of sticks across to the other, something strange in her stance, as if she had to lean back from her own wide hips. She wore an apron around her middle, ill-fitting, refusing to lie smoothly, and a scarf around her head, knotted at her throat.

"Here's the blow-up detail, just her," Clarence said.

Now her true wrongness began to emerge. Her face was mostly shadowed, just enough visible to make you wish you could see either more, and know what she really was, or less, so you didn't have to entertain doubts. The only features that caught the sidelight were a bulbous nose and a blocky chin that appeared to thrust forward from a lantern jaw. The rest was suggestion, and all the worse for it. Something about the way the features all fit together seemed . . . off. Like something carved from wood, and badly. The mouth looked grim and straight across, wider than wide. And given the scarf and direction of the sun, he could think of no reason her eyes should gleam with glints of light. Will Senior had been photographer enough to not bother using a flash outside like this, if he'd even possessed one.

Paulette was still shuffling from one print to the other. "Last shot on the roll, you said. What were the others?"

"Just landscapes. Nothing distinctive about them.

Paulette tapped the blow-up. "Well, Nana Ingrid used to say she wasn't really a woman at all. Or maybe not anymore, or maybe she told it both ways. Just something that dressed like one. To hide. Stories like that, you believe them when you're little. That's why they work, you don't want her to get you. Then you get a little older and you think it's just talk."

"What kind of stories?"

"Oh, you know, the usual threats. How if I didn't behave, she was going to come steal me, cook me. Or throw me down her well. Which of course was bottomless. Or use my bones to make a nest for her vulture. Nana could be creative sometimes."

"What did she call this woman?" Clarence asked. "She had to have a name."

"Old Daisy. Never just plain Daisy. Usually Old Daisy. Sometimes Crazy Daisy, if she was going for a laugh."

"Daisy? Seriously?"

"I know," Paulette said, and tapped the detail photo again. "That's the most undaisified woman I've ever seen."

Will leaned toward her from across the table, and she mirrored him right back, as if the two of them were already excluding him. "How old was your grandmother when she first knew about Daisy?"

"She grew up around her. So, from the time she was a little bitty thing until she was close to my age."

"What happened then?"

"She got hitched and moved a few miles away and squeezed out my mom." Paulette swept the photos together and shoved them at Clarence. "Better put these up for safe keeping. We're about to get nine kinds of messy here."

He slipped them into their folder as the food arrived, beef ribs and pulled pork and slaw and onion rings made with jumbo Vidalias. A couple of bites in, he was willing to admit that, okay, Paulette knew her barbecue joints.

"How close did Ingrid live to her?" Will asked.

Paulette shrugged. "Down the road, is all she used to say."

"How far does that mean?" Clarence said.

"I have no idea. You know country people. 'Down the road a piece' . . . that can mean just about anything."

"But your grandmother saw her, right? These weren't just stories to her, too?"

"Saw her all the time. Never up close, though. Nobody ever saw her up close. There's some people, you know, they're just not neighborly, so you let them be. Back then, I guess it was seen as more peculiar than it is now. Now it's just a way of life all over. But even then, there had to be people like that, and I guess they didn't push it. She did fine on her own, puttering around that old place." Paulette grinned, recalling more. "That didn't stop the area boys from trying to look. Nana Ingrid's brother was one of them. They'd dare each other to sneak up close to Old Daisy's property and try to get in a peek, and they'd get a good scare. Before they got too close, she'd spot them and screech at them and they'd scatter. In fact, that's what some people thought that crazy singing she did was all about. To keep people away. Same as a rattle-snake shaking its tail."

"A threat display."

"And I guess it worked," she said. "Have you got it? Can I hear it?"

She wiped her fingers with a Wet-Nap as they handed over the Walkman and the earphones. The tape was already cued up, and unlike many people, Paulette didn't shut it down early. She hung in there until the end.

"I gotta say, that's not what I was expecting," she said while stripping away the headphones. "That doesn't sound like a crazy person. It hardly sounds like a person at all."

Clarence had always thought the same thing, but never liked to lead people to the conclusion. It was always more validating to see them arrive at it on their own.

"Maybe I'm just dense, but there's one thing I'm not getting here," she said. "If nobody ever saw your grandfather again, then how do you happen to have his last pictures and recordings?"

"The greed and kindness of strangers," Will said.

"The camera was something he got while he was in the army. He epoxied a nameplate on it, so it wouldn't be as easy for someone to steal," Clarence said. "Three or four months after he went missing, our grandmother got a call from a pawn shop in Hays. The family had raised all the hell they could out here, her and our uncles . . . filing missing person reports, and they got it in some newspapers, and on the radio, a little TV. So the pawnbroker recognized the name when some vagrant brought in the camera and tape recorder in the same bag our grandfather used to carry them around. Oilskin, so it wouldn't soak through if he got caught in the rain. The story the pawnbroker got out of him, once he got him past the bullshit about how they were his, was that he found the bag on a junk heap along the side of the road someplace west. By that time, he'd been carrying them around a couple weeks or more, until he could find someplace to sell them, so he couldn't pin it down where he found them. Nobody got a chance to press him on it, because once he realized he wasn't going to get any money for them, and maybe there was a murder investigation in it too, he was out the door and gone."

Will cut in to finish as if he were feeling sidelined. "The pawnbroker wasn't a big fan of the cops either, so he got in touch with our family directly. Said he'd get our grandfather's things to them and let them decide what they wanted to do about that."

"Decent of him," she said. "What'd they do?"

"They had the film developed, had prints made, and copies of the tape. They sent them out to different departments. It didn't help. Since there was no body and no car, I don't think they were taking it seriously, once they understood that these trips of his weren't anything new. I think they just figured he liked it that way and decided to stay gone. Start over somewhere else. He wouldn't be the first."

Paulette narrowed her eyes. "Wait a second. Nobody ever found his car, either?"

"No."

"Doesn't that seem weird to you that both him and his car vanish, but his camera and tape recorder get found?"

Will appeared mystified she would even ask. "That's just what happened."

"Yeah, but . . ." She pecked at the folder holding the photos. "Say Old Daisy is responsible. Somehow, some way. Somebody is, so let's say it's her. She gets rid of him. Obviously. She knows enough to get rid of his car, too. That's pretty cunning. You can't drop a car down a well. But then this bag of other things that could be tied to him, she's so careless with it she just tosses it aside like it doesn't matter? Even though she stood right there facing him as he took her picture? Does that make sense to you?"

Clarence stepped in, locking ranks. "Like he said. That's how it happened."

But Paulette was right. Sometimes it took an outsider to point out the obvious. It had never gnawed at him until now. He'd known the story since childhood. Had grown up taking every detail for granted without appreciating what some might actually imply.

"Daisy didn't know what a camera was?" he mused. "She knew what cars were, she could see that, even if she didn't drive one herself. But the camera and tape recorder . . . no. She didn't know. In 1963, she didn't know. How is that possible?"

"Like *I* said. She kept to herself and they were glad to let her do it."

Clarence moved the decades around in his head like blocks. "How far back are we talking about with your grandmother, anyway? How old is she?"

Paulette did some quick calculating. "She'd be seventy-five, seventy-six now."

"So if she grew up around Old Daisy, that'd be as far back as twenty years before our grandfather disappeared. Give or take. And she was old then?"

"That was the story. It sounded like she was one of those people who'd always been around, as far back as anyone could remember. But you know, some people, they look and act older than they really are, so that's how it gets to seeming that way. And if you don't see them up close . . ."

"Did you ever see her?"

"God no. I never wanted to. Nana Ingrid talked like she was still around, but this was at her married home, miles from where she grew up. She must've been making it up. She'd step out on the porch sometimes and stare down the dirt road like she was watching for the old hag, like she might spot her passing by and call her over if I didn't behave. But that was just part of the threats. This was, what, thirty, forty years on from when she was living out there, so the woman had to be dead by then."

Had to. Yes.

"It's a hard old life, out like that."

Had to. Unless a woman wasn't what she was at all.

"You say Ingrid's still with you?" Clarence said.

"She's in a home now. Good days and bad days. But yeah."

"Could she tell you where Daisy's place was? Exactly? And how to find it?"

Paulette hesitated before answering, like someone who hated to let people down but would do it anyway. "Look, I was glad to help if I could, if it didn't take too long, but I'm not looking for a new project to take on. And that Wal-Mart produce aisle isn't going to run itself."

"We'll pay," Will blurted. "We'll make it worth your time."

Clarence wondered how obvious it would be if he kicked his brother under the table.

"'Worth your time' is like 'down the road a piece,'" Paulette said. "There's lots of wiggle room in what it means."

Two days later, on the word of Paulette's grandmother – on one of her good days, he hoped – they headed out into the prairie wastes again, deeper than they'd ever had reason enough to go. There had never been much point to going where people were so few and far between that the land hardly seemed lived in at all.

It had once, though. The rubble and residue lingered. Along roads that had crumbled mostly back to dirt, they passed the scattered, empty shells of lives long abandoned. Separated by minutes and miles, the remains of farmhouses and barns left for ruin seemed to sink into seas of prairie grass. The trees hung on, as tenacious loners or clustering into distant, ragged rows that betrayed the hidden vein of a creek.

"I think this might be it. Where Nana grew up," Paulette said from the back seat. "Can we stop?"

She'd been guiding them from a hand-drawn map that took over from where the printed map left off.

Clarence nosed the car toward the side of the road, sniffing for where the driveway used to be, and found it – a weedy land bridge between stretches of clogged ditch. He didn't go far past. Any debris could be in that grass. He killed the engine and they got out to stand in the simmering silence of the day as Paulette compared the place as it was now with a photo borrowed from an album at her parents' home.

"Is this it?" Will asked, and he sounded so tender.

"I think. I don't know. But it should be. It's just hard to tell."

Of course it was. The picture showed life. However hardscrabble, it was life: a troop of skinny children, boys in overalls and girls in plain dresses, clowning around a swing fashioned from two ropes and a slat of wood. That could be the same oak, right there, sixty-odd years bigger. The sun-blasted, two-story farmhouse looked as though it could be the corpse of the one behind the children. It seemed to be the same roof, even though half of it was now gone, exposing a framework of rotting rafters. Unseen in the photo was a windmill out back that must've pumped their well. It still stood, a rusted, skeletal tower as tall as the house and crowned with a giant fan. A few of its sixteen blades had fallen free, while the rest ignored the wind, the gears too corroded to turn.

He reconsidered. There was still plenty of life here. It was just nothing human.

"It would kill her to see the place like this," Paulette said. "Literally kill her."

Which could have been an act of mercy. Yesterday's trip to the nursing home had left him with a new appreciation for living out like this until the end. It had to hasten things, a swifter demise than being warehoused in a stinking building devoted to death by increments, surrounded by people whose bodies and minds raced to see which could deteriorate faster, and the cruelest thing was having enough of a mind left to realize you were one of them. Out like this, fall and break a hip? He'd take three days of dehydration on the floor over years of the other.

Paulette had wandered ahead of them in a daze, as if time had slowed, exploring the trunk of the oak, the front of the house, pieces of the past hidden in the weeds.

"I came from here. I came from this," she said, although whom she was speaking to wasn't clear. "And I never bothered to come see. Thirty miles, and I didn't even come out for a look."

"Nice we can pay her for the privilege," Clarence murmured, not because he begrudged her the opportunity, but because he knew it would get a rise out of Will.

"Shut up. Don't you say anything more about that," Will said. "Besides, *we* aren't paying her for anything. *I* am."

And he didn't know why it rankled him so. Years ago they'd vowed to never pay for information. It could only encourage people to lie. For that matter, why did it rankle him so much that his brother was now bankrolling each year's venture? Because he could afford to, that's why. Right now, at least, cloud architecture was some of the best money in IT, and this was the way Will wanted to spend it, and the worst part of it was that Will pulled in six figures doing something he excelled at but didn't even enjoy. All the money in the world couldn't buy him what he seemed to want most: to live in a simpler time.

"I'm sorry," Clarence said. "I just want to get this done."

"I know."

"Except I don't know what *done* is supposed to look like. Even if we find that old hag's house and it's still standing, we're not going to walk in and find a skeleton at the table wearing Grandpa's army dog tags. It's never going to be that neat and clean."

At their feet was a decayed shard of post snarled in a rusty length of galvanized fencing that twisted through the grasses and weeds like a wire snakeskin. Will stared at it, seeming to ponder how he might straighten it out, make it all better.

"I know," he said again.

"I won't ask you to promise today, but when we find it, at least start thinking that maybe it should be the end of the line." He put a hand on his brother's shoulder. "We'll find the place in the picture. We found out who the woman was. We got a name, and there might be some old records where we can find out a little more. That's a lot. Maybe it should be enough to get to the last place Grandpa got to, and admit that the two of them are the only ones who know what happened next, and we just can't know. But we got here. We closed that circle. Can you live with that?"

Will thought a moment, then nodded. "I guess I'll have to. I just hope it'll be enough for Mom."

"Come on, slackers, let's go!" Paulette called over to them from the car. He hadn't even seen her return to it. "We haven't got all day!"

Under the vast and cloudless prairie sky, they prowled roads no one seemed to travel anymore. He recalled that the area had once been called Biggsby, and had been so inconsequential as to not even merit inclusion on modern maps. By now there was no indication this place had ever deserved being thought of as a town. Biggsby – it was the name of a hostile field sprawling between horizons, a forgotten savannah where animals burrowed and mated and devoured each other undisturbed.

Paulette's map seemed not quite right, maybe a casualty of faulty recollections: a curve in the road that shouldn't have been there, an expected crossroad that wasn't. They tracked and backtracked, futilely hoping to find things waiting just as they were in a photo shot fifty years ago. If only it could be as certain as spotting that inexplicable gauntlet of branches from Will Senior's last photo.

Even Nana Ingrid, who remembered it firsthand, hadn't had an explanation for that.

"She kept it in good repair, whatever it was for," Ingrid said from her wheelchair. "We used to call it her cattle chute. Even though she didn't raise no cattle."

They stopped to explore a series of ruined farmhouses that seemed like possible candidates, each little different from the others, all sagging roofs and disintegrating walls, collapsed chimneys and wood eaten to sponges and splinters by the onslaught of the seasons.

"Even if she did, you wouldn't want to bring the cattle straight to your door."

They found sofas reduced to shapeless masses erupting with rusty springs, and boxy old televisions whose tubes had shattered, and it was these castoffs that made him think no, none of these were the place, because as old and neglected as these features were, they were still too modern.

"What about there?" Will said, back on the hunt and pointing at a spot they'd passed twice already.

It was the gentle slope of the land that first made Clarence suspect they'd found it at last. The place was farther off the road than anywhere else they'd tried, and if these were the same trees in the background of Willard's photo, then they were willows with another fifty years of growth behind them, nearly sweeping the ground now to screen the house from sight from the road.

House? What they found was a slumping hovel, a single-story dwelling made of both durable stone and vulnerable timber. It seemed far older than the other ruins they'd inspected, something a pioneer might have built as a first outpost for taming a wild frontier. Behind the willows that bowed and bobbed in the wind, it sat in the midst of an immense stillness pregnant with the whispers of rustling leaves and insects whose chirring in the weeds sounded as sharp as a drill.

It felt right. This was the place. It felt right because something about it felt deeply wrong. This was a place poisoned by time.

And now that they knew, Young Will went back to the car, parked along the side of the road, to retrieve Will Senior's heirloom camera. The vintage Leica still worked. They'd been built to last decades, to survive wars. He brought it with him every year, but until this moment, Clarence had always assumed it was some sort of totem, the only physical connection he could have to the man whose name he'd been born to carry. He'd never mentioned an intention to actually use it.

His brother stationed himself down below, camera at his eye as he framed up the incline, until he was satisfied he'd found the vantage point from which Willard had shot his final photo. He then pointed at a spot on the ground that had once been striped by a ladder of shadows.

"Stand there," he told Paulette.

"What for?" She didn't sound happy about it.

"For scale."

She complied, but seemed to find the act physically repugnant, as if Daisy had left behind contaminants that would infect anyone who stood where she had. Good luck. If she'd lived here as long as legend suggested, there couldn't be a square inch of earth her gnarled feet hadn't cursed.

Clarence was more captivated by the thought of where Will Senior had hidden away, probably the night before, to make his recording. He'd gotten close, perhaps within twenty yards. There was a hint of distance in the sound, but not much; for comparison, they had the voice of Willard himself, the parts they never played for anyone else.

He pondered the ground he stood on. *From here.* Maybe the old man had hunkered low and listened to what he should never have heard and sealed his fate from right here.

They moved on, toward the remains of the house, finally ready to touch it. It was a shelter no longer, the outside world having invaded long ago, through the glassless windows and crumbling walls and the entrances whose doors had fallen off their hinges. Where the roof had drooped inward, it was open to the sun and moon alike. Weeds grew in every crack, and generations of predators had denned in the corners to gnaw the bones of their prey.

Yet even in its disintegration, traces of the life once lived here lingered: a chipped mug, a blue enamel coffee percolator, a salvageable spindle-back chair and the table it accompanied. A row of large cans, rusted almost to lace, remained on a cupboard shelf. In an alcove that might have been a closet sat a battered washtub whose accumulated filth couldn't quite hide the suggestion of ancient stains.

Gutbucket – the word came to him before he knew why, then he remembered it from his own digging into Willard's obsessions, as a folk term for a cheap upright bass made from a washtub.

He kept coming back to that improbable row of cans.

"Did she ever die, that anyone knew of?" Clarence asked.

"You got me," Paulette said. "If she did, Nana never heard about it."

"Wouldn't it have been news if she had?" He squatted in front of a block of iron, half hidden by weeds and tumbled rafters, and realized it was a wood-fired stove. "She kept to herself, okay, but one day, someone's got to realize nobody's seen her out for a year. Somebody's going to check eventually. They wouldn't let her rot in here forever."

"Maybe she just walked away," Will said.

"To go where? Where do you go from here?"

"You'd have to ask her," Paulette said, quieter now. "Maybe that's why Nana was always looking for her on the road."

They made their way around back, where the land rolled away into fields of nothing. A minute's walk in one direction led to a heap of fungus-eaten wood, the collapsed shell of an outhouse. It made his stomach roll to speculate what might turn up if they started scraping through the dried-out layers down in the trench. A minute's walk in another led to her well, the bucket and rope long gone, but the mortared stone wall around it remained intact. It was too dark down the well's gullet to see. He pried a rock from the grassy soil and lobbed it in, and seconds later heard a splat of thickest mud.

"How stupid are we, we didn't even bring a flashlight?" he said.

But there would be nothing to see, would there? He doubted she would poison her own well with a corpse. This was someone, something, resourceful enough to make a Chevrolet vanish, so surely she had better options for her dead. And it occurred to him that while he still thought of her as female, at some point he had ceased thinking of her as a woman.

"Clarence. Get over here."

He hadn't realized that Will and Paulette had drifted back to the house, where they both stood peering at the foundation.

He must have listened to the full recording a thousand times throughout his life.

It begins with the sound of clunks and fumbling, and spread atop the creamy hiss of tape is an ambience of crickets and tree frogs. If fireflies could make a sound, he imagined it would've captured them too.

"There we go. Missed it. Shoot. Not used to doing this in the dark." *Willard's voice is close and hushed, the voice of a man hugging the ground.* "Welp . . . if she's gonna do it again, she better do it while the batteries are

*still good." His disappointment is palpable. "Now that I've heard it, I don't
know what to make of it. Nothing about it seems to point to any tradition I
ever heard. That just might be my own gaps." He falls silent, musing as the
night fills in around him. "The feeling I get from it . . . it . . . it's like some
kind of lamentation. There's sorrow in it. Sorrow and rage." Then a minis-
cule break in the sound as Willard pauses the tape. When it resumes after an
indeterminate recess, his whisper is taut with excitement. "Here she goes
again."*

*He lets Old Daisy have the next three minutes to herself. Only once does
he interject, not meaning to, but unable to halt the shaky sound of a
sharply drawn breath as her voice peaks to a terrible warbling crescendo
that could strip the trees of their leaves and claw scars across the cold
white face of the moon.*

*Until the night is still again, and even the crickets and frogs seem
cowed.*

*"Jesus, Mary, and Joseph," he whispers. "That poor woman. That poor
soul. How does . . . is she deformed, is that how . . . ?"*

*He lets the tape roll awhile longer, with nothing more to add that the
infinite night can't say better, and with a greater sense of awe.*

Along the house's foundation Will had cleared some of the rampant
weeds and dirt and build-up of wind-tossed leaves, and still it wanted to
not be seen: a rough-hewn door into the earth.

"Storm cellar. Where we're standing right now is smack dead center
in the middle of Tornado Alley," Paulette said. "You ever see *The Wizard
of Oz*? It's not like that."

They cleared away more, untangling the weeds from a heavy chain
that held the entrance closed, lashed across the door in a sideways "V"
whose point was threaded through a lock nearly the size of his fist,
rusted but still sound. Even if they found a key, he doubted it would
turn. The chain's ends were anchored into the door's hinge plates, and
here was the weak spot. The wood along the edges had rotted enough
that they were able to tug on the chain to rip up the hinge plates, bolts

and all. They heaved the door open, opposite the way it was meant to swing, and the storm cellar exhaled a musty sigh of roots and earth, like the smell of a waiting grave.

"Watch those steps," Will warned him. "They may not be any sturdier."

But they held, a dozen of them sloping down to a floor of dry, hard-packed earth and walls so coarsely cut they looked like adobe.

With the door open, enough light spilled down inside for them to see. They barely had room to stand beneath the crude rafters, black with creosote, that kept the hovel above and the tons of soil between from falling through.

He wished it had all failed long ago. He wished they'd never found this place.

"Jesus, Mary, and Joseph," his brother whispered. One trepidatious step at a time, Will moved to where it dwelled along one wall – did it sit? or did it stand? – and when he was close, began to reach.

"Maybe you ought not touch it," Paulette said.

He stilled his hand. "Why not?"

"Because I wouldn't."

Again: "Why not?"

"Maybe I've just got more sense than that, I don't know."

Clarence was with her on this one. And Will withdrew his hand.

That it was some sort of sculpture was obvious, yet he couldn't even tell what it was made of, much less what it was meant to represent. It was as tall as he was, with features and symmetry, but far more bulky. To look at it was to understand it had to have come from someplace, been worked by sentient hands, and realize he could never know enough about the world and its shadowed quarters to fathom who or where or why.

Was it metal? Stone? It appeared to be a mixture of both, marbled into each other under the temperatures of a blast furnace. Aspects of it glinted in the light that the rest seemed to swallow.

"A meteorite, maybe?" Will said. "That's my guess."

As sculpture, it was pitted and rough, but that it had been shaped at all seemed miraculous. It must have been incomprehensibly hard to work with. Its weight had to be immense. It was contradictory, various parts suggesting man and animal, mammal and mollusk, demon and dragon, a creature fit to dominate anywhere, be it ocean, land, or sky. It was a nightmare rising from a slag heap left over from the formation of the galaxy.

"So nobody else is going to say it?" Will asked. "Okay: 'I don't think we're in Kansas anymore.'"

But Kansas wasn't any reference point here. For no reason he could defend, Clarence knew beyond a doubt that this grotesque effigy predated even the idea of Kansas. It predated the nation, maybe the continent, the mountains to the west and the great bisecting river to the east. For all he knew, it came from an epoch when the land was one mass, a single crucible of primal forces surrounded by one titanic sea, the globe like a turbulent eye staring back at the affront of creation.

Then how had it come to be here and now? Perhaps it was as simple as waiting out the eons, impervious to time, until it was unearthed in a field.

He sensed it all in the presence of this thing. The thoughts were in his head as if it had forced them. He couldn't have been the first.

"We should leave," he whispered.

"Guys? Check it out."

Paulette was pointing at the rafters. With their eyes better accustomed to the shadows, they were ready to see what hid in plain sight when the statue was all they were prepared to notice. It was everywhere, on the rafters and the upright timbers bracing the earthen walls and beneath the dust on the steps, a single message repeated over years and decades: COME BACK. Etched into the wood with the points of knives and awls, a thousand utterances of the same plaintive incantation: COME BACK COME BACK COME BACK.

"That thing?" Will jabbed his finger at the statue. "Did she mean that thing? It was real, it was here?"

"I don't think so." Paulette cut an impatient glance at him as if she pitied him for his misunderstanding. "I bet she meant her people. Family, friends, neighbors. Her people. Her . . . world."

Funny. He'd always considered her a loner, a freak who reveled in her isolation.

"Maybe Nana was right after all," Paulette said. "Maybe it really wasn't just Old Daisy out here once."

Will stared at her. "She said there were more like her?"

Paulette nodded. "Nana said there used to be a whole passel of them. This would've been way back. Kept their heads down, hid their faces, wore sacks, some of them. Didn't want to be seen, didn't want to have anything to do with newer neighbors, didn't want anyone else even coming close. People like that, they were like moonshiners used to be, and meth cooks now. You learned to steer clear if you didn't want a load of buckshot coming your way."

For the moment, Clarence quelled the urge to leave. "You didn't say anything about this before."

"Because it wasn't something I grew up with, all right? Nana never said a thing about it when I was little and she was telling her stories to keep me in line. And she only said it the once. This was after they put her in the home." Paulette sighed with exasperation. "It wasn't a serious talk. We were laughing about it, how scared of Daisy she had me. I thought it was just some notion that got in her head after she started to get dotty enough to finally believe her own stories."

"Maybe," Clarence said, "she was dotty enough to finally let it slip."

"If it was even true, they wouldn't have been people she'd ever seen. According to her, it was something she heard about from her own grandmother. So we're talking *waaay* back. Civil War times, or not long after. There's no way Old Daisy could've been around here since . . ."

She clammed up, not even wanting to say it. Maybe because she could no longer be certain of absolutes, and hated to lie.

Above him, behind him, and all around: COME BACK COME BACK COME BACK.

"Then what happened to the rest of them?"

"That's probably a dirty old secret that died out with somebody a long time ago." Paulette looked both solemn and sad. "What do you think?

You come from West Virginia. If I've heard stories about what used to happen in your mountains there, then I know for sure you must have."

There was that. Yes. People who trekked up into the hollows to nose around where they didn't belong, and never came out again. Or one group taking such a dislike to another they decided they could no longer abide living side by side. The population had always been sparse out here, and he supposed there was a time when not a lot could come of rumor and a mass of unmarked graves.

Especially if the dead were . . . different.

And if there was a sole survivor, killers left them for all manner of reasons, by accident or as reminders or to soothe their consciences that what they'd done wasn't actually genocide.

God damn. Will Senior had sensed it simply from listening once in the dark. *It's like some kind of lamentation. There's sorrow in it. Sorrow and rage.*

Young Will trudged across the cellar and slumped onto the steps, heedless of the dust, then shot a baleful look at the statue. "A lifespan like that? The way she looks in the photo? This thing *did* that to them?"

Clarence couldn't bring himself to agree. Not out loud. Not to Will. Impressionable Young Will. "Do you hear yourself, what that sounds like?"

"Well, I've sure as shit spent my life hearing what *she* sounded like." He turned his gaze on Clarence, no less spiteful. "That thing's not natural, not one bit. There's something coming through it. Don't tell me you don't feel it. I can see it in your face. You're the worst liar I ever met."

Clarence approached the stairs while Paulette watched as if she suddenly feared both of them blocking the only way out. Nobody could fight like brothers.

"Come on. Let's go," Clarence said, as gently as he could. "We're not going to learn anything more here. We've already learned more than we ever wanted to."

Will fixed him with a look that nailed his feet to the floor. "He's not even dead. You realize that, don't you? I'll bet you anything he's not. He could still be alive even without that thing's influence. He'd be, what, around ninety? It's no big deal to hit that anymore. All this time we've taken it for granted he would've come home if he could, but what if family didn't mean as much to him as everyone assumed it did. We never even met him, you and I. But think about it. Doesn't it sound like home just turned into a place for him to plan the next trip? And song-catching, maybe that was only the surface of what he was really out looking for."

Clarence's first impulse was to argue, until he realized he had nothing to wield. He'd bought it all on faith. He'd never considered this alternative. Not seriously. He'd swallowed the easier story to accept and let it dictate his life.

Maybe it was Willard Chambers all along who had made sure his car was never found, and that his Nagra and his camera were. If he didn't need them anymore, maybe they'd prove more useful as circumstantial evidence of death.

"He loved Mom," Clarence whispered. "He loved Grandma. He loved Aunt Jane and Uncle Terry. He did."

"And then he found something that meant more."

Will stood up, finally, as around them, the storm cellar grew thick with the weight of eons.

"I was named for a deserter. Mom hung that on me." His face curled with the disgust of betrayal and a life of self-told lies. "He may have done his duty in war, but back home? He was a deserter." Will nodded, confirming it to himself. "But there's a side of me that can't totally blame him for it."

When he looked at the statue again, his anger was all but dissipated.

"It must've been worth it."

He shouldered past, and when Clarence hooked a hand around his arm, Will whirled. Next thing Clarence knew, he was sprawling across the hard-packed earth with a dull, throbbing ache in his cheek, as somewhere out in the blur, Paulette gave a startled cry of warning that plunged into sorrow.

When his vision cleared, he saw Will gripping the statue with splayed hands, tense as a cable but motionless, until his head tipped slowly, ecstatically, back and he made a reedy sound that seemed to come from a much older man. His bladder let go in a spreading dark stain.

Though sunk in the earth and surrounded by walls, the statue had brought its own climate. Clarence felt it deeper than skin, a gust of particles and waves, the solar wind from a black sun. Outside was August, but down here was a numbing gust of absolute zero, the point where every molecule froze, everything but thought, and the invitation beckoned: *Come . . . join with it . . . step outside the boundaries of time. It only burns for a little while.*

His instinct, still, was to intercede, the way he'd always done. It was what big brothers did, pulling their little brothers out of traffic when they stepped off the curb, and out of the deep water when they fell in over their head. Maybe he could do it without harm, and Will was not yet a conduit for whatever was coming through that timeless chunk of shrapnel from the cataclysm that birthed the worst among gods.

And maybe he couldn't. But it had always been expected of him to try.

Then Paulette was at his side, clutching his wrist, levering his arm down again. He'd never have dreamed he could let her do it so easily. He knew she was going to join Will before she seemed to realize it herself. As their eyes met, and from a place beyond words she urged him to let his brother go, he saw the conflict play itself out, then the resolution: that she preferred the vast unknown to a life she didn't want to go back to, as long as she didn't have to do it alone.

For all he knew, Will had even been counting on it.

They stayed down in the cellar a long time, long after Clarence had made it up the steps. He sat with his back to the hole some twenty paces away and shivered in the August sun. He didn't want to look. He didn't want to listen. Yet he didn't want to drive away without knowing what, exactly, he would be driving away from. If there was a chance, the slightest chance, he still had a brother he recognized.

And when their shadows fell across him, long and distorted, he had time to wonder if he hadn't made the last mistake of his life.

It didn't seem particularly lucky that there would be time for many more.

"I don't think I'll be going home for a while," Will said. "You probably guessed that already."

He knew their names. *Will. Paulette.* He knew their faces. He knew their clothes and the sound of their voices and the smell of them after a long, hot day. He just didn't know who they were. To see them now was like looking with one eye off-center. The halves of the image didn't quite line up.

"What am I supposed to tell Mom?" he asked.

"You can tell her whatever it takes. I haven't lived at *home* home for years. How different will it be?"

"Except for the part where you call every day."

"I could still check in from time to time." He looked down at the dirt with a murky little smile, as if it had whispered a joke. "It won't matter that long, anyway."

This from a son who could barely be coaxed into admitting his mother had two years, at best, to live.

Then Will held out the camera, the well-traveled Leica that had led them here, full circle after half a century. Its last shot from earlier, around front – Clarence didn't know if he could ever bring himself to get it developed. Until Will took him by surprise, so he would have no choice.

"Go on, shoot one more. Both of us," he said. "Show Mom I'm okay. Show her that we're happy."

Clarence steadied himself and shot it, the camera alien in his hand, like someone else's heart. It had passed to him, but it wasn't his. It would never be his. Behind them, these imposters in familiar skins, the hovel sat as it always had, slumping into itself year by year, as patient as decay, and the land stretched empty for miles.

"Here," Clarence said. "You're staying . . . here."

To Paulette, nothing seemed more natural. "It's got everything we need."

And that was that. They turned their backs on him, returning to the cellar, and the last he saw of Young Will was his arm, reaching up from below to swing the rotting wooden door closed again. As Clarence remembered the other day, not without shame, telling Will that he and Paulette didn't match.

They would. One day, they would.

On the drive back to the motel, solitary and endless, the pain worse than if a piece of him had been amputated and burned before his eyes, he passed the same dead barns and farmhouse ruins but saw them differently now. Had that really been him, last week, talking of breaking one down for the wood?

It was inconceivable now. No telling what such a place might hold. They only looked dead from the road.

Maybe she just walked away.

To go where? Where do you go from here?

She had her pick, didn't she? There were so many, all waiting like carcasses for the flies to come and settle and breed.

His eyes started to play tricks, imagining he caught a glimpse of her in this one, that one, and the next. Peering out at him from between fungus-eaten boards, and then there were worse tricks to come, as he divined it wasn't just her. No, she had a companion, a man the likes of which they didn't make anymore. A changed man who wouldn't even know his own grandson if he watched him drive by.

Because there were so many more lasting things worth knowing.

The phone calls started three weeks later.

But the first came at nearly four o'clock in the morning, so Clarence missed it, and it went to voicemail.

I was right. He's out here. Somewhere. I can feel him. I can feel him passing by in the night. It's happened twice. Sure as god made little green apples.

But I don't think he wants to be found. Maybe it's because I'm not worthy of finding him yet. You think so? Hello? Are you there?

After that, Clarence got a new phone for everyday use, and let the earlier one go straight to voice mail. Permanently. He wanted the connection. He just couldn't hold up his side of the conversation.

If you were dreaming the dreams of a mountain under the sea, how could you tell anyone what they were so it would all make sense? That's what this is like.

He went to Boston, where he shut down as much of Will's life as he could, and took over the phone bill, so the conduit would remain open. How Will was keeping a charge in the phone was anyone's guess.

We're getting closer. I can feel him. He's a mighty thing. I wonder if he'll be proud or angry. Paulette says hello. I think that's what she meant.

The months passed, and the calls came in when they came, infrequent and random, no pattern to it, other than the way every time he thought Will had finally stopped, *surely* by now he'd stopped, another message was waiting a day or two later.

I was wrong. This isn't what I thought it was going to be. I just don't know if it's better or worse. It's . . . it's the knowing that changes you. Like a download of information wakes up something that was always inside. I never could buy it that what they call junk DNA is just junk. Are you even there anymore? Why don't you ever answer?

And it was Will's voice – he would recognize it anywhere – yet something was different about it each time. It was more than how each call sounded a bit farther away, fighting past a little more static and noise than the previous time. It was in the resonance of his throat, and the tones it produced.

Mom's gone. Isn't she. I don't know how I know that, I just do. Don't be sorry for her. She's lucky. She's beyond what's coming. You should be too. I shouldn't be telling you this. You should kill yourself, though. Rochelle first, then yourself. You should be okay then. I know you, you won't want to do it because she's pregnant, but you'll be glad you did.

That day will come. If you can't trust your baby brother, who can you trust?

A thousand times a day, he thought of cutting the connection. But never could.

I shouldn't tell you this. When they come, they'll look like meteors. But that won't be what they are at all. When the sky changes color, it'll be too late. Nothing will make any difference then. They'll already have you. That's when you'll wish you'd listened to me. Don't ask what color, I can't really describe it. But out here, I've seen the kind of green the sky turns before a tornado. That's a start.

We're really getting close now. I wonder if Daisy will let me call her "Mother."

And when it had gone nearly a year between calls, and so much had changed, and Clarence was a father now, with a father's fears, he knew better than to think the calls were done. They would never be done. Even when they no longer conveyed any words he could understand.

Since coming home from Kansas for the last time, alone, he hadn't listened to his grandfather's tape any more, the longest in his life he'd let it idle. There was no more to learn from it. He would rather forget.

But there was no forgetting such a song. He knew it, still, the moment he heard it begin, coming through miles and static and time. He would always know it.

Yet now there was a difference. He could no longer hear the lamentation in it. Just the rage. It was a song of endings and rebirths, a song for green skies and streaks like blue-white fire among the clouds. A song he would never be fit to join and sing.

And, finally, it was coming from more than one throat.

He counted two the first time.

He counted four the next.

In the end, he counted a choir of multitudes.

Helen Marshall is a critically acclaimed Canadian author, editor, and medievalist. Her debut collection of short stories, *Hair Side, Flesh Side* won the 2013 British Fantasy Award for Best Newcomer. Her second collection, *Gifts for the One Who Comes After*, was shortlisted for the Bram Stoker, the Aurora, and the Shirley Jackson Awards. She lives in Oxford, England, where she spends her time staring at old books. Unwisely. When you look into a book, who knows what might be looking back . . .

"One of the finest books I have read in recent years is Shirley Jackson's *We Have Always Lived in the Castle*," she notes. "Merricat Blackwood is a bizarrely engaging narrator with her love of her sister Constance, and Richard Plantagenet, and *Amanita phalloides*, the deathcap mushroom, and the mixture of naiveté, love, loyalty, and killer instinct that she shows in the novel has always resonated with me. When I was asked to write for this anthology, I had one of those wild, improbable titles that made me giggle to myself with enough manic glee that I knew I was onto something – *We Have Always Lived in the Cthulhu*. But what might have been nothing more than an amusing pastiche began to take on more and more depth as I explored alongside Caro and her grandmother the spiraling shell of an ancient ocean-dwelling creature and the terrible secret at the center of it. What has always fascinated me about Lovecraft's stories is the madness that accompanies any sort of genuine knowledge – but the question I have always wondered is what happens afterward? How do we live in madness? How do we accommodate ourselves to knowing too much? Much like Jackson's delightful black comedy, which finds something redemptive and oddly touching in the apparent insanity of the Blackwood family, this story seeks to provide some sort of answer – albeit a very strange one."

Caro in Carno
Helen Marshall

—————

"That is not dead which can eternal lie . . ."

– H. P. Lovecraft, "The Nameless City"

My name is Caroline Eve Arkwright and I am thirteen years old. I prefer to be called Caro over Caroline and I don't like the name Eve at all. I've insisted to Nan that I be called Caro because I've recently begun to learn my Latin declensions: *caro, carnis*, which means *flesh*, *the body*, and *low passions*. I don't know much about *low passions* but I'm much more knowledgeable when it comes to *flesh* and *the body*. The body is the house in which the soul lives; and so I myself am like a house and I'm also the person living inside the house. This presents a conundrum, which I like very much. How can I be both a house and the occupant? Nan will not answer me. Nan has never enjoyed conundrums as much as I do.

Nan and I have always lived in the house and Nan tells me this is how it must always be. Our house isn't like the houses in the village, Nan has told me, for it is *caro, carnis* as well. It is a big house. How shall I describe it? The walls are white, like the chalk cliff, but even more beautiful than that for they shine different colors in the light and are perfectly smooth. The floor is curved as well. From the outside the house appears as a giant hole opened in the cliff, but on the inside it has a series of chambers or *cubicula*, which spiral inward, each smaller than the last and curved as well. The house then is an *orbis*, which means *ring, disk, coil* – but most of all – *world*. I've spent many hours exploring the house but I've never gone beyond the eleventh chamber.

The village sits atop the cliff, not so close by, for the villagers are afraid of the ground giving way as it did once before. Their houses, which I've seen for myself, are neither *orbes* nor *carnes* but rather *saxa*, which is stones, and *quadrata*, which is squares. They have wooden roofs. They have windows in the attics with lights that come on and go off when I pass them. The people inside are *caro* or rather *caro in saxo*, but I am *Caro in carno*.

The way to the village is dangerous. The cliff is sheer and there are all sorts of other seashells and such visible there. None are as large as my house. The view of the ocean from the steps is very beautiful but if I'm not careful I could fall. Nan says this is what happened to Mother and Father, that they were not careful enough and so they fell. I don't know if this is true but I've chosen to believe it. We must all choose to believe something, mustn't we, even if it's bad? Nan is too old to make the journey now and so I must make it alone. I try not to look down. Below me is *mors, mortis* which does not mean fall but *death*.

It's my job to collect supplies from the village. Mostly this means onions and potatoes and flour and sometimes a pound of sugar and two pounds of coffee but these last are only for special occasions. I've been instructed to touch neither fish nor fowl, nothing that has lived and nothing that has died. I find these instructions somewhat confusing. Both the onions and the potatoes have lived, as I understand it, but Nan is firm that it's not the same sort of living. She says this is an issue of vocabulary but I confess I've not pressed it further. Without onions and potatoes our cellar would be very bare! But it does seem to me that there ought to be a word that says more than *mors, mortis* to denote the different kinds of death such as *death by falling* or *death by disease*. This could be done of course with the addition of further words but it would be much more elegant if one word encompassed all these meanings. Perhaps there's such a word in Greek or Egyptian or one of the many other languages I shall learn but I've not come across it yet.

In the village is a grocer who weighs the sugar and the coffee. In return I must give him a small pouch filled with salt that we scrape from the walls of the house. I've been told to watch him very carefully. Sometimes, Nan says, he likes to put his thumb on the scale. If he puts his thumb on the scale, then either I must make a second trip to the village before the appointed time or else we must make do without sugar or coffee. The grocer has a boy who counts out the onions and the potatoes but Nan says I must not look on him lest I fall into *caro, carnis*, that is *low passions*. Which is quite hard for he's *very* handsome.

"Good morning, Caroline Eve Arkwright," he's accustomed to say to me. I think he likes that I have three names, for no one else in the village seems to have more than one. He's called Tom, which, I think, is an excellent name. "How are you today?"

"I'm doing very well, thank you."

"And how many potatoes will that be? The usual number?"

"Yes, please."

"Not one more? Aren't you a growing girl? It seems to me that you're growing day by day!" Tom's always saying something like this. I can't tell if he's mocking me. Although I think Tom is handsome, I keep close to my heart what Nan has said about the people from the village.

"The usual number, please, just as we have agreed. No more and no less!"

"Not an apple for the way back?" This is tempting. I've always thought that apples look very beautiful. They come in all sorts of different colors. But I know that I must refuse.

But I don't refuse, not yet. "Do the different colors have different tastes?"

Tom looks at me for longer than I'm used to and I find that I'm blushing. Sometimes I feel so *ignorant* around him and this is one of those times.

"This one," he says at last, "tastes *green*. And this one? *Red*. Red is the best taste, don't you think?"

"I've never tasted red."

"Never?"

"Never."

"Would you like to?"

Tom polishes the apple very carefully on his sleeve. Now the skin is red and gleaming. But he has a look in his eyes like perhaps he's mocking me. Perhaps he'll take the apple away if I ask him for it.

I can't help myself. I take the apple from him. It feels very smooth. It is a beautiful feeling to hold that apple. I think, *I can hold this but I must not eat it*. Tom smiles as he watches me holding the apple and I smile at Tom. The skin of the apple reflects both of our smiles, like two crescent moons. But then Tom stops smiling and I'm left to wonder if I've done something wrong, if I should not have taken the apple, if he'll take this as a sign that the contract is voided.

"My mother'll be coming to you," Tom says after a little while. "Will you take care of her properly? Do you promise?"

I've seen Tom's mother before. Her hair is light and yellow and it drapes like silk all the way down her back. Sometimes she measures out the coffee and the sugar for me and she has never, not once, put her thumb on the scales. It makes me sad that his mother will be coming to me soon. I can see that it makes Tom sad as well. I touch his hand, very gently, in case he pulls it away but he doesn't and so we stand like that together for some minutes.

"Thank you for the apple," I tell him shyly. But I don't put in my satchel. Instead I leave it on the porch of the grocer's shop. I know now I should not have taken it. *No more and no less!*

But sometimes *caro* is no friend to Caro.

There is a large hoist at the top of the chalk cliff, which swings out over the ocean below. The supplies from the village are much too difficult to manage on the steps, and so I load them onto the platform beneath the lifting hook. Once I've lowered them to the house, Nan will carry them inside. Nan says that the villagers used to lower the supplies themselves once, but after Mother and Father died, they wouldn't do it anymore. So now Nan or I must go to remind them, and since Nan can't go anymore, it must be me. But this is good, Nan tells me, because the villagers ought to become accustomed to me. They do not suffer strangers very easily.

Nan is waiting for me at the bottom of the steps. She worries for me when I make the climb even though I'm always very careful. She has prepared coffee for me and so we sit together in the *vestibulum*, the largest of the chambers, where the mouth opens out toward the ocean. This is my favorite place because the noise of the waves is very soothing. Part of the cliff has fallen away on one side of the *vestibulum* and so the floor sticks out, smooth and gently crenellated, just like my lower lip if I'm sulking. Underneath this lip is the best place for gathering salt, though it can be got from further in the house as well, only with more difficulty. The floor isn't very curved here. It is easier for Nan.

"The grocer's mother will be coming to us soon," I tell Nan.

"How do you know, Caroline?"

"Caro," I remind her. She's always forgetting.

"How do you know, Caro?"

"The grocer's boy told me so."

"Well." And after a time: "We will greet her when she comes. Are you ready? How are your Latin declensions progressing?"

"*Optime*," I tell her.

"Then perhaps you ought to join me when we greet her."

I don't like this very much but there is nothing I can say. I shall try to do my best for Tom and his mother. I shall try to greet her properly.

Several weeks pass before Tom's mother comes to visit, which is later than I expected. It's almost time for me to return to the village again. It's the sound of the winch that tells me she's coming. Outside the noise isn't so loud but when I'm inside the house the noises become louder and louder and louder, even as the chambers become smaller and smaller and smaller. Sometimes I think that if I were to come to the end of the house then the noise would be so deafening I'd die!

I run through the chambers as quickly as I can, but carefully too, for the floors are more curved where I've been working. Nan keeps our library far away from the *vestibulum* where the salt and rain would destroy our books. As it is, they aren't in very good condition and the oldest of them have fallen to pieces. If I had string, I'd mend them, but we don't have very much string, so the best I can do is to wrap them in strips of my old shifts. As Nan says, *waste not, want not!* And if we're to want for nothing, then we must waste nothing.

The noise of the winch echoes like a screech as I make my way through the deep passages to the outermost chamber. My feet hitting the floor make a *bum, bum, bum* sound. When I reach the *vestibulum*, Nan has already begun to remove Tom's mother from the platform. She's covered in a pale blue blanket but I can see the edge of her hair draped over the heartwood.

"What is the word for death?" Nan asks me.

"*Mors, mortis*," I tell her.

"Can you conjugate it fully as a verb?" Nan unhooks the platform from the lifting hook and I help settle it down. The platform is set on wheels so it can be more easily maneuvered into the house with us.

"*Morior*, which is *I die*, and then *moriris*, which is *you die*, and then *moritur*, which is *she dies*—"

"And if it is in the perfect tense?"

"—then it would be *moriturus est*, which is *she has died*."

"Very good, Caroline."

"Caro," I remind her.

"Very good, Caro," she says. "Now what does it mean that the grocer's mother has died?"

This is more difficult for it goes beyond knowing the pattern of words to knowing the meaning of words. And I've only just begun this, but I will try. If Nan corrects me then I shall be wiser than before at any rate.

"*Mori* is a word used by the ancients to indicate the passage of a creature from one state into another. It's something like *transire*, which is *to go across* but it isn't about movement outside or over but rather movement inside."

I'm very proud of this description. I look at Nan very closely to see if it has satisfied her but she's busy with maneuvering the platform onto the rails that run lengthwise down the center of every chamber.

"This won't last much longer," says Nan as the wheels of the platform sing out an unpleasant note. She's right. One of the wheels has gone wobbly and so the load is badly balanced. When it tips, Tom's mother begins to slide toward the edge. I lay my hands upon the long folds of cloth in which she's swaddled. The blanket is more brittle than I had supposed and much more coarse. At last, Nan turns back to me. "That's a very good description of *mori*."

"I've a question," I tell her. "If *mori* means an inward movement, is it very like *somniare*, which is *to dream*? That's like an inward movement too, isn't it?"

"What do you dream about, darling?" She's not looking at me but rather at Tom's mother underneath the blanket.

"Sometimes I have a dream that I'm dead, or that death is a thing very close to me, but it isn't so much a passage as . . . a breath, which is, I suppose, a movement of the air from inside to outside, and so it is *like* a passage."

"And how do you know that you are dead?"

"Because a great voice whispers it to me. *Moriris*. You are dead."

Now Nan looks at me very closely and I can see a strange yellowish cast to her eyes, which seem folded in dark and heavy flesh. "Each of those things is very like death, but it isn't the same thing."

"I've another question," I tell her, "must all *caro, carnis* suffer from death?"

"All things suffer from death except salt." She eyes me warily.

"Why not salt?"

"Salt has never lived."

"I've another question," I tell her, "if all *caro, carnis* must suffer from death and I am *caro* and this house is *caro*, does that mean that I've suffered from death and this house has suffered from death?"

Nan clucks again with her tongue, which is the sound she makes when she's thinking.

"When your mother and father died, did you suffer?"

I think about this for a moment. I don't remember Mother and Father very well. It has been Nan for so long that it may as well have been Nan *ab aeterno*, which is *forever*, like the salt. But then I think of the dream I've been having, and how the breath is very warm on my face and how it smells very nice and the dream whispers *I am your mother* but for some reason this isn't a happy thought but a sad thought.

"I think I did," I tell Nan.

"Then you have suffered from death."

I can tell that Nan's being wily with me. She has only answered a question very like my question but not my question at all.

The path through the house is long. There aren't any branches in the path, no need to navigate – only the task of setting one foot in front of the other. We pass through the *domus*, which includes the pantry, and the sitting room, and the bedrooms, each one marginally smaller than the last.

"Would you come along the rest of the way with me, dear?" Nan asks in a kindly voice, for I've begun to fall behind her. I've never gone beyond the eleventh chamber before and the prospect of further travel frightens me a little although I can't rightly say why. And Nan has never asked me to before. In fact, she often distracts me from the thought, saying I must learn the Latin, and then the Greek, and then the Egyptian afterward. Perhaps I'm progressing beyond her expectations.

Or perhaps it is something else. The grocer's mother was much younger than Nan is now, and I've seen the hump growing upon her back. The way it twists her spine.

"Don't fret, Caroline—"

"Caro," I remind her.

"—I shall manage well enough without you, I suppose. The grocer's wife isn't so large as some of the others. But am I warm enough, do you think? It gets so very cold . . ."

Nan glances down at the grocer's wife, and, for a moment, I'm a little frightened that she'll snatch the sheets away. Her hands are trembling.

"Take my shawl, Nan, I won't need it. Not today. The weather hasn't turned yet."

"That's nice, dear," she murmurs as I tuck my shawl around her shoulders. She pats my arm very gently.

The days pass easily after that, almost indistinguishable from one another. Soon I've produced passable translations of Apuleius, Pseudo-Quintilian, Marcellus Empiricus, and Pliny the Elder – and then Nan tells me it is time to return to the village again.

The weather's been growing colder and darker and so I must begin the climb early in the morning as soon as there is light. To avoid thinking of the fall, I repeat to myself another conundrum: If when I dream I can see figments, then is it possible those figments may also dream? And if so, isn't it possible that I'm a figment of another's dreams? This is very like the problem Plato proposed to Glaucon about the prisoners who saw shadows upon the wall of the cave for the shadows are very much like dreams. And yet Plato never asked if the shadows themselves perceive – but it's certainly possible that they did!

I feel quite clever in coming up with this conundrum. I wonder if, perhaps, no one else in the world has ever thought this particular thought before.

"Hello, miss," says Tom as he begins to count out my share of potatoes. He has on a black jacket, which I've never seen before. I confess it shows off his broad shoulders rather well. He has slim black trousers too and black shoes that shine as if he has polished them with his sleeve.

"You look uncommonly fine today, Tom," I say to him with my best smile. "I would not have taken you for the grocer's boy at all, but rather for a prince or perhaps for a duke!"

"That's very kind of you to say, miss."

It's the second time he has said that to me. And, indeed, he has said nothing about my best smile. Perhaps he's in a mood, and I may draw him out of it.

"May I ask you a question, Tom?"

"If you'd like."

"It's a problem, really, a very difficult one. One that takes ages and ages to solve. But I'll tell you my conundrum because—" And now I feel quite shy I've begun this line of talk with him. "—because you yourself made me think of it."

I won't tell him the rest. I won't tell him that sometimes I dream about him and that the things he whispers to me are very nice. Instead, I try to explain to him the conundrum about the dream and the dreams and the cave and the shadows but try as I might I can't make it exactly clear what it is I wish to say.

But Tom seems not to notice my missteps. "We solved *that* one years ago," he says carelessly. His eyes are a very delicate shade of blue. I've not noticed this before, but then I've not noticed how peculiarly changeable Tom's moods may be.

"Will you give me the answer?"

"I'm near shocked you haven't solved it for yourself, and you being so learned too, miss!" His tone is cruel. "*We* are the dreamers."

"And me?" I'm trembling.

"You'll see, won't you, when we wake up! And we will, you know, we shan't be so dozy about what goes on below us forever."

His smile is quite terrible. He will not look at me, he only counts the potatoes, one by one and places them into the sack for me.

"Are you very angry with me?" I say softly.

"You're a murderer," he hisses

"But how can you say that, Tom? I've never murdered anyone!"

He glances at me, all sly now, like he's playing a trick. "You wake in the night, don't you? So there's someone you've murdered, there must be!"

"Please don't be so unkind, Tom, I can't bear it, not from you!" I'm clutching at the hem of my dress now, just like Nan does. And then, softly: "I'm so sorry about the apple. I shouldn't have taken it from you."

"What apple, miss?" he sneers. "You didn't carry off no apple of mine, did you? So there's no debt between us, nothing exchanged except that which was promised. My mother's gone to visit you, she's gone down and down and into the mouth of that awful beastie. You've done with her what you've done with all the others, it's monstrous!"

"It's not monstrous what Nan did, I promise and I promise!"

"Oh, go on and take your potatoes," he says, "go take them and feast on them, Caroline Eve Arkwright." He's shoving the potatoes into my arms and his mouth is so twisted, it's evil looking. "But just think on this, will you? I got these potatoes from deep underground, I dug them out special for you. These potatoes, they been growing amongst the worms and spiders and every nasty thing, and I just pray some of those nasty things're living in there still, small and deadly, just like you, like you and *her*!"

I stumble away from him with my arms all full of potatoes. How I want to cry, but I mustn't cry because Nan has told me I must never show the villagers I'm afraid of them. But what am I to do? Oh, Tom! I turn away from him very quickly. For a moment he looks as if he might strike me! And thinking that, I start to run – I know I shouldn't but I can't help myself. *Dum, dum, dum* go my feet as they hit the cobblestones but the noise is very little, almost nothing. I run for at least a mile before I can stop myself from running any longer.

It is only once I've reached the edge of the village that I remember he has not given me the onions at all.

Nan is disappointed with me, I can tell from the way that she scowls ever so slightly and clutches at the hem of her cardigan but she'll not tell me that I've done badly.

"They're a vicious lot, absolutely *vicious*! But they daren't harm you, dear, not an Arkwright, whatever that boy might've said."

"Then—you don't think he might've put something in the potatoes? He was so *angry*!"

It's this thought that has been haunting me, that perhaps he's poisoned them.

"It's not a thing to be worried at."

"But you didn't see him, Nan. Not his face, or his— his eyes! I've never seen him like that before. And he might've put something in them, mightn't he? And if he did, what could we do? There's little enough left from before and I didn't even remember the onions, there'd be nothing at all to eat for days and days!"

"I expect we'd manage somehow. There are things you don't know," she says.

There's a way Nan has of shaking her head when she has well and truly had enough of my questions so that the skin wobbles around her neck. This is the headshake she's given me now but I can't stop myself from going on and on.

"But how? What other provisions? Not fish, nor flesh, nothing that has lived and nothing that has died, nor any other thing but what they give us, isn't that right?"

"Look to your studies, Caroline—"

"Caro," I remind her.

"Shush now, granddaughter, I don't like that other name! It isn't a good thing, whatever you might think, and I shan't call you by it. You're far too loose with your words. A thing is what it is. You can't change it just by asking and you are *Caroline* Eve Arkwright. Now enough of all this fretting, I'll go to the village tomorrow and be straight with them."

"But you *can't*, Nan!"

Now I'm thinking of her shuffling walk. I'm thinking of the sound her chest makes when she breathes in and out heavily.

"I'm not so far gone as you would have me, not yet. There's still some good I can do. It's like when they put their thumb on the scale, they know it doesn't break with the bargain. We're allowed the onions and they must give them over."

"But the potatoes?"

"He hasn't poisoned the potatoes, Caroline! Now hurry along and fetch your books. We'll try the passive periphrastic today. Your mother made such a fuss over that in her day, but we'll see if you can't master it quicker than she did!"

*   *   *

It has been three days since Nan went to the village.

For three days I've eaten little flour pancakes. To start with they were as big as my fist, but now they're no bigger than a mussel shell. I tried to make the coffee just as Nan does, but my hands were shaking so badly that I spilled the grounds. I've tried to collect them, but I can see plainly that it isn't only coffee I've got but salt too.

And I haven't dared to touch the potatoes, whatever Nan said!

Nan came to visit me this morning. I'd been so anxious I could hardly look at my books! But then I heard the winch turning and turning and I knew it was her coming back to me at last!

The villagers wrapped her in a beautiful, winding sheet of red silk. I've only seen that color once before. Nan told me that it was called *carmine* and that it can only be made with the shells of certain insects. It's very expensive.

The word *carmine* is very like the word *carmen*, *carminis* which is *charm*, *prayer*, or *oracle*.

Her body was very light, so light I thought, for a moment, that perhaps there was nothing wrapped in the silk at all – but when I moved her, the silk fell away and I saw her hand. The nails were a color-less yellow and the veins were a colorless blue and I've no other words for what I saw except that I knew the hand could belong to no other.

It was a kindness they did her, wrapping her up in red silk.

I took her in my arms very gently and still she was so light.

I unhooked that platform just as she used to do but Nan was so much better at it than I am! It's very hard when you're all by yourself. The hook was difficult to manage and the fourth wheel was broken off completely. But they wrapped her in red silk and that was kind, I think, for they mightn't've done that.

They might've taken her away and never sent her back to me at all.

Still I can't come to the thought properly.

Moriturus est.

She has died.

The platform moves very slowly.

It isn't balanced very well but I don't know how to make it better. I don't want to touch Nan. I can't bear the thought that she's underneath the red silk. It's as if she were sleeping and not actually dead. It's as if she could wake at any moment. But when I touched her she didn't wake up, when I shook her she was so still! Her skin was very cold and it made me think about what she said last time, about how it's very cold where we must go and I take a blanket for myself and the blanket is pale green with golden flowers and it's one of my favorites but then I think I don't want to take my favorite blanket because then I'll always be thinking on the red silk when I wear it, so instead I settle for my second favorite blanket which is old and gray.

But then the blanket is bulky and it's difficult to move in. It keeps getting trapped under the wheels of the platform. At last I let it lie beside the rail. I shall return for it eventually. I must come this way again.

But am I being foolish?

"Will I be warm enough, do you think?" And then: "I'm frightened of the way. Please. Please wake up. I don't want to go by myself."

Her silence is terrible.

I decide not to leave the blanket after all. Instead I wrap it around myself the way I've seen the Romans in the pictures do it so that it falls like a heavy dress around me. If I had string I would cinch it around my waist but I don't have any string.

I pass the pantry and the sitting room. The blanket catches again and I must adjust it. I pass the bedrooms. The sunlight is still very bright here. It echoes the way that sound echoes and sometimes the colors it makes upon the walls are beautiful. There are all sorts of colors but none is the same color of red as the winding sheet of silk.

And then we are moving into darkness – past the eleventh chamber where I faltered, past the twelfth chamber and the thirteenth chamber. I never asked Nan how far the way was. I never asked Nan what must come next. I don't think I'm brave enough for this but I must be brave enough because there is no one else to do this for her, no one but Caro, Caro passing into *car* . . .

From the darkness comes a new kind of light as if the walls themselves have begun to shine very softly. They are all studded with silvery white blooms that remind me very much of the flowers I've seen in the village in springtime, all clustered together in little beds. Or perhaps these things look like teeth. Or snow. There are long shining spindles that hang suspended and I must be careful when I step underneath them. Some have broken away. Their edges look very sharp. When I look at them I can see myself carrying Nan reflected a thousand times, perhaps ten thousand times, but each image I see isn't me exactly.

I touch my eyes. They begin to water and burn dreadfully. My hands are almost white, the silk sheet is almost white.

This is what death looks like, I think, and it is a very frightening thought: but I've never seen anything as white as this!

Around and around, through chamber after chamber, the walls shrink around me until I feel as if I could reach out on either side and touch them. At the same time they begin to feel larger and larger as if there were some method by which I can detect the dimensions of the room which relies upon neither my eyes nor my fingers. It is strange to think I'm perhaps not so very far from my own bedroom. I'm within the place I've always lived. It shouldn't be frightening for all around me are the places I've walked all my life. But they aren't this place, are they? This place stands in the center of all that. The air stings my eyes, it tastes like the ocean air but much sharper.

Now there is shadow, and with it, the sense of something deliberately obscured.

I feel very giddy. It is impossible to continue further.

But I remember what Nan said to me when I was afraid of going to the village the first time. She took my hands in hers, but they were warm then, very warm, and she said: "Listen, Caroline, no one there will hurt you, no one will touch you, I promise and I promise."

"But they hate us so much!"

"Oh, no, darling, no, no – it isn't hatred! It can't ever be hatred, it goes beyond hatred or fear or even love what they feel for us. It is only that there is a voice that whispers to them in their dreams and it makes them all so terribly afraid. But they shan't hurt you, they won't, I will never, ever let them touch you."

"But what does the voice whisper, Nan? What makes them so afraid?"

"It whispers *morieris*, dearest, which, as you shall learn, means all things must die. *Caro, carnis*. Everything dies except for salt."

And I think perhaps it's comforting, what Nan said, and I say to myself: "Don't be afraid, Caroline, no one there will hurt you, no one will touch you!"

I even use my own true name just as Nan wanted me to.

But it doesn't make me braver. For now there's a noise I can hear or I've been hearing it for some time now, I can't tell exactly. Perhaps it is only the sound of the ocean reflected inward, the deep and heavy *huff* of the waves. It sounds very much like breathing. But as I strain my ears, a second noise becomes clearer to me: a sharp *tap-tap-tapping* sound that I don't like one bit, for it becomes louder and louder, maddeningly loud, so that I must press my hands against my ears lest I begin to shriek!

A hot blast of air gusts through the chamber, but from where it comes I could not say only that it's as if I'm in my dream and this is Mother's breath, warm against my skin and sweet smelling.

"Mother," I cry out. "Oh, Mother!"

But I can't see her! It is as if the air around me has begun to heave and writhe. But it isn't the air, it is clouds of white dust, sharp and stinging – the walls billow, but it isn't the walls, it is clothes of all different colors, blues and oranges and purples and yellows and green and they are all fluttering around me as if I've become lost within a flock of birds!

Then the wind dies away and all the clothes come to settle once more only they don't lie properly as they did before. I can see now, I can see what lies beneath them. Nan never lied to me! For here they are, just as she promised, the ones from the village – all our visitors! There are so many of them! Some I recognize like Tom's mother with her hair as golden as wheat but there are so many of them and I think to myself that I could not possibly have seen so many for they go on and on and on into the darkness. Those closest to me are just as they were in life, all pale and pretty with white, white cheeks – but those further are as strangers to me. Their flesh has withered and hardened into a yellow-veined shell – like *saxa*, which is *stone* – and all I can see are their jagged teeth set in the widened, black circle of their mouths.

And one by one by one it is as if I can see lights coming on within.

They are tiny at first, the barest glow, but they become brighter and brighter, each of them smaller than my smallest finger, set in a gilded carapace like a Roman soldier! And they are moving, oh, they are moving! In and out they go, scuttling on a thousand tiny legs, through the mouth, through the empty holes of the eyes and the nose, over the fingernails and the ribs.

How enchanting these creatures are, how absolutely beautiful!

There is a part of me that has become very happy. I know I should be frightened but these little things with their *tap-tap-tapping* don't frighten me one bit. How is it that I've not thought through this particular part of the conundrum? A person is not only a person, a person can also be a house. *Caro in carno.* Just like me. And all the villagers have become like houses, row upon row of tiny houses: each with their own towers and colonnades, their own hushed streets and marvelous gardens. It seems perfectly obvious to me now! The soul is merely a single occupant, and when the soul has fled, of course, something else shall come to lodge itself within them.

They are very small and even if there are so many of them all wiggling around I know that I could crush them if I wanted to, I could press my fingers down upon them until they bled. But I shan't do that, shall I? I shan't, even though I could. They are so little, just like babies! And they are mine, aren't they? I am Mother to them – and it shall be my voice that whispers, "*Morieris*" to them in the night. But they needn't be afraid, for perhaps death is not so terrible a thing, perhaps it is only an inward movement, the casting away of the veil of dreams.

And so I take Nan gently in my arms and I bury my fingers in the smooth red silk of her covering. When I lay her upon the salt shelf I'm careful to wrap the cloth around her frail body. I loved her very much. But the world isn't an apple. It isn't sweet and perfectly formed – or if it was once long ago then it has fallen away into rot. It is a shell, a husk, an infinite spiral – *caro in carno*, all of it moving inward, passing over, ever slumbering, ever waking.

But I shall be *Caro in carno* no longer. I've heard the voice which whispers, you will die, and I'm not afraid; for to me it whispers sweetly, *come to me, beautiful child, and I shall cradle you as you sleep, I shall watch over your dreaming and you shall at last be safe.*

I've gone to the village for the last time now. It is true that I've come to love the stone houses with their pretty wooden roofs, their straight flowerbeds, the people all milling about, tending to the day's business. There is a simple charm to the world they inhabit, how their years are governed by the planting season and the reaping season and yet it is amazing how little they know of the true mechanisms of the earth! But that is unfair of me for they are hardly scholars and perhaps only the barest gleanings of nature's operations are enough for survival if one requires little enough.

The grocer would not look at me. His face was a red mask of suffering and I could see the way his fists clenched. He would have hurled stones at me if he could. "There shall be no food for you, Miss Arkwright, not ever again. So don't you come back, d'you hear? No more of that devil's bargain, there shall be nothing given between mine and yours, not ever!"

But I did not make the journey to speak with him and so his curses meant very little to me. It is as Nan said, they will not touch me, not ever – for it is they who are afraid and their fear is well deserved.

Tom has filled out very nicely even without his handsome black suit. His hands are strong worker's hands with thick pad on his thumbs. He has been raised coarsely but even I can see there is finer stuff within.

"You there!" I call to him.

He's mute.

"Tom!"

"What is that you want, *miss*?"

"I wanted to tell you about your mother."

"My father is watching us right now," he tells me sullenly. "He'll go get the others if there's any trouble. The deal's broken now, isn't it? We don't want no more of it. You shouldn't be here."

But I ignore all this. The agreement isn't necessary any longer. I've found a way to manage on my own. I have looked to my studies just as Nan said.

"Don't you want to know what your mother had to tell you?"

He looks at me uncertainly. I know this is cruel, that I'm teasing him a little, but he was cruel to me once as well. I can't help it.

"Very well then."

"Wait!" he calls as I begin to cross the street. "Please! Wait, miss! What did she—" he's almost shuddering now "—did she say something to me? Did she give you a message?"

I turn to look at him once more. He's standing at the edge of the porch, straining forward. I can see that he's breathing very heavily and his eyes are wet and shining like glass.

"She said she loves you very much. She says she longs to hold you in her arms once more. Will you come to her?"

I do not tell him the truth. I know what she whispers. She whispers, "*Morieris*" – and so it is, but not yet, not yet.

"I don't know what you mean, miss." I watch his Adam's apple bob up and down.

"You know well enough, Tom." His lips are very red. It is lonely without Nan, oh, not so lonely as you would think – I have my studies after all! – but still lonely enough.

"Come if you like, Tom," I say, smiling my very best smile. From here I can almost taste the salt of his tears. How magnificent you are, I want to tell him! You carry within yourself the stuff of eternal life – and yet you shed it so easily! "The way goes down and down and down but it isn't so difficult. And we shall be ever so happy to have you join us for a while."

Sandra McDonald's story draws specifically on H. P. Lovecraft's ideas and language, albeit in a unique way. Its setting is R'lyeh, the city under the waves with its "slimy green vaults," a place that calls to the darkness in all of our hearts.

McDonald served as a commissioned officer in the US Navy for eight years and remains fascinated by issues of tradition and protocol. More than seventy of her short stories and eight novels are in print, ranging from young adult to military science fiction to paranormal romance. Her first collection of fiction, *Diana Comet and Other Improbable Stories*, was a *Booklist* Editor's Choice, an American Library Association Over the Rainbow Book, and winner of a Lambda Literary Award for transgender fiction. She holds an MFA in creative writing from the University of Southern Maine and teaches college in Florida.

The Cthulhu Navy Wife
Sandra McDonald

___

Security

Sometimes the nature of your husband's work means you will not know exactly where he is going, or for how long, or what he will be doing in service to the Old Ones. He may not be able to answer questions you pose or discuss other details of his deployment. You might roll over in bed one gray, dreary morning to find him already gone. Perhaps he will return shortly, or several months from now, or not at all. But the little ones need breakfast or changed diapers, so get up with good cheer and face the day. A Navy wife never shirks from duty.

Many times your husband's job will be "classified" and the details available only to those who "need to know." As a Navy wife, you do not "need to know" anything beyond what it takes to keep your husband satisfied and your household run efficiently here in the city of R'lyeh under the waves. Put aside your worries and focus your energy on activities such as church, scouting, and baking contests. You and your family will be happier if you keep busy and useful.

Do remember, however, that effective security is the best way to protect our way of life and keep the Earth secure. This protection can only be as strong as the citizens who use common sense in their actions and speech.

Therefore, never press your husband for details about his job. Do not gossip with the other wives about ship schedules or activities, even when taking tea with the captain's wife. Do practice the good habit of saying "I don't know" if asked unnecessary questions by strangers. Do not be curious.

An important part of being a military wife is understanding that there are some things you can not know. Your life depends on it.

Moving and Travel

A military career requires many transfers and promotions. Details of your moving and transportation allowances will always be made available to you. Here is a word of advice from experienced wives: smile! We genuinely mean that. Your changes in station will be much less nerve-wracking if you keep your sense of humor and appreciate the uniqueness of each new location.

For instance, when you first moved here to R'lyeh you were frustrated by the narrow streets and alleyways that fold back on themselves like the long slimy tentacles of a mammoth sea creature. The foul climate and frigid waters made you long for the days of your girlhood, when the sun still shone in skies still blue. The thick mud and foul ooze that cover the city made it difficult to keep your carpets clean, and the reverberant bells from broken church spires gave you headaches that took root deep in your skull and blossomed with thorns.

Now, however, you drift through the city on currents of complacency, content to be pulled by forces beyond your control. You let the cold waters seep into you without struggle or concern. The ache in your head has faded to a dull throb that only flares when you think of those blue skies and lost sun. You beat the carpets with stones and soak in the gray-green sludge that fills your ceramic tub.

We know you are happy here in R'lyeh under the waves. We watch you with our unblinking eyes.

Yet one day your husband may come with news that you are transferring to Arkham or Innsmouth, or perhaps even Providence. Be flexible, as the move may be quite sudden. Set aside any grimoires or tinctures that you wish to carry yourselves. Cooperate with the movers and packers. They'll appreciate some sweet iced tea or hot coffee while they work. Freshly baked cookies are always a nice treat.

Be aware that throughout your husband's career, the way you furnish your house or apartment will reflect on him and your decorating skills. Versatile furniture works best. For instance, chests of drawers inscribed with ancient runes can be used in living rooms as well as bedrooms. When shifting from one home to the next, keep in mind that a bucket of paint can cover wall glyphs to better blend with family furnishings passed from generation to generation. If you are renting, however, don't even paint a shelf until the landlord (and your husband!) give permission.

During your transfer between stations, you might find it practical to pack a small bag for your little ones to hold cards, paper, pencils, crayons, and sleep aids. A small suitcase can be useful to keep diapers and bibs for the baby as well as your own cosmetics for freshening up. Some families prefer to travel directly, while others make time to visit family or picturesque sites.

Of course, there are no picturesque sites anymore, but that doesn't stop puny humans from dreaming of them.

Ceremony

Upon occasion your husband's captain may host a "dining-out." This is a formal dinner to which all officers and wives will be invited. All members of the wardroom are expected to attend. A written request to be excused may be submitted, but will not be approved. The captain traditionally serves as president of the dining-out. As a junior officer, your husband may be asked to serve as "vice." The vice is in charge of sending invitations, overseeing the menu, sounding the dinner chimes, making the toasts, and arranging all sacrifices.

Your job is to support him as needed. If you have a steady hand, perhaps you can draw the seating chart that will be posted in the cocktail lounge. If your voice is clear and sweet, volunteer to sing the national anthem. If you are good at cleaning (and you should be!), you might ensure all flags and standards are free from any bloodstains from the last dining-out.

During the weeks prior to the dining-out you may find yourself working closely with the captain's wife on matters of protocol. Pay close attention to her speech and actions, especially in private. You may be asked later to recall conversations or facial expressions. Your close observations may be handsomely rewarded.

Your husband's uniform must be immaculate for the dining-out. Medals must be polished and appropriately placed, and his white sword-knot tight and carefully draped. Wives should wear long dinner gowns with tasteful jewelry. Women's gloves are optional. During the dinner, refrain from smoking. After dessert is cleared and the wine glasses refilled, the president will authorize the smoking lamp to be lit. The president will also light the guest of honor's cigar.

The first toast will always be to Cthulhu, our Commander in Chief. Each officer must stand with raised glass. Remember not to drain your glass until the last toast, which is traditionally bottoms-up. Do not ask what liquid you have been served.

During the bloodletting, remain attentively in your seat. The captain's wife excused herself last time, setting a poor example for others and bringing her to our cold attention.

How Ships are Named

A standard naming convention applies to ships of the fleet. Destroyers and frigates are named after deceased academics and scholars, such as *Angell*, *Webb*, and *Pabodie*. Cruisers are named for cities and towns, such as *Dunwich*, *Pawtuxet*, and *Salem*. Aircraft carriers are named for famous individuals including *Wilbur Whateley, Barnabus Marsh,* and *Charles Dexter Ward*. Spaceships are named for the Old Ones whose names you cannot pronounce. Submarines honor the Deep Ones, who extend their slimy, webbed hands in an invitation to breed with them.

Wives' Clubs

At most stations, there are wives' clubs for the spouses of enlisted men, Chief Petty Officers, and commissioned officers. These clubs offer a ready-made social group and greatly contribute to the civic health of the community. You may also find clubs for squadron wives, Supply Corps wives, medical staff wives, and wives who are Prisoners of War/ Missing in Action. Membership is always open except for the POW/ MIA Club. That group is special invitation only.

Although there is no rank among wives, a junior officer's wife should always show courteous deference to older women and senior officers' wives. When you are in doubt about etiquette or procedure, a senior officer's wife will offer sage advice. After all, they had to learn these hard lessons, too, at one time.

While your husband is away, you will find the support of these wives invaluable. They can share helpful tips about the traditionally male domains of paying bills, repairing appliances, and disciplining children. Your leisure time is important, too! Recreational activities you can partake in through your local club include bridge, mah-jongg, gardening, antiques, chorus, and gourmet cooking. Hobby groups will be plentiful for crochet, knitting, macramé, embroidery, and ceramics.

You might even find classes for watercolor or oil painting. Remember those dreams you once had of being an artist? In high school you painted a ballerina's feet *en pointe*, her satiny slippers pale pink on the canvas. The painting is long gone but sometimes surfaces in your restless dreams. You run and run through the dark halls of a dead museum, frantic with dread as you search for the girl who painted it.

You mentioned that dream last week to the captain's wife. You'd both drunk an extra glass of wine at a Hail and Farewell function at the officer's club. You were standing on the back deck sharing an illicit cigarette while the cold wind whipped against you and the oily waves crashed on the pilings underneath. You don't like tobacco, but you liked the upsweep of her blond hair and the sly look in her dark blue eyes.

"I have the same nightmare every night," she said, lifting her wine glass to the steel-colored sky. "I'm stuck in a city under the sea, and there's no more sun anywhere."

You laughed, although there's nothing funny about the truth. If your life had been very different, you might have reached out to touch her smooth face. You might have been tempted to kiss her red lips. She might have kissed you back, filling that void inside that your husband has never been able to satisfy.

But you didn't touch and you didn't kiss. Instead, she fixed her gaze on you for a long moment and then turned toward the gray horizon. She said, "Sometimes I dream of changing things."

Inside the club, music and conversation and too many bodies made the air thick. Standing with her, you felt like you could think more clearly. You felt a glimmer of something that might have even been hope. But that was just the wine, and in the morning you made a telephone call.

Religion

We do not actually consider ourselves gods, but it may be useful for you to regard us as such.

Certainly our age, wisdom, and power far outmatch any of the frail system of idols and myths that mankind has invented for itself. We rule the stars. We transcend time. We are more than capable of delivering the "miracles" you ascribe to your religious saviors, but we don't perform on command. We grant life and death on the basis of our own whims and reasons, and only some of us are swayed by silly prayers or slaughtered innocents. Do not make the mistake of believing that in our ancient genes we carry any traits resembling compassion or pity.

The military supports the free exercise of religion, no matter how feeble it may be. Here in R'lyeh under the waves you may attend Protestant, Catholic, Jewish, Muslim, and Buddhist services. As a guest at a meal or special event, you may be called on to participate in a simple religious observance such as a blessing. If asked to pray while in a home of a differing religious affiliation, be sincere with your own favorite grace or stay respectfully silent.

The base chaplain is available to all service members regardless of faith. You may call upon him with questions or concerns, and in many cases your conversations will be kept confidential. The chaplain's aide is a young woman named Petty Officer Windstern. Females in the military service are rare these days, but they serve with the same patriotism, enthusiasm, and devotion as their male counterparts. They are accorded the same respect as their peers, more or less.

Order of Precedence

Precedence is the logical order of rank when dealing with matters of protocol at an official function. All military personnel understand the importance of rank, but matters may become complicated when civilians are present. In brief, any Old One automatically assumes highest precedence and must be accorded every traditional honor. They also receive head-of-line privileges while shopping for groceries at the base commissary and get the best reserved-parking spaces.

The traditional descending order of precedence is Old Ones, supernatural creatures, half-breed supernatural creatures, creatures with just one gray drop of supernatural blood, male humans, male humans with aberrant tendencies, humans made male through surgery or other modification, male children, and female humans.

Remember that social niceties are important from the first moment you follow your husband's footsteps to a new duty station. Social calls must be made and accepted. Respond promptly to RSVPs by note or telephone. Formal receptions celebrating promotions, retirements, and other special occasions will allow your husband to make important political connections, and you should make every effort to be pleasing to the eye. Cocktail parties are more informal, but it is important to dress appropriately. Avoid awkwardness by paying close attention to the difference between casual wear (coat and tie for men, afternoon dress for women) and informal attire (sports shirt for your husband, blouse and skirt for you).

When hosting an event, spend considerable time with menu selection. Never try out a new dish on guests, for something will invariably go wrong. Learn the different grades and cuts of meat. Keep your pantry well stocked with staples. For *hors d'oeuvres*, keep them simple. Men like good, filling appetizers, such as shrimp with piquant sauce, small knobs of cauliflower, or potato chips to be dipped in Roquefort dressing. Do as much planning and preparing as you can in the morning after sending your husband off with a good breakfast. When he returns, he will appreciate your wanting to be in the living room with him, even if it is only to sit by and watch him read the newspaper.

An important tradition in the officer corps is celebrating the promotion of an officer with a dinner party or other event called a "wetting-down." Soon your husband will put on his lieutenant's bars, so definitely share his success with your friends and neighbors. Guests should include his captain. To avoid unpleasantness, do not comment on the absence of his wife. He may not wish to reflect upon the day the military police took her away and certainly can't answer any questions as to her current whereabouts. He has no "need to know," and neither do you.

What is a Navy Wife?

A Navy wife must clean the house, wash clothes, cook meals, tend to the children, and provide for the needs and comfort of her husband. He has the right to good reading lamps, clean ashtrays, and peace and quiet at the end of the day. A Navy wife learns to find satisfaction and happiness in a job well done. She accepts the challenges of the military life with enthusiasm and optimism, and values the traditions and customs passed down to her from earlier generations.

A Navy wife does not dwell on her mistakes. She does not stand on the rocky shore with her coat wrapped tight, contemplating drowning herself in the unforgiving waves. She does not close her eyes and remember dark blue eyes and upswept hair. She does not dream of helpless screams in the city under the sea.

A Navy wife knows that freedom is a fragile thing and must be closely defended.

A Navy wife serves the Old Ones, as does all mankind.

"One of the great appeals of the Mythos – intuitive to those of us who can so easily google the inhuman forces that dominate the twenty-first century – is the idea that knowledge is both irresistibly tempting and overwhelmingly dangerous," according to **Ruthanna Emrys**. Her story, "Those Who Watch," is, she says, "a love letter to the Necronomicon, the Pnakotic Manuscripts, and all those remarkably well-preserved books buried in cyclopean archives beneath the Australian desert."

Emrys lives in a mysterious manor house in the outskirts of Washington DC, with her wife and their large, strange family. She makes homemade vanilla, obsesses about game design, gives unsolicited advice, occasionally attempts to save the world, and blogs sporadically about these things on LiveJournal and Twitter. Her stories have appeared in a number of venues including *Tor.com*, *Strange Horizons*, and *Analog*.

Those Who Watch
Ruthanna Emrys

———

On my third full day, the library marked me. I should have been holding down the desk – I'd been hired for reference – but instead I was shelving. After a year with an MLIS and no prospects, you don't whine. Deep in the narrow aisles of the back stacks, the air conditioning struggled against the sticky Louisiana heat outside. I gave up on my itchy suit jacket, draped it over the cart, and tucked *Cults and Sects of Eastern Bavaria* under my arm while I hooked a rolling stool with my ankle. And felt a piercing sting against the inside of my elbow.

I screamed, almost dropped the book, caught it but lost my balance. My ass is pretty well padded, but now I felt a nasty bruise start up to go along with whatever mutant mosquito had snuck in from the swamps to assault me. I set *Cults and Sects* gently on floor and examined my arm.

The skin swelled, red and inflamed, around a tiny spiral galaxy of indigo and scarlet flame.

I've never so much as pierced my ears. I hate pain. A lot of days I hate my body, too, but it's mine and I don't expect it'd improve anything to ink it up or poke extra holes in it. But I've got braver friends, so I could tell this was unmistakably a tattoo, right about the point some people take off the Band-Aid – a little too early – and send you close-up selfies to make you wince in sympathy. I touched it and shrieked again, a little muffled because I expected the pain this time.

I prodded the book, turned it carefully with the tip of my finger. No needles hidden between pages by urban legend psychopaths, or protruding from the spine like some literary assassin's poison ring. An ordinary book, cloth bound and stamped along the page ends with "Crique Foudre Community College."

"Elaine! Are you all right?" My boss hurried around the end of the row. I scrambled to my feet, nearly tripping again, left hand clapped over the evidence of whatever screw-up I'd managed.

"Sorry, Sherise," I managed. *Sherise*, she'd made clear when I started, not Sherry or Miss Nichols or any of the other variants people had tried – she liked her name and she used it.

"Let me see," she said. When I didn't move, she pried my fingers away from the offending spot. She hummed as she traced the swollen area. "Better get the first aid kit to be safe. Come on."

She strode confidently through the stacks, a maze I'd already gotten lost in twice that morning. Florescent light gleamed off her brown skin and the darker maps winding around her arms – hers were probably from an actual tattoo parlor. Her hair puffed over her ears; big gold rings strung with lapis beads dangled underneath. I struggled to keep up.

A few more turns, and we'd come all the way around the shelf-lined halls that surrounded the library's central reading room, back to the staff office with its institutional carpet and laminate desks. Sherise's, in the corner, stood out by being bigger and uglier than the others, and topped by sort of an old style wooden card catalog, dozens of tiny drawers with brass pulls. She opened one, pulled out a box of what looked like alcohol wipes. She tore open a sealed pack, labeled in an alphabet I didn't recognize. It smelled of wintergreen and ashes. She rubbed the cool pad over my arm, and stinging gave way to a softer tingle.

"There, that should keep it from spreading. Be careful with the religion books. Powers want respect, and so do the words around them."

"Okay." My last semester at Rutgers I'd applied to jobs all around the country – and the same for a year afterward. It was August now, and plenty of hungry new graduates would be glad to move to rural Louisiana if I didn't work out.

CFCC had been a miracle of double-scheduling, tacked onto a disastrous interview at the smallest and most obscure branch of Louisiana State University. The LSU staff started by asking whether I had any family in the area and what church I liked. Their library was a disaster, too: a modern brick monstrosity that turned off the climate control at night to keep under budget, and never mind if mold ate away their skimpy collection. After that, just about anywhere would have been an easy sell. The CFCC library, endowed by an alumnus-made-good with distinctly non-modern architectural tastes, about made me cry with gratitude.

At CFCC, they didn't ask about my family. They threw a dozen weird-ass reference queries at me in rapid succession, and seemed pleased by my sample class on databases. They did ask my religion, but "sort of an agnostic Neopagan" – I was through being coy after LSU – seemed like an acceptable answer. By the time they brought out an old leather-bound tome from their rare books collection and wanted to know if the font gave me a headache, I didn't much care. I was past wanting a job, any job – I wanted to work somewhere that actually cared about being a good library for their visitors. I wanted a *space* that cared, and never mind if outside the doors waited mosquitoes and killing humidity and drive-through liquor stores.

Sherise didn't send me home, which I kind of thought might have been justified. On the other hand she didn't yell at me, which would probably have been justified, too. I'd been disrespectful to *Sects and Cults*, after all, whatever that meant. I retreated to the reading room.

The circular, high-domed room at the library's heart was a legacy of the generous alumnus. According to Sherise, this benefactor had traveled the world collecting antiquities, and decided that American education neglected the values that had made the ancient world great. "By ancient he meant Greece," she'd said. "Maybe Baghdad if he was feeling really broad-minded. But still, you won't find another building this pretty closer than New Orleans." And she was right: in the middle of a campus of shoebox buildings, the library stood out like a dandelion breaking through a sidewalk.

Each door to the reading room was crowned by cherubim bearing a motto on a banner – in this case: "The temple of knowledge shapes the mind within." Actual cherubim, not putti; I had to look up the original descriptions before I believed it. Inside, the room went up three stories. The center held the shelves and work stations and computers you'd expect, but allegorical sculptures of Cosmology and Determination and Wisdom, Agriculture and Epiphany and Curiosity, gazed down over the doors. Above them a bas-relief ribbon detailed stories related to these virtues. Some I recognized: Oedipus and the sphinx, Archimedes in his bath. In others, humans and fabulous monsters played out less familiar myths. A tromp l'œil thunderstorm stood over all, making the room feel dim and cool even with the lamps turned up bright. A few professors bent over oak desks, and I felt self-conscious as I craned my neck.

The sculptures had been a definite selling point for the school, one that helped me work up the guts to come out as Neopagan – though it's not always a trustworthy sign; a guy screamed at me one time for pointing out Minerva's owls atop the Chicago Public Library. People don't like admitting they're taking advantage of other people's temples, maybe even worshipping just by walking through.

It was Determination I wanted – to get through the day, to do my work right so I'd still have a job and an apartment and insurance when David's visiting professorship in Chicago ended. There was a little spot between two shelves where I could get near her with no one watching. I sat heavily on a stool, looked up. She wore armor, and aimed her spear down at my seat. In her other arm, she clasped a book protectively, and she gazed with narrowed eyes, daring anyone to come up and try something. But someone had: carven blood spilled from a wound in her side, the only spot of color on the white marble.

When I first saw her, I assumed she got that wound from some enemy's weapon. But it was awfully close to the book. I opened my mouth to whisper a prayer, and couldn't get anything out.

The advantage of being agnostic is that you can pray to whatever you like. A stream, a statue, an abstract concept, a fictional character – if it feels like it ought to be a god, if it does you some good to think about how it might see your problems, you can just go ahead and babble. But I couldn't doubt the muddy multichromatic swirl pressed into my skin. Some power, aware or otherwise, had decided that was a good idea.

I knew enough stories. Gods, if they actually exist and don't mind letting you see the evidence, are scary fucks. No damn way was I *praying* to one. My arms slipped up to wrap around my chest and I scooted to the side. I felt ridiculous, but I also felt like at any moment Determination might shift her spear. Maybe she wanted to make sure I didn't misuse another precious book. My heart sped, and I started to feel dizzy. I pushed the stool farther back, checked the aisle behind me and saw Epiphany, globe upheld in one hand and wings spread, other hand on her robe. But her eyes – like Determination's – focused on me, mocking. I scrambled up, kicking the stool against the shelf, flinching as it banged into the wood. Backed away, then fled through Wisdom's door to the staff room, not daring to look either at her or at the professors who might've noticed my outburst.

I shouldn't have taken the prayer break in any case. I should've gone to work the reference desk – in the middle of the reading room – or back to the pre-semester re-shelving. But I still didn't know what I'd done wrong, and after a few minutes trying to swallow a growing lump of nausea, knew that I couldn't face either today. Sherise had left the staff room and I'd only get lost looking for her. I scribbled a note: "I'm feeling sick and need to go home early – I'll make it up later in the week. Sorry for the short notice."

As I gathered up my things, I imagined her reading the note. I had no idea what rare sequelae might result from book tattoos – would she call an ambulance? I went back and added: "It's a problem with the dose on my medication; I'll get it fixed." She knew I was on meds; I'd deliberately let her see the sertraline when I took my morning pills. Another thing I didn't feel like being coy about. And it was true about the dosage problem. After a year with no insurance, my new doctor wanted to start slowly; the amount I was taking now might work for an anxious supermodel, but for a big girl like me it barely made a dent.

Outside, heat slammed my lungs. I squinted against the blinding afternoon sun, trying to catch my breath. Halfway to the parking lot, sweat soaked my shirt; just walking felt disgusting. Skin and cloth stuck to each other and peeled away, again and again. By the time I got to the car, my legs were shaking and my heart still hadn't slowed. I felt short of breath, and couldn't tell whether I was hyperventilating or just having trouble with the humidity.

The first blast of AC cleared my head enough for me to realize that no way in hell should I drive like this. After a minute of circling the need-to-get-home/can't-go-home paradox, I gave in and called David. Skyped, actually – still just in range of the campus Wi-Fi, I needed to see him more desperately than I needed him not to see me in sweat-stained dishabille.

The phone sang its reassuring trying-to-connect melody, less reassuring as it went on and I wondered if I'd misremembered his class schedule. Or he could be with a student, or in a meeting, or just too busy. But finally, with a satisfied plink, the video came through.

"Hey, gorgeous," he said. "Are you okay?"

"Hey, pretty boy." It was ritual exchange, but at least my end of it was true. My fiancé was a beautiful red-haired Nordic type who could rock a Viking helmet or a slinky dress with equal aplomb. What he saw in me was still a mystery. I tried to explain what was going on, managed only: "I hate Louisiana."

"I don't blame you." He leaned closer. "Are you having a panic attack?"

I shook my head, then nodded, then shook it again.

"Okay. Take a deep breath. I'm right here, I'm holding you. Let it out. Breathe in."

I imagined his arms around me, imagined lying together in the shitty little apartment we'd shared near Rutgers. It made me feel lonely, but it gave me something to think about besides the heat and the tattoo and my boss and the job that might be too weird for me to handle. The breathing helped. My head cleared further, and keeping the car on the right side of the road no longer seemed like an overwhelming prospect.

"Thanks, that helps." I wanted to show him the tattoo – but the thought made my mouth feel dry again. What if he demanded I quit my job and come to Chicago right away? Or worse, what if he couldn't see it at all? Hallucination isn't supposed to be a symptom of generalized anxiety disorder, but it was actually the most rational explanation I could think of. "What do you do when your job gets weird?" I asked instead.

He leaned back, obviously pleased to have been of use. "Research, mostly. Or diagnose my colleagues' personality disorders on insufficient evidence, depending on the brand of weirdness. Is someone being nasty?"

"No. Just, um, trying to figure out campus culture."

"Lots of alcohol and not enough drugs, probably."

We chatted a little longer, and then he had to get back to course prep. I let him go, and didn't tell him I'd called in sick. Nothing bad happened on my drive home.

Outside my apartment complex, I found the heat still intense, but now that I was calmer (and before I hit the barricade of smokers by the door) I took a moment to breathe. I can't stand the way Louisiana looks or feels, but the smell is amazing. Silt and decay like endless autumn, overlain with orchids and citrus and cypress and a million other trees and vines and roots bursting from every available surface. I can't face the swamp in person. Giant bugs to bite you or leap in your face, mud to slip on, alligators just lying around hoping you're weak enough to be worth a sprint. But I love the smell.

I drowned my sorrows in chocolate and a *Criminal Minds* marathon, and it helped. Sherise sent an email to say she hoped I'd feel better, and I stared at it for five minutes trying to figure out whether she believed me before giving up and going back to the TV.

But calling out sick only works for so long, and I've learned the hard way that if I let myself do it two days in a row it's easy to get inertia and stretch it for a week. So the next morning, lying in bed, I tried to put my thoughts in order.

The tattoo remained, stubbornly, on my arm. It still felt tender, but the dim light filtering through the blinds showed that the swelling had gone down. So I would go with the assumption that I wasn't hallucinating, if nothing else because I wasn't checking into any hospital without David there to look respectable for the doctors.

If the tattoo was real . . . then I still wasn't sure about the statues. I'd been spiraling, and I couldn't even trust my judgment of live people when that happened. How the hell was I supposed to predict allegorical virtues? But the tattoo, all by itself, meant I didn't understand how books worked. Probably it meant I didn't understand how the world worked at all, but I'd always known that. Books, though, I thought I had down.

When his job got weird, David did research. For him that meant digging through sociology databases and endless stacks of journal articles. I didn't know what database covered this situation – but if the library had untrustworthy books, it ought to have resources to tell you about them.

"Imagine it's someone else's reference question," I said aloud. Talking to myself feels stupid, but never speaking aloud at home feels a lot worse. "Miss, I've got a report about book attacks due in three hours. Can you find everything for me? Yes, damn straight I can."

*   *   *

Sherise nodded when I dropped my lunch in the staff room, and asked casually after my health. I told her I was fine today, tried to parse what she was thinking. Probably I ought to have gone ahead and asked about the book. But she hadn't told me when she cleaned the tattoo, and maybe there was a reason for that. Either it wasn't the sort of thing she could explain properly, or she assumed I already knew.

One of David's psych grad friends, a year ahead of him, figured out – halfway through his post doc – that they'd hired him thinking he'd studied under a different professor from the same department. They'd never asked, he'd never told them, and he'd struggled to keep up the whole year. But it wasn't exactly the kind of thing you could come out and say. Suppose one of the Rutgers library science professors was secretly a Predatory Books specialist? Or more plausibly, suppose Sherise assumed this was something Neopagans just knew about? Either way, I didn't want to make her feel stupid – or like hiring me had been a mistake. I'd just have to paw through the databases myself until I found what I needed.

Walking into the reading room was hard. My body believed, even if I wasn't sure, that I'd faced a threat here. Bodies like to preserve themselves; mine wanted me to go back to my cave where it was safe. I told my body that it was stupid, and went in. I couldn't help glancing at Determination. She didn't seem about to spear me, but I still sensed something watching. The sense of attention seemed to pervade the room, all the allegories judging our choices of study. I shivered, tried to ignore what was probably just my neurotic imagination, and turned on the ancient reference computer.

The library's generous funder wasn't nearly as fond of technology as of architecture or hard copy, so I had far too long to sit in the crossfire of allegorical gazes without the screen to distract me. When I finally got the browser running, I looked over the library's scant list of databases. Medline? Likely to support the hallucination hypothesis. PsycInfo? Worse. Maybe JSTOR or the always over-general Academic Search Premier? Eventually I decided to start with databases I'd never heard of – if a community college with a lousy budget for online services subscribed to something really obscure, there was probably a reason.

I found a few, in fact. Mostly the weird ones claimed space in world mythology and folklore, though there was one in biology and another in physics. MythINFO turned out to be perfectly pedestrian, though kind of awesome: it let you search by a drop-down menu of Stith Thompson Motif Index entries. Several looked relevant – various "transformation" archetypes, magical books – but turned up only articles on fairy tales, drowned in the deep jargon of literary analysis.

PYTHIAS, though, seemed more promising. Various combinations of "book" and "tattoo," suitably modified by "AND" one thing and "–" another, got me nowhere. But an exasperated "bibliogenic illness" turned up a long list of books in the Zs. I scribbled down call numbers for those available locally, took a deep breath, and fled the reading room for whatever lurked in the stacks.

My first few days in the library, I could get lost by blinking. The stacks wound back in all directions, and I could never quite figure out how straight rows added up to a circular building – except that the rows seemed to curve subtly, sometimes, and the turns weren't always right angles. Today for the first time, a map stretched out in my mind; I couldn't see the edges, but could feel the shape and logic of how the rows spread from where I stood. Beneath my skin, the tattoo pulsed with soft heat. I touched it, gingerly, but felt nothing from outside.

I hadn't been back to the Zs – the "index" section whose self-referential topic is books and libraries – since the whirlwind tour during my interview. But the warmth in my arm seemed to increase along what I vaguely recalled was the right path. I gave in and followed it, trying not to think too hard about what I was doing.

The AC was managing better today, at least as far as temperature. The stacks felt cool and shadowy. But in the corner of my eye fog seeped from below the shelves, never there when I turned to look though I felt it against my skin. It sometimes seemed about to coalesce into more solid form and draw me to a particular shelf, a particular volume – but it never did.

My map grew as I walked; at last I saw that the stacks were not so much neat rows as a galactic spiral, linear only to the cursory glance. And at the far end of the western arm, I found an alcove lit by buzzing fluorescents and lined with tightly packed mahogany bookshelves. Tiny paperbacks pressed against oversized leather-bound tomes, and the half-imagined fog cleared in favor of archival dryness. A circular stained-glass window, wider than the span of my hands, filtered light through an abstract pattern of magenta and midnight blue. The colors shifted as shadows moved beyond – probably leaves from the grand row of hollies and live oaks between library and parking lot. My arm burned, pain flaring as I stepped into the coruscating illumination. I whimpered and bit my lip.

I wanted to move away from the window and get my books. Instead, unwilled, I knelt. As in the reading room, I felt again the attention of some presence. This one seemed less judgmental, more curious. Not friendly curiosity: a biologist examining a noisy DNA sequence, perhaps, or me with a particularly recalcitrant new database. The attention sharpened, and I felt uncomfortably aware of my body: not only fat ass and weak ankles, but heart thudding and guts clenching and nerves struggling to keep up. All pus and blood and static, acid and slime and brittle bone.

And I felt the examination grow more active, as whatever attended through the window started to prod at my flaws and cracks.

The tattoo had been quick, done before I knew what was happening. Not so, here. This thing wanted to change me, though it clearly didn't care about my opinion on the specifics – probably didn't even consider that I might have one. I gasped, but still couldn't rise from where it held me bent almost to the floor, stomach compressing uncomfortably and legs cramping and falling asleep. Worse, a part of me didn't want to. I've never liked my body, not the ass and ankles and skin and face I deal with every day, and not the inside bits now suddenly forced into my awareness. Any change might be for the better – at the very least wouldn't be anything I could be blamed for.

But the part that knelt willingly was all conscious. A wave of revulsion and fear surged up to overwhelm any other reaction; my whole body shook and my pulse came so fast it hurt. In the throes of the panic attack, my instincts broke through whatever held me down, as they did everything that might have intent about it. I threw myself from the illuminated circle and scuttled backward until my back pressed against the nearest shelf. If the books wanted to bite me, I'd be ink all over.

Slowly – no Sherise to interrupt my reactions, no David to talk me down – I started to think in words again. I stared at dust motes floating in the light from the window, made swirling nebulae by the colors. The light hadn't moved while I curled frozen beside it. I'd lost track of time, but sunlight ought to have shifted across the floor. Maybe there was another room beyond this one, even if my unlikely map told me otherwise.

If I got up and went closer, I might be able to glimpse whatever lay on window's other side. That seemed like a bad idea.

Maybe the books could tell me.

I pulled myself to my feet, terrified every moment of toppling back into the light. My arm still ached with heat. In the panic's aftermath I felt washed out emotionally, just numb enough to actually consider sticking around for what I'd come to get.

The Nature of the Word was bound in calfskin, fine yellow-edged pages typeset save for hand-illuminated letters at the start of chapters. I winced at the yellowing; this ought to be in the rare book room, not the ordinary stacks. *Palaces of History* was library bound but looked like a reprint of something much earlier, each page imaged from a neatly handwritten monograph with intricate – if disturbing – illustrations. The simply named *Libris* looked like a Penguin Classics paperback, except that it came from Sarkomand Translations, a publisher and imprint I'd never heard of.

I found a library cart lurking in a back corner, odd reassurance that the alcove existed for other people, too. Maybe they all knew to avoid the window, or maybe it liked them better. Or maybe I ought to report it – like telling someone when you spot a leaking pipe. I trundled the cart back toward the galactic core.

I ducked my head at Determination and her companions as I settled at my desk. Powers want respect, Sherise had said, and until I knew what I was doing it was probably safer to give them at least a little. Epiphany's gaze stood higher now, no longer focused on those of us below. I caught myself staring at her left hand, the one holding her robe. It wasn't just a pose, I realized: she stood ready to bare her chest to Determination's spear, and it was her opposite's eye that she sought to attract.

I shivered, and forced my attention back to the books. I started with *The Nature of the Word*: at any minute, I expected someone to come along and tell me it needed to go into protective storage until I could prove my need to touch its fragile pages. Selfish but not sociopathic, I did snag a pair of nitrile gloves from the check-out counter.

> *Those who believe the universe was created, believe it was created with words. Those who know it for an accident still understand that language, once created, becomes a force in its own right. Fifteen million years before humanity's birth, the Tay-yug claimed that miserly gods hid favored words in the hearts of stars, making them unstable and scouring life from worlds that spun too close.*

I sat back, breathing hard. It was a story, of course it was a story, a myth I'd never heard before. A myth of gamma ray bursts, in a book that looked older than the phenomenon's discovery – but how much did I know about the history of physics? I ought to keep reading. Would, in a moment.

When I was a kid, for a while I got really into urban legends. Even though I knew better, I'd sit up late reading about chupacabras and the Loch Ness monster. The one that really got to me was the Mothman. It was sort of a humanoid with big bug wings, and people would look out their windows and it would just be hovering there, staring at them. That was it – it never broke the window or hurt anyone, at least not who reported it later. But I'd pull my shades down tight, eyes squeezed shut so that if anything was out there, I wouldn't see it. Knowing that if I hadn't read about it, if I hadn't known it was out there to look for, the windows would have been perfectly safe.

Of course I already knew, now, that there was something outside.

I scanned, sampled, turning pages cautiously but skimming as quickly as I could, looking for what I needed – something that would explain what had happened to me. Instead, I learned about books that started plagues or imprisoned their readers, and others that, read in the right place and at the right time, would let you cast your mind out to travel the stars. Stories that could leave your mind a husk colonized by parasitic characters, single words that could rewrite memory.

I did not slam the book shut. I closed it, carefully, like the rare archival volume that it was. I could *not* give up reading, wouldn't blind myself to what it offered, just because there might be monsters inside.

I hadn't found anything about tattoos, or stained glass windows – maybe another book would be more relevant. You've got to focus when you're doing research, can't just let yourself get sucked in by whatever seems shiniest. And "terrifying" is a lot like "shiny." *Libris*, with its two-tone paper cover, looked reassuringly pragmatic.

"How did you get ahold of that?" Sherise's voice, sharp and angry, froze me with my hand on the cover. My eyes shifted toward *The Nature of the Word* and I felt my cheeks grow hot. But it was *Libris* that she snatched from my desk.

"I'm sorry," I said. "I found it in the Zs. I was trying to look up some-thing about—" I pushed up my sleeve to show the galaxy tattoo. It was, I realized, the same shape as the stacks, the same colors as the window. And I'd just made my ignorance obvious, too. "I'm sorry," I repeated.

"I'm not mad at you." She ran a finger across the cover, frowning. "But this shouldn't have been shelved in the regular stacks. A bit past anything you need to be handling, right now."

"Does it eat your brain?" I felt my cheeks flare again, worse for the knowledge that it showed like a beacon.

She smiled. "Not this one, no. But it's not translated from any human language, and it's safer to know what to expect before you get into it." She tucked it under her arm, though not against bare skin.

At this point, she could tell anyway that I didn't know what I was doing. Still, it took a few dry swallows before I could get the words out. They were angrier than I'd intended. "Am I *supposed* to ask? Or am I supposed to figure it out all on my own and hope I don't unleash a plague on the whole Gulf Coast?"

She leaned against the edge of my desk, put *Libris* back down, patted the offending volume a couple of times as if to reassure herself that it was still closed. Then she pushed her cloud of hair away from one ear. The whole outer curve had been sculpted into tiny scallops, like waves of flesh, and faded to cheap newsprint gray. It stood like a scar against the warm brown of the rest of her skin. She let the hair spring back.

"Happened my first day at Crique Foudre. I can hear the books, and hear people and other things thinking when they mean to do harm. Prophecies, sometimes. And people arguing in whispers down the block when I'm trying to sleep. The gifts have sharp edges. There's no way to know beforehand who can handle it all and who can't, and we've learned the hard way that you have to find out most of it for yourself. If someone explains everything straight up, it always ends badly."

"Suppose I quit?" I swallowed, because again I hadn't meant to speak so bluntly, and because I knew the answer. I'd show up at David's studio, and he'd support me as best he could – no one in Chicago was hard up for librarians – and he wouldn't criticize me for not being able to cut it in the real world.

"You could do that. The lady before you left at two months – that's why we were hiring so late in the summer." Nothing about how I'd leave them in the lurch if I quit just before the semester started, though it didn't really need saying. "This is riskier than holding down a desk just about anywhere else. The best I can offer is that if you stick around, you'll become something special. We all do. Whether that special is more like yourself, or less, depends on luck. And on your own choices, at least a little."

I didn't know whether I ought to be tempted by the "more" or the "less" – or whether I was even crazier than usual to be tempted by either. "What *can* you tell me? Without things ending badly?"

She sighed, fidgeted the beads on her earring. I wondered if they drowned out the voices of the books. "That's always a gamble, but I'll give it a shot. You know about our patron."

"Yeah. Although no one's told me his name. Or her name. I'd think there'd be a plaque or something – is this one of the things it's dangerous to know?"

"No, he just likes to keep a low profile. You might meet him, one of these days." She closed her eyes and inhaled sharply. "Maybe that's not the place to start. I'm sorry. I don't feel like I've explained this right to anyone, yet. Maybe this'll be the time – unless you want me to shut up and let you track it all down for yourself."

I shook my head, a bit spooked by her uncertainty.

"Well. The universe is a dangerous place. It's not trying to be dangerous, and it's full of things that have never heard of humans and wouldn't much care if they did – but not caring can do at least as much harm as hatred, from things that can break you just passing by. The safest way, for a species that wants time to grow up, is to make a few places that can focus the strangeness, draw it away from everywhere else, and help keep it from getting out of control. People have been doing that on earth for millions of years, maybe longer, each learning from fragments left by those who came before, and doing just a little better as a result. This library is one of those places for humans."

"Out in—" I just stopped myself from asking what – if she wasn't just making this up – a vital shield against extinction was doing out in the middle of nowhere, in a state that most of the country couldn't even bother to protect from floods.

She smiled wryly, making me think I'd been pretty transparent. "Safer this way. Crique Foudre is heir to Zaluski Library in Warsaw. Our patron traveled there in the 1920s, and when the Nazis destroyed it he knew we'd need another one. He thought, a place that isn't the capital of anywhere or the center of anything – it would be a lot safer from other humans."

"So we're the quiet heroes who protect the world from terrible cosmic monsters?" I'd seen that show; I would have been happier to leave it on the screen.

"You've been to the edge of the stacks. It's not that simple. Sometimes we just keep the monsters happy, or distract them, or find a use for them, or study them to learn what else is out there. Sometimes we're bait. Sometimes we can't do a damn thing other than watch. And eventually we'll lose the fight – either to other humans, like Zaluski, or altogether, like the three other species on this world that we know about before us."

I shivered. "One more thing to worry about."

"That's one way to handle it, sure."

"What do you do?" I asked.

"I go for distraction, personally. There are so many things to *learn* here, that you'll never find in another library that isn't doing the same work. Things to become. As long as you're doing your job, the larger cosmic picture kind of takes care of itself, whether or not you grieve over it."

"Do you ever worry about asteroids?" I asked David. I was home, curled up with my laptop on the couch, insufficiently distracted by my pretty boyfriend.

"Like the one that got the dinosaurs?" he asked. "Not really. It doesn't seem like something that happens very often, and I'm not in a position to do anything about it in any case."

"Very logical." I drew up my knees, watched him pass back and forth across the screen as he made French toast. "Suppose you *could* do something. Or thought you could?"

"You mean like a desperate space mission to steer a comet away from Earth? Yeah, I would worry about that. I worry when there's something

I can try, and it matters if I screw up." He smiled gently. "You've got to pick your battles – there's only so much worry to go around."

"Unless you're me."

"Even for you, gorgeous."

Later, I realized that I hadn't asked if he'd rather be in a position to try something, even if he thought he'd screw up, or whether he'd rather do work he was better at, and not have to look.

On the first day of classes, humidity spilled over the banks of the sky into a spectacular thunderstorm. I eased my car around puddles half-grown into lakes, breathing slowly through the constant strobe of lightning. I arrived ten minutes late, suit soaked through in spite of my umbrella. The AC set me shivering, but Sherise and the other librarians were talking and laughing in the staff room and one of them tossed me a giant beach towel.

Sherise nodded at me and said, "We're gonna get slammed even with the rain, so you know. And there are still a dozen professors who need pinning to the wall 'til they hand over their reserve lists." By the time I got the last math professor to confess the identity of his textbook, and started on the English department, umbrellas filled the foyer and students swirled through the reading room.

Most of the morning's reference questions were about what I'd expected. Students wanted their course reserves and panicked about their first day's homework and didn't know how to manage the catalogue. But a lot of them seemed to realize they were in sacred space. I saw a dozen conflicting rituals. People blew kisses to the statues, or stood under the trompe l'oeil ceiling with arms raised. One student fussed at my desk for five minutes while I grew increasingly exasperated, then asked hesitantly if I could leave her offering "for the loa Epiphany" after the library closed. She slipped me a sandwich bag filled with cookies and tiny slips of calligraphed poetry, then wanted to know whether we'd fixed the PYTHIAS bugs over the summer.

After the students cleared out at last, I stayed at my desk for a few minutes trying to catch my breath. Even the allegories seemed tired.

Determination's spear might have drooped a little, unless it just pointed at where some student had annoyed her. I got up and started to put the reference section back in order, then went to give Epiphany her cookies. In the wall below each statue, just above eye level, were little niches that I'd never noticed before. They were easier to spot now, as plenty of people hadn't bothered with an intermediary for their offerings. There were flowers and pebbles, photos, cupcakes, a thankfully unlit candle, tiny jars of liquor that I was just going to assume came from faculty. I stuck the baggie in the appropriate spot.

"Hey," I told Epiphany. I still wasn't sure about talking with them, but ignoring them didn't seem wise, and the students knew the place better than I did. "Long day. Keep safe, okay?" I felt her attention on me, and knew that safety didn't interest her at all – not to give, and not to receive. I trembled: equal parts awe and anxiety, both uncomfortable. Her companions seemed to perk up, their notice sharpening. The air brightened with storm-tinged ozone, and my ears ached as if I'd gone up too fast in an elevator. I felt again the urge to kneel. But I'd spent the day doing my job, and doing it mostly right.

I looked around, found myself alone in the reading room. "I'm not just going to do what you want," I said. No response. I shivered.

"I'm not ignoring you," I went on. Then, swallowing. "I'm not running away, yet. But we're going to work together on this, or it's all going to fall apart."

Still no response – maybe Sherise would have been able to hear one – but the pressure lifted a little. My ears popped, painfully.

"That's better," I said. I kept the shakes out of my voice, knowing I would pay later – if not through some screw-up here, then through breaking down when I got home and thought too hard about the whole thing. But then, I'd have paid that price whatever I did. "All right. Was there something you wanted to show me?"

I left through Epiphany's door, and followed the pulse of my little galaxy out into the stacks.

Laird Barron is the author of several books, including *The Croning*, *Occultation*, and *The Beautiful Thing That Awaits Us All*. His work has also appeared in many magazines and anthologies. An expatriate Alaskan, Barron currently resides in upstate New York. *Slate* has aptly said of his short fiction: "Relentlessly readable, highly atmospheric, sharply and often arrestingly written – Barron's prose style resembles, by turns, a high-flown Jim Thompson mixed with a pulp Barry Hannah – and situated in a dizzying assortment of precision-built worlds."

As for his contribution to this anthology, Barron explains: "Lovecraft's fiction covers a broader spectrum than many people realize. It's important to keep his versatility in mind when tilling this particular patch of earth for a themed anthology. 'A Clutch' isn't meant to emulate Lovecraft, but rather to respond to certain elements of his work – black magic, corruption, ancient secrets best left buried, and lurking doom. I filtered these elements through my own conception of a weird tale. Crack the shell and have a look."

A Clutch
Laird Barron

———

The man on the straw bed was done for, for sure. The young woman saw it plainly in his knotted muscles, heard it in his wet and ragged coughs. Moss lung, the wise women called the malady. Woodcutters, such as her uncle, risked it by hewing into fungi-encrusted cedars and firs. He gleamed with sweat. Three white hens clucked and fluffed themselves on their rack near his naked feet. The dog grumbled by the hearth, lost in a dream of the hunt.

"I am dying," her uncle said. "Come near. You took me in and gave me shelter. Allowed me to call you daughter . . . You are a precious ornament to my worthless life. O my sweet fair one! Scrubber of pots, burner of suppers, nurse to wounded forest creatures, radiant of heart, and pure of virtue!" He relapsed, head lolling.

The woman ignored him until she finished stoking the fire. She gathered her skirts and came to kneel at his side. She laid her hand upon his brow. Hot as a skillet. It wouldn't be long. Death whetted his culling knife out in the night gloom, ready to cut another soul off at the knees. She uncorked a bottle of whiskey and dribbled it over the man's scabrous lips until he gagged.

"My parents are dead these nine years. You have stood in their place. You have cut the wood and killed the wolves. You were my father's blood returned home at our darkest hour. O Uncle, of course you may call me daughter."

"Uncle. Yes, uncle. That was the story." The man tugged her sleeve. He seemed to gather his innermost reserves, for his expression smoothed and he spoke with a cold, uncharacteristic serenity. "The moon will roll like the bloody hub of a chariot through the branches of the crying sycamores. On nights such as this when the wind roars in the trees and the hearth coals glow like the eyes of the Black Dog itself, you and the whiskey are a comfort. The cottage seems so rude, the candle glow of our souls so feeble, yet from your cheerful mien I draw courage. You resemble so much your mother now, Creator rest her.

"Gazing upon the accumulated trinkets, my bitten axes, the salted venison, the burlap and the barrels, storm chests and sealed urns, and the painting of your mother in her maidenhood, I am struck by how little there is to show for the generations of labor, for the missing thumb, the broken back, the lungs infested with devil's club spore. My drunkard's breath rasping, slower and slower.

"You are a good girl. Alas, I must tell you something nevertheless. My deathbed confession. Before you came along, I swore I'd be crisped in the fires of hell rather than sire offspring. You are dearer to my heart than any golden treasure. I should have kept my word."

"Sired offspring?" she said. "I don't take your meaning."

"I fear it will come to you."

When I was young, the Emperor's Highway ended a few leagues south of the Black Forest. Not like today where the road cleaves right through the middle and is lined with hostels and cheery inns thanks to the many reforms of the Empress, Creator bless and keep her from harm. No, in the olden times all you got were deer paths and howling darkness once you set foot off the porch. Men hunted in groups with flintlocks and spears and packs of hounds. Boar, bear, wolf, and worse, lurked. Even a few of the trees and some of the mossy boulders couldn't be trusted. Vile spirits were loose in the world. Hapless travelers vanished. Burly hunters, too. The children are what bothered everyone the most.

Ours has ever been a family of foresters – hunters, trappers, fellers, every one. My great-great-great grandfather Abernathy Ruark settled right here on the southern verge of the forest just after the shouting ended over the botched succession of King Theobald. Abernathy and his kin were a band of scofflaws and partisans who fled north when the revolt went sour, but half the kingdoms were in the same pickle and a couple generations later all was forgiven, if not forgotten. Most of the wood folk returned to the cities once the Interregnum ended. The Ruarks stood fast and continued to carve a living from the banded oak and red walnut that southern lords and fat-bellied merchants hold so dear. We hunted the razorback boars and skinned the bears-that-speak-the-tongue-of-men. We will continue until the last of us has shuffled into the Hinterlands.

James Dandy was a friend in my youth. Yes, yes, the very highway-man and brigand who got himself hanged in King's Grove two winters gone. Last of his line. He grew up hard as nails. His parents were put to the ax and his brothers taken in chains to Sad Island. The Kouadoi would have bagged him, too, if he'd not squirreled away beneath a pile of dung until they tramped down to their ships and went back over the sea to their great ruined empire of caverns in Mount Thrall. That marked him, surely it did. Not a bad sort, but not a good one either, and now he's worm food with all the rest but yours truly.

Our misadventures were mainly his doing, or that of his cousins Manfred Hurt and Ike Lutz, both of whom had fled Westhold under a dark cloud. Man whores, the pair. Hurt convinced me to leave home and travel the kingdom in search of adventure. For a year I followed him around like a puppy, growing leaner and meaner with each passing week. We survived by laboring when there was labor, stealing pies from windowsills, whoring ourselves to monied folk, and so forth. I learned much of Dandy and his cousins. Much indeed.

I'd resigned myself to another dose of boot-leather soup when Dandy waved a handbill he'd snagged from the gutter. He proposed that we four should join a troop of other stout lads to answer the King's call for a march into the worst part of the Black Forest – The Fells. Aye, *The Fells, The Fells where the Jumping Jack dwells* . . . The Ministry of Coin wanted to scour the ruins of them old fallen holds that lie sunk into the muck and mire. There'd been a war, always a war, and it drained the treasury. Matters were so dire, palace servants had taken to melting royal dinnerware for the gold. Shameful.

Eadweard Mingy sat the throne in those days. King Mingy's mother died birthing him and he was raised by a witch from the Far East. The bat gave him a taste for the black arts, maybe for the Dark itself. What a wretched court his must've been. Damned if that warlock Jon Foot didn't curry his favor all the years Mingy reigned. Jon Foot's folly is why I'll never step north of the Hunt River so long as I draw breath. Creator blast him.

After a roaring drunk, my friends and I got fresh tattoos and signed up with the Royal Army. They were pleased to snatch our service since we were accomplished woodsmen, or close enough for their uses. I hoped to see home again. Foolish boy was I.

Away we went – a full company of soldiers, laborers, potboys, and whores. One of a dozen such companies sent to spelunk for gold and precious relics and jewelry in the abandoned strongholds of the dead lords. Whispers were that the leaders of the expeditions reported not to the chancellery, but to Foot himself. He sought something other than mere gold or trinkets among the ruins.

Woe to us who discovered it for him.

We marched. North and north through the tilled and green lands around Great Port. North and north over the Tumwater and though the Wolverine Mountains a day's ride from the sea. North and north again until we passed through Sterling and entered the Black Forest in the region known as Cottonwood Vale for the cottonwood trees that line the River Fetch.

Our troop was led by Captain Vanger – well known throughout the army as a genuine hard ass. Vanger the Incorruptible, Vanger the Whip. Captain brooked no nonsense among the ranks, squaddie or civilian. Carried a blacksnake whip at his belt – as the men all do in Carlsbad, which is where he'd been brought bloody and screaming into this evil world. Loved that whip, Vanger did. Could snap a fly off a man's cheek at seven paces. Nobody was safe from it, either. That's how Manfred Hurt lost a chunk of his earlobe – old Incorruptible popped it like a cherry over some trifling infraction or because he didn't care for the look on the lad's face. No, it didn't teach Hurt much except to use a bit more stealth when fucking about. Only a bit.

North and north. Five days along the Left Hand Path where the canopy closes like an iron trap and sunbeams are wan. That way cannot be found anymore; it has overgrown and some sprats argue it only exists in the addled minds of old men. Sprats with fewer teeth than before they say it to me, I aver.

Our scouts, a squad of Peloki warriors who wore topknots and red ochre war paint, had their chores cut out for them. You think our homely shack lies in the wilds, now, do you? Back then, the Left Hand was the only trail except what the animals made. Before the grand massacres that exterminated them once and for all, Malets and Hillmen skulked from the moors and hunted the forest. Not for game, mind you. Plenty of that in the highlands. The savages collected scalps from unwary southerners they caught with their breeches at half-mast.

None of us snot-noses had seen a genuine blue-belly, and despite the grim mutters among the veterans, we eagerly hoped to catch a glimpse. Some shit-eating fairy always lurks in the wings, waiting to grant an errant wish. Horses and donkeys went missing. Patrols spotted malevolent shadows flitting among the wagons and drove them away with torches and shouts. Finally, the Malets captured two lads on graveyard watch – snatched those unlucky boys smooth and quiet as weasels in the coop. Captain Vanger forbade any rescue mission into the deep undergrowth. He'd fought in the Battle of Thornwood and a dozen more on the Ynde subcontinent where tigers and their cults of worship roam the jungles. He knew the score. We marched onward and dusk came in a rich crimson blush through the foliage.

Deter Johansen and Marvin of Saltlick, those were their names. Healthy lads with good strong lungs. The boys' screams echoed for two nights. *Still* echo in my mind sometimes.

Three more days northwest and we forded the River Hunt and soon came upon a marsh of pale moss. Across this bog spanned a rough path of rotted planks. Here lay the beginning of The Fells. The savages harried us no more. Even they were wise enough to stay clear of that cursed land with its toads, spiders, and poison clouds from the Fifty Years Fires.

The trails crisscrossed the Fells like veins in the back of a crone's hand. Some called those paths The Gray Fingers, others, the Long Trail Winding. They branched every which way and as far as I know, wound on forever. Nobody can say who slapped them down in the first place. Perhaps it was the ancient kings or surveyors from the time of Argead of Enathia or his usurper son. What I do know is the horses and donkeys hated them. The soldiers hated them, too, but to step off the planks was sure death. The mud had no bottom and would suck a man straight down to hell.

More days of stumble and slog. Mosquitoes blacked the nets at night. Bloodsuckers droned so loud, you couldn't hear the comrade snoring at you shoulder. Everybody had the shits. Lost four men and an entire string of horses to the bog water.

Autumn north of the Wolverine Mountains is dreary. Rain, muck, and leeches are what you're in for. Our camps became restless as the priests argued with the officers on the matter of performing rites sacred to the season. The men were not particularly thrilled that the Feast of the Dead fell upon us as we journeyed across a land laid low by sorcery. We feared to offend the Powers, yet we dreaded to commence ceremonies that by necessity draw the attention of the Dark. Captain Vanger compromised by doubling wine rations and permitting the chaplain to affright us with gruesome tales of how the inhabitants of the region had all gotten themselves exterminated. The chaplain painted with broad strokes; the men were bumpkins and nitty-gritty details would have been wasted.

On the next to last evening of autumn, the army camped atop a butte that heaved from the quagmire. West lay the ruins of Castle Warrant. Warrant's towers had crumbled and pieces of carved granite were embedded in the slope of the ridge it occupied. The vision of that night remains: a half dozen campfires in an encircling ring around the crown of our bluff, smoke rising into the grin of the skull moon; shattered battlements of the castle silhouetted against stars smashed so densely close together they formed bands of white and pink and smearing red. Gelid cold of the dark between the stars seeped across the void and stole my breath. I slept little.

At dawn, the soldiers dug earthworks. Captain Vanger hadn't lived to earn silver in his whiskers by playing the fool. No guarantee the blue-bellies wouldn't return in force or that the giant troglodytes of the deep swamp wouldn't boil forth to ravish the men and slaughter the animals. We civvies were divided into small parties overseen by squads of light infantry and dispatched along vectors of approach.

Manfred Hurt and me were sent to a breach in the southern curtain wall. Dandy and Lutz got sent elsewhere with other laborers. I never saw Lutz again. He fell into a crevice. Plop.

With picks, axes, and pry bars we spent the hours until dusk chopping through thickets and rolling aside boulders to reach the outer courtyard. Mossy walls loomed overhead. Hurt asked me if I knew of the Warrants and why their castle was so damnably massive. It went against my grain to admit any sort of book learning to the oafs of my acquaintance, thus I broke wind and shrugged. Da had taught me to play it close to the chest. On the other hand, *Ma* had taught me to read, semi-educated lady that she'd been before her logger-love swept her away from civilization. I could've instructed my chum that this fortress had once held the Northwest Marches against the Noord, those fathers of Malets and Grethungs and the Peloki, indeed, a hundred other tribes that fell to barbarism when the great *Empire Across the Sea* receded into itself. They called her Castle Warrant, yet she'd served as the steading of many a noble family until the Belfours lost her during the Interregnum.

I could've also mentioned the rumors of madness and depravity that possessed the Balfour family decades before the wars. My grandmother waited on the famed historian Grote of Lygos, and she read over his shoulder when he recorded the Red Treatise of Diebold and the North. She'd muttered of bloody orgies and foul sacraments that occurred in many of the north holds of a certain era. A vile cult infiltrated the ranks of the noble families, corrupting those fair knights to the ways of evil, and ultimately destroying them from within. *Traffickers with the Dark,* Gram said of the cultists. Were she yet living, she would not have approved of our traipsing about the ruined estates of those who'd perished in the thrall of wormy perversions.

No way could I speak any of this to loutish Hurt. He cursed the Crown in one breath and praised it with the next. Over a supper of boiled oats and salted pork, a strapping blacksmith's son named Henry Bane gripped my shoulder in his ham hock fist. "Don' go back in the morn," he says to me. I ask why not and he says he beheld a crow peck the eye from a dying mule. The crow winged through the mist toward the western tower. Henry Bane took it for an ill omen. "Somethin' right terrible will happen tomorrow," he warned.

Fuck me running if that clod wasn't dead right. The horror acted on a delay. It fastened upon me, aye. I finally understood, in the fullness of time and all that. More and more every night when I lie awake and listen to branches scratch the roof.

The courtyard sod had grown brittle. A royal engineer marked a spot and we yoked a team of mules to an auger and bored until we'd punched a hole into a vault. Me and a score of other lads descended on a series of lines knotted together. Down and down into the bowels of the earth with our picks and our lamps, hearts pitter-patting in our throats. We knew what to search for – coffers of jewelry and objects of art and ancient precious coins tarnished or bright, ceremonial blades begrimed by rust and verdigris, and panoplies of ancestral armor.

A grand cavern spread beneath the foundations of Castle Warrant. Stalactites oozed primordial slime. Shelves of granite and quartz blazed in the torchlight and fell away into utter blackness. A river clashed over distant rocks. Colonies of bats shrilled as they funneled into the abyss. Echoes traveled for leagues. Our party unhooked from the belays and clung to the damp spine of bedrock, followed its curve around to a landing and came to a flight of steps carved from the very stone itself. One case spiraled downward into the heart of the earth. The second case corkscrewed upward into the ruins of the castle proper. Our party split. I ventured up with nine comrades. A lonely feeling to watch the torches of our other fellows sink and dwindle to specks floating in oil, then snuffed.

In case you're wondering, we never saw them again either.

Hurt and I took point. We climbed. Three hundred steps. Cracks every which way. *Deep* cracks stuffed with millipedes and pill bugs and wet, cancerous moss that smelled worse than the stuff in the swamp. Clung to our boots and squelched like mud as did the pale mushrooms in their beds of hollowed step and splintered masonry. Earthquakes had tumbled stones from the vaulted roof. We scrambled over them, or went around, climbing, climbing, until at last we traveled through an archway into the basement.

Mind you, Castle Warrant stood for a millennium before the Interregnum. Emperor Innocent II himself ordered it built. As one of the great keeps of the North, Warrant contained smithies and barracks and stables to house lancers of diluted Xet stock who rode warhorses imported from the west. And dungeons. Many, many cells, many chambers of interrogation and woe. The rock was a honeycomb full of bones. An ossuary of damned souls. None of the prisoners of war were released during the final days before the Fires. Men, packed into cubbyholes, were left to gnaw one another like starved rats. Their skeletons moldered, locked in the eternal struggle.

Oh, how we tiptoed past the bones. Our shadows, tall and cruelly sharp, capered and spilled across the walls, mocking us. Grown men, with daggers and swords, we huddled together and held hands like children passing through that crypt. Halls crissed and crossed and doubled upon themselves. Sergeant Bakker broke out the chalk so we wouldn't become lost forever in the warren.

The stairwell to the main floor had collapsed, confining our search for riches to those lower levels. I filled a burlap bag with coins. Brass, bronze, copper, reliefs worn smooth and shined to a glow I could see in the near dark. I swept all kinds of bullshit into that sack on the chance it would fetch a kind word from the Captain or at least spare me from the lash. Pewter cups and pewter plates, mostly cracked, but who gave a rip? Metal tongs and shattered candlesticks. Hurt rejoiced to find a trunk he thought would be jammed with valuables. Alas, mostly dirt and moldering cloth. He saved a moth-eaten tapestry that had grayed with antiquity.

Smoke hung in the fumy haze of our torch. More slimy lichen covered the walls. More slimy white mushrooms puffed beneath our tread. My breath huffed forth, and I sucked it and the torch smoke and the pall of the mushrooms in again and my thoughts revolved around themselves and my mood lightened even as a tear of desperation leaked from my eye. Intoxicated, dear daughter – no matter the source – is one way to pass the time in hell, should you ever need to know.

Hurt and I struck it rich in a dead end passage. I leaned against the wall to rest my sore backside. The stone crumbled and sloughed away and there in a queerly shaped cell, were two-dozen obsidian eggs stacked within the remnants of rotted crates. I'd seen their like once at a jeweler's shop in Victory City: hollow for the placing of a gem or prayer scroll while other others contained several smaller versions, each nested within its kin. Richies collected them in sets of fanciful design and jewelers crafted them in a drover's dozen lands.

I lifted one and turned it over. Different from the fabricated pieces I'd encountered, yet similar enough to give me hope of high value. Hard and edgy as the obsidian it resembled and seamless as any true egg. Something inside rattled the way a musician's gourd rattles.

"Why'n hell they got no latches?" Hurt said the way a child will of a Solfest upon discovering there's no gifts on the breakfast platter.

Surely the exotic nature of the eggs would fetch a fair coin. We'd get double rations at camp and that pleased me well enough to clear my foggy brain. I admit to a larcenous nature – knowing well that Hurt was too dumb to count, I socked away three of the eggs with the intention of smuggling them back to civilization and brokering a fortune of my own.

Hurt gathered our comrades while I set about fashioning a travois to transport the other goods we'd gathered. Soon the others arrived bearing their own dubious treasures. We stowed our spoils and proceeded for the surface. A train of scout ants dutifully transporting crumbs back to the colony.

Somehow, and maybe the brain-fog returned to beleaguer me, I lost the way. I'd taken the hind teat of our column as I dragged a carpet-load of junk treasure and no one wanted to trip over it in the gloom. One moment, Hurt trudged a couple paces ahead, and then I stubbed my toe on a loose stone and the men went around the corner, gone. Grunts and laughter and curses quit upon an instant as did the glare of their lamps and torches. The sudden stillness sobered me right smartly.

I shouted to them. My voice echoed through the labyrinth. It didn't rebound; it kept on going without answer. Then I felt in my pockets for flint and in moments ignited a brand from a sconce. A feeble reddish hue flickered from that ancient pitch. Nowhere did I spy Sergeant

Bakker's chalk marks. I thought of all those skeletons in their cells and the weight of the rock overhead, and of the mold and slime oozing in the cracks. Somewhere, wind moaned through a crevice. Dread coiled around me, sure as the noxious smoke.

Hold still, young Ruark. Someone whispered from the shadows. *Hold still, child. I'm almost with you.* My father's gruff voice, though he'd died several winters before, crushed beneath the felled trunk of an oak. Later, I became convinced it was my imagination, but in the moment, that coldly eager whisper was enough to get me moving. I abandoned the load and set forth with alacrity.

The hall wound this way and that and tightened until rudely carved rock dug into my shoulders. I squeezed through and stumbled into a cavern. Saints know how big – couldn't see far as the brand smoldered to a nub. Earth crumbled away from the toes of my boots into a pit. A foul breeze moaned up from that abyss and snuffed the dying flame.

Sapped of fight, I curled into a ball and fell asleep right there on the lip of oblivion. Chill and damp woke me. Didn't know what else to do, so I crawled. Crawled because I dared not risk tripping into sudden doom. I rested often; so thirsty I sucked at water seeping through rock, so hungry I licked the salty blood from my scabs, so weary I'd slip into dreams of the home cottage and Mother's honey porridge before the miserable cold roused me and I crept onward without direction or hope. The hunger became terrible. I sorted through my pockets, mad for the smallest crumb, and came across three of the obsidian eggs I'd stuffed in there and forgotten. I nearly pitched them away, until something stayed my hand.

Strangely, the jagged edges had smoothed and softened as unfired clay does over time. The shell curved, pliable as leather as I caressed it. In a daze, I obeyed a mindless command and cracked the egg and took its clabbered bounty in a gulp. The darkness was complete, thus I couldn't discern what yolky, blood-warm mass sludged down my throat, nor what fine bones and bits crunched between my teeth. The taste of it, horrible and delightful, a rancid ambrosia, smoldered in my guts.

The next two went down the hatch with more ease. I heard my own grunts and gulps echoing from the rocks around me. Horrible. And I licked my fingers and the ground for any drooling trace, and when I'd done, crawled onward.

The Dark looks after its own.

I found a chimney vent and wriggled my way until I popped out on the surface. I wept and rolled in that bog mud. You've seen the scars upon my back. You know how Captain Vanger greeted me upon my return to camp. After twenty lashes at the whipping post, they clapped me in the stocks for a night and chalked it off as a lesson learned. The Captain said I reminded him of one of his stupider nephews.

I wasn't the only sod who disappeared. Only one who vanished and then *came back*, though. Vanger ordered the company to withdraw. Apparently he took a gander at the obsidian eggs Hurt and the other lads hauled out of the depths and made the call right there. Loose talk spread through the ranks – Jon Foot wanted the eggs, had sent us into the wilderness for the very purposes of securing them, gold and gems be damned.

Damned.

The company made good time on its return journey. The weather stiffened and that sent the blue-bellies into their warrens for the cold season. On the eleventh sunset when we camped near the Thrush Meadows, I went forth to fetch wood for the bonfires. Dreadful pains stabbed through my innards. A foul, sickly sweat oozed from my entire body and made my clothes sodden. Phantasms of delirium cascaded through my mind. I bolted from the work part and squatted behind a log and voided my bowels.

Women groan about the agonies of giving birth. Well, lass, they have my profound sympathy. Shite and blood burst from me. I thought myself liable to split apart at the seams, as it were. Miracles and horrors! Three eggs dropped from me and lay in the muddy stench. A clutch of my very own. Each glistened in the muck; roughly the size of a hen's and translucent. Shrimplike embryos coiled in jelly. I recognized the black wisps of my hair, the imprint of my own coarse features, my own eye gone molten yellow that flashed with unnatural awareness. Within a few heartbeats, the eggs crusted over, sealed by a jagged black shell.

Feral cunning overtook me, reduced me to an animal. I scooped handfuls of dirt and dead leaves over the abominations, then slipped back among my comrades who'd made merry at my cries of gastric distress. Life in the Legion is cruel.

Nightmares lashed me, surely as Vanger's whip. I was shorn of rest and sanity, condemned to drift as a voiceless spirit while doppelgangers assumed my life. Brazen, evilly grinning doubles doted upon by dear mother, my friends and colleagues. Each new dawn found me shaking in my bedroll. Only Jim Dandy and Hurt noted my ghastly pale countenance for I strove mightily to conceal the nature of my ills. The instinct that compelled me to bury the eggs also warned that I lived in the shadow of some obscene, circling terror. Should anyone discover my secret, I would be undone in spectacular fashion.

The moral I learned from this experience, is always heed your suspicious inner voice.

On the seventeenth evening Jon Foot himself materialized from the whirling smoke of our main bonfire. The dogs barked with insane fury and then cowered at his sandals. Two sentries pissed themselves. Most depictions of the warlock are exaggerated. Artists render him as a monster: red eyes, spiked horns, a death's head. Eight feet tall, razor talons and a lizard's tail. In private, he may strip his costume and resemble exactly thus a demon. However, when I met him, he appeared altogether ordinary. Softening into middle age, his hair receded and his belly rounded. Brown of eye and mildly spoken. His black cloak smelt of sulfur and he smiled too much. He smoked a clay pipe. That was the extent of his nefarious comport.

Soldiers vacated a tent on the edge of camp. Jon Foot quartered within. Shortly thereafter he summoned, one by one, those of us who'd ventured beneath Castle Warrant. The interviews were brief. Men emerged from their audiences none the worse for the wear, although none would speak of what had transpired nor meet the eyes of those who inquired. Vanger's lieutenants roamed among us and boxed the ears of those who pressed the point. Soon enough, the gossip stilled and the men fell into sulky routine.

My turn rolled round after midnight.

Jon Foot's tent fumed with smoke from an iron brazier and his pipe. He reclined upon a stone chair carved into the likeness of a centipede rampant. It much resembled the one I am told existed at court in the Privy Council. The warlock took my measure with a long polite stare. He finished his cigarette and lighted another from the small flames of the brazier.

In that lull, I realized the sounds of camp were not muffled by the tent walls. Nay, we inhabited a bubble in a sea of silent darkness. Cozier than my terrifying span trapped in the caverns, yet much the same.

"Master Ruark, so good to make your acquaintance. I'm sure this will be the high-water mark of my day." He affected the cultured tones of a highborn. His politeness smacked of malice. Or, perhaps his tepid certainty and unwavering gaze preyed upon my guilt. His demeanor suggested that he knew everything about me all the way back to the rainy morn I dropped from Mama's womb. He laughed and said, "Yes, yes. I know much. *Much*, however, isn't the same as *all*. I cannot see what happened to you in the dim cellars of Henry Belfour. You were lost and now you are found. How does this happen?"

My intent was to mumble an inoffensive lie or three, to deflect and prevaricate as peasantry has treated with the rich since the beginning of time. Foot, black magician, must have cast a geas upon me, for matters took a bizarre turn.

"I got hungry and I ate three of them fucking eggs you're on about," I listened to myself say. Every other muscle in my body froze. I swayed, rooted in place.

"Damn. Captain Vanger counted the haul. A perfect set if not for the ones you abandoned. And the ones you devoured, alas."

"Too bad. They hit the spot."

"Thank you for your honesty, son." Jon Foot levitated to his feet. "Apparently you met an old friend of mine down there in the cellars."

"Aye, someone else was there. Whispering."

Jon Foot nodded wisely. "Others sought the Clutch. Bad ones. Ethan, Julie the Fifth, Carling . . . Phil Wary. Black sorcerers, each. It would be no matter to disguise themselves and walk among your comrades. To divide and strike. You were befuddled and cut from the herd. Mere chance delivered you from doom . . . Did he speak to you? Surely, he did."

My mouth opened again, though I resisted mightily. "Aye. My father came upon me in the dark."

"Your *dead* father."

"As a doornail."

"This won't do. I'm sorry." He actually did seem a trifle melancholy. Then he took a small skinning knife from his pocket and sliced me from crotch to sternum. I cannot emphasize how disconcerting it is to watch in hapless wonder as the cut is assayed and one's intestines slop onto hard-packed dirt. What's worse? The warlock crouched, poking through the mess the way priests divine the future from pigeon entrails. The shock awakened my muscles. I regained sufficient control to stagger backward through the tent flaps.

Jon Foot watched me go, knife dripping in his hand. "Come back here, son. I want to hug the shit out of you!" He spread his arms and smiled with pure joy. His shadow against the wall coiled most unnaturally. It bristled with barbs.

Me and my train of guts paid no heed of his imprecation. Three steps took me across the threshold. I collapsed near a cook fire where soldiers just off watch gathered to warm themselves. The last moment I recalled of that particular life are their shouts, their expressions of panic and disgust. Sweet oblivion swept over me, and I was dead.

I revived, blanketed in slimy leaves, in the woods behind this very cottage. Naked and bloody and stinking, but whole. The pink flesh of my belly was without blemish, its cleaving wound had perfectly healed.

They say that home always seems smaller when a man returns. This was the opposite. Trees loomed, the night stretched wider and deeper.

Guided by memory and habit, I emerged from the woods and knocked on the door. Ma swooned at the sight of her son, gone nearly two years. *More* than surprise smote her. More than alarm at my gory visage. Far more, as I discovered upon glimpsing myself in yonder body mirror. Upon departing to seek my fortune in the wide world, I'd attained middling height and shorn my whiskers daily with Da's razor. Now, my form had reverted to that of a child of no more than five winters. My face had altered into a somewhat familiar stranger's. Partially my grown self, partially a changeling's. Mom would remark later that for a several moments she took me for her grandson.

Days of confusion followed. My thoughts buzzed. Waking proved difficult to separate from dreaming. I raved of centipede men and eternal darkness. Mother tended me as my strength and wits were gradually restored, and by the end of a week I'd grown fully into my father's old logging clothes. I began to feed myself. I shaved again. She gently inquired what I recalled of the time between my murder and awakening. What she wanted to know was if I'd witnessed the afterlife, if I'd gone there and dipped in a toe.

I shook my head and claimed ignorance of aught save a smooth, formless void. How could I tell her the truth? I recalled the formless dark. Indeed, I also remembered the licks of fire shooting through its depths, the black rolling back to reveal a deathly white, an iris of bones of men fused together unto eternity. How could I speak to her of the awesome cold, or of the death groans of hidden stars? How could I articulate the sense of folding into myself, of being trapped inside an egg, drawing sustenance from its yolk as a chick does?

I lacked the courage to describe a vision of rebirth wherein my eggshell cracked in half and I floated upon a woodland stream near a summer twilight. Willows entangled themselves against a red sky. Other reborn souls rode the current in their shells. They cried to one another, mewling as babes. Bitterns jigged between the reeds, their tarnished bills poised for the killing stroke. The towering birds pecked and stabbed at tiny prey and swallowed piteous shrieks of my fellow travelers. I met the glaring, avaricious eye of fate as it plunged its bill toward me and the red sky cracked as the eggshell had, and tarry black spilled forth instead of light. I drowned in blood, not water.

My weary mother deserved a fairer tale. All mothers do. Thus, I spun a pretty yarn about warmth and quiet and the peace of the womb. I had changed enough from the son she bore and raised that she had little choice but to accept the lies as one might from a fresh-faced stranger. Wearing a new face and armed with bitter experience, my gift for fabrication was much improved. Despite the uncanniness of the situation, it proved easier for her than I might've suspected. We were able to make a fresh slate of it.

As the doldrums evaporated, I realized the starkness of Mom's situation. Since Dad's untimely demise and my departure, she'd become haggard and mournful. Our ancestral hut had gone to wrack and ruin. Where had my younger brother Marlon gone? Four summers my junior and a forester in the making, I assumed his absence meant he was afield cutting wood or away at the market in King's Grove. Mom covered her face and wept. The gods demanded balance – three nights before my return, Marlon vanished while logging a nearby hillside. He'd been in the company of fellow woodcutters. They searched for him in vain. The men concluded he'd run afoul of wolves, which were particularly ravenous of late.

Immediately, I dressed in my father's work clothes, gathered meager supplies, and set forth with his bearded ax slung across my back. The hillside wasn't far. I supped with the loggers who toiled there. These were men slightly younger than myself alongside whom I'd labored and feasted in days gone by. None recognized my countenance, although each embraced me as a Ruark for I bore an unerring stamp of the family bloodline. I introduced myself as a traveling cousin and was thus reborn full and true. Solved my problem with the Legion. The functionaries hate it when folks they've killed turn up alive and well. Their foreman told me how Marlon walked into the bushes and vanished. He didn't figure I'd have any better luck turning up a corpse, but gods be with me in my task.

I sought my brother high and low. Scoured the nearby hills and hollows. Finally, I kicked over a pile of human bones deep in a thicket. Couldn't tell whether they belonged to him or not – hacked and charred too badly. Reminded me of something. I buried the bones and said a few words in case the gods were watching.

Reinvention and a newfound loathing for travel served me well. I put my faith in the fates, relegated miseries to the past, and set to work. Strong whiskey and back-breaking labor kept me on the straight path and with scant time for contemplation on matters best left undisturbed.

Soon, I became an accomplished logger and attracted a crew of strapping lads. As you can see, riches didn't follow. Nonetheless, we did well enough. I was content to dwell here in this cottage alone for a score of years. Over the years, I sought out Dandy, Hurt, and the others and introduced myself under this new identity. Never did I choose to wander, however. Nor did I pine for the company of a wife. Not until I met your mother in King's Grove by happy accident. Charm, wit, beauty. Youth! Too good for a woodcutter with white in his mane and sap in his beard, I vow. She smote me with a bat of her lashes. Long after our honeymoon, I harbored the notion she'd merely taken pity on a poor boy. In hindsight, it's more likely she fled demons of her own. City life is as treacherous as any bad stretch of the forest. Eventually you came along, my dear, our only child.

Despite an abundance of joy, I occasionally dreamed of death and of things worse than death.

The second time I died was on a midsummer's night, nine years gone. Like my father before me, I chopped a tree and it corkscrewed beyond control and crushed me to jelly. You and your mother wept. Then she disappeared. I imagine how it went – a strangled cry jolted you from nightmares. Though you desperately searched this hut, though you combed the yard and the woods, you discovered nary hide nor hair of her. You collapsed near the hearth ashes in despair. Calamity upon calamity! What would become of you?

But three nights later you opened this door to soft knocking and found me, naked and delirious upon your step. I claimed to be your uncle. What choice did you have other than accept providence? Parents dead or missing. No man to protect you, no man to provide. A girl alone in the wood is easy prey for beasts. Besides, there could be no question of our kinship. I am inalienably a Ruark. Sad to say I am also a wee bit more than that.

This second death had traversed a similar arc to the first. I envisioned an abyss of terrible cold and darkness; I floated a stream as a fingerling babe upon a half shell and was devoured alive by bitterns. I clawed back into this world in the bog just yonder. The only real difference being my transformation from toddler to graybeard occurred as I stumbled along the path to your door. You accepted me and my hastily contrived tale of prodigal uncle, home at last. Robbers stripped me and left me beaten bloody. By the grace of the gods had I managed to reach sanctuary . . .

The moment I learned of your mother's disappearance, I finally possessed an inkling of the horrible nature of the black eggs, if not their unholy provenance. Once a man departs the mortal realm he can only be restored by the subtraction of another soul. Rebirth via the egg claimed the flesh and blood, the very consciousness, of those whom I cherished. My suspicions were confirmed when I located her skeleton in the blackberry tangles that border the meadow. My wails of anguish scattered birds from the trees. A dark cloud blotted the sun and rain lashed the field.

Full to the craw with dread, I went to the bog that twice vomited me forth and beheld the remnants of the obsidian eggs. Animals steer well clear of that plot. Pieces of broken shell lay there, perfectly preserved. After a bit of rooting around the bed of decayed leaves and mossy loam, I uncovered the third egg. It nestled in a patch of muck, glittering like a flinty gemstone prized free of the Dark Lord's own tiara.

Gods help me, I intended to destroy the egg lest you one day feed its unnatural hunger. I failed. Each time I bore the egg away, it slipped from my pocket and reappeared in the bog by some malignant supernatural trickery. I kicked it, smashed it with my ax, piled tinder wood atop and set it ablaze. All useless; no measure so much as scratched the gods damned egg. I even resorted to prayer, if you can imagine your old man upon his knees, yammering to the invisible powers with the zeal of a penitent. What a farce.

Despite these theatrics, a small voice in my head was pleased. My soul and my thoughts are corrupted, you see. To eat of the black egg is to be damned.

Both times I've rowed back from the abyss, my essence mingled and consumed an innocent sacrificial soul. In the process, some essential piece of my own being was replaced. Cold and darkness seeped into my bones. That cruelly selfish portion bid me to quit my attempts to destroy the egg and speak of it no more. It promised to ease my nightmares, it swore I would forget, but only if I played the fool, the supplicant. To my everlasting shame, I heeded this whisper. Grateful as a dog for the whipping to end.

Light burn me, I've tried to be a good father. Once in a blue moon, I ignored my instincts and summoned the courage to perform one last valorous deed before the bell tolls an accounting. Perhaps Jon Foot's dark magic could reverse this damnation. Too bad he's dead and beyond the reach of all men. The names he mentioned – Julie, Ethan, Phil Wary – are mysteries that confound solution. With rare exceptions, sorcerers tend to keep a low profile.

There have been times, such as last night, fortified by loneliness for your mother, or by the powerful spirit of the jug, that I crept out to the bog and sat cross-legged in the moss and schemed of ways to slip this noose around our necks. Generally though, it's much easier to live the life of a garrulous drunkard and cheerfully wait for fate to run its course. Yes, so much easier to not dream of bitterns pecking my eyes and balls for eternity.

Soon, I shall die. Then, I shall return and *you* will be gone. You will vanish as my brother and your mother did. After you, there is no one. I will reside here, an unfamiliar ghost of myself, alone.

He slumped against his pillow. The effort of reciting his tale of woe had drained the man and turned his flesh a chalky white. Bruises around his eyes and nostrils lent him the aspect of a corpse about to endure ritual mummification. He coughed. Blood speckled his beard.

The woman held his hand. The fire had burnt low, casting a shadow across her face. She said, "Uncle, I mean, Da, that was an amazing story. Especially the part about Jon Foot. Did you really meet him? Was he so very ordinary? Surely, you never met him."

"Merciful . . . Did you listen to a word?"

"You are a sweet, confused sod. Fret not over damnation nor curses, nor phantoms. *I* ate the egg."

"You what?"

"*We* ate the egg, to speak true. Did you suppose I slept through your blundering around the cottage at all hours? What matter to follow you? And what matter, after you'd come and gone, to examine the item you coveted in your fevered state? A great white goose egg. Pristine as snow awaiting my eager hands to pluck it from the nest. Pluck it I did; *plop* into my apron and borne home in a trice."

"No." Horror twisted his countenance. He covered his mouth against a deeper, ripping cough, and blood came freely between his fingers. "Oh, daughter. There are no geese here. No geese. *Nothing* lives in the bog."

"Our luck was good," she said with placid determination. "The omelet we enjoyed this morning contained rich red yolk and a lump of half-formed gosling to boot. Praise to the Light. It is the first meat we've enjoyed since you took ill."

He moaned and tossed his head in terrible negation. The woman stroked his brow. She soothed him until he ceased thrashing. His breathing slowed. After a long while it stopped. She squeezed his hand. How sad it was to lose one's sanity with age as one lost his or her teeth.

She wiped her eyes and composed herself. There were practical matters to attend, such as acquiring a husband to chop wood and hunt game and run off the ever-lurking bandits. Pickings were slim in this neck of the woods, so she'd long delayed accepting a suitor. Now she feared it would come down to one of the inbred Slawson brothers or a gap-toothed hick from among the Smyths who dwelt a couple of hollows over . . .

The dog growled. His mangy fur stiffened until he was more porcupine than mutt. The woman told him to be still and then the shake roof peeled away with a grinding clatter. The stars were gone, replaced by a sky that glowed hellish red. A bittern, as tall and wide as a windmill, warbled mightily and slithered its long neck and broadsword of a bill through the gap and skewered the man's corpse, lifted him on high, and flicked him back down its throat. A second bird echoed the hunting cry and muscled in, its smooth dark eye glinting with the murderous crimson light of the firmament.

"Well, shit," the woman said. The black bill unhinged as it plunged to take her.

Gradually the swollen red light dimmed and stars sprinkled the heavens. The dog waited until he hadn't heard any more screams or those piss-inducing bird cries for a while. He crept from beneath a table and sniffed around warily. Cold hearth, empty beds, no humans but for their fading scents. Tragic, although the mongrel had only wandered into the yard that spring. Scraps were less than plentiful of late, and the woodcutter had been free with his hobnail boot after a few drinks, so the dog wasn't overly invested in the arrangement.

He jumped through the open window and trotted away into the night.

Crawford Tillinghast, a researcher of the "physical and meta-physical," appears in H. P. Lovecraft's "From Beyond." It is the first of several stories with the theme – to quote S. T. Joshi – of "a reality beyond that revealed to us by the senses, or that which we experience in everyday life." **John Shirley** – who has also written several works of fiction with that as a subject, perhaps most notably in his novel *Wetbones* – uses "From Beyond" as a springboard for this imaginative tale. Shirley also recalls being enchanted by "The Dream-Quest of Unknown Kadath" around age thirteen: "I've used Lovecraft's concept of psychic exploring in novels like *Bleak History* and *Demons*." His original Lovecraftian stories have appeared in many anthologies including *Black Wings II*, *World War Cthulhu*, *The Madness of Cthulhu*, *Searchers After Horror*, *Innsmouth Nightmares*, *Gothic Lovecraft*, and periodicals such as *Weird Tales* and *Spectral Realms*.

Emmy-nominated Shirley is the author of the Bram Stoker Award-winning collection *Black Butterflies* and the highly regarded collections *Living Shadows* and *In Extremis*, as well as over thirty novels and numerous short stories. His latest dark fantasy novel is *Doyle After Death*. A collection of his Lovecraftian fiction is forthcoming. John Shirley was co-writer of the movie *The Crow* and has written television including scripts for *Poltergeist: The Legacy*. His Lovecraftian-themed lyrics for the song "The Old Gods Return" (and others) were recorded by the Blue Öyster Cult.

Just Beyond the Trailer Park
John Shirley

I seen that Mr. Tillinghast since I was a five-year-old boy. Now I'm almost twelve, I finally I know him.

Mr. Tillinghast got that old house of his granddad's just cranked up off its foundations and moved over here from Benevolent Street because they was going to tear it down, him being behind on some taxes and it being ugly and not fitting in over there and ordinances. That's what Providence town people said about it. So he got it up on those jacks they used, and had a big tractor-trailer pull it over here, next door to the Cumberland Glory Trailer Park. We're out by the new Walmart. My dad said there's a money end of Cumberland Avenue and a no-money end. We're at that no-money end.

My dad said Mr. Tillinghast must have a big ol' bucket of money to do that. Said he would talk to him. My mom was drunk asleep, I didn't want to stay around with the TV broke and Mama snoring with her mouth open, so I decided to follow Dad down there, and he never noticed if I did that.

It was cold out, but no snow yet. When I went out the door I wished I had a coat on but it was lost in that mess on the closet floor.

I followed and I seen Dad talking to a man strapping boxes from the back of his big car to one of those hand trucks. The man was dressed in a sweater and slacks and a bowtie. First time I saw a bowtie except on Mr. Rogers. That man did not act like Mr. Rogers.

Dad said, "I could help you carry them boxes in, won't charge you for that. But I do some handy work for cash, now 'n' then."

"Don't touch those boxes," the man said. He had white hair cut real short, like he didn't want to bother with it. Even though he had white hair he had a young face. But also when he frowned he looks older, hella older. You can't tell a lot for sure about Mr. Tillinghast till you know him some.

"Well if there's anything else I can do," Dad said. "Glad to help. My name's Lenny Forest. Live right next door." He had his hands stuck in his pockets when he said it because it was cold. I could see his breath coming out like smoke. "I'm in trailer seven over there, in Cumberland."

That's exactly what he said, too. I remember everything, always. My mom says I've got a memory like flypaper. I remember what the emergency doctor said when I was two and I had that virus and I remember what people said when I was three and four.

When Mr. Tillinghast just frowned some more like he wanted my dad to leave, Dad said, "I sure was blown away, seeing you wheel this whole house out here. Look at that, you already got the crew to set it down on foundations, and she's all set. Everything running okay?"

Mr. Tillinghast looked at the house with his eyes real squinty. "Fools didn't get the pipes right. Water's not right running."

"You don't say! I've done my share of plumbing and I got the tools. How about I hook it up for you, and you can pay me a hundred dollars, cash, if it's done right and not before then. How'd that be?"

"And if you make it worse?"

"I won't. But if I do, I'll get people in to fix it."

Even back then I wondered who that would be, who my dad could get in there to fix it. He was bluffing I guess.

"I have no time to fix pipes." Mr. Tillinghast made a grunting sound. "So be it then."

I never heard anyone say *so be it* but Mr. Tillinghast.

"You come in one hour," he said, "and I'll show you where the pipes are. You will come around to the back." Then Mr. Tillinghast went on with hand trucking his boxes.

My dad turned around to go home and he saw me and got mad that I was standing there staring with my finger in my nose and yelled at me, "Get your ass home, Vester!" My name's Sylvester, after Sylvester Stallone, but they call me Vester or Ves.

Dad was about to give me a smack but I ran home, wondering what was up with that man who trucked his big house into the lot on the other side of the maples. I was in a trailer park and I knew you could move those houses but I was amazed anyone could move a big one like that. It looked like it could tip over if you pushed it. Two and a half stories tall, and missing most of its white paint and all kind of squeezed together looking.

Now looking back, I wonder that Mr. Tillinghast trusted my dad, that day, because Dad had old sneakers on, and no socks, and his raggedy jeans and Iron Maiden T-shirt. It was cold but Dad didn't have the sense to put his jacket on, and he was grownup. And he had all those tats on his arms and that beardy face. But then again, I found out later that Mr. Tillinghast didn't trust anyone who wrote stuff down about him. You get some guy from a fancy-ass plumbing company – like Cumberland Glory has for maintenance – they always look like they're writing things down.

Dad fixed that pipe all right and Mr. Tillinghast paid him and we went and had hamburgers and French fries and milk shakes that night. Sometimes Dad went over there and cut the grass on the lot, for twenty dollars, so the city people wouldn't come and bother Mr. Tillinghast about the yard ordinance.

But I heard my dad say more than once, "That's not a friendly man, that Tillinghast."

My dad wasn't always friendly neither, especially when he was smoking the glass pipe and drinking. He would do that and stop doing it and do it and stop doing it. He couldn't just forever stop doing it. Sometimes he went to special meetings about it and then he'd stop smoking for a while. When he started again, my mom bitched at him about it and he would give my mom a "teaching smack" on the face. But then when he was in the stop-doing-it time, he was okay and he would do some work in construction. He took me to see *The Expendables 4* at the mall when he got in a check, just last year. He'd drive me to school sometimes, because the bus stop is so far from here. I liked going to school and he told me once he thought it was good I liked it. "Me," he said, "I never liked it. Wished I did."

But he would start up smoking the glass again. So late spring last year, he got taken to jail, because of not wanting the repo to tow his truck off, and he hit that repo guy with the tire iron, and fought the police when they came, and broke a cop's collarbone. They tazed him, and cuffed him, and I haven't seen him since, except one visit with Mom.

He won't be back till I'm twenty-seven because it was also some kind of probation violation, and because he was holding, and because of assault on a police officer, and assault on the repo guy, and resisting arrest.

My mom's still around, but she likes to drink, and sometimes there's pills, too. She's asleep a lot. She has a boyfriend, part time, since last month. She goes to his apartment.

I have a sister, Dusty, who's fifteen, but she left with Barron from Trailer 2, they took his dad's old El Dorado and we haven't seen them for almost a year. Mom hates Barron. She cries and talks about killing him when she's about half a gallon into that red Carlo Rossi.

I saw Mr. Tillinghast many times, but didn't talk to him till last year. I heard the humming from his house and the sound like way too many bees, but it didn't bother me. Other people in the park said the humming and buzzing would shake their trailers and give them headaches. Mom didn't seem to notice it but she used to live next to a stock car racetrack.

I could feel it when he was running machines that made the humming and that noise like too many bees buzzing. It was a weird feeling, but not so bad. It gave me dreams that were better than some movies I've seen. I called it the dream hum. I wasn't even really asleep when that happened – just halfway. The hum and the buzz gave me ideas, too, but it's hard to explain what they were. But I always liked to look in the back of televisions and radios and Bebe's dad told me sometimes how they work and I looked up some on the school internet.

Now Dulesta Finch, she's my Mom's friend, from across the park. Her daughter is my friend Bebe.

On the Fourth of July, last year, I heard Dulesta say, when we were at their barbecue, that Mr. Greel who owns Cumberland Glory was going to send the police over to the Tillinghast house because he said it wasn't zoned for some equipment, and that kind of gear could interfere with airplanes flying over. And she said she heard on the news some pilots were having radio trouble, when they were flying over here.

My dad was only a few months in jail, then. I was noticing him not being there, that night, on the Fourth of July. He used to take us to the free fireworks at the beach park every Fourth. But there was Dulesta's barbecue and we had sparklers, me and my friend Bebe, who's kind of my girlfriend but kind of not, and we had some firecrackers. Mrs. Finch got mad when we used a firecracker behind her trailer, it made her fuzzy little white dog hide under the doublewide and cry, so she yelled at us and we run off.

Bebe and I slowed down when we got to the fence between the park and the Tillinghast property. I was feeling wicked sick to my stomach, then, for running after eating too much barbecue and maybe something else that was just in the air.

Then I looked past the fence and I seen Mr. Tillinghast up on his roof. I could see him pretty good between the trees, because that time of year, it's not so dark yet after dinner. He was putting some kind of metal mesh thing on the roof.

And then it came over me, like, *Boom! I know what I'll do.*

I told Bebe I was going to go over there and tell Mr. Tillinghast the police were going to bother him. Warn him. Get his back.

"You are crazy to go there." She shook her head. That always made her black braids fly around. "Don't be a dumbfuck."

"I'm going. The police are going to bother him just for nothing. He's gonna get bagged! He helped us, he hired my dad!"

I was thinking about my dad. We never liked cops much and now I felt, about cops, just, *Fuck you.*

I started climbing over the fence.

"No, Vester!"

But I climbed over the fence and left her there and walked off. Maybe I was showing off some even though she said it was a bad idea.

I crossed the lot and walked under the trees and yelled up at him. "Hey, Mr. Tillinghast!"

He went all twitchy up there and I saw him grab at a chimney. He almost slipped off the roof.

"Sorry, Mr. Tillinghast!" I called. "I just wanted to tell you—"

"Get out of here, boy! You! Go!"

I felt slapped, when he did that.

I turned around and started to walk off, then decided that because Bebe was watching, from over the fence, I had to say something else. I turned and yelled, "They're coming out to bust you is what!"

I was almost over the fence when he called again, from the house. "Boy! Come back here and tell me what the devil you're talking about!"

He's the only one I ever heard say, *What the devil*.

It smelled like mold and dust and burning wires and something else I never smelled before. That's what the attic smelled like. Tasted like it, too, on my tongue when I breathed in.

Mr. Tillinghast was looking at me like he was thinking of taking a bite out of me. "They're coming tonight? You are certain it was to happen *tonight*?"

"Yeah," I said. "That's what she said."

He looked at the ceiling, like he could see right through it. "I just put those insulation baffles on the roof. They will address the problem. The signals will not penetrate aircraft now." I didn't know what meant by *address* it. I've learned a humongous lot from the way he talks since then, though. (But I have to use spellcheck on this.) He gave me a big frown and pointed his finger at me. "But if the authorities come rooting through here, they will find devices that break a variety of their paltry regulations! Indeed, frequencies that might interest Homeland Security. Not that they should fear me but . . . one can explain nothing to those people. They see nothing but what is in front of their noses. And even that they do not see."

(I told you, I remember everything people say.)

"Can you hide that stuff?" I asked.

"There is no time . . . That is – no time, working alone."

"I could help."

"That is a possibility – that is why I brought you up here. Your father was discreet. Are you?"

Discreet was another word I didn't know then. But I could tell he wanted me to say "yes." And I remembered he paid cash money.

"Yes," I said.

"I shall reward you! You're small, but—forty dollars?"

Forty! "Where you want to start?"

It was hard. The machines parts were larger than my mom's old HP computer, and made of heavier stuff. Some were missing panels and inside them I saw *vacuum tubes*. I knew they were real old.

It was hot in there, and I was coughing from dust and my fingers was getting slick from sweat but I carried what I had to. We took certain machines down from the attic, all the way to the basement, and he set them up there. We had to make five trips.

By the time I was back down with the rest of the equipment he had four pieces of gear set up, wired together. I seen the wires looked really old, they were doubled and winding around one another and they had cloth on the outside. He stripped the ends of the wires with a knife and twisted them to each other's with needle-nose pliers, so the units was all connected up. I was, like, what?

"Good, good, put that one on top of this unit, here. We'll set up our camouflage antenna, ha ha, and it will be transmitting before they arrive."

I know what camouflage was and I started to get what he was doing then.

Pretty quick the vacuum tubes were lit up and there was a smell of hot copper wire in the air. There was a big cluster of lightbulbs, all wired close together. Some of them were broken. There was a "transmitter" made of an old TV antenna and a hum came out of one of the machines. Mr. Tillinghast chuckled as he turned the humming part up as loud as it would go. That humming came and went but it wasn't the hum from the attic.

We had set it all up between a bunch of dirty wooden boxes under a light fixture so low he knocked his head on it and the fixture broke and we were in the darkness. He switched on a flashlight so he could replace the bulb. While he did that he cursed with some words I never heard before.

Then he arranged the "units" a little more. "The key unit isn't here," he said. "But they won't know that."

Just when he got the arranging done, there was a banging on the front door above.

"Coming, coming!" Mr. Tillinghast shouted. He whispered to me, "Wait in the attic if you want to be paid right away. Otherwise – slip out the back and come back when they're gone."

I went toward the back door because, after all, *cops* was coming into the house. But I couldn't help going around to the basement window, laying down in the dirt there and listening. I could only see a man's shiny shoes and suit pants down there next to the equipment.

I heard Mr. Tillinghast say, "Very well, here's my equipment! But why should the FAA come here?"

The woman said something about interference with the radios of jet planes passing overhead. And the other person, who had a deep voice, said he was a Federal Marshal and he had a warrant.

"You see the only transmission devices I have," Mr. Tillinghast said. "When I patent this device I shall be wealthy! It will send radio signals through the center of the Earth! No satellite will be needed!"

Damn he was good at sounding like a cranky old nut.

The Marshal said, "I see!" He sounded like he was trying not to laugh. "I am sorry but we're going to have to confiscate this equipment, Mr. Tillinghast. I have all the permissions right here."

"What! My life's work!"

"After it's inspected, and pending approval, you can work on it in a safer location, sir."

"The Devil, sir! And it is he who has arranged this! My equipment may indeed show the actual physical location of hell below the crust of the Earth! Do not look so incredulous! The Devil exists, sir!"

"I am sure he does, Mr. Tillinghast!" The man said that all chuckling.

"And when you pass into his realm, even should it be a hundred years from now, he will be waiting to *chew on the bones of your soul*, you pompous ass! Do you suppose the soul does not have bones? In *that* realm it is does, I assure you!"

I always loved the way Mr. Tillinghast talks.

"I'm going to ask you to unplug this equipment, please. Mary, could you ask the removal team to come in? They'd better wear gloves, this stuff is pretty old, could have lead or mercury in it . . ."

But in half an hour they was gone. I seen them just driving away in their van, with pieces of his granddad's equipment and some stuff he took out of an old stereo.

I went to the back door. It was still a little open, and I yelled out, "Mr. Tillinghast!"

In a couple minutes he came puffing up, his face red and all sweaty, and he had a smile on his face that I think would've scared Bebe. "We baffled the fools, boy! They took my grandfather's equipment – only the parts that don't matter. Of course the key piece was destroyed." He was digging out his wallet. "Long ago, destroyed. By an oaf."

I asked, "They didn't take the stuff that shakes makes that hum, the dream hum?"

"What's that you say? *Dream hum?*"

He had the money halfway out of his wallet. He was staring at me like I just said I was working for the cops.

"I . . . that's what I call it. When your equipment makes that noise like bees and that other hum and I feel a little sick but then I get a tingle in my head and then I start to have those dreams." It all came out at once like that. I felt stupid.

"A tingle. Where in your head."

I tapped my forehead, between my eyes.

"You feel it there – that is an indication of extrasensory activation of the pineal."

I shrugged. I was wondering, back then, what a *pine-eel* was.

"Yes," he went on, looking at my head like he might want to do one of those frog dissections of it. "The tingle. I know it well. One feels it between the eyes, inside the skull – but it originates deep in the vertebrate brain, between the cerebral cortex and the midbrain you see. At the pineal! Yes."

I was looking at his hand. It was still frozen to that money.

"Oh, your remuneration!" He took the money out and handed it to me. "You did a fine job. We cut it fine but we fooled them, boy."

"My name's Vester."

"Indeed? What is the derivation of the name?"

"Derivation? Oh. It's from . . . Sylvester."

"Then why not go with Sylvester! I like it much better! Or *Syl*, perhaps?"

"Syl – I like that better."

"Syl it shall be. This business of . . . dreams. What sort?"

"Like . . . at the aquarium."

"You dreamed you were at an aquarium?"

"No. The dreams – sometimes I dreamed of giant things like the jellyfish from the Providence aquarium. But I seen big ones right in the room with me. But not exactly jellyfish. And a slow-motion exploding thing. Like in a video game if they show a explosion playback. You know?"

He was gaping at me. "Good lord. You saw all this *over there*, at the trailer park?"

"Yes."

"Remarkable! Do come in, boy, we'll have a glass of wine and discuss it."

Wine?

I was suddenly wondering if I should trust him. Maybe he was going to get all handsy on me.

But we went in the living room, that had only two old chairs in it, that smelled like someone's grandmother, and he poured us two glasses of something he called red port. I'd had beer before, and some of my mom's Carlo Rossi, but not this. I liked it.

"Only one glass for the youngster, ha ha," he said. He said *ha ha* that way when he was in a good mood. "This is old port, old like me. I like old things, apart from the productions of science. I am, like my father, an antiquarian yet I like technology that is quite modern – if only my grandfather had computers!"

Then he started telling me about Crawford Tillinghast, his grandfather, and how he was a genius but "a vile person, in himself" so that Grandmama – he pronounced it *grandmahMAH* – ran off from him when she was pregnant. She had a baby, who was Mr. Tillinghast's father. A letter came to her from someone with a story about Crawford Tillinghast and someone who shot his machine because of what he saw. And Grandmama told Mr. Tillinghast's father that the letter was true. It was a story of how he had a machine that used "resonance waves" to transport some secret frequency – that's Mr. Tillinghast's words. *Secret frequency*. He sent it right to the pineal gland in the brain and it allowed the person to see a world that's all around us, real close, but you can't see it.

"Yes yes yes, the servants were affected, they attracted a predator from that world, yes yes *yes* they died, but what of it? *That was not Grandfather's intention!* All truly vital research entails risk! His research was unprecedented! It was of vital importance to science and then it was rudely interrupted. Such a tragedy. So much to explore!" He gave out a big sigh at that. "Of course, I have continued from precisely where he was forced to stop." Mr. Tillinghast drank some more of his port and smacked his lips like he was tasting what he was thinking. "Consider, Syl! There is the microbiological world we all know of. Bacteria, viruses . . . Yet imagine how startled the first researchers were to realize these tiny creatures were everywhere! And then there was the hidden worlds of radio waves and X-rays and cosmic rays. Naturally there are other kinds of hidden worlds with organisms quite unknown to us and I do not mean the worlds to be found in other planetary systems! I mean a hidden world right here, Syl! Oh my grandfather knew – yet there's so much Grandad Crawford did not know! Why, consider quantum effects and neutrinos. I have gone much further than he! I have superior equipment, I have annuities from Great-granddad's oil wells, I have endless time for research . . . but I am beginning to grow old, child." He looked at his hands. "Arthritis troubles me. And I do not trust physicians." He gave me that weird smile again. I guess it should have scared me but it didn't. "I shall need an assistant! Someone like you, who evidently can see the truth and not go mad! But perhaps youth is the key to keeping sanity when exposed to the secret world as youth is not mentally ossified." (I still haven't looked up *ossified* yet.) "Still – why not test this hypothesis?"

"Yeah. I guess." I wasn't saying much. I was, like, whoa, how did this guy get so talkative? He always seemed like he never wanted to talk to anybody. But I guess he didn't have anybody he could talk to about this stuff before.

Then I seen he was looking at me like he was waiting for something.

When I didn't say anything he said, "Well? Are you willing?"

"Willing to do what?"

"To test the hypothesis about your gland."

I was looking at the front door thinking yeah, I should run for it . . .

He made a kind of "oh, sorry" noise in his throat. "To be clear – your *pineal* gland. Within your brain! Your ability to see the . . . you called them dreams. They are not dreams, however. You see, the pineal gland, though deep within your brain, is a kind of sensory organ, Syl. It has other functions, too, but when properly stimulated it allows you to see more than anyone else – a whole new world alongside ours! The Alternating World!"

"Oh. Yeah that's okay," I said. "Can I have a glass of water first?"

After moving all that stuff I was really thirsty.

"You can call me Oswald, if you like, Syl," he said, as he powered up the equipment.

I sat on an old kitchen chair set up at one end of the attic facing the equipment. There were little wired up circles he called *monitoring devices* taped to me. He promised they wouldn't hurt.

The attic was long and narrow and it surprised me how big it was. There was equipment in I had never seen, but I haven't seen much. One piece had a screen that showed waves on it. There was something in the middle of the attic pointed upward that reminded me of a satellite antenna. There were windows in the walls at either end of the attic but they were covered up with sheet metal.

I was starting to feel scared. But I was thinking about him saying, *You can call me Oswald, if you like, Syl.*

That felt good. I liked being called Syl. Even my dad had always called me Vester. (*Sly* would've pleased my dad more, but so what). And I liked that Oswald was talking like a friend, like we were just as good as each other. So I stayed where I was.

Mr. Tillinghast – I can't get myself to call him *Oswald* yet – was using a computer mouse to turn up a digital control on a screen, and as he did that I heard the bees start buzzing. Like the biggest hive you ever could imagine.

When Mr. Tillinghast spoke, he sounded like he was far away in a tunnel somewhere. *"My system is based on my grandfather's . . . I have his blueprints . . . but I have taken it to another level of power and control . . ."*

The bees sounded angry. That sound made me shiver. The walls were vibrating a little so that some dust fell off. But then he switched on the dream hum.

I felt a little sick, for a minute. And then the tingle came. I felt it right between my eyes, and inside my head.

Then I seen a colored light that wasn't coming from anywhere, really. It isn't a color I knew. I don't know how to say what color it was. Darker than purple but not dark purple. It went dim for a few seconds and then it got bright again, and then dim and then bright. Every time it got brighter I seen more things. More *new* things.

They were living things and they were flapping and floating. They were floating around these big pillars, like you'd see in a huge old museum building holding up the roof, but they seemed like they grew out of the ground way down below and they went on up above us forever. And the flopping floating things were floating between them. The floppers had these long strings made out of rubber or glass floating from the bottom, and one of them stretched out the strings to grab another flopper and pulled it close and sort of gobbled it up. Which made the gobbling one grow some bigger.

There were other things, too – they were slithering around the bases of the columns. These were like centipedes with hundreds of little feet but they seemed to be made of smooth soft-looking skin except it was gray-colored spotted with blue that wasn't blue and they had human eyes on the front but no nose and mouth. This hose came out from under their chin and they ate with that. I seen they were feeding on stuff that was on the floor under our floor – see, I could see *right through* the attic floor. There was another floor, or a ground, under the attic floor, about three feet down, and these big centipedes slipped around on it like snakes. They were bigger than boa snakes. I seen something else, too – kind of like those seeds with little wings that go all twisting when they fall down from trees, but these went up and down, up and down, and they were as big as my hand and they would connect with one another into shapes that were like writing, and then they would erase that, flitter apart, and write something else.

All these things came through the attic walls and floor and ceiling, like it wasn't there.

The buzzing sound *was* there but it was like I couldn't exactly hear it – I *felt* it instead, in my bones and in my stomach and head. I couldn't hear the humming anymore at all.

I heard Mr. Tillinghast's voice all echoey say, "*Your vital signs are elevated but you do not seem to have succumbed to panic.*" (I had to look up *succumbed* at a dictionary site, later. I thought he was saying I didn't suck or something but I didn't see how that fit with the rest of it.) "*You will have observed several organisms. Perhaps the blue-spotted slitherers are alarming in appearance, but they are harmless, and even friendly. They are aware of us – the more intelligent creatures in the Alternating World are aware of us, as soon as we are aware of them.*"

"How can they be here and be so big and we can't see them without your machine?" My voice sounded strange in my ears.

"*Think of it this way: our universe happens in beats. Let us say that for every other one millionth of a second our universe's reality does not exist; then it does exist, then it doesn't, all in millionths of a second. Or cut the fractions even finer than that! Less than momentary – and yet our reality appears and reappears in the stream of time so fast we do not detect its going*

and coming – it seems continuous. Let us then say that this other world,
which you are seeing now, vibrates in and out of existence, too, but it is here
when ours is gone, and ours is gone when the Alternating World is here! The
particularly potent resonance waves my grandfather distilled . . . and the
even more powerful and malleable waves I have distilled . . . have rendered
this world visible, so that we can see their appearance and ours at once –
and made a great deal more possible, as you may learn, some day. It creates
a tunnel between those two realities."

I still don't understand what he said. Not real well. But that's what
he said.

I was thinking about it – and then one of the blue-spotted slitherers
reared up and looked me right in the eyes. Up close.

"Do not be afraid, Syl!" Mr. Tillinghast yelled. *"He is friendly!"*

I looked into the slitherer's eyes. They were a color that was sort of
like green but not.

Then the blue-spotted slitherer laid its head in my lap, and wriggled
against my stomach, and looked up at me.

I don't know why, but I scratched it on the head. It pushed back
against my fingers to get some more. It liked the scratching.

"Good lord! They do not take to me so! You have made a friend!"

I was starting to feel dizzy; my head was hurting. It ached deep
inside. My stomach felt like it was turning inside out.

It wasn't the slitherer doing that. I just felt like I'd had that buzz
feeling and tingling too long.

Then I was gagging. The slitherer slipped away and I felt sicker and
sicker . . .

I heard a loud click and the buzz feeling stopped – I heard the
humming and then it stopped, too. The room was rocking like a boat
when the wind comes in. Then it stopped rocking and I threw up.

I tried to tell Mr. Tillinghast I was sorry for puking but he had helped
me up and took the monitors off me and he said, "It is I who should
apologize." There was a ringing in my ears so loud I could barely hear
him. "I was swept away, all too intrigued, by your apparently gifted

pineal capacity, Syl! I should not have proceeded with the experiment so precipitously, but these opportunities come so rarely. Come along . . ."

He helped me down the stairs, which was good, because my knees were wobbly. He gave me some water and I said I wanted to go home and he said, "Certainly, of course, but Syl – please – may I trust you to tell no one? Remember that if you *do* speak of it they will take you to a doctor and give you some horrible antipsychotic medicine and you will not like it, I assure you."

"I won't tell." He was right, no one would believe me. They'd think I was psycho. I couldn't even tell Bebe. Not all of it.

So I went back to the trailer park. I didn't see Bebe waiting around. I was glad. I didn't want to talk to her yet. I went in our doublewide and it felt all strange there, the television and the smell of some real skunky weed and my mom sitting with some guy I didn't know, like it was the strange world and not the one I seen in the attic. My mom's lipstick was messed up and her hair was, too. But that's not what was strange. It's just that everything I seen a million times looked like I never seen it before. The cigarette butts in the ashtray looked like some horrible little dead animals.

She said the guy's name was Merk. He just got here from California. He was a friend of her friend Belinda who moved to California.

"What up, little dude," Merk said. He looked older than my dad, and drunker than my mom. He had long, bleached blond hair and tattoos of women who looked like whores. His eyes were kind of saggy and red. He had a can of Bud in one hand and a blunt in the other.

I remembered that this Merk was hanging around the Fourth of July barbecue. He had a can of Bud in one hand and a blunt in the other then, too.

Mom, sitting real close to Merk, didn't look that happy to see me. "I thought you were out with Bebe."

It was hard to hear Mom talking over the ringing in my ears.

"She's . . . Bebe went home."

I could tell I wasn't supposed to be there so I went for a walk. The sky over the avenue was way overfull of stars. I didn't think all of them were supposed to be there. Sometimes they slipped around and made the shapes of faces. When I looked at the ground, I seen slitherers slipping by. My ears were still ringing.

I seen something else, too.

It was standing out in the field between the park and Mr. Tillinghast's house – it was a two-legged thing and it had this big fan of spikes around its neck like some guy in a metal band, and it had toothy tongues for fingers and it had a face like a goat but sort of dinosaur, too. It was about a hundred feet from me.

It looked at me with eyes like a goat. Looked right at me. I could feel it seeing me.

But then the ringing in my ears stopped and that thing went away, too. Just blinked out.

I was only scared of it after it was gone. I ran back to the Cumberland Glory and found Bebe on her front steps. I sat down below her and told her a little.

But not everything.

I almost didn't go back to Mr. Tillinghast's. I got more scared the next day, from what I seen in his attic. It was like, the night I seen it I wasn't feeling like I was real, right then, and after, so I couldn't be scared, because what could hurt you if you weren't real.

But that was wrong.

I was real and they were real.

I thought, later, maybe it was like seeing stuff on dope. That happened the two times I smoked pot, the squirmy stuff that wasn't really there.

But I didn't think it was like those little weed hallucinations like wallpaper moving. And I wanted to know what it really, really was. There was something wicked cool about it. And I didn't want to be in the trailer park because, what was there anymore? A month after that night, Bebe's mom took her away. They just pulled up and moved out. Bebe texted me for a while but then my phone broke and my mom couldn't get me another one right away.

I didn't have any other friends around there. And that *dude* Merk was there most of the time. He was swallowing his blue pills and smoking and banging my mom in her bedroom. They didn't care if I was in the trailer anymore they just shut the door and turned up his Van Halen.

So I went back to Mr. Tillinghast. "Can I help?" I asked when he came to the door.

"I am quite relieved to see you, my boy. Would you like to join me? I have a simple repast prepared."

"A what?"

"Hamburgers. Would you care for one? I can easily make another for you. Afterward we can discuss electronics. I have some books to show you."

It's more than year since I wrote all that earlier stuff.

Merk is still here, living in the trailer now. When he takes off his shoes, his feet stink bad. He doesn't wear socks. He has this really girly sounding laugh when he gets high or when he's trying to laugh something off.

About eight months ago I told my mom I saw him feeling up a drunk lady at the bowling alley and she asked him about it and he made that laugh and then he came outside, when I was out there on the steps and he said, "Kid you don't fuck with me, I won't fuck with you. But if you fuck up my thing I'll fuck you up. You know?"

I laughed and he slapped me on the back of the head, hard.

I jumped up and tried to hit him back and he pushed me over. I got up and backed away and then I just left.

So I went to Oswald's house. To Mr. Tillinghast's laboratory.

We worked on the blueprints and I fixed the resonator with him. He needs my help for soldering. His eyes aren't that good up close. He won't go to an eye doctor. He doesn't like how they write things down about him.

Oswald used the resonator many times. We went to the Alternating World, and some of it came to us. Spot, my slitherer, seems like he waits for me. He knows me good, and sometimes I hear his thoughts. He says he will always be my friend, that it was intended by the stars who speak.

Me and Oswald have learned we can breathe the air over there, in the Alternating World, and Oswald believes we can find things to eat there if we want longer trips.

Oswald showed me his bestiary, he calls it, of that world. He drew it himself. It has really good pictures of the flappers and the slitherers and the crepuscules and the linkages and the akishra and the dancing monoliths and the weeblers and the thing he calls the Baphomet. I looked up Baphomet online and I told him, that's not exactly what it looks like to me. And he said, "I know, my boy. But it seems like a relative. The diabolic goat man, don't you know."

"Kind of like a dinosaur, too."

"Rather more intelligent, I believe, than a dinosaur, in a malign sort of way. Fortunately we have the counter rings."

The counter rings are actually more like bracelets. We put them on our wrists and they give out a resonance that keeps the Baphomet from getting too close when we're in the resonation field. The Baphomet comes a little ways off and looks at us like he wants to taste us but he doesn't come any closer. Sometimes if I look at him too long, he comes closer to me. Once I thought, "I wish you'd go behind something" and he did. Like he would do what I would think.

Here it is, almost Christmas. I am getting more used to the Alternating World, and less used to ours. Cars and cigarettes and televisions and cell phones all look sort of strange to me. When I saw people looking into their cell phones it was like I could see an eel coming from the cell phones, licking their brains, and it's wearing their brains down like a hard candy. They didn't know it was there, but I could see it.

One night last week I told Oswald about this eel thing, as we worked over a new amplification circuit, and he looked worried.

"Oh dear. That was a crossover beast."

A crossover beast is one that can come into our world for a little while. To feed on things. Normal people can't see them. There aren't very many.

He scratched his nose and said, "It was an *akishra*. You shouldn't be seeing such things in our world, without the resonator going – or without having used it quite recently."

"I told you I saw them before without it."

"But that was soon after you'd used it – you saw the akishra three days after you were here last! And out of the blue!"

"Yep."

"So there it is. Well we may have to embrace the transition, after all – if you choose to. I will not make up your mind for you."

He was going to tell me about the transition but then my new cell made a text ding. I should have said I gave my mom most of the money that Oswald gave me but not all of it. I made her get me a new cell phone with some of it. It's pretty tight.

"My mom says I have to come home."

"We shall speak of it later."

So I started walking home, across the field.

I could see Christmas lights blinking on our trailer, over there. And lights in the little fir tree in the middle of the Cumberland Glory turn-around. Greel puts up those lights every year.

I knew Merk was there and I was fantasizing again about feeding him to the Baphomet. I could lure him up to the attic when Oswald wasn't home. *Dude, there's shrooms up in that attic. Tillinghast grows 'em. You can get high.*

Merk wouldn't have the countering rings. But killing him might put Oswald in danger. You can't just kill people. You could get bagged.

I looked up at the stars – and they started roiling around. I was getting the tingling and I started seeing things flying by up there. One of them I hadn't seen before was like entrails with wings. It made me sick to see it. Another one was like a big ugly baby that was floating along eating some little furry animal and it was eating it alive.

There were the floppers up there, too, and the crepuscules and there was the slow-motion exploder that kept rewinding back and exploding all over again and there was The Yellow Fog That Hates. (That's what Oswald calls that fog creature.)

I didn't want to see that stuff, not then, and suddenly, between looking at the Christmas lights and seeing those flying entrails – I didn't want to see that kind of stuff anymore.

I would miss the feeling I got from working with Oswald. But I had to choose my mom and my world. I had to choose Christmas and summer vacation and learning how to fix cars and having a girlfriend.

I got nightmares, sometimes, from Oswald's attic. It seemed worth it, then, but now, looking at the Christmas lights, I thought, it's not worth it. I need to forget that stuff or I won't ever come back. Maybe I'll get crazy like Crawford Tillinghast and get stuck in some place in my mind so they take me away and give me that antipsychotic shit.

Thinking about that, I really wanted to see my mom. I climbed over the fence by our trailer and then I saw my mom was driving away. I could see she was crying. I ran up and tried to wave her down but she wouldn't stop and the side mirror on her old Chevy coupe clipped my arm as she went by. I don't think she knew it. My arm wasn't broken but it really hurt and I felt like I was falling in a hole.

I found the trailer door open and I seen Merk in there under my mom's artificial Christmas tree, opening all the presents. He got most of them open already.

"You looking for shit to steal?" I asked.

He turned around, fast. He looked wicked hammered and mad. "She owes me money."

"Not much to steal there. We haven't got much. Steal from somebody rich, down the road."

He stood up, and staggered, and fell back against the Christmas tree. Bash, it went over. Christmas tree bulbs broke. "Come here, kid, you little fucker." He was getting up, pulling tree lights off him. "Fuck!"

He was standing in the middle of Christmas, kicking it.

I guess it was always kind of stupid anyway. Christmas.

I said, "Man I wish I could feed you to the Baphomet."

He didn't know what I meant.

I turned around and ran around the trailer to the fence, climbed over, jumped into the field, ran down the trail. Only then did it come to me, whoa, I made this trail, me alone, to Oswald's house.

Then I was close to the house and yelling for him. For Oswald.

He came to the door and shushed me. "Do you wish to alert the authorities? Come in, come in, then. What of your mother?"

"She left. I don't want to talk about that shit."

"I do wish you wouldn't use that vulgar, ah, lingo. Well, well, well. Come in, then. Perhaps we shall discuss transition."

I'm going to write this out and leave it in resonant-blocking shield we have, and during transition it'll fall right through the floor and land in the field. If you're reading this then somebody found it.

I am not going to say too much more. I guess I got in the habit of being secret, like Oswald.

I'll tell you a few things. We set up the fuel cells Oswald collected for the generator, to use after full transition, and we increased the output of the resonator, so that it does more than letting us see that world, and a little physical contact with it.

It can take us there all permanent so we don't have to come back.

It can take the whole house, too. It's a portable house, I guess. Like a trailer. But it rides vibrations into another world.

First we had to do what Oswald calls a *preliminary attempt*, while we still had a way to get back if we wanted. So, Oswald started up the machine and put it on the new setting that would really open up major big time to that world. We had to go transition careful so careful, shifting in space Oswald said, in a way that wouldn't get the animals in the Alternating World stuck in our bodies and we'd show up in a place where there was room for the whole house. That was part of the preliminary.

But one thing went wrong. The Baphomet showed up, during that test, when we were almost completely into that world, and because of the wider resonation field, we opened a door for him, and he went totally right the fuck into our world.

And the walls were transparent, I could see them but they were like dirty glass. And I seen the Baphomet running over to the Cumberland Glory Trailer Park. He was running right to our house. My mom's car was gone. But Merk was still there. I knew he was there because I knew I had called that Baphomet in some way, to go find Merk. I don't understand how. But I did. Like that time I made him hide behind something. He went where I wanted. And he went to my mom's doublewide because of me. And he went in it.

I couldn't hear Merk scream, but I could feel it.

"Is something wrong?" Oswald asked me. His voice sounded normal now because we were becoming part of that other wave system. "Are the police coming? You seem to be looking through the walls."

"No," I told him. "Nothing's wrong. But Oswald, if something gets through to our world from that other world, like something that could hurt people, because of us, does it just stay over there?"

"Have you seen such a thing?"

"Maybe." I shrugged. "Not sure."

"If it came through it might do some damage but once we're gone, the gap will close and it will be drawn through, back to the Alternating World, as the gap closes – a kind of energy suction. Are you concerned about someone?"

I looked away from the wall, and went back to looking at the monitor, to check wavelength ratios. "No. I'm not concerned."

So right now, we're taking a break, and I'm writing this last part up in this notebook, and then I'll put it in the insulation covers, and let it fall to the field. And we'll see what happens now, as soon as we finish the transition, and we go over there for good.

But Oswald and me, we are partners. Nothing will stop us.

And when we're tired of that world, there are more.

But we can never come back here, Oswald told me. He said I have to choose.

It's okay. Because, I choose that world, the Alternating World. I choose it, and whatever else we see. I choose the world of crepuscules and The Yellow Fog That Hates and the slow exploder and the slitherers and the floppers. I have a pet, waiting for me there. My own blue-spotted slitherer. Spot.

We have tools, and weapons. The Baphomet, I know, will be there, and it will kill me if it can, just like it killed the servants of Oswald's grandfather.

I don't care. It's still better than my own world.

Almost anything would be better.

"The Sea Inside" is **Amanda Downum**'s response to Lovecraft's "The Thing on the Doorstep." "It's one of my favorite Lovecraft stories," she states, "but I'm very skeptical of the events as presented by Daniel Upton. This is my first rebuttal, and probably not the last."

A resident of Austin, Texas, Downum is the author of *The Necromancer Chronicles* series, published by Orbit Books, and *Dreams of Shreds & Tatters*, from Solaris. Her short fiction has appeared in *Strange Horizons*, *Realms of Fantasy*, *Weird Tales*, and elsewhere. One day she will return to the sea.

The Sea Inside
Amanda Downum

———

"[O]cean is more ancient than the mountains, and freighted with the memories and the dreams of Time."

– H. P. Lovecraft, "The White Ship"

The sky above the gulf was the color of oysters, a pale, sunless stretch. It might have been late morning or late afternoon. Verdigris waves rolled over bone-grey sand, leaving behind a lace of foam and swags of rusty sargassum. The wind gusted warm and sticky off the water. Beneath the brine, it smelled faintly of decay. The shore was empty save for a few distant beachcombers, a couple swimming, a man and a dog.

At the edge of the beach, between the dry sand and Seawall Boulevard, a woman sat at a picnic table on the weathered gray planks of a shrimp-shack patio. A plastic cup sweated at her elbow, leaving rings on the wood. She stared at the sea through dark glasses. The damp wind pulled her hair loose from its braid and set it frizzing around her face.

A car idled by the curb on the street above the strand. It had been there ten minutes. Finally the engine died and another woman stepped out. Younger, sleeker, also wearing sunglasses. The wind had its way with her styled hair. She stood beside the car for a while, staring at the water. Then she made her way down the steps to the beach. Her expensive, impractical shoes sank into the sand.

The older woman didn't stir except to lift her drink. Moisture dripped off her fingers. When the younger woman sat down opposite her, she turned. Each pair of dark plastic lenses reflected the other.

"You're the one," the young woman said at last.

The other woman smiled, a flash of white in a light brown face. "I am."

"You know why I'm here."

"Yes."

"You can really do this?"

"Are you hungry?" The woman lifted her cup again. Ice rattled. She raised a hand and a stooped, balding man stepped out of the shack.

"No." The young woman reached into her purse for a cigarette and a lighter. A diamond glittered on her left hand, brilliant even in the wan daylight.

Dark glasses tilted. Brown lips pursed. "Do you think you should do that?"

"Why—" The angry question died away. She looked down at the cigarette she held between two manicured fingers. "They told you."

"I have to know if I'm going to help you." The bald man had arrived at their table. "Are you hungry?"

The young woman frowned. "Shrimp," she told the man. "I don't care what kind." She lifted her chin. "And a beer."

The man turned away, shuffling across the warped deck. "Can you?" the young woman asked when he was gone. "Help me?"

"I can change things. You have to help yourself in the end."

"Did they tell you why I'm here?"

"Some. The details don't matter. People only have one reason for finding me in the end. You need out."

"This is crazy."

The woman shrugged. "You don't have to do it."

"Then what?"

"Eat some shrimp. Drink a beer, if you want to. Go home and wait."

"Just like that?"

Another shrug. "It's a nice day, and I have all the time in the world."

"I have money."

"So do I. I'll take yours, though, if you want. It's useful."

The young woman fell silent, staring at her unlit cigarette. Slim fingers tensed and the paper cylinder crumpled. Flecks of tobacco danced on the salty wind. "Money solves problems. But not this one. He'll find me."

"You don't have to go through with it. With me. With him. With . . ." She lifted a hand and let it fall. "Any of it."

"It doesn't matter if I do or don't. He'll find me. He'll find you if you help me."

The woman grinned. She showed a lot of teeth. "I don't care."

"The worst thing is . . . part of me still thinks I can go back and everything will be fine again. Just like before." She shook her head, tucking a strand of hair behind her ear. The wind whipped it loose again.

"You can't go back from this," the woman said. "Only forward."

The old man returned, one sandaled foot dragging softly across the boards as he walked. He set down a paper basket full of breaded shrimp and a plastic cup of pale beer. The young woman handed him a bill from her purse. "Keep the change."

He nodded. The creases on his weathered face never shifted. The money vanished into his pocket and he returned to the shack.

She picked up a shrimp. It crunched between her teeth and she exhaled a short, hot breath. "Coconut." Her voice lifted with surprise. She touched the cup of beer, studied it for a moment, then sighed and inched it away from her.

"Why? Why do you do this?"

The older woman watched the waves roll in. White foam surged against the sand. "For the same reason. But this way it's on my terms. I know what it's like to be trapped."

"What's it like? What you do, I mean."

Brown shoulders lifted in a shrug. "It can be perfectly simple, if you let it. Or it can be hell. It's what you make it."

"Really? Perfectly simple?"

"Well." Her lips curled, a lopsided smile. "Not perfectly simple. But easy enough. You can't have your old life back, but you can make a new one."

"Really?" the young woman said again, softer this time.

"Yes."

"What will happen to . . . everything?" One hand settled in her lap. She put it back on the table again. "If things were different – less complicated – I could take care of it myself. I know lots of people who have. Some of them say that's simple, too." Her mouth twisted. "Or maybe I wouldn't. I wanted a family, once. I thought it would all be so easy." She laughed, and the sound rose high and wild over the steady crush of the waves. "Did you ever have a family?"

Plastic lenses reflected the sea. "My mother left when I was young. My father" – she made a soft, ugly sound – "taught me a lot of things. Part of me always wanted a daughter. I know I'd leave, too, eventually, but I'd at least make sure she was in a good place when I did."

The young woman sighed. "It doesn't matter, I suppose. I just don't want . . ." She trailed off. "You'd leave her in a good place? With people less selfish than me?"

"With people less selfish than either of us."

"Let me see your eyes."

The older woman turned to face her and slowly removed her sunglasses. The other woman did the same. They studied their reflections in each other's eyes.

"How does it work?" the young woman finally asked.

"Give me your hand."

She reached across the table, but stopped halfway. She stared at the diamond flashing on her finger. Her lips peeled back from her teeth and she twisted the ring free with three sharp tugs. It traced a glittering arc through the sticky air, vanishing somewhere in the damp sand and foam. She rubbed at the crease it left on her finger. Then she extended her hand.

They sat for several moments, two women under a cloudy sky, holding hands and watching each other wordlessly. The man and the dog walked behind a pale line of dunes in the distance. The swimming couple had disappeared. The man inside the shrimp shack didn't look up from his crossword puzzle.

The older woman jerked, chest hitching. Her eyes widened.

The younger woman blinked once, twice. She lifted her left hand and studied the careful manicure, the fading ghost of a diamond ring.

"Look in your purse," she said. Her voice was slower, lower. "Do you have everything you need?"

The other woman sorted for the bag beside her on the bench. With shaking hands she fumbled through its contents: wallet, driver's license, cash, passport, a keychain full of keys.

"A car?"

"Parked down the street. You'll find it. Not as nice as the other one, but it will take you wherever you need to go. How do you feel?"

"Fine." Her voice rose uncertainly. "I feel fine," she said, steadier. "It's what I make of it."

The younger woman smiled. "That's right." She reached into her bag and slid the cigarettes across the table. "Here. I should go. Enjoy your food. Enjoy the day. You have time." She picked up her sunglasses, and plastic eclipsed her eyes. One hand rested briefly against her stomach.

"Like a sea inside," she murmured.

She toed off her expensive, impractical shoes and hooked them with two fingers. Her toes dug into the warm sand as she walked away.

A woman sat alone at the picnic table. The shutters had been pulled down on the shrimp shack, and a *Closed* sign shifted in the breeze. A glass of beer sweated at her elbow. After a moment she lit a cigarette and took one deep drag. She laughed, high and wild, and the sound and the smoke drifted away in the salty air. The cigarette burned down between her fingers as she watched the sea.

She continued to laugh while her shoulders trembled, and tears tracked slowly down her cheeks.

John Langan is the author of three collections of short fiction: *Sefira and Other Betrayals, The Wide, Carnivorous Sky and Other Monstrous Geographies* (both from Hippocampus), and *Mr. Gaunt and Other Uneasy Encounters* (Prime). He has written a novel, *House of Windows* (Night Shade), and with Paul Tremblay, co-edited *Creatures: Thirty Years of Monsters* (Prime). He lives in upstate New York with his wife and younger son.

For Langan, one of the key elements of Lovecraft's stories is the forbidden text. "To be exposed to this text is to have your eyes opened to another world, one whose intersection with ours leaves your perspective forever changed, generally for the worse. I suppose 'The Necronomicon' is the best-known example of this, but there are other stories – 'Pickman's Model,' 'The Music of Eric Zann' – where another means of expression is the source of revelation. We've all had the experience of the tune that will not leave us alone. What, I wondered, if there was more to it than that?"

Outside the House, Watching for the Crows
John Langan

Dear Sam,

I know: who writes a letter, anymore?

I suppose you're used to the mail as a conduit for care packages from your mom and Steve, or Liz and me, but if you're anticipating any written communication from us, you'll check your email, or your Facebook account, or even Twitter. I thought about sending this as an email. Actually, I did more than think about it. In the "Drafts" folder on my laptop, there are a couple of paragraphs I obsessed over for several hours after our last conversation, then for several more hours the following night, before I decided it would be better to sit down at my desk with a pad of legal paper, an extra-fine Precise V5 (black), and compose a letter to you. (For reasons you'll understand later, the social media options never were.) This is the way I plan out a case, spread all my notes around me and arrange the facts they relate into a coherent structure.

I don't have any notes, now. What I have is your question, "What's the weirdest thing that's ever happened to you – I mean, the *weirdest*?" which (I admit) I speculated might have been prompted by your experimentation with substances I probably don't want to know about. Yet the answer that instantly occurred to me seems to come directly from such an experience. To be honest, I'm almost embarrassed to tell it to you. For one thing, it's so extravagant you may suspect I've finally started the novel I've been threatening. For another, it doesn't show me in the best light, and while I know you've been aware of my clay feet for a long time, I'm reluctant to call attention to them. At the same time, there's a part of me that's been desperate to relate this story to someone since it happened. I thought I had long since learned to control that urge, to suppress it, but your question threw open the doors and let it loose. By writing this, I suppose, I'm giving in to my need to confess; although I'm doing so in such fashion that I still have the option to delete it once I'm finished.

So: it begins with the answer to your question: at the beginning of the summer between my junior and senior years of high school, I attended a concert by a band called The Subterraneans at The Last Chance, which was a club in what I guess would have been called downtown Poughkeepsie. There weren't many other people present. Aside from me and the friend I'd met there, maybe two dozen bodies filled the space in front of the stage. At the beginning of the show, I had positioned myself toward the rear of the open area. About halfway through the band's set, in the midst of a keyboard solo that went on and on, I felt a breeze tickle the back of my neck. I glanced behind me, and saw the section of the club there, under the balcony, had changed. It was completely dark, except for a strip in the middle opening into a narrow alley right through what had been the club's bar. I was not hallucinating – at least, I hadn't ingested anything that would have allowed this to be a possibility. The breeze blew out of the alley against my face, carrying with it the smell of the ocean, brine and baked seaweed. I looked away, but the odor persisted. When I turned around, the alley was still there. I took a step toward it. Around me, the keyboard, sounding like a manic pipe organ, continued its solo. Bright moonlight picked out scraps of paper skittering across the alley's cobblestones. At the far end of the passage, a group of tall figures stood in silhouette. I advanced another step. I didn't like the way the moonlight slid over those tall shapes, but this didn't stop me from continuing in their direction. I was wondering why none of the rest of the audience was noticing this when Jude, the friend I'd met here, shoved past me and walked right up to the verge of the alley, where he stopped – waiting, I realized, for me to join him.

There isn't a great deal more – though there is something – but what I've related is incomplete, devoid of the context that brought me to that moment. If I'm being frank, then I have to admit, I'm not certain how much those details explain the events of that night. But it feels wrong to relate this portion of the narrative without what came before. I need to back up, to an aging manila envelope I've kept for twenty-five years, through moves from apartments to rental houses to my own house. It contains an audiocassette tape, a ticket stub, and a Polaroid faded almost beyond visibility. The tape has been unplayable since it unspooled in my car stereo and became so hopelessly entangled in the deck's mechanisms that I had to snap it in several places to extract it. Although I spent I can't tell you how many hours attempting to repair it, smoothing its creases, gluing its ends together, winding it back onto its wheels, it was too far gone. Nor could I replace it, since it was a copy of a bootleg recording of which, as far as I know, there was only one original. (I'm not even sure about that, since I never saw the tape it was copied from.) And yes, I've searched online for it, and no luck. When it still played, the tape contained fifty-nine minutes of the band I mentioned, The Subterraneans, performing a live show at The Last

Chance. The ticket stub is for another concert by the same band at the same place on 21 June 1986.

The Polaroid is not a picture of the band. It's of a group of people I spent Friday and Saturday nights hanging out with during the spring of my junior year of high school. Even with the damage two and half decades have done to it, I can identify everyone in the photo; though my memory supplements details that have deteriorated beyond recognition. Were you to look at it, I imagine you'd see a collection of pale ovals like a talented child's approximation of faces, each one ornamented with a tag screaming "Eighties!" Long hair hair-sprayed into exaggerated pompadours in the case of the guys; short hair spiked and/ or dyed purple in the case of the girls. Short leather and denim jackets festooned with buttons displaying the names of bands, the anarchist "A," slogans like "Sticks and stone may break my bones, but whips and chains excite me." Jeans and Doc Martens, or ankle-length skirts and Keds, or leather miniskirts and fishnet stockings with Docs or Keds. Clunky jewelry. It was Punk meets New Wave meets Proto-Goth.

No, I didn't dress like that. However much I may have wanted to, I was far too self-conscious, too much of a conformist, to abandon my Polo shirt, jeans, and Converse, not to mention, my blue-and-yellow varsity jacket, an article of clothing I'd worn in all but the hottest or coldest weather since lettering in spring track my sophomore year. My clothes didn't exactly make me fit in at school – my shirt and jeans were whatever brands were on sale at Marshalls or Kmart – but they didn't make me stand out. They were like a kind of low-grade camouflage. The jacket drew a few startled looks from the self-identified jocks and their girlfriends; that was all. It might have made me a little less visible as a target for ridicule, which was about as much as I hoped for.

So if I was so obsessed with invisibility, why did I spend my weekend nights in the company of people whose clothes, hair, everything drew all eyes in their direction, right? To start with, there was a girl. Her name was Lorrie Carter. She was my date for the junior prom. When I asked her to go with me, it was as a friend, because she cocked her head to the right, narrowed her eyes, and said, "As boyfriend–girlfriend, or as friends?" and I said, "As friends," the tone of my voice implying, "Of course." Lorrie was attractive. I would have been happy to invite her as boyfriend–girlfriend, but I was reasonably sure she was seeing someone who wasn't a student at Mount Carmel, and I was desperate for a prom date. To be honest, even had I not suspected she was dating, I would have given the same answer. Unlike you, by the ripe old age of sixteen, I had yet to have a girlfriend. I hadn't even kissed a girl. During the games of spin-the-bottle I'd taken part in at the couple of sweet-sixteens I'd been to, the neck of the bottle never seemed to point exactly at me; instead, the guys to either side of me saw their nights improve. Too much information, I suppose. The point is, as far as girls went, my self-confidence was nil.

But Lorrie agreed to go to the prom with me, and about two weeks before the event, she invited me to join her and some of her friends for Chinese food on a Friday night after I was done with work. (I had a part-time job at a Waldenbooks, which I'm not even sure exist, anymore, in a mall that I know doesn't exist, anymore.) Your grandparents were only too happy to give their permission. Until I turned sixteen, they strongly discouraged me from dating anyone. Once my birthday passed, however, they began to inquire and even nag about my romantic prospects. They had looked dubious at my description of my prom date as a friend. For me to be meeting her for a meal was more in keeping with their expectations.

If they'd been there for the actual meal, though, any comfort they felt would have evaporated. I met Lorrie and her friends in the main parking lot of Dutchess Community College, whose location I knew but to which I'd been only once, the time I accompanied Uncle Matt to the County Science Fair there. The parking lot is at the foot of the hill on which the campus sits. I remember being surprised at the lights still shining in the windows of the college buildings, the number of cars in the parking lot at nine forty-five on a Friday night. Lorrie and the quartet of friends with her had already picked up their order of Chinese and were passing the open white containers back and forth, some using the chopsticks the restaurant had provided, others opting for plastic forks. Lorrie had the door to her old Saab open and was perched on the edge of the driver's seat, legs extended, ankles crossed. To her left, a tall guy whose white-blond hair rose above his head in a rooster's comb leaned against the car, while the remaining guy and pair of girls sat in a half-circle on the blacktop in front of Lorrie.

At the sight of me, sporting the ubiquitous varsity jacket over my shirt-and-tie work clothes, a collective tense stiffened the group, until Lorrie's face lit with recognition and she proclaimed, "This is my friend, Michael. He's my *prom date*," and everyone relaxed. One of the girls sitting on the ground held up a carton of food. I took it and the chopsticks Lorrie handed to me. I hadn't seen chopsticks outside Sunday afternoon kung-fu movies on channel 9, but I slid them from their paper wrapper, snapped them apart, and gave it my best try. The container I'd taken was full of large slices of mushroom and green pepper floating in a spicy blue-gray sauce that numbed and stung my tongue at the same time. Mushrooms weren't something your grandmother served on a regular basis, by which I mean ever, and I didn't like the way these ones squirmed in my mouth. I ate enough not to be rude, then exchanged the carton with the sitting guy for one full of fried rice, whose taste I greatly preferred; although I spilled more of it than I ate. I hadn't known to bring anything to drink with me, but no one else had a beverage, either, so I guessed it was okay.

It was a strange night – the hour and a half of it I spent with Lorrie and her friends before I had to speed home to miss my curfew by only a little. I guess it's always a bit awkward when you meet a new group of people, but the few times this had happened to me previously, it hadn't taken long for me to flip through my list of general high-school-related topics and find one that would allow us to pass the time pleasantly if blandly enough. Where do you go to school? How is it? Really? Or, You listening to anything good? Bryan Adams? Yeah, I love the video for his song, "Heat of the Night." (Don't you laugh at Bryan Adams.) These guys, though – it was like talking with people who spoke, not another language, but a dialect so profoundly removed from your daily speech, you could pick out only every third or fourth word if you were lucky. School? With the exception of Lorrie, everyone there went to a different private school I'd heard of but otherwise knew nothing about: Heartwood Academy, Most Holy Temple, Poughkeepsie Progressive School, George Rogers; although, from their conversation, it wasn't clear how much any of them knew about their individual schools, since their days apparently consisted of skipping class, in-house suspension, and blowing off school altogether. If I tell you how shocked I was to hear people comparing notes on the best way to forge a hall pass, I realize how naïve, how sheltered that will make me sound, but I was both of those things. I might have thought about missing Calculus, but fear of being caught – and punished – by your grandfather kept the thought from becoming action. Parents, though, and any reprisals they might threaten, were of scant concern. Even Lorrie talked with cheerful disregard of calling her mother an uptight bitch for asking her why there were so many absences listed on her last report card.

As for music . . . I liked to think of my tastes as fairly eclectic, extending from Michael Jackson to Prince to Bruce Springsteen to Madonna (although I wouldn't admit the last one), plus a few bands who were mildly off the beaten track: INXS, U2, Talking Heads. (While I'm sure my examples will seem painfully parochial to someone of your generation, I would make the case that, say, *Bad*, *Sign o' the Times*, *Tunnel of Love*, and *True Blue* cover a much larger musical terrain than you might grant them credit for.) In fact, when talk turned from school to records, I felt a brief flare of hope that I would be able to break what had become a long and uncomfortable silence. However, except for a nod when the guy with the rooster-comb – whose name was Jude – asked if I knew INXS's *Listen Like Thieves*, I remained outside the discussion. Bauhaus, Love and Rockets, Dead Can Dance, Pixies, Throwing Muses: I had never heard of these bands, let alone anything they'd done. Other bands – Depeche Mode, The Psychedelic Furs, Siouxsie and the

Banshees – I recognized as names attached to songs I'd listened to on the radio, none of which had impressed me one way or the other. You know how it is when you're talking to your friends about a shared passion. You speak in shorthand. While perfectly intelligible to you, it leaves anyone unfamiliar with it with the sensation of listening to a radio broadcast clouded by static, so that only the occasional phrase or sentence comes clear. It's the type of thing for which lawyers are constantly criticized, speaking "legalese," but really, there are a multitude of examples.

Two events redeemed the night. When a check of my watch showed it was time to go, Lorrie walked me to my car. After I thanked her for inviting me, I'd had a good time, her friends were cool, she said, "I've been thinking about the prom."

At those words, my stomach lurched. She was about to announce her decision not to go with me, after all. Tonight had been a test and I'd flunked it with flying colors. I wondered if I'd be able to find another date in time.

Lorrie said, "Remember when I asked you if we were going as boyfriend-girlfriend, or as friends, and you said, 'Friends?'"

I nodded. "Sure." She was going with her boyfriend. Was it Jude? The other guy?

"I think we should go as boyfriend-girlfriend."

For a moment, I literally did not understand what I had heard. Then, when the meaning caught up with the words that had delivered it, I said, "Really?" I like to think my voice wasn't too high-pitched and incredulous.

"Uh huh," Lorrie said, and stepped forward, raised up on her tip-toes, and kissed me on the lips. It was brief, almost chaste. Before I could respond, she said, "See you Monday," and was walking away. Fully twenty-five years, a quarter century, have passed since that night in March, and the soft give of Lorrie Carter's lips is as vivid to me as if she had pressed them to mine this minute past.

All right, all right: once again, too much information. The other thing that saved the occasion occurred as I was nodding to everyone, saying my goodbyes. Jude stepped away from his position on Lorrie's car, his right hand held out to me. At first, I thought he was offering to shake my hand, which wasn't something my friends and I did, but when in the DCCC parking lot . . . until I noticed the black plastic cassette tape in his fingers. "Here," he said as I took it, "if you like *Listen Like Thieves*, you might get this."

"Thanks," I said, and slipped it into my jacket pocket. There it stayed until the following morning, when I was searching for my car keys. Do you know, I never asked Jude why he gave the tape to me? There were several moments later on when I could have, but the question always seemed to slip my mind until it was too late. And then it was.

The fact I'd been handed the cassette in the first place had vacated my thoughts, pushed out by the memory of my first kiss from my first girlfriend. There have been a lot of happy events in my life since then: your birth, my wedding to Liz, completing law school, opening my own practice – those and plenty more, but I'm not sure any of them made me happy in exactly the same way I was after that kiss. My first impulse is to compare the emotion I experienced during the drive home that night to what I felt as a child at some unexpected pleasure, say, your grandfather surprising Uncle Matt and me with a trip to the Roosevelt to see *Star Wars*. But that's not it. The smell of Lorrie's perfume, floral (lilacs, I think) without being overpowering; the faint taste of the mushroom and pepper dish she left on my lips; the momentary press of her body against mine – obviously, none of this is anything like sitting in a darkened theater as spaceships arc across a starscape, exchanging dashes of red and green fire. What is the same is the quality of the happiness which infused each occasion, a certain . . . the word that occurs to me is "purity," which is accurate enough for me to set it down; although further reflection suggests "uncomplicated" wouldn't be a bad choice, either.

By the trip to work the next day, my emotion had moderated, though the early sunlight that made me squint and flip down the visor seemed more intense, more charged with raw, unprocessed beauty, than I'd noticed before. I'd brought the tape with me. There was writing on it, a single word I couldn't decipher beyond the extravagant "S" from which it unspooled. The word was repeated on the other side, no more legibly. I slotted the cassette into the tape deck, adjusted the volume, and waited.

Considering how important the tape was to become to me, you'd think my first listen to it would have been an experience to rival Lorrie's kiss. It wasn't. The quality of the recoding wasn't particularly good. A low-level hiss underlay a fuzzy collection of longish songs built around an electric guitar whose heavy reverb kept getting in its own way, keyboards whose pipe organ tones clashed with the guitar, and a singer whose nasal whine frequently disappeared into the competing noise. Neither bass nor drums were especially clear, and what was audible through the din sounded basic, uninspired. Had I been told this was a garage band playing in an actual garage, I would have accepted the description without question. I left the tape on for the twenty minutes or so of the drive to the mall, not so much because I thought the music would improve – hope springs eternal, yes, but there are some albums, just as there are some books, movies, TV shows, that you know early on will not change. They may become more of what they already are, speed further and faster down the road they're on, but they aren't going to veer off it. I was more curious to see if I could deduce what had prompted Jude to pass this tape to me. Yes, he'd mentioned INXS, but this was nothing like *Listen Like Thieves*. That record was crisp, clear, the band's assorted instruments working with one another and Michael Hutchence's voice to construct each song. At least on a first listen-through – which I completed during the ride home from work that night and the drive back the following morning – I couldn't hear any obvious connections. I wondered if the cassette was meant as a corrective to the more popular album, an example of the kind of music I should be listening to. I entertained the possibility it was some kind of joke; although if this were the case, it seemed unnecessarily obscure. Unless that was the point, to demonstrate to me that I was not part of the group. As far as explanations went, it fell pretty firmly under the paranoia column, but such is adolescent psychology.

When I started the tape a second time, on the way home Sunday afternoon, it was because I was no closer to understanding what I was supposed to take away from this music at its end than I had been at its beginning. To anyone in a similar situation, then or now, my counsel would have been, "Don't worry about it," but this was advice I myself was (and am) unable to accept. If someone tells me a work of art's something special, I will stick with said piece of art until I: a) decide the person who recommended it was right, b) decide the person who recommended it was wrong, or c) decide I need more time with it. If something requires more time, I'll take as much of it as I require, to the point of years. After my first listen to Jude's tape, I was pretty close to option b), but enough doubt colored my impression for me to conclude another listen was in order. It didn't hurt that the guy who'd handed it to me was a friend of my newly minted girlfriend.

However, the most my repeat play accomplished was to leave the cassette in the tape deck, resulting in a third and fourth exposure on the drive into school, the drive from school down Route 9 to work, and the drive home from work. Nothing clicked. There was no magic "Ah-Ha!" moment when understanding dawned on me. But by the time I was back at the beginning of the tape for run-through number five, a vague sense of what was so significant about the music on it had started to suggest itself to me.

That music. Once you accommodated yourself to the clash of the guitar and keyboard, and could concentrate on the melody they were fighting over, you realized the band's songs were basically the kind of music that had filled the airwaves of 1950s radio, the bluegrass-inflected R&B gathering itself into rock n' roll through the ministrations of Buddy Holly, the Big Bopper, and of course Elvis Presley. In an odd way, The Subterraneans – it would be another couple of weeks until I deciphered their name – were doing something comparable to what a band like the Ramones was – only, where the Ramones were trying to refine the rock song down to its simplest, purest state, these guys were trying to widen it, start with those simple chord progressions, basic melodies, and throw open all the doors and windows. Had I known anything about jazz, then, I would have identified the parallel of starting with a straightforward progression of notes, stretching them into new configurations, and returning to the original arrangement. As it was, I just thought they were addicted to long, strange solos. The more used to the music I became, the more of its lyrics I was able to decode; although large patches of every song remained opaque to me. There were references to feeling like death, and to litter on the street, and to puddles of black water, and to walking around at two am. Someone named Jo-Jo lived in an apartment that was a great place to crash at. There were several mentions of standing outside the house, sometimes a church, and the words "in-between" seemed to find their way into every set of lyrics. At least once, the singer proclaimed, "You've got to watch out for the crows."

Looking over what I've written, I realize I've failed almost completely to do justice to the music I listened to constantly, every time I was in the car, and soon when I was in my room – I dug out an old cassette recorder that had a single earplug for quiet listening which practically took up residence in my left ear. I've made The Subterraneans sound like a concept band, an exercise in performance art, and conveyed nothing of their immediacy, of the immanence in their songs, the overriding impression they gave that there was something they were on the verge of saying, a revelation they were on the cusp of delivering. I went to sleep with their music filling my ear, and their songs followed me into sleep, into dreams where I stood on the streets of a city I did not know while the wind chased paper bags and Styrofoam cups across the pavement.

The following Friday, Lorrie invited me to join her and her friends. If she hadn't, I would have asked to. Of course I wanted to meet her outside of school, where our respective schedules permitted us to see one another in only a few classes, but I was eager to talk to Jude, as well, about the tape whose songs were playing in my head whether I was listening to them or not, which had become the soundtrack of my life – or, I'm not sure if this will make any sense, but it was as if my day's activities had become an extended illustration of the music, a feature-length video for it.

The principle difference between this night and the previous Friday was I spent it sitting beside Lorrie on the hood of her car, my feet resting on the front bumper, hers crossed under her legs, so she had to lean against me to keep from sliding off. I wasn't daring enough to put my arm around her, but I placed my hand on the hood behind her and pretended to support myself with it, when its actual purpose was to allow a maximum portion of me to come into contact with a maximum portion of her as unobtrusively as possible. An hour and half with a pretty girl pressed into me was more than sufficient compensation for the remainder of the night being a virtual repeat of the week before, from another carton of vegetables in a strange-tasting and spicy sauce to further conversation to which my contribution was minimal. In addition, Jude was not in attendance. I asked Lorrie about his absence while she walked me to my car. She shrugged and said, "He's got a lot going on." I wasn't exactly disappointed, especially since the kiss I received at this departure was significantly longer and – more involved, I guess you might say. But when Lorrie suggested I might like to meet with her and her friends the next night, some small measure of what prompted me to say, "Sure, yeah," was the prospect Jude would be present.

He wasn't, and since the weekend after was the prom, I didn't see any of Lorrie's friends. I saw her, and the large house where she and her parents lived, and D'Artagnan, her standard poodle, and her parents, who were younger than mine and glowed with money, and the elaborate royal blue dress she wore. Your grandfather had rented an Oldsmobile to ferry us to the prom, held in the catering hall of the Villa Alighieri, an Italian restaurant. Later, he chauffeured us to an after-prom party being held at someone's house out in Millbrook, and still later to retrieve us from the smoldering embers of the party and return us home. Lorrie and he hit it off, and the night went as well as these things do. The meal and music were adequate, the company at our table pleasant.

What I remember most about the prom is that The Subterraneans' music colored it, too. In fact, were it not for my subsequent experiences at The Last Chance, I likely would have identified a moment at the dance as the weirdest thing that ever happened to me. It occurred while the DJ was playing the prom theme (for the record, Madonna's "Crazy for You"). Lorrie and I were slow dancing, her head resting on my chest. Underneath the homogenized sentimentality of Madonna's lyrics, The Subterraneans' singer was declaring it was *always* Halloween, here. The space around the dance floor dimmed, as if the lighting there had been lowered almost completely. Where the tables and chairs had been, tall forms moved from left to right in a slow procession. I had the impression of heads like those of enormous birds, with sharp, curving beaks, and dark robes draped all the way to the floor. Then the light returned, and the figures were gone. What I had seen was weird with a capital W, but it also vanished so quickly I was able to blink a couple of times and put it out of my mind. The girl leaning against me, in her stockinged feet because she'd removed her uncomfortable shoes, swaying in time to the theme, facilitated this. For the remainder of the prom, the vision did not return, nor did it during the after-party events, when I was engaged in more pleasant pursuits. The night concluded with a good-bye kiss on the front step of Lorrie's parents' house, after which, your grandfather took me for breakfast at McDonald's.

One month after the prom, Lorrie broke up with me. It was less traumatic than you might suppose. Although I had continued to join her and her friends at the DCCC parking lot for takeout Chinese on Fridays and Saturdays, school, sport, and work commitments kept me from seeing any more of her. Not to mention, one of the girls on the track team, a cute sophomore, had told me she thought I resembled the lead singer of the band, ABC, and he was *cute*. While I had never been quickest on the uptake when it came to such things (a fact to which your stepmother will attest), even my limited powers of perception could detect this new girl's interest in me. So when Lorrie called to say, "It isn't working," I found it easier to sigh and agree than I might have otherwise. I was still welcome to hang out with her and her friends, Lorrie said, which I took as a formality but appreciated nonetheless. I said I might. After I hung up the phone, I was sad, and briefly angry, at things not working out between Lorrie and me, but I was also more philosophical, more mature about it than I believe I have been about the end of any subsequent relationship, which is a strange thing to realize.

Lorrie and I remained friendly, although I returned to the college parking lot only once to eat with her and her friends. As luck would have it, Jude was there as well, for the first time since the night he had handed me the tape of The Subterraneans. I wondered if he remembered passing me the cassette, but of course he did. Since I was no longer seated next to Lorrie, it was easier for him and me to lean our heads toward one another and talk. He didn't ask me if I'd listened to the tape. He knew. He said, "Well? What do you think?"

"I think I can't stop listening to that tape," I said. "It doesn't matter if it isn't playing: I'm still hearing it, you know?"

Jude nodded. "Anything . . . else?"

"What do you mean?"

"Have you seen anything?"

"Have I . . . ?" But I had, the robed forms moving past the dance floor at the prom.

Jude caught it in my face. "You did," he said. "What? What did you see? The Black Ocean? The City?"

"People," I said. "I think they were people. They were tall – I mean, seven feet plus – and wearing these costumes, bird masks and long robes. At the prom," I added.

"The Watch," he said. "You saw members of the Goddamned Watch."

"Is that good?"

"As long as they didn't see you – they didn't, did they?"

Did they? "No," I said.

"Then you're fine," he said. "Holy shit. You know you're the first person I've met who actually saw something? Amazing."

"I don't understand," I said. "I'm sorry. I mean, I get that something important has happened – to me – but I don't know what it is."

"It's the music. It thins what's around you, lets you see beyond it."

I had read and watched enough science fiction to think I understood what Jude was talking about. "You mean to another dimension?"

"Sure," he said. "Dimension, plane, iteration, it's all just a way of saying someplace else. Someplace more essential than all of this." He waved his hand to take in the cars, the parking lot, the college, us.

"How— who are these guys? The Subterraneans? How did they do this?"

"I don't know. There are rumors, but they're pretty ridiculous. A lot of bands have messed around with occult material, usually as an occasion for some depraved sex. Fucking Jimmy Page and his sex magic. This is different. These guys are into some crazy mathematics, stuff that goes all the way back to Pythagoras and his followers. What they tried wasn't a complete success. Most of the people I've handed the tape to played it once and ignored it. A few became obsessed with it. Like I said, though, you're the first to see anything."

"Have you?" I said. "You have, haven't you?"

"Twice. Both times, I saw a city. It was huge, spread out along the shore of an ocean for as far as I could see. The buildings looked Greek, or Roman. A lot of them were in ruins, which made the place seem old, ancient. But there were people walking its streets, so I knew it wasn't abandoned. The ocean was immense. Its water was black. Its waves were half as tall as some of the buildings."

"Where is it?" I said. "Do you know what it's called?"

"No." He shook his head. "I spoke to a folklorist over at SUNY Huguenot. He'd heard of the city. He said it was called the Black City – also the Spindle. He thought it was another version of Hell. He was the one who told me about the Watch, the guys in the bird masks. Said you did not want to attract their attention."

"Why not?"

"He didn't spell it out. I'm guessing a fate worse than death."

"Oh."

"They're coming here, you know."

For a second, I thought Jude was referring to the Watch, then I understood he meant the band. "Here? Where?"

"They're playing a show at The Last Chance. Late June, I forget the exact date."

"Are you going to go?"

"Are you kidding? You have to come, too."

"Me?"

"Look at the effect a recording of their material had on you. Imagine what hearing it live could do."

"I don't know." To be honest, I was as worried by the prospect of what your grandparents would say as I was any further visions. Depending on their moods, they had a way of making a request to do something new sound as if it were a personal injury to them.

"You cannot be serious," Jude said. "You're standing on the verge of . . ." He threw up his hands.

"Of what?"

"Does it matter?" he said. "Really? Does it? Even if this place is a district in Hell, isn't that more than you're ever going to find, here?"

I was religious enough for his example to give me pause, but I understood and sympathized with the underlying sentiment. It was what I responded to in The Subterraneans' music in the first place, in so much of the music I liked to listen to, the sense that there was more, to what was outside and to what was inside me. "Let me see," I said.

As it turned out, your grandparents raised no objection to my attending the concert. They ran through the standard questions: Where was it? When was it? Who was I going with? Who was this band? All of which I answered to their satisfaction. Their biggest concern was that I understood I would still have to wake up for church the next morning. I said I did. Having cleared this hurdle, my principle dilemma was whether to invite Adrienne – the girl from the track team, with whom I'd been going out for a couple of weeks. On the one hand, I wasn't sure what I might be exposing her to. On the other hand, she might be angry at not being invited to a concert with me. Yes, my priorities were not what they should have been. I decided to play the tape for her and let her decide for herself. The expression she made when the first note of the first song burst from my car's speakers told me her decision before the song was done: this was not her kind of music. I could have insisted she listen to the remainder of the cassette, but I was relieved she hadn't liked the band and didn't press the issue. It meant I could attend the show with her consent, and without having to worry about her.

This left Jude and myself to be concerned about. Not only did The Subterraneans' music continue to form the soundtrack to my life, to the extent that whatever was taking place around me seemed to occur less for its own sake and more as an illustration, however obscure, of the lyrics of the moment, but I experienced a second vision. It occurred while I was lying on my bed, reading for school (*Waiting for Godot*). The earplug was in my right ear, the cassette nearing its mid-point. Beyond the foot of the bed, where my desk was jammed against the wall, the air darkened, wavered, as if a sheet of black water was descending from the ceiling to the floor. I put down my book and sat up. A figure stepped forward, almost through the water. It was one of the Watch. This close, it was enormous, nearer eight feet than seven, wider than my narrow bed. The beak on the bird mask shone sharp as a scimitar; the glass eyes were black and empty. The mask left uncovered the figure's mouth and jaw, white as fungus. Its body was hidden by a heavy cape covered with overlapping metal feathers, or maybe they were scales. A long moment passed, during which my heart did not beat, before the figure and its watery aperture faded from view. Once I could see my desk again, my heart began hammering so hard I was afraid I was going to vomit. Jude's words, "As long as they didn't see you," sounded in my ears, temporarily drowning out The Subterraneans. What if the Watch saw you? What if one of its members stood at the foot of your bed and leveled the glass eyes of its mask at you? What did that mean?

Nothing good, obviously, something Jude confirmed when I called him. I asked him what the SUNY professor had said about the Watch.

Not much, it seemed. According to him, the Watch dealt with invaders to the City. Don't worry, Jude said, I was probably fine. I said I didn't feel fine. "They're trying to scare you," he said.

"Well, they succeeded," I said. "I'm thinking maybe we should give the show a miss."

"Are you kidding?" he said. "We have to go."

"Did you not just hear the story I told you?"

"What do you think is going to happen if you stay home?" Jude said. "Do you think everything's going to go back to normal? You are inside the music now. We both are."

"And what do you think is going to happen if we go?" I said. "If the music has us, then how will going to its source help us?"

"Listening to the tape started something," Jude said. "It isn't complete. That's why we're catching glimpses of the other place, instead of seeing it whole. If we're in the presence of the actual music, it might finish the process."

As far as logic went, Jude's argument left a lot to be desired. But so did the entire situation. In the end, I decided to attend the concert, after all.

It may have occurred to you to wonder why I didn't share any of this with my parents. As your mom and Steve, Liz and I have done with you, throughout my childhood and adolescence, your grandparents routinely assured me that I could always come to them, there was nothing I couldn't tell them, no matter how bad. I think they meant it, too. The times I had taken them up on their advice, though, had gone less than swimmingly. When I struggled with math or science, your grandfather, who was something of a math prodigy, couldn't understand how what was in front of me wasn't perfectly clear, and had trouble finding the words to explain it to me. When I brought home a failing grade, my protests that I had tried my best were dismissed, because if I had tried my best, then I wouldn't have failed. When I complained of being teased by other kids in school, my parents asked me why I was letting it bother me. From the distance of years – not to mention, the perspective I gained raising you and your little brother – I understand and appreciate that they were doing the best they could, as do most parents. At the time, however, it meant there was no serious chance of me approaching them about what was happening to me. What would I have said? I couldn't stop listening to this tape? I was seeing tall men dressed as birds?

So after I signed out at work on Saturday, 21 June, I drove up Route 9 to Poughkeepsie and The Last Chance. The moon hung full and yellow in a violet sky. I knew the club from the concert calendar the DJs at the local rock station read off twice a day. It had achieved notoriety as the place The Police had played on one of their early US tours – it may have been the first – to an audience of half a dozen people. (There was a snowstorm that night, or so the story goes.) I hadn't been to it, but this was because the bands and singers I wanted to see were playing the Knickerbocker Arena in Albany, or Madison Square Garden to the south. The club reminded me of my high school auditorium, a long, rectangular space overhung by a balcony for about half its length, with a curtained stage at the far end. There was a bar along the back wall, but the fluorescent green band around my wrist restricted me to overpriced Cokes. Underneath where the balcony ended, the floor dropped six inches. A few tables and chairs were positioned around this abbreviated ledge. By the time I arrived, they were occupied by couples in various states of fascination with one another. Maybe fifteen feet in front of the bar, the sound board was illuminated by its own set of lights. A skinny guy who didn't look much older than I was stood holding a pair of head-phones to his right ear while he slid a lever steadily up a slot in the board. Cigarette smoke clouded the air at the bar, where I stopped for a Coke and to survey the club. I was wearing my work clothes; though I had removed my tie; but I didn't stick out as much as I had feared. What audience there was appeared slightly older, college age, and were dressed in jeans and casual shirts. It was easier than I'd anticipated to find Jude, who sighted me at the bar and came over to join me. He was wearing a torn *Anarchy in the UK* T-shirt, camouflage pants, and Doc Martens. His hair stood up like the crest of some tropical bird. I had missed the opening act, he said, but that was no loss. Some guy with long hair whose guitar strings kept breaking; already, Jude had forgotten his name. He guessed the band would be on in another forty-five minutes, maybe an hour.

We passed what was in fact an hour and a half making small talk. Much of it concerned Lorrie and the other people I'd hung out with in the college parking lot. It was gossip, really. Apparently, Lorrie was seeing a guy who'd been a senior at our school. I recognized his name. He'd been in the drama club. I didn't know him, but Jude considered him an asshole. "She should've stuck with you," he said. I thanked him, but told him the decision to break up had been mutual. This was a surprise to him. Yes, I said, I was seeing someone new, too, so really, everything had worked out all right. Despite the music playing in my head, everything seemed normal, mundane. We were a couple of friends out to listen to some live music, discussing our mutual friends. The weirdness that had enveloped me for so many weeks seemed far away, dream-like.

The appearance of The Subterraneans, themselves, bolstered my sense of the ordinary. There were four of them, drummer, keyboardist, guitarist, and lead singer, who strapped on an acoustic guitar which spent the part of the show I saw hanging at his side like a prop. The four of them wore black jeans and plain black T-shirts. Their hair was long, but not so much they couldn't have worked most day jobs. The curtain parted, and they emerged from backstage nonchalantly, picking their way through the cables on the stage to their respective instruments. Without introduction, they started into their first song.

The cassette had given a fair impression of the band's sound. What it had not conveyed was the intense focus with which they performed. In my car, on my bed, listening to the guitar and keyboard clashing with one another, I had imagined a group whose members were struggling for control of whatever they were playing, and I would have predicted a certain amount of tension, if not outright animosity, amongst them. (Think Oasis.) Everything The Subterraneans did, however, was deliberate and smooth, intentional. The antagonism between the pipe-organ keyboard and the surf-rock guitar, the way the singer's voice overrode and was overridden by them, the drums' steady, almost monotonous beat, all were precisely as they were supposed to be. The band finished their first song, and, before the audience had started applauding, slid into the next one. This was the way they acted, as if the club were empty and they were performing for themselves. Maybe they were annoyed at the low turnout for their show; though I had the impression that had the place been filled, they would have behaved in the same manner.

When the band took the stage, my internal soundtrack was about two-thirds of the way through their tape. By the opening notes of the second song, however, my interior music had synchronized with the concert. The sensation was strange, as if I were the margin where two versions of the same song by the same band converged. I kept to the rear of the space in front of the stage. Jude stationed himself at the stage's foot. In such a confined area, the sound was overwhelming, deafening. As The Subterraneans progressed through their set list, the stage lights went from white to a deep blue that had the effect of rendering everything on stage fuzzy at the edges, as if it had slipped out of focus. At the same time, I seemed to hear the music in a way I previously hadn't. The keyboard and guitar weren't fighting; instead, the keyboard's chords were creating a vast space off whose walls the guitar's notes echoed. The drum buttressed the enormous structure, while the singer was the point around which the great architecture arranged itself. A feeling of the sacred – sublime, terrifying – swept through me.

This was the moment the breeze tickled the hairs on my neck, and I turned to witness the alleyway that had replaced the bar. It seems incredible to me that I should have walked toward such a thing, but I couldn't come up with any other response to it. As my feet crossed the floor, I noted the tall forms gathered at the far end of the passage: members of the Watch, there to meet any trespass. Air moved over my face, filling my nostrils with the damp smell of the sea. My body felt curiously light.

Then Jude shouldered past me and strode to the edge of the worn cobblestones. There, he stopped and glanced over his shoulder to see if

I was coming. I wanted to, but it was as if his contact with me had robbed me of my ability to move. Not to mention, the Watch had shifted into the alley proper, and there was something about the way they moved, a kind of liquid quality, as if they were ink rather than flesh, that filled my stomach with dread. I hesitated. Jude did not. He turned to the passage and crossed its threshold. I took one step, two, closer. The keyboard's solo rang off the alley's walls. Jude must have seen the black figures drawing nearer, but he did not alter his pace. The Watch allowed him to reach the halfway point of the alley – it may have been a border they had to observe – before they took him. One second, they were ten, fifteen yards from Jude; the next, they encircled him. It was like watching a group of snakes, of eels, slither around their prey. Jude looked from side to side, his eyes wide, his mouth moving. I couldn't hear what he was saying, nor could I read his lips. The guitar echoed up the alleyway. The members of the Watch raised their cloaks; although it looked more as if their cloaks raised themselves. Their masks rippled, the beaks lengthening, the eyes melting into them. Jude lifted his hand, begging for more time, perhaps, asking them to hear whatever else it was he had to say. The Watch fell on him. His hand kept its position amidst the black swirling around the rest of him. I could swear I heard high, hysterical laughter, worse, it was Jude's. I ran for the alley, but it was already gone.

Instead, I collided with one of the bouncers, who was first annoyed with my clumsiness, then panicked by my shouting about what had happened to my friend. Drugs, I'm sure he thought. He ejected me from the club, and told me to get lost before he called the cops. I did, because I couldn't think of what else to do. I'm not sure how I made the drive home. The following morning, after rising for church with my family, I claimed a bad stomach and spent the day in bed. I was exhausted, but I couldn't fall asleep for any length of time. The image of those tall figures lifting their cloaks, their masks flowing into blades like scythes, would not leave me. When I did sleep, I dreamed of crows, hunched around some poor, pale thing, their beaks poised to strike. I was horrified, by what I'd seen and was certain had happened to Jude, and by the prospect of his parents, or worse, the police, showing up at the front door and asking me what I knew about his disappearance. Alongside my horror, guilt gnawed at me. I wasn't responsible for Jude's fate, not directly, but I hadn't done anything to stop it, had I? Probably a lawyer could argue the case for my innocence, but I knew better. I was complicit in what had befallen my friend.

Secretly, I wanted the cops to ring the doorbell. I wanted to confess my role in the events at The Last Chance and be punished. For all my disagreements with the Church over the years, I have always granted it the power of the sacrament of Confession, and the penance that accompanies the rite. It's what the law provides, or can provide, on the secular side of things. No police appeared, however. If Jude's parents knew he'd intended to meet me at the club, they chose not to follow up on it. I actually went to Confession the next Saturday, but after listening to an abbreviated version of what I've written here, the priest gave me a prolonged lecture on the perils of drug use. Had I attempted the same thing with your grandparents, the result would have been approximately the same.

I considered trying to find my way back to that alley; though I'm not sure what I thought I would find. Jude's remains? Evidence he was still alive, held captive in some alien prison? Whatever I hoped for, the other world was closed off to me. In the days after the concert, I realized that The Subterraneans' music was no longer playing its endless loop in my mind. When I listened to the cassette, the songs refused to stay in my memory. In the weeks to come, as the summer unfolded, I continued to play the tape, hoping the air in front of me would waver, and I would once again see the alleyway opening in front of me. It appeared Jude had been right, though. Whatever had been started by the recording of the band's music had been completed by its live performance. Eventually, the week before my senior year was to begin, the cassette unspooled in my car's tape deck, and was so badly damaged as to be unplayable, its songs lost to me.

For years afterward, every time I was in a record store, I kept my eyes open for a copy of The Subterraneans' tape. At the same time, I was on the lookout for information on the band, itself, who its members were, where they were located. I had no luck with either search. Last year, I spent a couple of days researching the band and its music online, but found little of any use.

As for Jude: at the start of senior year, I joined Lorrie for lunch in the senior lounge. We exchanged pleasantries about our respective summers, the classes we would be taking. I turned the conversation to Jude. How was he doing? I asked. Oh, she said, no one had seen him around for a while. Supposedly, he'd left for Boston, which he'd been talking about doing for years. Boston, I said. Yeah, she said. He wasn't very happy here. He had a lot of stuff going on at home. Well, I said, wherever he was, I hoped he was happier. "I doubt it," Lorrie said. "Some people just aren't, you know?"

I said I did.

As I told you at the outset, I've never shared this story with anyone, not your mother, not Liz. Maybe I shouldn't have with you. If it's easier – if I send this letter to you – you can trash it, pretend I answered your question in some other, innocuous way. That might be better. I'm not sure what more there is to say about any of it. That is, except for the questions I still can't answer.

Love,
Dad

For Fiona, and for JoAnn Cox

Simon Strantzas says of "Alexandra Lost": "The story may take its title from Leonard Cohen, but it takes its trappings from old Howard Phillips. I found myself thinking of 'The Case of Charles Dexter Ward' and of the essential salts that so many are reduced to in that tale, and I began to wonder about how much salt there was in the world, and the part it played. There's an inevitability in 'Alexandra Lost' as there is in the best of Lovecraft, and a suspicion that we are all cast in a play we don't know the ending to, and our lines are being written by something beyond our comprehension. I hoped to explore that here, while also drilling into the head of someone who has never been anything but lost. Perhaps it's that, the sense of never belonging, that cuts most to the heart of Lovecraft. All I can say for sure is it cuts most to the heart of me."

The author of four collections of weird and strange fiction, including the Shirley Jackson Award-nominated *Burnt Black Suns* (Hippocampus Press), Simon Strantzas is also the editor of *Aickman's Heirs* (Undertow Publications), *Shadow's Edge* (Gray Friar Press), and guest editor of *The Year's Best Weird Fiction, Vol. 3*. His writing has been reprinted in various "best of" anthologies; has been translated into other languages; and has been nominated for the British Fantasy Award. He lives with his wife in Toronto, Ontario.

Alexandra Lost
Simon Strantzas

————

The sunlight through the windshield bounced and refracted, filling Alexandra Leaving's eyes with wriggling stars. Leonard drove his Chevrolet across upstate New York with his foot pressed firmly to the floor, and though she pleaded with him to slow down, he met her protests with further, more dangerous weaving. She eventually stopped asking, and instead kept her eyes focused on the map.

"How much longer do you figure before we reach the coast?" he said.

She checked the clock.

"It's about ten hours from Buffalo, but we hit that traffic so now I have no idea."

The map in her hands was the most important thing she owned. She clung to it: her tether as she drifted out into the unknown. She would not use a GPS – technology could not be trusted to tell her where she was going. Only a paper map made sense, something on which she could chart their route, drawing for hours before they left. Every hour on the page marked; she knew where they were supposed to be each step of the way. Her father had become lost when she was seven; lost and never found. She was terrified the same might happen to her. Having their journey carefully plotted made her feel safer. But she hadn't anticipated how fast Leonard would drive, and how that speed would compromise the work she'd done. "We'll get there faster," he assured her, but it was impossible – they didn't have a clear idea where they were. If they missed the ramp to the next highway, she worried they would never realize it and simply drive on forever.

"There's an end to the highway," Leonard said, reading her thoughts. "As long as we keep driving we'll get there. At the end of every highway there's an ocean waiting to be found."

She smiled, anxious. For a moment, she forgot how much of a mistake she'd made. For a moment, she remembered why she'd let Leonard take her so far from home. She did it for him. To prove that despite the anxieties and worries that clouded her head, she was good enough for him – even if she didn't believe it. When he realized she had never seen the ocean, he spontaneously decided he had to take her, and she pretended she was spontaneous enough to go.

"I read this article about a couple who just flew off to Europe for a few months without packing anything but their phones and a charger," she said, explaining all the research she'd done before they left. She saw his lip quiver, but she wasn't sure of the cause. "They bought new toothbrushes wherever they went, washed their clothes in strangers' houses, and just met as many people as they could. It was like there was this whole world of people working together to help them get by. It was surprising."

"Surprising, how?"

"I don't know," she said. She ran her hand over her shorts to dry it. "I guess I asked myself if I'd do the same – if I'd help a stranger like that."

"I think you probably would."

She didn't say anything. She wanted to believe he was right even if it sounded unlikely. But more importantly, she wanted him to continue believing that sort of thing about her. It was important he not know what kind of things dwelt within her head. He wouldn't understand. No one had ever really understood. Not her father when he was around, and certainly not her mother once he was gone. "My little lost girl" was what he'd called her as he held her tight in his arms. They sat in their warm backyard as the sun set earlier each summer day. "My little lost girl," he said, and squeezed her the way no one had squeezed her since. And she didn't know what he meant, not until he was gone. Then she knew the feeling well.

She looked out the window at the passing scenery. She and Leonard had not spoken in some time, and she liked the quiet rhythm of the wheels on the road. Between the Chevrolet and the horizon the grass dipped and sloped upward, and tiny farms dotted the distant landscape. Farther still lay a series of hills obscuring what lay beyond. All she knew of that land was it was occupied by giants. Wind turbines, more that a dozen in a row and sprouting upward, blades moving in slow endless circles. They stood so far away that Alexandra could not fully grasp their enormity.

"You can tell how big they are by their spin," Leonard said. "If they were closer, the blades would be moving a lot slower. Those turbines are huge – you just can't tell how huge things are from so far away."

"I can *feel* how huge they are, though, if that makes any sense. They make my head loopy."

* * *

They almost missed the ramp onto the interstate. Unending miles of highway banked with forest, giant trees too thick to see between, covered in oranges and reds and golds like a burning sunset. Alexandra felt insignificant beside them, no better than the insects crushed against the Chevrolet's windshield. When those trunks petered out, she saw, in the distance, the glint of cars moving away.

Her map – she needed to consult her map.

There, the forest was demarcated with a faint brown line, and almost upon it the blue ink of her pen where she'd traced their route onward. She looked from the map, afraid it was too late, and saw the green sign on the shoulder pass in an instant, hanging branches covering its warning. The ramp was imminent.

"Here. You want this exit here!"

"What?" Leonard slurred as though awoken from a dream. Alexandra watched the exiting lanes rush toward them. Panic seized her.

"This is it! This is the ramp. Take it. Take it. Take it."

Leonard snapped awake, pulled the wheel hard after the marked lanes had already split. A symphony of honks trailed, and the Chevrolet shook from the forces pulling it in multiple directions. Alexandra was flung aside as the car wrenched itself into the proper lane, and as Leonard tried to straighten its path, the tail began to wag. He spun the wheel all the way to the left, then again all the way to the right, trying to keep the car from skidding as the horns blared louder. Back and forth, back and forth, the tail swung until finally, with only a minor tremor, he regained control over the car. He accelerated away from the complaining motorists.

Once safely out of danger, Leonard turned with another grin.

"I hope we didn't go the wrong way," he said.

Alexandra did not understand Leonard's obsession with the ocean. He hadn't been born on a coast; he had lived in the same small dry town as Alexandra long before she met him. The ocean never arose during their courtship's early months, and why would it? It was not typical dinner conversation. And yet, he seemed aghast when she reveled in passing that she had never seen the ocean herself. His dumb silence eventually gave way to incredulity, and it was from that point that his dreams became consumed with taking her there.

"Wait until you see it," he promised. "It's so immense you'll feel completely insignificant."

The idea terrified her.

Water was never something Alexandra was comfortable around. Small amounts of it for cooking and bathing didn't bother her, but once the bodies became larger – fountains, pools, lakes – her anxiety increased. It wasn't a phobia – she did not fear water like some feared snakes or spiders – but instead it seemed to whisper to her whenever she was close. The words were too quiet to make out, but they left her with an unfathomable urge to submit herself to it. To walk bare-footed into the waves and let them consume her. Mind. Body. Soul. The water unnerved her because the water wanted her submission, wanted her to lose herself to its power, and the sensation that swirled in her head was as suffocating as any drowning.

They pulled off the interstate for dinner at a small unnamed restaurant, dark branches draping over its burnt-out sign. Alexandra folded her map carefully and placed it in her bag where it would be safe at hand. Leonard watched her, the hint of amusement twitching in his lips, but said nothing. When she stepped from the car Alexandra realized the parking lot was nearly empty, and inside the restaurant, it seemed no more than three of its dark wooden tables were occupied. The rest had places set and menus out, prepared for occupation by a host of souls who would never arrive. When the teenage hostess finally greeted Alexandra and Leonard, her hair tied in a tight bun against the back of her head, Leonard immediately asked where all the customers were. The girl shrugged as she marked their table off her list.

"I guess not as many families are traveling right now since it's so close to school."

Leonard nodded, satisfied, but the hostess didn't wait long enough to see it.

She sat them in a booth by the window. Alexandra saw the western sky and the sun change color like autumn leaves.

"I still can't believe you've never been to the ocean," Leonard said over his menu, not lifting his eyes from the rows of barbecued meat and pasta. "You've never felt the urge? Not even once?"

She shook her head.

"It's never really been a priority, I guess. I've never been much of a traveler."

"Wow, that's amazing. I feel like I'd be happy if all I did was travel. You know: get on a plane and hop from one place to another – like that couple in the story you told me about earlier. Maybe stick around for a few days. When I was just out of school, I took a trip around Europe. It was fantastic!"

She nodded, not sure how to explain that she'd never felt the same drive. The idea left her queasy. Already, she felt so lost, so untethered, that the only way she could hang on was to surround herself with the familiar, the comfortable. At home, she knew where her favorite restaurants were, where to get the clothes she liked. At home, she knew how far it was to the office and how long it took her to get back in the evening. At home, she was safe, and the constant gnawing fear that seemed so much worse at night, in the dark, behind her closed eyes – that fear that she was anything but safe, adrift in the void of the unfathomable universe – was a muted shout from deep within. The terrors squirmed inside of her, but she was able to keep them contained.

Leonard couldn't understand. He clearly *enjoyed* the sensation.

"What's great about Europe is how old everything is." He looked at her, but his eyes saw something more. "We don't have that same sense of history here. You walk around a European city, you *feel* part of how ancient everything is. It's all stood for so long you begin to wonder if it was there before there were people to see it. The old world is so close at hand, yet it's so distant and unknowable. You walk by buildings with the most beautiful and ornate carvings – even those half in ruin – and they seem so impossible. Yet, there they stand, and *have* stood through riots, revolts, and marches; man has done so many things by uniting into a single force, both for good and evil. It's amazing to be in touch with all of that."

"I've always thought about going," Alexandra lied, "but I've just never done it. Maybe one day."

"We should totally go. I'd love to show you around. I think you'd really get a kick out of it."

She smiled. Then the waitress arrived with their drinks.

"Are you sure this is right?"

They'd driven for an hour after leaving the restaurant, and in that time traffic had thinned and the dark orange sun had reached the horizon. The encroaching dusk only heightened her panicked anxiety.

"I don't know," she said. "We're still in upstate New York, but I can't figure out where. Nothing matches the map." Worries swam in her head in frenzy, and she couldn't stop herself from feeling she'd made horrendous mistake in her calculation, and her precious map was wrong. If that were true, she truly was adrift, and the feeling of the earth widening around her made her limbs stiffen, her breath wheeze. If Leonard feared the same, his face did not betray it, covered as it was by deepening shadows.

"Maybe it's time to pull over for the night. We can't be that far from the coast – maybe a few hours? Let's stop at a motel and get a new start tomorrow when we have light."

It took another twenty minutes to find a motel, and by that time the highway was so dark the motel's glowing red sign shone brighter than the moon. Leonard pulled into the parking lot, and helped Alexandra out of the car. After traveling for so long, she felt unsteady, as though her body was still hurtling forward along the highway, and it took a few steps before she saw the world through human eyes again.

The man behind the counter couldn't have been more than eighteen, his face spotted and blotched, his curly hair shaved near the temples. He was courteous, but he was bored and tired and went through the motions because he had to. Even when, for her peace of mind if nothing else, Alexandra asked him to show her where on the map the hotel was, he did so with a vague point, and wouldn't be pressed to do more. He seemed more interested in whatever he'd been doing as they arrived, and when she looked over the reception desk partition while he entered Leonard's name into the computer, she saw textbooks lying spine-flat beside the phone. The titles were upside down, but the pictures looked like star charts.

"So you *do* know something about maps. Are you studying astronomy?"

He didn't bother looking away from the computer screen. He simply and unceremoniously slid his open notebook to cover the page. She looked at Leonard, who shrugged nervously but said nothing to the boy. Alexandra hated herself for backing down. She even thanked the boy when he gave them the key.

Later, in the motel room, she remained fuming at the small wooden desk, trying to retrace the route on her map. All the lines looked the same to her, all the roads feeding into the highway like rivulets. Leonard off-handedly dismissed her unhappiness.

"He was probably worried you were from head office or something, checking to make sure he was doing paid work and not school work."

"I don't know," she said, looking from her map as he buttoned his shirt. "It didn't *feel* like that's what he was worried about."

"Well, what else could it be?"

She didn't know. And, she supposed Leonard was right. It didn't matter. "All that matters is that we're here, together," he said. He ran his fingers through her hair and she put down her pen and looked at him. She touched the side of his warm face, felt the stubble scratch her fingers. He took her hand.

The room was small. The only other furniture was the uncomfortable queen-sized bed, and its springs creaked with each small movement. Leonard suggested they move the blankets onto the floor, where it was quieter, and it was lying there that he moved his hand under the front of her nightshirt and placed it on her bare breast. He then lifted himself onto his other arm and placed his mouth over hers.

He tasted of salt, but mixed with the sweetness of his saliva Alexandra didn't mind. His tongue found hers, invading her mouth tentatively, and the flesh was rough and soft and made the hairs along the back of her neck stand. Her mind drifted for a moment, swaying as though in a dream, and she had to focus herself to remain in the present with Leonard and not recede into her crowded thoughts.

Leonard's face twisted as he pushed into her, as though willing himself to occupy the same physical space, to join with her on a quantum level. Yet though she bit her lip and arched her back, and though she felt her flesh warm to the point of fire, she felt herself powerlessly being pulled away from him all the same, cast backward into her mind, a powerless witness to events unfolding. Leonard's breath hitched, his brow knitted, he cried some unintelligible word, and she felt the warmth of him flooding into her, coursing through her body like an violent tide, reaching each extremity. Her fingers vibrated, her scalp raised. Leonard continued thrusting afterward, but she couldn't tell for how long while lost in her muddled head. When he finally rolled off, out of breath, she had returned to the surface of her thoughts, and felt aching sadness, but she did her best to throttle it as he perched his head on his bent arm and brushed the hair from her face with the other. He said it was so he could see her better, but she saw nothing in the dark.

"Are you enjoying the trip so far?"

"I think so," she said. "I like that we're doing it together. I don't think I could have done it alone."

It wasn't until she spoke the words that she realized how true they were. Her father's leaving had done more to keep her tied down than anything else, and she had succumbed until she was no different than those giant shadows of slow-spinning blades she and Leonard seen fixed to the horizon, in motion yet unmoving. They were the reason she let Leonard take her away from where it was safe. If she didn't try to rebel against the sickness she felt the farther from home she traveled, he would surely be the next person lost to her. So she followed him into the unknown, with only her thin overdrawn map as protection, and did her best to endure.

Leonard stroked her hair as the two lay in the dark of the motel room. He whispered to her encouragingly, trying to ease her terror, and she struggled to concentrate on what he said and not get lost in her own anxieties.

"I keep thinking about how much you're going to love the ocean. You'll absolutely freak when you see it – especially if we take a boat out to watch the whales. I went once before with a—well, she was a girl I knew. It was a few years ago. Anyway, going out on the ocean is a trip, pure and simple." He paused, uncertain he should continue, giving her a chance to ask about who that other woman was. She wondered how many women he'd taken there, how many before her had there been. But Alexandra was succumbing to the warmth of his touch, and his droning voice. She didn't want to disturb it by speaking.

"Even if you don't see any whales, you see all sorts of other crazy things. When I was out there, I just happened to be on the boat with a marine biologist, and she pretty much became the *de facto* tour guide for us. There was this school of fish . . . Have you ever seen a huge school of fish before? Maybe on television? It was larger than that. It was massive. All those sleek black bodies slicing through the water, all moving as one." He moved his hand away as if to illustrate the size, but even if it weren't too dark to see, Alexandra did not open her eyes. "They say the reason a school of fish can react so quickly is because they act together, each fish part of a single super-mind. They're much more of a hive than bees are, I think. The school stretched out so far I couldn't see its edges, as though they encompassed the sea – millions of lithe bodies becoming one giant creature beneath the waves – all sharing a single thought, all using a single voice. It was so beautiful. I really hope we get to do that – go out on the water. You have no idea what it's like!"

Leonard's disembodied voice continued whispering nonsense to her in the dark. It was warm and comforting, so she let him ramble on as the day's journey finally found her.

* * *

In her dreams, she and Leonard drove the length of an extended high-way bridge, flanked on both sides by endless water. The wheels hummed as they passed over the asphalt, so filling the car with volume she heard nothing else. Not the radio, not Leonard beside her, not the black shapes that crested the water's turbulent surface before submerging once more. She heard nothing but the teeth-gnashing drone. Even her shouts were inaudible over the noise. Lost and panicked, she felt they'd been driving that road forever. They were moving too fast, and when she looked down she saw her own foot pressing the pedal to the floor of the car. Reflexively, she lifted it, and the throbbing in her head intensi-fied in response. The only way to quell her nausea was to press the pedal harder, move faster, burn along the solitary bridge. She looked beside her but the passenger seat was empty; she alone was driving. She alone was crying. And she drove. And drove. And drove.

And she did not wake well rested. She felt drained; her swollen, tired eyes nearly impossible to open. At some point before morning Alexandra had moved into the bed, dragging a single blanket with her, and from beneath it she watched Leonard perform his morning rituals. She rolled her sour tongue and wished she had some water, though the notion of drinking anything made her ill.

"Good morning," Leonard said. "I'm pretty much ready if you want to hop in the shower now."

"I think I might lie here a bit longer. I'm not ready to get up yet."

"Er . . . okay," he said. "But we've got to check-out, so don't leave it too long."

"Why? I thought we had until eleven."

He stopped his preparations to look at her. "What time do you think it is?"

She rolled over and checked the display on her cell phone. The digits didn't immediately make sense. How could it be nearly half-past ten?

"Why did you let me sleep so long?"

"Let you? How was I supposed to stop you? You wouldn't budge this morning. That must have been some dream."

Fragments surfaced in her memory, flashes of that expansive body, the foreboding of what lay ahead. She felt restless and agitated, possessed by a tension nearly at its limit

"Yeah, it was pretty crazy," she said, then stretched her arms as far as she could and sat up. The discomfort in her head worsened. "Ugh. I feel horrible."

"Take your shower. You'll feel better once we eat."

She rubbed her palms against her face, doubtful.

Out the Chevrolet's window the trees had returned, though they kept a cautious distance from the highway. Leaves slipped off in the breeze in a steady stream, golds and scarlets in long spiraling chains through the air. Alexandra and Leonard continued eastward, and with each mile traveled the tether Alexandra felt tightening since she awoke, the tether to her home in the dry country, stretched thinner and thinner. Staring out the window, trying to keep her eyes open while her skull tightened, she felt something like a soft pop, and her vision filled with light. Somewhere ahead, somewhere distant, somewhere future, a soft gentle roar echoed. The waves, the surf, the vastness. Leonard was right. There was power in the ocean. She heard its whisper for the first time, urging her onward. Fingers wriggling inside her head.

"How long before we get there?" she asked. Her condition hadn't improved since waking, but the discomfort had become a dull ache behind her eyes. Her mouth parched, head throbbing, she did her best to hide it from Leonard.

"Only a few hours. Maybe two? You're the one with the map."

She nodded and looked down at it, but the brightness of the sun seemed to flare, and no matter how she squinted she couldn't see the lines she had drawn. Everything was escaping, fluttering into the ether, and no matter how desperately she tried to catch and draw it back they merely slithered through her fingers.

"I know you have everything plotted out," Leonard said, nodding his head toward her without taking his eyes from the road or the cars he was weaving among, "but it's amazing how much has come back to me. I remember that hill over there—" He pointed off to the left at a large incline, the peak of which was a new horizon across the cloudless sky; "—and how shadows moved across it. This place, where we are right at this second, is so beyond real that I can barely process it. Some people say there are extra senses? This must be what they're talking about, because I can sense how much we belong together, on this journey, right now."

Alexandra nodded, though barely understood him as he continued. The pain rattling through her skull intensified. But instead of dulling and distancing her from reality, it drew the world into sharper focus. The rush of the ocean a hundred miles away echoed in her crowded head, quelling her lifelong displacement and isolation. The car traveled quicker toward the coast, quicker than she'd thought possible, and while Leonard spoke Alexandra's eyes returned to the over-bright map crumpled in her hands that was coming into focus. The folds condensed the lines she had plotted, shortening the distance between where their trip had begun and their final destination. The truth of the journey slipped into focus, and Alexandra finally understood. Eased of the nag of dislocation, the knowledge of where she was – of *when* she was – became clear. And it felt *good* to finally understand. Beneath the discomfort of her throbbing head she wondered if that was how the rest of the world felt. Present. Aware.

Cars whizzed past as the Chevrolet raced across the highway, barely slowing for the austere toll booths. Leonard's face was serene in the bathing sunlight, while Alexandra's was covered by jittering hands working her throbbing temples. When the pain became too unbearable, Alexandra asked if they could pull into a rest stop so she could use the washroom, and there she splashed water on her face and took some chalky tablets, but the endeavor did nothing. She remained in excruciating pain, and yet was terrified Leonard might stop if he learned the truth. The risk was near incalculable, so instead, with the taste of bland chalk still on her tongue, she smiled and told him everything was fine. But even as she did she barely saw his face behind the stars that had gathered in her vision. His muted voice asked her twice if she were okay, and Alexandra responded with forced casualness. She hoped she didn't look as pale as her reflection in the washroom mirror has suggested, or speak with the slur she certainly heard. But if Leonard noticed either, he was too polite to say, and they were soon back in the car speeding toward the ocean.

The highway signs increased with the amount of traffic, forcing them to slow down, but it was clear they were closing in on the coast. Commuters clogged the lanes beneath a sun risen to near its height, and the heat in the car steadily increased. Leonard seemed unbothered, but Alexandra had to remove her jacket and cardigan in an effort to cool down. The spasms in her head multiplied.

"The earliest we can check into the hotel is three o'clock, so we might as well go to the ocean first. There a little town off the water called Bearskin Point that would be perfect. It's where I caught the whale-watching boat, so we can find out when it runs as well."

Alexandra's headache knotted itself, but she kept her face calm. "Sure," she said. It was all she could manage without betraying distress.

After a time, Leonard stopped asking questions as he navigated the merging highways to Bearskin Point. Alexandra looked down at her map through squinting eyes as the lines contorted and skewed. Each time she thought the car was off-course, a landmark passed suggesting the opposite. She asked Leonard how he knew where he was going.

"I don't. I'm just following the signs." But even with the throb in her head, she knew there were no such signs. The map had been important until then, the foundation on which she'd been able to survive for so long. But the ocean, too, called to her, its quiet voice growing, and she didn't know which she could trust.

Leonard drove on with unerring confidence, at once quieter and more intense. Alexandra's face was turned out the side window, watching passing cars drag boats away from closed summer homes, her face grimaced in pain. She had traveled too far from home, her tether stretched near its breaking point, and as Leonard drove faster that tether continued to stretch thinner still.

She asked herself why she didn't speak up, why she suffered quietly. Racing thoughts screamed something was wrong, but they were buried deep in a tangle of pain, slipping away with every second the Chevrolet closed in on the vast ocean. She had spent so many years – too many years – cooped in her small dry town, never moving beyond its imaginary walls, a bird in a cage. It was only as she approached the Atlantic and felt the difference in the air, the openness in the contrasted sky, that she began to suspect there were bars.

She had never felt so untethered, and it was terrifying. And yet, for all her freedom, she felt anything but lost. Her map was clenched to her chest, a symbol of her clarity; her life *was* the map, laid out in an exact path, the end-point of its journey set. The inevitability was itself a structure to which she was bound and soothed, and she felt no more in control of it than a bottle in the surf.

The transition from highway to street was seamless, and from there to side road even more so. Leonard guided the car through turns and stop signs without once stepping on the brakes. The tires squealed with each jerk of the wheel, and the momentum reignited Alexandra's disguised pains, but she bore through them. Despite the pull back to where she had come from, back to where her father had stroked her hair one last time before becoming lost for good, she was convinced that her freedom lay in seeing the ocean, that it was only that sight, witnessed until then solely in dreams, that would ultimately and finally find herself. Leonard had to be right. Once she was able to stand in the water and look eastward toward where the sun emerged, she would finally stop running away from the world, and stop being afraid of running toward something better. On facing that immensity, her longing pains would reach their end.

Bearskin Point appeared no different than any small town she had seen, but Alexandra's head swam so that she no longer trusted her vision. Behind the white and grey façades, she saw a large shape loom, its wide wings stretched outward, but in an instant the shape dispersed, the clouds that comprised it pushed apart by warm winds.

Leonard drove the car slowly along the short road to Bearskin Point, passing small stores with local crafts and paintings displayed in the dark store front windows, the warped glass reflecting strange shapes and colors moving. No one walked the abandoned road, and Alexandra wondered if she and Leonard were the only travelers left in the world. A sharp pain punctuated the thought – a charge through her head that Alexandra was unable to contain. The smallest moan emerged.

"Not much farther," Leonard said.

Bearskin Point was a small circular outcropping into the ocean. Despite her draw toward it, Alexandra traveled the remainder with eyes closed, struggling to contain her encroaching delirium. Her tether was stretched to a thin gossamer thread, and she felt every tug on it, every twang. With clenched, bloodless fingers around the car door handle, she felt beads of sweat slip down her neck, steam off her chest. That thread was so taught, so painful, that it blocked the vision from her eyes. Blind, her body felt it continuous motion, falling into the depths of nothing, fading from a spiraling world of teeming shadows.

"We're here!"

Leonard's voice jarred her awake. She opened her eyes, though initially wasn't certain she had.

She stepped out of the car onto her shaking leg. Leonard rushed to help, but she remained upright, never prying her eyes from what was laid out before her. All pain and discomfort forgotten.

"It's . . ." She couldn't think of words to follow.

The surface of the water stretched outward, encompassing the horizon. There was nothing else; only a line that met the clouded sky. It seemed unreal, the dark contrast of elements separated by that thin sliver; it went on and on forever. And, yet, there was something else out there, something more, moving toward them. She could not see it, but it was coming. Something large.

"Leonard, can you—" she looked at the wasteland of rocks between her and the water. "Will you help me down to the beach? I don't think I can do it alone."

"Yes," he said, and held out his hand.

They took the first step onto the rocks together, then one at a time as he led her down to the ocean's edge. With each successive step, she looked at the water's calm surface, knowing what was out there was ever closer.

"Careful you don't get your foot trapped," Leonard said. "These rocks can be dangerous."

"Okay," she said.

It took ten minutes to reach the edge of the water, and when Alexandra's foot first sank into the wet sand she felt an electric jolt travel through her. The air smelled as it did after a thunderstorm, wet and cold, and the standing hairs sent shivers over her arms. All sound ceased; she simply existed, as much a part of that place as were the rocks and sand and air. As much as the water and everything moving under its surface. She was at one with everything as she had never been before. Not in her own home, not in the arms of her father, not beneath any lover or among any friends. She struggled for a word that described it all, but as soon as she had it, it was gone, swimming away.

She released Leonard's hand and stepped forward, each foot leaving a fading print in the wet sand. She stepped to the lapping edge of the ocean and then continued onward – the water rising first to her ankle, then to her knee, then halfway up her thigh. She stood alone in the water, watching the endless horizon, waiting for what was to come.

It did not take long.

She doubled over, unable to keep upright as waves of excruciating pain traveled from the frigid water around her legs. Leonard stood behind her – somewhere on the land or perhaps holding her, she couldn't be sure – and she tried to scream but no words emerged. Or, if they did, they were inaudible over the rushing sound of the surf churning beneath her. It was as though she were being lanced by a burning metal rod forced though her skull one inch at a time, burning hotter the further it traveled. Her head was thick with pressure, and behind her tightly squeezed lids stars refracted and filled her vision. There were shapes in the endless field, enormous masses that moved in the distance, eldritch things that watched from the depths of a between-space she only now saw was connected to the ocean, the primal force of the drowning earth. And behind them all she saw *him* on the horizon, elephantine arms reaching out to draw her in close. Alexandra forced her eyes open, unable to bear any more, and the tears rushed forward, falling into the water. There, in the waves, each transformed into a silvery-sleek creature that darted away. More tears fell, more creatures darted, as though a tear between worlds had opened behind her eyes, and through it fell children of another place, all of whom were streaming toward the great thing that approached from out in the distant depths, something no doubt older than the earth, than even those ancient things behind her watering eyes. They swam forward in the churning ocean and she didn't know why, didn't know what it all meant, didn't know where Leonard was or how many times he'd been there before, or when she had been impregnated with the horror. So many questions, burning inside her cracking head, so many tears falling she could not stop, and she prayed the pain would end and that she could once more be blind to the foulness she was a portal for. But she knew it would not happen; she knew it was too late. Whatever was inside her, whatever emerged from the beyond, would not stop until she was consumed, transformed from flesh and blood back to the essential salts that had formed her, left to mix and dilute, returning home at last to find herself within the great ocean of tears beneath which some unfathomable future approached.

Yoon Ha Lee first discovered H. P. Lovecraft's writings in a collection in his high school library. "I was fascinated by the strong sense of place, particularly the creepy, inward-facing nature of the communities (human or otherwise) he described. I wasn't so impressed by the Cthulhu mythos' One Ones' indifference – not even malevolence, just indifference – to beings so far beneath their notice, because I was all too used to reading astronomy books and the universe is a big place that probably doesn't notice me. In a sense, I feel that human indifference is worse because there is a conscious choice involved. 'Falcon-and-Sparrows' takes place in what I think of as the rural Koreanish equivalent of that setting, and describes the destruction of history by an uncaring force that people have bowed to – when they don't have to."

Lee's first collection, *Conservation of Shadows*, was published by Prime Books. His fiction has appeared in *Tor.com*, *Clarkesworld*, *The Magazine of Fantasy & Science Fiction*, and other venues. He lives in Louisiana with his family and has not yet been eaten by gators.

Falcon-and-Sparrows
Yoon Ha Lee

After the first shock of my mother's death wore off, I traveled to Falcons Crossing. It was only two days' journey by train – the Kheneiran Peninsula is not large – and I hardly noticed the small discomforts of travel.

My mother had come from a tiny village near Falcons Crossing. I had not first heard of the town from my mother, due to her reluctance to talk about her past. I'd learned of my mother's origins from an unfinished letter I had found in her room. To my frustration, she had not addressed it to anyone by name, only a diffident honorific. I had brought it with me, tucked into my coat.

Now I looked out the window of the train. You could scarcely tell there had been a civil war in the past generation. Cranes stood like pale slivers in the rice paddies; if I had been outside, I would have heard the deafening chorus of frogs. I almost wished I could stay on the train forever. I would reach my destination in a few more hours, however.

My mother had never spoken of what had led her to have an affair with a foreign soldier. Even as a child I had only dared to ask once. Seeing her go white had convinced me never to mention it again. Yet she had kept a silver bracelet he had given her, so I always hoped that there had been some thread of affection between them. I never found out whether it was true that he had died in the unrest following the war that divided the Kheneiran Peninsula, or if he had abandoned her for some wife back in Ulo.

The bracelet was not the only gift my father had given her. Another Ulowen soldier, one of a contingent left behind to discourage a second outbreak of war, had told me that my father had secured my mother a job as a secretary at the military outpost. My mother was quick with languages, and her Ulowen cursive had precise, beautiful swells and flourishes. It wasn't until I was older that I figured out this meant my mother, cast out by her own family, didn't have to prostitute herself to bored Ulowen soldiers.

The other consequence of my father's odd thoughtfulness was that my mother had ready access to paper. She often brought home flyers and memoranda that the Ulowen had no further use for. As a child, she had learned paper-folding. She taught me the mountain and valley folds, the trick of buffing a crease with my fingernail so it became crisp. She guided me in everything from simple boats to lilies whose petals could be curled gracefully with the aid of a chopstick or pencil.

While the variety of objects that can be emulated in paper is limited only by the skill and imagination of the artist, the one that fascinated me the most was the humble glider. I began with the simplest designs and later experimented with more outlandish ones with asymmetrical wings or flaps. Most of them flew drunkenly when they flew at all.

This brings us to the matter of Falcons Crossing. For many years I had thought little of it. But Kheneira's Royal Historians – back in the days when there was a crown, anyway – had archives going back almost seven hundred years. During the civil war, some of those archives had been evacuated from the then-capital to Falcons Crossing because it was far removed from the front lines. Then the capital fell to West Kheneira, and no one ever got around to moving the archives to some more illustrious location.

The National Archives were not my specific interest, even if I had heard of them. Rather, the migrations were.

As I grew in years, I had participated in the new capital's migrations – what we called the glider contests. My mother, bemused, had given me her encouragement.

Even today I don't know what had led East Kheneira's Cultural Preservation Council to choose the migrations as a designated cultural treasure. But the contests were held every year, not just in the capital, but in a number of towns. Glider artists from Falcons Crossing dominated the contests. I was not the only one to study their methods, desperate for some hint as to their mastery. It was unlikely to be in their designs, which were conventional. They used the paper provided for the contests, so that couldn't be it either. Perhaps, as some said, it was their devotion to the art, which had a longer lineage in Falcons Crossing than elsewhere.

I had come to the town itself in hopes of finding the answer. What I expected to discover, I don't know. But anything was better than lingering over my mother's possessions, trying to puzzle out the mysteries that had led to her dying with no one to mourn her but a half-Kheneiran, half-Ulowen child.

It was a relief to collect my luggage and make my way to the platform. The confinement had been getting to me more than I had realized. I was only one of two people to get off, and the other hurried away without looking me in the eye, a reaction I was accustomed to.

The sky, unevenly cloaked by clouds, was darkening already. At least it didn't smell like it would rain tonight. The train platform was hung about by low lanterns, which should have looked festive, but instead gave the place a sense of gloom imperfectly warded off. I resolved to get to a guesthouse as quickly as possible.

There was supposed to be a migration in four days. I had timed my travel accordingly. I'd expected that some sort of decoration would announce the event for out-of-towners, and indeed enormous banners had been hung about the station, but I wasn't sure they were related to the migration. Anywhere else there would have been calligraphy. Here, the banners displayed paintings of birds, detailed down to the feather, but holes had been ripped into the fabric where the eyes should have been.

Perhaps the guesthouse keeper could tell me what was going on. From a newspaper account some years old, I had obtained directions to a guesthouse I hoped still existed. I rounded the corner from the station, luggage in tow, and was confronted by a sight the clipping had not prepared me for.

My first impression was that, by some misappropriation of angles, I had stumbled into the town square. What rose before me appeared to be a gallows tree of fantastic proportion. Streamers dangled from its limbs, stirring in the fitful wind. I had a vision of a storm of eyeless birds plunging earthward, barbed feathers, sharp beaks.

Someone bumped into me and hurried past without apologizing. This freed me from my imagination, and I saw then that the gallows tree was a shrine. I laughed ruefully at myself.

The shrine had been hammered together with blackened nails. The streamers were braided cords dyed red and black. Despite the initial shock of its appearance, it was not so different from the shrines I had seen in the past. There, people used bright ribbons to tie prayers written upon slips of paper to the branches of holy trees.

Here, people had tied paper folded into gliders and knotted the cords through their pointed "beaks" in such a way that I thought of eyes. I wondered what was written inside the gliders, but it would have been taboo for me to open one up to look.

As a child, at our neighborhood shrine, I had once broken the taboo. I had been disappointed by the ordinariness of the prayers. Most Kheneirans are literate, the result of a cultural fervor for education and the classics, but not everyone is equally skilled with brush and ink. Some of the prayers had been scratched out with a stick of charcoal or graphite; others were written in calligraphy so fine that I was sure a local scribe, versed in the formulas of piety, had been paid to do the work.

People had asked for loan sharks to develop forgiving hearts; for injured relatives to regain enough mobility to work; for the rainy season to bring rain, but not too much rain. For healthy babies, for well-favored marriages, for high scores on critical exams. Even as a child I knew how these stories ended. I slipped back home, secure – as only a child could be – in the knowledge my mother would take care of me. No doubt the prayers here were much the same.

I made my way past the shrine of Falcons Crossing, determined not to be intimidated by it. Strangely, I counted not one scribe booth near the shrine, but four. Were people especially devout here? What was more, each had a sign marked simply with the traditional drawing of brush and inkstone, but no example verse to demonstrate the scribe's skill. In addition, banners hung from each one, their color indeterminate in the low light. I would have to ask about the booths when I had the opportunity.

The guesthouse was where the newspaper had said it would be, flanked by two enormous wisteria trees. At this time of year they weren't in bloom, but I inhaled the evening air deeply, remembering the heady scent from my childhood. I contemplated the guesthouse's sign as I did so. To my puzzlement, it had no writing on it, only a painted lamp.

I had worried that I'd arrived too late – especially in smaller towns, people go to bed early – but the guesthouse keeper let me in. He was a wrinkled man who spoke with a wheeze. I paid ahead for the two weeks

I planned to stay. Before I asked if there was any leftover rice I could have, he said he would have a dinner tray sent up to my room. At this hour the common room wouldn't be open anyway.

"Does it ever get busy this time of year?" I asked, the most direct way I could think of asking if there were other guests.

"We do well enough," the guesthouse keeper said.

I couldn't tell if I had offended him. "I have another question."

He looked at me with unrevealing eyes. "Strangers often do."

Not exactly encouraging, but he hadn't told me that I *couldn't* ask. "Why are there so many scribe booths by the shrine?"

"Saves the rest of us from having to learn," he said. "Myself, anytime I need any of that done, I get my daughter to do it. My late wife was from" – he named the nearest city of any size – "and she insisted on teaching the girl. I put up with it just to get some peace."

I blinked at the foreignness of this attitude, but just then my stomach complained. Dealing with provincial backwardness was not my affair. I indicated my desire to retire to my room, and the guesthouse keeper gave me the key after reiterating that dinner would be brought up to me.

The food was more than satisfactory. Despite having grown up listening to Ulowen complaints about the native cuisine, I liked it. Even here the rice was not poorly cooked – Kheneirans have an unspeakable contempt for people who cannot produce a decent bowl of rice – and the marinated anchovies, combined with the seasoned sautéed spinach, provided enough counterpoint to satisfy the tongue.

I placed the tray just outside my room when I was done and closed the door. The hour was too late to visit the guesthouse's bath, so I would attend to that in the morning. Instead, I unfolded the sleeping mat, changed, and lay down.

Sleep came quickly, yet I awoke in the middle of the night gripped by a frantic exhilaration. I paced to the window and opened it. The moon was not visible from this angle, although I knew it would be a waning crescent. Parts of the sky were scarved with cirrus.

Against that dark-light sky, I saw a vast migration: gliders whose size I had trouble gauging, gliders that seemed to silhouette the moon-crescent, soaring to some unguessable destination. I could not tell whether any of them had eyes.

The local migration contests would not begin until the end of the week. But I had to know what was going on. I pulled on my shoes and flung my coat on over my sleeping clothes, then hurried outside. The chill hit me immediately, and I shivered, huffing steam into the air.

A single lantern guttered out, like a stabbed eye, as I made it past the wisteria trees. Moonlight silvered the peaked roofs, the rough stones of the street. I regretted not taking the time to dress more warmly.

I hurried after the gliders. The formation flew in an eerily constant direction. I navigated by them as though they were a sailor's true-stars. They could have led me into the cavern mouth of a tiger and I wouldn't have paid heed until it was too late.

The gliders took no notice of me. I might as well have been chasing seed puffs. For all that I hurried, they were soon out of sight. With the cold wind at my back, I continued to run after them, heart hammering, panting from the unaccustomed exertion. My calf cramped. I went down.

I landed badly despite flinging my hands out to catch myself. For a moment I could scarcely breathe. Then, as my palms began to throb, I staggered back to my feet.

I could keep going after the gliders. Not that I expected to catch up to them – it had been ridiculous to think I might. Now that I considered it, the chase might be hopeless, but I could trace their path *backwards* and figure out where they had come from.

This time I walked. Maybe people with paper cuts on their hands awaited me, people discussing omens and staring into the far haze of night for signs of – what?

I heard the piercing cries of a night-bird, which fell silent as I approached. The insects' shrill song was almost as tangible as the bite in the air. The towns' lanterns flickered unnervingly as I passed them.

Perhaps I should have anticipated this, but the path led me to the shrine. Its sharp angles and jutting beams intimidated me even more than they had when there had been a trace of sunlight. I pulled up short despite the twinge in my knees.

Even in the uncertain light, I saw what had changed, where the gliders had come from. None of the eyeless gliders that had been tied to the shrine remained. All the beams were barren, and the cords floated freely in the wind.

I'd never heard of this variant of the ritual. At all the other shrines I'd encountered, you let the elements dissolve the slips of paper to carry the prayers to the small gods of rock and rill and rain. But then, it was naive of me to believe that religious practice was the same throughout the peninsula. In a town where people didn't even take interest in their own language's writing, who knew?

The variant should have thrilled me. The idea of prayers flying into the sky had a certain elegance. Yet I remembered the eerie flock of gliders, sailing distances that should have been inconceivable without the guidance of some otherworldly force.

By that point I had finally realized how inadequate my coat was against the cold. I stared up at the shrine and wondered how I could find out more about what was going on.

Perhaps I could insinuate myself into the proceedings. Moved by phantasms of superstition rather than logic, I searched the scribes' booths. They had left none of their supplies, and it felt sacrilegious to tear a strip from one of the banners.

Then I remembered the letter tucked into my coat. It wasn't that this was the last memento I had of my mother. I had the silver bracelet, and a butterfly hairpin she had liked. But there's always something personal about letters, about the vagaries of an individual's handwriting, the way they write in neat or drifting columns.

I didn't know how long I stood there, hesitating. But eventually I drew the letter out. The folded sheet was crinkled from the journey it had made with me. I smoothed the paper as best I could, then unfolded it.

It was difficult to read the letter by the scarce moonlight. Still, I knew its contents by heart. A few barren lines: The date and address. Trivialities about the weather, the price of barley, a quick sketch of a cat. Then, the unexpected stab of the pen's nib into the paper, the splayed streak of ink. I could feel the hole in the paper with my fingertips.

What sudden emotion had overtaken my mother? Had she drafted a new letter and sent that instead? Or had she set this one aside to complete later, pretending the hole didn't exist?

I punched through the hole with my index finger, enlarging it. I almost expected to *feel* something as I did so, as though paper had an anatomy of blood and muscle and skin. But no, it was only paper.

Long practice made it easy for me to fold the glider after that. I devised a design that placed the hole at the glider's "eye," although I had to jab again so it went all the way through. Silently, I asked my mother's forgiveness.

It's only paper, I told myself. *It's only paper.*

That was little consolation as I made my way to the shrine and, with trembling hands, knotted a cord through the glider's eye: my offering.

After that, I returned to the guesthouse. I thought someone might stop me – but no one did.

There's a game played in Kheneira, the game of falcon-and-sparrows. The Ulowen call it *tag*. The Kheneiran version involves the following chant (loosely translated):

> *Falcon, falcon, can't catch me*
> *Falcon, falcon, one two three*
> *Falcon, falcon, don't touch my hand*
> *Falcon, falcon, nowhere to land.*

In Falcons Crossing, the falcon is blindfolded; and yet the children run fast, run faster, as if the blindfolded child's outflung arms are tipped with talons.

In ordinary games of falcon-and-sparrows, the children being chased sometimes dart close to the falcon, shouting taunts.

Children in Falcons Crossing learn from the time they can stand that they must run from the falcon, even if the falcon is nowhere near them, even if the falcon shows no interest in them.

I woke early the next day, nerves thrumming. The first thing I did was go to the window and peer outside. The sky had cleared, and the faintest of gray light pearled the horizon.

After folding up the sleeping mat and blankets, and putting them away, I took my bath. No one else occupied the bathhouse, to my relief. Then I ventured to the common room, wondering if anyone would be up yet. There was one other guest, an older woman, who pointedly ignored me, so I sat away from her.

The guesthouse keeper served me rice porridge with chicken and vegetables. I gulped it down without even seasoning it with soy sauce, and only realized it when I caught the guesthouse keeper studying me with pursed lips.

There was no reason to linger, so I ventured into town. Its people paid little heed to me. Others looked like they, too, must be in Falcons Crossing for the migration, wearing clothes with elaborate knotwork embellishments or embroidered patches, fashions from other parts of the country. A few times I asked about the migrations, but answers were curt, factual. No one took the pride in the event that I had expected. The other outsiders, listening in, seemed just as puzzled, but as a half-Kheneiran I was wary of approaching them for further information. I doubted they knew more than I did, anyway.

I wound up, where else, at the shrine. Even from some distance it dominated the square. Even sitting in a noodle shop several streets away eating lunch, I couldn't help thinking of its silhouette, the swaying ropes, the punctured eyes. I don't think I finished the bowl before I stumbled out, drawn to the shrine in spite of myself.

Three of the four scribe booths were occupied, with lines at each. The expressions of the people in line, from a woman with two children pulling at her coat to a stooped older man, bothered me. They didn't want to be here. I couldn't identify the emotion I saw on their faces. Fear? Resignation? Stupor? Even the children, while not precisely well behaved, scuffled quietly, without looking directly at the shrine.

The shrine's beams were already festooned with prayer offerings. I spotted mine with its ragged hole. I selected the least hostile-looking scribe, a tidy woman wearing a shawl of magenta and lilac, and got in line.

By listening in on the scribe's transactions, I learned what she charged for her services. My mother had left me everything and money wasn't a concern, but I wondered about the people in front of me.

I noticed something more curious when I peered at the booth: the paper. There was a whole stack of it, weighted with a carnelian seal stone in the shape of a plunging falcon pierced through where its eyes should have been. It wasn't the quality of the paper that bothered me. Rather, it was that the top sheet appeared as though it had been trimmed out of a book. I wasn't great at reading upside-down text, but it seemed to describe a stillbirth. (The relevant word vanished beneath the falcon seal.) The upper part of the pile seemed to be the same. Below that the pile became ragged, sheets of different proportions and sizes, not even neatly aligned.

I had expected the scribe to go through the pile in order, but she liked to flick through it and pull out a sheet at random. Each piece of paper had something on it. I caught sight of a poster with a lopsided representation of the East Kheneiran seal, and a doodle of a train in the margin; a letter in hasty script; a shopping list. And more pages out of books.

A horrible suspicion rooted in my mind, and would not be dislodged.

Soon enough my turn came. The scribe's ledger caught my attention. I knew something of accounting and was surprised that she used the simplest of tally marks. I told myself not to be narrow-minded. If the tally marks worked for her, what was wrong with that?

I had been hoping to glean some clue from the scribe's handwriting. But as far as I could tell, she didn't write anything on the paper at all, even though she had an inkstone and water and a brush. The brush's bristles were unstained, as though they had never seen use. Were they merely for show?

I opened my mouth to ask about the procedure.

The scribe frowned quellingly. She set her brush aside – I approved of the gesture's fussiness – and lifted her arm to point unerringly at my glider where it dangled from the shrine. "Sunset," she said. That was all.

I reached for my purse anyway, intending next to ask her about the bird banners, but she was already gesturing toward the next person in line, a man with a broken nose. She caught my eye and said, more emphatically, "Sunset."

Despite the lack of animus in her voice, I flushed. Still, I couldn't help asking, "What happens next?"

"The migration," the man said with distinct impatience. Then he began telling the scribe about his sick younger sister.

I took the hint. I walked a little way from the line and squinted up at the shrine. A child of indeterminate sex was being held up by a broad-backed man so it could tie up a prayer. The knot looked like it wouldn't last long against a wind of any strength. The man lowered the child but didn't do anything to secure the knot. The two of them walked away side by side but not hand in hand. Before they turned away, I saw their faces: each held the deadened resignation I was becoming familiar with.

Next I visited the town hall so I could inquire after the fate of the national archives. According to tradition, even the queens and kings of the old realm were not permitted to read the Royal Historians' chronicles, so that the historians' objectivity would not be compromised. I doubted the historians had been able to enforce this, but the myth meant something.

After dealing with two older clerks whose lack of interest was palpable, I tracked down an assistant, a woman perhaps a few years younger than I was. She seemed genuinely distressed that she couldn't answer my questions. "I'm sorry," she said. "I'm told there was a lot of confusion during the civil war. The person you would have wanted to ask was—" The name she gave meant nothing to me. There was no reason why it should have, yet I felt a pang of disappointment. "She was in charge of the archives and, as far as anyone knew, she wasn't terribly interested in the job, but no one else was either. After she passed away, people let them slide into neglect. That's all I know."

"Did she worship often at the shrine?" I asked.

She blinked. "I—I think so, yes. She was known for being very devout."

I told her where I was staying and asked her to send word if she found anything more.

But I already knew I would not hear from her.

I returned to the guesthouse early, stopping at a stationery store on the way to buy some paper just in case. No clues here: just ordinary blank paper. In my frustration, it was tempting to poke holes into one of the sheets, or wad it up, or tear it to shreds. My mother had taught me frugality, however, so I resisted the urge.

The hours until sunset passed half as a blur, half as a crawl. If the guesthouse keeper hadn't called me to the common room, I would have forgotten to eat. His daughter, whom he introduced perfunctorily, asked several times if I wanted anything specific. I was picking at my food, too jittery to down most of it, and had to keep reassuring her that no, I didn't want anything else.

After dinner I hurried to the shrine, noting the way people lifted their heads to stare at me. It was a marked difference from the way they had ignored me earlier. Moths flitted around the lanterns, and their shadows danced across my path.

I might as well have taken my time, despite my prickling awareness of the sun's arc. After a childhood of taunts and ambushes, I had come prepared to fight if I had to. I had imagined that shamans of the high places would await me, or the scribes with their unstained brushes, or a tumult of followers barring me from the shrine.

Instead, the shrine was abandoned, the scribes' stalls empty, just as before. The banners stirred weakly as the wind gusted around them; that was all.

I had been counting on finding someone here to ask questions of. Even walking the perimeter revealed nothing useful. The buildings in the vicinity were shuttered and showed no sign of occupation, and I would have felt ridiculous pestering the locals by knocking on doors.

I returned my attention to the shrine – specifically, to my own offering. It was no mystery to me. But what of the other offerings? Just what was on all those sheets? Had any of them been written on?

Maybe the fact that nobody was here – nobody I had spotted, anyway – worked in my favor.

Before I could talk myself out of it, I strode up to the shrine's lowest beam and snatched at one of the gliders. It floated out of my reach in response to a sudden gust, as if it was shying from my hand.

The lines from that children's game whispered in my mind:

> *Falcon, falcon, don't touch my hand*
> *Falcon, falcon, nowhere to land.*

Then I understood. The glider wasn't a falcon. It was *fleeing* the falcon.

On the second try I ripped the glider free, destroying its eye. My hands shook as I unfolded it, eager to discover its secrets. For a moment I thought I heard the distant cry of a night bird. Then I laughed at myself: it was the train's whistle as it approached Falcons Crossing, nothing more.

The train whistled again as I righted the paper and read it. It looked like a recipe for pickled cabbage. Who would ask for a prayer about pickled cabbage? I let the mutilated paper fall. It almost seemed to twitch limply as it did so.

The next glider I harvested was more interesting. Whoever had folded it must have had long experience coaxing old paper into shape, for it was brittle with age. In better light I imagined it would have a yellow tint.

This one was a letter from some soldier to his wife. It spoke of his sergeant's callous sense of humor, of pranks involving mismatched socks; it asked about their children. It said without saying it outright, *I am afraid I will never make it home.*

I folded it back up and flung it into the night. It soared onward, finally disappearing from sight. It would fly far, I thought. The letter was full of fear. People run fastest when full of fear. I doubted a sparrow would do any differently, and Falcons Crossing was the falcon's home.

I pulled my coat more tightly about myself as the wind picked up. The sun was sinking beneath the horizon, like an eye being blotted. I reached for another glider, then another, reading them, then folding them up again and launching them.

When I examined the first – twelve? twenty? – my hunch was right. The scribes hadn't bothered writing anything at all, despite the trappings of their profession. After that I stopped examining the gliders. I had already figured out that people in Falcons Crossing didn't trust writing; that they preferred to parasitize documents already in existence.

In a frenzy, I freed the rest of the gliders, the eyeless gliders, flinging them into the air. Some of the gliders dropped quickly to the ground, while others sped away as though pursued. Only when I came to my own did I stop.

Carefully, I unknotted my mother's letter. I had almost ripped it down and flung it away. But I had stopped in time. I tucked it back into my coat.

I became aware of the old children's chant rising around me, of the people who had emerged to circle the shrine. "Falcon, falcon," they called to me.

The scribe I had visited earlier in the day walked toward me. She held her unstained brush out to me.

"No," I said. I would not take up her profession.

As terrible as the indifference of the gods is, the indifference of people is worse. All that history folded up into gliders, offerings to an unlistening power. I could not stop it, but neither would I participate in it. Now I understood now why my mother had left. I walked away and did not look back.

It gives **W. H. Pugmire** "a kind of perverse pleasure to pen
stories that are audaciously Lovecraftian, in that they reference
H. P. Lovecraft's superb stories and then weave my own diabolic
twist into the tale. It's a delicious pastime. My story herein is set
in Lovecraft's notorious witch-town and mentions his infamous
artist, Pickman; I play with Lovecraft's cosmic themes in my
own fashion."

Wilum Pugmire has been writing Lovecraftian fiction since
the early 1970s, at which time he began to read Lovecraft and
correspond with the surviving members of the Lovecraft/*Weird
Tales* Circle. Since then he has published twenty books of explic-
itly eldritch fiction, the latest of which is *Monstrous Aftermath*
(Hippocampus Press). He is presently at work on his second
collection for Centipede Press.

A Shadow of Thine Own Design
W. H. Pugmire

———

"This thing of darkness I acknowledge mine."
　　　　　– William Shakespeare: *The Tempest*, Act 5, Scene 1

Malcolm Elioth sauntered across the Garrison Street Bridge and
stopped midpoint, leaned over the sturdy railing and watched the play
of moonlight on the Miskatonic River below. He listened, and wondered
why the flowing water seemed to call to him with liquid voice, as if
trying to coax him over the barrier and into its depths; yet Malcolm
resisted the call, for there were other pools of darkness into which he
wished to plunge.

Continuing his amble, Malcolm raised his swarthy visage to the
moon and imagined his eyes were drinking in her cool luminosity.
Although she appeared very bright, he knew that her surface was

dark, and this added to his feeling of kinship with her. He felt as isolated as she appeared, far away from the common horde that crawled upon the earth.

Pursing lips, he began to whistle an obscure tune as he continued to Water Street and approached the antique house that was his destination. Stopping to study the structure, he contemplated the woman he had arranged to meet, the figure he was perhaps to paint. He knew little of her, for she was a creature of mystery and myth, incredibly old and never seen, except on rare occasions in deepest night. He recalled a line from Ovid of which he was fond: "Blemishes are hid by night and every fault forgiven; darkness makes any woman fair."

Yet Edith Gnome was not any woman. No one knew how old she had been in 1925, when Richard Upton Pickman had painted her; and his canvases were certainly no indication, for in some she looked very young indeed, little more than a teenager, while in the most famous painting she had been depicted as a mature woman seated at a spinning wheel.

Miss Gnome had earned a slight reputation as a Bohemian poet in Boston, but Malcolm knew of her because of his obsession with the sinister painter and his work. Pickman was reputed to have completed thirteen canvases of the woman before his mysterious disappearance in 1926. Using his underground connections, Malcolm had obtained the smallest of these paintings – one of a series – in which Miss Gnome was shown as an adolescent surrounded by dog-faced ghouls who were instructing her in the art of feeding like themselves. Malcolm's fixation on the mystery of the sitter resulted in his obtaining a copy of the very scarce volume of her poetry that had been published in a very limited edition. To his amazement, the person who sold him the book mentioned nonchalantly that Edith Gnome yet lived, incredibly aged, in Arkham.

"She is rumored to hate being photographed, you know, and yet my friend who visited her was allowed to take one snap of the poet at her wheel. I was one of the lucky few who were given copies, after vowing never to allow it to be reproduced. This is from last year."

Malcolm reached out for the small photograph handed him, shocked at the image that had been captured; he had imagined the mysterious poet would have an ominous appearance in keeping with her legend, yet the woman in the picture looked like a simple peasant woman of European origin seated at a primitive spinning wheel. Her plain attire of long dark skirt and white blouse was of no particular era; the shawl covering her shoulders appeared to be embroidered silk. A lace bonnet covered the wisps of white hair that framed what at first seemed a nondescript countenance; and yet the longer Malcolm gazed at her elderly face, the more he seemed to sense something in its expression that excited him subtly. He had the strangest sensation that the eyes in the photograph were returning his scrutiny.

A cloud obscured the moonlight, and night darkened. Malcolm blinked memory away and approached the house, climbed the porch steps and tapped lightly on the six-panel door. His rapping was answered by a fey fellow of indeterminate age who resembled Aubrey Beardsley and held a taper. Softly, the fellow spoke Malcolm's name, stepped aside and allowed him egress into the dark domain. They passed flickering candles held in bronze sconces fastened to yellow walls, moving silently through dancing shadows in a hallway leading to immense double doors that opened into a large room with walls of paneled oak. Malcolm saw no spinning wheel. It would have been out of place in the elegant room, just as Miss Gnome, who now appeared to be far more aristocrat than peasant, would have been equally out of place spinning. The petite creature sat on a cushioned chair of red fabric, attired in a long ebony gown and with a black and silver snood covering her pale hair. The sight of her withered face with its high forehead and jade eyes shocked her visitor, for he had never encountered anyone so incredibly aged. Yet, through the signs of age, the woman still possessed a frail loveliness, although it was a morbid beauty because her facial flesh was so thin one could easily discern the skull beneath her features. Smiling, she motioned to a chair, into which Malcolm lowered himself as the manservant exited the chamber.

"Welcome to my home, Mr. Elioth. Do take off your jacket and set your knapsack on the floor. My, how young you are!"

He returned her smile and said, "At twenty-seven I no longer feel so youthful."

"And that is absurd, young man. When you have existed for more than a century, then you can speak of lost youth. You gaze at what Shakespeare called a 'cormorant devouring Time' and marvel that you have yet escaped time's appetite. You peer into the dim past and see those moments that still exist as shimmering memory. And although youth is a far-off incident, particles of it exist within you still, especially when you dance."

The woman shut her eyes and nodded, and delicate music filtered into the room. Turning to the sound, Malcolm saw that the manservant had surreptitiously re-entered the room and had lifted the lid of an ornate music box. Malcolm heard a rustling noise as the old woman rose out of the chair and began to move about him like some thing of dainty shadow. Her small soft hands reached out for his, and he took them into his own. She led him into what was, for him, an inept and clumsy dance. They moved as one for some few moments, until the music slowed and ceased.

The tall fellow looked down at the diminutive woman and sighed.

"I'm not graceful on my feet, I fear," he told her, laughing. "I regret never having learned to dance properly, gracefully, as they do in the old movies. I watch those Fred Astaire and Gene Kelly films and it seems like watching the past dance before my eyes."

They regained their seats and, for no conscious reason of which he was aware, Malcolm said, in more somber tones, "I often feel as if I were born in the wrong era . . . that I was not intended for this century. Wouldn't it be wonderful, to be able to dance out of time, to step into a different era or an alternative existence if one wished?"

Miss Gnome's eyes shimmered with queer luster. "Wonderful indeed."

Malcolm leaned over, unzipped a pocket of his bulky backpack, and pulled out the rare edition of Edith Gnome's verse, the sight of which moved her to moan a little. "Will you honor me with a signature?" She took hold of the booklet and hesitated a little as she turned over its leaves. She then accepted his proffered pen and scribbled an inscription on the title page.

"I feel a vague precaution before signing my name. It probably stems from my witch heritage. The signing of one's name can be a potent – at times a parlous – thing."

The young man nodded, a dark corkscrew of hair falling to his brow. "Yes, I've noticed the recurring sorcerous motif in your verses."

Outlandishly, she cackled. "Yes, that is something Richard Pickman and I shared: Salem ancestry. He actually painted a certain gathering pertinent to our kind, which no one has ever seen, myself excepted. Would you care to?"

"It would give me intense pleasure," was his enthusiastic reply. Malcolm could hardly believe his good fortune: he'd not dared hope for any discussion of her poetry, let alone the revelation of an unknown Pickman. Of course he had not expected to partner her in dance either.

"Follow me. I have a special hallway wherein I keep my collection." Malcolm followed her out of the room and along a series of hallways, until they came to one that seemed especially wide and well lit compared to the duskiness of the rest of the house. His excitement became a palpable taste in his mouth as his eyes took in the series of framed works fastened to the hallway walls. He stopped before one large canvas and studied it in the dim light of the corridor. He knew the painting was entitled "Gallows Hill," for he had read a description of it in some catalogue. A ring of baying ghouls raised their canine faces to a witch who hanged from a frayed length of rope that had been secured onto a primitive-looking post. The hanged woman, however, was not the hag Malcolm had expected to see depicted, but rather a young and lovely corpse modeled after a youthful Edith Gnome.

He felt the elderly creature lean against him gently. "That was a long and grueling pose," she told him. "Richard had actually constructed a low gallows with dangling rope for me to position myself with. I love how the moonlight is reflected in my wide dead eyes, and how my eyes resemble the emerald orbs of the pack that pay homage to their murdered enchantress. Richard understood the connection that exists between witches and ghouls. You may know his four-times-great-grandmother had been hanged on Gallows Hill in 1692 as Cotton Mather looked on. Mather was the inspiration for this next canvas." They moved a short distance down the hallway. "This is me sitting on Mather's tomb in Copp's Hill Burying Ground. Notice how my face is mostly obscured in shadow, except for the green patina of my eyes? Richard worked from a photograph, as I obviously couldn't pose for any extended time with a man positioned as the ghoul who sucks my breast."

"The suggestive play of shadow all around is effective," Malcolm responded. "It is Pickman's talent for evoking shadow that entrances me. To look at those shadows is to feel a longing to become a part of them. When I express that to my friends they think me, well, weird – but maybe you understand."

She nodded. "I like that – 'evoking shadow' – that's exactly right. You see, I was not merely Pickman's model, I was his student. He instructed me in certain ways, and from him I learned new . . . appetites." She smiled coyly at the word. "It was he who instilled within me a love of fabulous darkness. I have not seen the wretched light of day for many decades. I exist in the living light of candle flame, and in the shadows such flame 'evokes,' as you phrased it. And there is a deeper shadow that can also be induced; it was such a shadow that inspired him to create the work at the end of this corridor. You see it there, the mammoth mirror encased in golden frame? It was so original of Richard, to use mirror as a canvas of sorts. Wait, before approaching it – we must see it in proper lighting."

Malcolm looked down at Edith as she shut her eyes and began to hum, a sound in which there was no music, being merely a buzzing. Strangely, the flames from the candles in their sconces altered, darkening into embers of unearthly violet hue. He experienced sudden vertigo and reeled to one wall, finding he was leaning against a canvas. Pushing away from it feebly, he saw it portrayed the image to which Miss Gnome had referred: sharp and life-like, painted in Pickman's realist technique, blasphemous shapes danced below a monstrous creature, far more ghastly than any merely satanic being ever imagined. This hideous fiend stood with arms upraised, one hand holding a carmine-dripping knife – each drop of blood glowing like a ruby. On the stone altar beneath lay a gory sacrifice. Although the body was obviously lifeless, its emerald eyes were opened wide.

He felt a hand clasp his, looked down and saw the green-hued eyes from the painting peering into his own as living liquid orbs. Not speaking, Malcolm allowed himself to be guided down the corridor, to the wall on which the enormous mirror was fastened. It looked like some gigantic canvas encased by golden frame.

"I never knew if Richard found the mirror or had some friend construct it, for you see that the glass is curiously half-blackened although still reflective. Aren't they intriguing, the spirals of bizarre luminosity scattered about in it? He told me this piece was inspired by something he had seen in some abandoned church in Providence. It has a haunting aspect, does it not? Look how beautifully your sable skin wears that tint of purple sheen in your reflection. Marvelous. Your white shirt is a bit of a distraction, don't you find?"

Entranced by the massive mirror, Malcolm allowed her to unfasten the buttons of his shirt and pull it from his lean torso. He stepped nearer to that blackened glass and observed the odd shadows that moved within it. They were Pickman's shadows, alive and expressive. He watched, as their preternatural pitch moved from out of the glass and onto the paneled walls of the hallway.

"How strong is your desire, Malcolm Elioth, to dance out of time? Shall I instruct you, as Richard tutored me? It's easily done, if one has the keen compulsion. Titus – play."

Malcolm turned and observed the unworldly manservant had appeared, an oddly formed flute pressed to his mouth. The corridor filled with eerie music. The weird woman moved about him to the sound, as she had danced earlier. As she moved she reached out to the shadows now frolicking all around them, clutching portions of their gloom, wrapping it around her being, until she was little more than formless shadow herself. An extremely slender obsidian branch of blackness reached for Malcolm and enveloped his hand, chilling his flesh exquisitely. He did not falter as he was pulled out of the hallway, through the haunted mirror, entering into the realm for which Pickman's enchanted glass served as threshold.

One thing **Norman Partridge** has always found curious about Lovecraft's fiction is that "there's really no reflection of his time – no sense of the Roaring Twenties or the Great Depression or the hardscrabble realities most Americans faced in those days. Along with that, I've always wondered how HPL's other-worldly horror might have played if injected into other pulp forms of the day. So I dropped a chunk of Lovecraft's mythos ("The Hound") into thirties hardboiled territory, tossed in a pair of armed-and-dangerous California migrants on the run, and let things roll from there."

Partridge's first short story appeared in *Cemetery Dance* 2, and his debut novel, *Slippin' into Darkness*, was the first original novel published by CD. Since then, he has written a series novel (*The Crow: Wicked Prayer*) which was adapted for the screen, comics for DC, and six collections of short stories. Partridge's Halloween novel, *Dark Harvest*, was chosen by *Publishers Weekly* as one of the 100 Best Books of 2006 and has become a seasonal classic. A third-generation Californian, he lives in the San Francisco Bay Area with his wife, Canadian writer Tia V. Travis, and their daughter Neve. His latest novel is *The Devil's Brood*.

Backbite
Norman Partridge

——

The Depression had been hitting California hard for years, but that year the rains hit harder. The peas turned black on the vines, withering like arthritic fingers before migrants like my brother and I could pick them with our own. Stone fruit didn't fare any better. Peaches, apricots . . . all of it disappeared in one brutal season. Night after night and week after week a black dog of a wind howled through every orchard, and sleet rattled down and gnawed the fruit off the stone, and those dead stones hung tight to branches, inclined toward the mud like the skulls of lynched men.

Those stones weren't worth anything to the growers, and that meant they were worth even less to men like Russell and me. Men who stooped and picked and boxed and carried. Most people said Russell wasn't worth anything at all, just some mangled halfwit who couldn't be trusted with a sharp spoon. Even I had to admit that my older brother hadn't been right in the head since he'd come home from France, missing an eye and a chunk of his face thanks to a German bayonet. Of course, Russell never talked much about that. All he said about the war was that he spent it digging trenches and killing in them, but it was living in them that taught him some homes were as welcoming as the grave.

Bleak poetics aside, that wasn't saying much at all. I figured the truth of it was that the mustard gas had done a real job on Russell, but no one wanted to hear anything about that. No one wanted to hear anything about anything in those days. Talk didn't buy you much, and a sweet lie beat out the truth any day of the week. But Russ and I weren't the kind who had any sweet lies in us, even in the best of times.

By the time the rains came, we didn't have much left in us besides a whisper. There wasn't a way out, and the words that might have found one were hard to cough up. Honest explanations, sob stories, alibis . . . even the truth seemed like begging. Russell couldn't do it, and I didn't want to. If you asked me, our words belonged in our bellies the same as our guts. Our stories, too. Wrapped up in our skins, locked in bone houses we'd built for them . . . way down deep.

Like they say: to each his own. It was that way for me and it was that way for Russ. We fell into silence. Summer slipped into fall. The black wind howled, and the rain beat down. The fruit rotted on the vine. Russell got a cough. I listened to it night after night in one tent or another, and soon I heard little else. The cough rattled, and it made me think of a desperate man trying to pick a safe, twisting the dial 'round and 'round, the tumblers never falling in place. But the dial spun on, and the storms drenched the land, and our work washed away in a flood. And soon there was nothing to do but turn our backs on the fields and orchards, the rain and the mud.

We found a new way of doing things.

A way that let us put away our words for good.

No more honest explanations. No sob stories. No alibis.

We started over.

We did our talking with a gun.

The first one was a .38 missing the pistol grips. Russell took it from the labor contractor who tried to cheat our crew out of one last payday, a mouthy little runt named Koslow. Russ also took the bankroll Koslow was going to pocket for himself. Only the idiot didn't get the message. He figured he was still the boss, and he started jabbering about company muscle and cops and what was going to happen to us.

So Russ smacked him around with the busted pistol. As big as Russ was, it was like watching a tiger bat around a house cat. Koslow was lucky it ended that way. Russell carried a German trench knife in a steel scabbard that hung from his belt, and I had no doubt he knew how to use it. Anyway, the bastard was smart enough to shut up before it came to that, and we took his car keys to seal the deal.

We never paid a price for what we did. At least, not the kind of price you'd figure. And if what we did felt good, Russell didn't say so and neither did I. I didn't say anything about how the roll of greenbacks felt tucked into my pants pocket, either. But the truth is that having those bills in my jeans gave me a hard-on . . . the first one I'd had in months. Jesus, life is funny.

The stolen Ford took us north of Fresno. We bought some groceries at an Armenian market along with a few bottles of bootleg wine. I picked up a local paper and a local map. Pickings were slim, but I knew what I was looking for. I checked the obituaries and circled a few addresses, and we drove around casing houses. The rain had slacked off at long last, but that black dog of a wind was still behind us . . . ahead of us . . . everywhere. It raged like a twister and wiped away the clouds, pushing them over the mountains to the east. The sky it left behind was as flat and gray and empty as the country roads we traveled.

The Ford's bald tires hummed over blacktop as we drove from one house to the next. I crossed addresses off the obit page as we went – most of the places were in town, with too many neighbors around. Finally we found an old ramshackle farmhouse just past the outskirts where the windows didn't light up at night.

The house was surrounded by overgrown fields, set back from the road down a gravel drive that twisted through an old stand of eucalyptus. We parked the car, and Russell yanked his German *Nahkampfmesser* from its steel scabbard. In his big hands it looked like a butter knife. Two seconds later he levered open the back door, and that was that.

Inside, there was nothing to greet us but a boxed-up sour smell – not like death, but the kind of feral scent that lingers in a house when there's an animal holed up in the crawlspace. Either way, the stink didn't bother me. Even a dead man's clapboard was a big step up from a leaky tent in a migrant camp. And anyway, the smell wasn't so bad on the second floor.

There were two bedrooms upstairs. We couldn't tell which one had belonged to the dead man. To tell the truth, I didn't care. The only thing that mattered to me was that my bed was soft, and I slept better in it than I had in months. My brother was another story. That lingering cough had Russell up and down all night. He must have memorized every corridor. Hearing him move around in the darkened house, I wondered if my brother had ended up in the dead man's bedroom, even toyed with the idea that Russell's cough was some kind of ghostly echo. That's the way things would have ended up in a pulp magazine. But I tried not to think about it, and eventually that twister wind spun over the old gables and took those sounds away.

The only bathroom was next to Russell's bedroom. It was a dull little pocket with a burned-out lightbulb and a little bit of a window set high near the ceiling. Most nights that window allowed enough moonlight to let you do what you needed . . . or maybe it allowed too much. In the middle of the second night, Russ smashed the bathroom mirror. He said he saw a shadow moving behind the glass. He slept better after that, though some nights I was sure I heard him rooting around in that dark bathroom, shifting pieces of that broken mirror in the sink like the pieces of a jigsaw puzzle. But Russ never said a word about it, and I didn't ask.

I'd get up in the morning, and the broken glass would still be there. I'd wash up, my eyes staring at me from the same broken shards as they had the day before. Russell never did clean up the mirror. Of course, I didn't clean it up, either. I could have, but I didn't want to mess with it. After all, I hadn't broken the thing, and I figured we'd earned letting things go at least a little bit after busting our asses to survive for so long. Even if it couldn't last, it seemed a stretch of rest was the least we deserved before we faced up to whatever was coming next.

Slice it up neat and clean: We both knew that we should move on. But neither one of us said it, and one day seemed to snake into the next before we could make a new start. I gained a few pounds eating the groceries we'd bought at that Armenian market. Russell drowned the last of his cough in wine. He'd developed a taste for the grape in France and slept sounder for it now, but it didn't help where it really counted. A couple slugs too many and Russ would end up out in the scrubby yard beneath the moon, staring at the stars with that lone eye of his, shouting at the cosmos in gutter *Deutsch* I figured he'd learned from a German whore. The dead man's house was in the sticks – there was no one around to hear but me . . . except the sky, I suppose – and it sounded like my brother was cursing the gods, or maybe their absence.

Those words spilled out, and across the fields, and into the night. Maybe there was nothing to understand in them at all. I just sat in the house and listened. There wasn't much else to do. We hadn't found a radio, and there wasn't a single book in the whole place . . . not even a pulp magazine. I loved those things, but no dice here. The only reading material was that local newspaper I'd bought at the market. I read it over and over, until I got the idea that simple act had set the whole world in stone. So I burned the paper in the fireplace. After that I fell asleep in an armchair while Russell drank and shouted at the stars.

Late that night I awoke to the sounds of my brother's screams. I crossed the room in two steps. Headlights washed the front of the house. A black Nash was parked on the gravel driveway. I snatched open the front door and the cold wind blasted me along with sounds that would have been right at home in a backwoods butcher shop.

But that didn't slow me down, because those sounds were coming from my brother. I crossed the porch and hit the scrubby grass in a dead run. Russell was down on his knees, his screams gone now, grunting as two guys worked him over with switchman's clubs. I tackled the first one before he saw me coming and rammed him against the Nash. His head hit the fender with a sickening thud, and that spelled *lights out*. By the time I grabbed the switchman's club from his hands and turned to face his partner, Russ had already gone to work.

Bark peeled as Russ shouldered his attacker against a thick eucalyptus. Then he moved in low, hooking to the belly like Dempsey, punching so hard I thought the stranger would spit up his liver. The guy was finished before he dropped, but Russ was just getting started. His left hand whipped back, fingers closing around the trench knife that hung at his side.

It took everything I had in me to grab Russ and pull him away before he could turn that German steel loose. Even so, the stranger shrank away like a dead man. His long black overcoat gathered around him as he collapsed, as if he were sinking through a trapdoor. Another second and he wasn't moving. Neither was the guy by the Nash.

We didn't need to yank their wallets to find out they were private cops set with the task of rousting squatters for a local bank, but we yanked their wallets anyway. They had thirty bucks between them. Toss in the Nash, and it amounted to a fair night's work. We dragged them inside the dead man's house and trussed them up. Then we closed the door behind us, and we left the two of them in that house with its feral smell, and the ashes of the last newspaper I'd ever read, and a busted bathroom mirror that tossed moonlight at the shadows.

Outside, the wind was dying off. The moon was brighter now. Pale, watching. The bats were out, circling in its cold glow, gobbling any insects that dared to flap wings.

I started the Nash and we backed out of the driveway. The headlight glow spilled across the front of the old house, and we left it behind us in the darkness.

It was time to move on.

Once we were clear of Fresno, we made a quick stop to search the car. There was nothing much up front – a couple salami sandwiches in a paper bag, a couple bottles of bootleg beer, and a map in the glove compartment that was folded up in a jumble. A town up north was circled in red, but its name – New Anvik – didn't ring a bell. Besides, any destination we might set would come later. At the moment all we wanted to do was put some distance between us and the dead man's house.

But first we'd finish checking the Nash. The real jackpot was locked in the truck – a pump-action shotgun and a couple boxes of oo buckshot shells. I guess it was just dumb luck the bank muscle had opted to start things off with clubs instead of the trench gun. We wouldn't make the same mistake. We stowed the Winchester in the backseat, tossed an old blanket over it, and headed north.

We blew through Merced and Modesto. Outside Stockton, we snatched a new license plate for the Nash. Breathing a little easier, we ate some burgers at a trucker's joint on the Delta just as the sun rose in a blue sky. I couldn't remember the last time I'd seen the sun, and it made me feel better . . . even kind of sleepy. We parked down by the water and I dozed a little, listening to birds call as a gentle breeze combed through the cattails.

Russ went for a walk. At least, that's what I thought he was doing. When I awoke I went looking for him, following a deer run that cut through the cattails. The first thing I found was a broken wine bottle, the last of that Armenian bootleg. And then I found Russ. He was down by the water where it was quiet, sitting there all alone. The sun beat down on him and he stared up at it . . . at least, that's what his good eye was doing. But whatever my brother saw, I was certain he was seeing it with the eye that wasn't there anymore . . . the angry red socket that was scarred over like a ravaged coffin lid.

The scar twitched and heaved. Even now, I can't imagine what Russ saw in his mind's eye. I only know that it was the last thing he thought he'd ever see, because he had that Winchester shotgun propped under his chin and his thumb was twitching on the trigger.

As gently as I could, I took away the gun. Russ didn't say a single word. Wherever he was, there weren't any words at all. I didn't have any words, either. But my hand closed around my brother's, and together we walked back to the stolen Nash.

I opened the glove compartment and grabbed the map. Unfolding it, the first thing I saw was that little town circled in red, a place called New Anvik. It lay to the northeast, just a few hours away . . . if we were lucky, anyway. Lots of pines and mountains up there, and summer cabins that would be shuttered for the season. The way I figured it, we could find a place to hole up in the sticks and get some breathing room. Then I could figure out what to do about Russ.

My brother didn't say a word as I drove. He just stared ahead, his one eye glazed as if a spider had spun cobwebs around his brain. A couple hours north of Sacramento the Nash overheated. I barely got it over to the side of the road, but I knew instantly we couldn't linger there. One look at us and even the stupidest cop would start asking questions. So I wrapped the guns in a blanket, handed Russ a sack with the sandwiches and the beer, and we started walking.

A gravel road cut away from the main one, and we followed it through a field. Eventually we hit some railroad tracks and trailed them north. The air was still. The sun shone down but the light it cast was flat and cold, so barren it didn't even glint off the railroad tracks. The only way to stay warm was to keep moving. That's what we did. Our boots thudded over ties and gravel, and we didn't move slowly. I set the pace, and Russ kept it.

The landscape was spare – fields rimmed by pine. We hoofed it a couple of miles and didn't see a single house. But with guns in our possession and little else, I was still wary of any kind of law . . . even a local yokel. I felt a little safer when the train tracks cut into a wall of pine. The ground within was as red as rusty iron, and the little forest seemed to hold a month's worth of frosty mornings. Which was another way of saying it was like a pine icebox in there, so we didn't slacken our pace. Instead, we doubled it.

The red earth disappeared beneath a carpet of rusty needles, muffling our footsteps as we moved deeper into the forest. The only other sounds were our breaths, which by now were just short of ragged. A sour scent greeted us about a quarter mile in – the same feral crawl-space scent we'd breathed for a week running at the dead man's house. The stink burned my lungs, and I have to admit that sucking it down made the hairs on the back of my neck stand up. We found its source soon enough – a dead boar lay to one side of the tracks, body mangled and partially devoured by god knows what, bristly coat heavy with frost as if its slayer had left it on ice for another meal.

I stared down at the carcass, but not for long. Fate might be pushing us, but there was no time to consider it. Not now. I wasn't going to gut the dead animal, spill its entrails, and give them a read. Not the way we were moving. The way I saw it we'd already placed our bet . . . wherever we were headed. And the chips could fall where they may.

So we skirted the dead boar and kept walking. Not far ahead, the forest opened on a circle of light. It was dull light, the kind only found in the shank of an afternoon, but it was light just the same.

Russell's lone eye narrowed as we stepped into it, and I got the feeling the cobwebs in his brain were melting away. A railway station lay ahead, just a little more than a stone's throw distant. The platform was empty, and a lone Ford was parked in the lot outside the office. If the place was as empty as it looked, we might be able to muscle our way in and steal whatever the station agent had in the cash drawer, maybe snatch a bag of mail from the warehouse . . . then keep moving. But all that was gravy. The main thing I wanted was the key to that Ford.

It was time to get it. The wind had picked up while we were in the forest, and now it was whipping cold from above and behind, driving the stink of that dead boar through the pines as if it were ready to gouge our heels with its tusks. Russ set down the bag with the sandwiches and the beer. We weren't going to need it now. We started toward the depot as the sun dipped behind the treetops. In an instant, afternoon slipped into twilight.

The wind didn't slacken, and the sign above the platform swayed on thick chains. As we drew closer, I recognized the station's name. New Anvik – the same town I'd seen circled on the map I found in the Nash's glove compartment.

Right now, it was our destination.

It looked like it had been all along.

Gravel crunched beneath our boots as we crossed the station lot. I brushed a hand along the Ford's hood as I passed by. The metal was as cold as a witch's tit, which meant the car had been sitting there a while. Russ trailed behind me as I climbed the stairs that led to the station platform, and together we followed a raised walk around the front of the building. All the while, a single hope stuck in my mind – that the depot was a one-man operation, and we'd only find the station agent inside.

That's exactly what we found, but not the way we expected.

"You'd better give me that shotgun," Russ said as we neared the door.

I stopped dead in my tracks, turning only to meet my brother's eye. It was as green as a piece of polished jade, and clear of cobwebs.

"Welcome back," I said, thinking I understood.

Of course, I didn't understand anything.

But I handed the Winchester to Russ.

And we moved toward the open door.

* * *

Deep notches marred the molding, as if someone had gained entry with a dull axe. I didn't have time to worry about that any more than I'd worried about the dead boar, because the Ford was still parked out front and I wanted the keys that cranked its engine more than I'd ever wanted anything in my miserable life. So I nudged Russ and he took the lead, stepping into the dark room like a golem with a trench gun.

His big shadow spilled across the floor, joining other shadows that pooled on the waxed hardwood. I flipped on the light as I followed my brother inside. With the shadows gone there was nothing much in the office except a couple of desks. It didn't take a detective to figure out they'd been moved – both rested at odd angles against the far wall, and the legs had gouged long scratches along the hardwood floor. As near as I could tell each desk had traveled about ten feet. And judging by the damage to the plaster wall the desks had moved fast and hard, as if they had been bucked across the room.

There weren't any car keys in either desk. No cash box, either. Between the two desks another open door waited, a large sliding panel that led to the warehouse. Maybe the keys to the Ford were back there . . . and maybe something else, too. Maybe some boxed freight we could snatch, or a bag of mail. If we could grab it fast, I'd take it . . . but I sure as hell wasn't going to hang around a second more than necessary.

Dull electric bulbs glowed from tin cowls set high in the warehouse ceiling, spilling yellow circles of illumination on the floor. In the middle of the largest circle stood another desk, its surface reflecting light from above in yellow shards, as if tossing sharpened knives back at the timbered crossbeams above. A broken mirror lay on the desktop – that explained the reflected shards of light. And in the middle of the desk, an open box waited. The box hadn't been opened neatly. Ragged slices crisscrossed the top, and rusty patches the color of dried blood had splattered the cardboard, as if someone had shattered the mirror and sliced into the box with the broken fragments.

Bits of broken mirror smashed against the hardwood floor as I brushed them off the desk. A glance at the top flap indicated that the package was addressed to a man named Smith in Auburn, California and had been mailed from a university in Massachusetts. That told me nothing, so I upended the contents. A sheaf of papers dropped out, followed by a statue attached to a chain.

The statue wasn't huge by any means, but it was large enough that I couldn't imagine anyone wearing it around his neck. Russ snatched the chain before I could get a close look at the thing. I only saw that it was fashioned from jade, and it looked like a hungry Doberman with the wings of a gigantic bat.

The chain swung back and forth as Russ dangled the statue before his good eye. Broken mirror-shards on the desktop caught the idol's image, and green light splashed against the warehouse walls. I barely noticed it because that sheaf of papers was still nestled between the reflected idols, and to me those papers were just as tantalizing as the statue itself.

I unfolded the pages and started reading. I didn't know if it was a letter or a story. All I knew was that the writer began by describing his strange partnership with a man named St. John, and then he turned to the subject of a statue they'd dug up in a European graveyard . . .

And just then Russ started reading, too. The jade statue lay cupped in his left palm like a miniature pet, and once again my brother's eyes were glazed with cobwebs. He was staring down at an inscription carved in letters I didn't recognize. His lips moved slowly, deliberately, and the whispered words that spilled from them were the same words I'd heard him use outside the dead man's house . . . the words I'd always taken for gutter *Deutsch*.

Quite suddenly, I understood those words weren't German at all.

They were another language altogether.

A language no one understood this side of hell.

In another moment, those words were buried by another sound . . . a scuttling percussion that erupted from a garbage can next to the desk. It was a twin to the night sounds I'd heard coming from the bathroom at the dead man's house, and a chill capered up my spine.

Russell's lips snapped shut, cutting off his words.

The garbage can tipped over and banged on the floor, dumping more broken-mirror shards.

A severed hand crawled through the mess, dragging a gnawed and splintered wrist.

The hand moved across the floor like a giant spider.

In another second it crossed through the doorway that adjoined the station office where the dead station agent stood, pointing at my brother with the bloody stump of his right wrist.

The agent was a bucket of gore dressed in a suit – face torn to ribbons, mangled lips hanging in shreds. Those lips slithered together like a pair of hungry grave-worms, and above them the thing's eyes shone with a stark blue brightness that made a glacier seem warm. Whatever the station agent had become wasn't anything close to human anymore. Its bloody teeth cut words in the absolute silence of that dark warehouse, and though I heard those words I knew they were meant for Russell alone.

"You unearthed the idol," the thing said. "You used its power to survive, and you hoped you had left it behind in the trenches with the corpses of all those soldiers you murdered in the Master's name. But you cannot escape the Master, any more than you can escape His talisman. It is risen from fallow killing fields just as the Master is risen, and it has found you just as He has found you, for the leash you occupy is a long one. The killing will never end, for this time the Master will bring you to heel like a prize bitch. This time you'll wear a brimstone collar, and you'll be forever at His side."

The words slapped Russell out of his daze, and he hurled the idol into the darkness. A quick whirling motion and the Winchester thundered in his hands. The agent's corpse flew backward in a red shower, thudding against the office floor. Before the smoke cleared, the scuttling hand disappeared into the shadows.

Russ and I exchanged a single glance – there was no time for words.

There was nothing to do but get shed of this place, the things in it, and whatever waited for us beyond its doors.

Russell turned and slid open the door that led to the station platform. An icy wind blasted through the doorway along with a cold stream of darkness, and it wrapped Russell in its grip and pulled him into the night.

Before I could take a single step, the warehouse door slammed in my face like a guillotine blade . . . but not before another black shadow blasted into the room.

It was the dead boar, and it was coming straight for me.

The boar raged through the darkness, crossing the room like a red torrent loosed from a broken dam in hell. I leveled the .38 and put two slugs in the creature, but it plowed over me before I could fire a third.

The pistol flew from my hand and spun through the jade shadows. Hoofs scratched over hardwood as the boar turned to attack again. I hadn't even made it to my knees, and the only thing within reach was a thick shard of broken mirror. Dizzily, I snatched it up as the boar closed on me – its face a mask of caked blood, its snout flared with exertion.

I drove the makeshift blade into the creature's right eye. Tusks raked my belly as the glass tore into my palm but my grip held firm, and I jammed the misshapen blade deeper as the monster smashed me backward. My head thudded against the wooden door, and a black galaxy opened before my eyes. For a second I was nowhere . . . and then in the space of a single blink I was back, just in time to see the boar topple to the floor.

I didn't wait for it to get up. The pistol lay near the door, and I grabbed it with my bloody hand. Tittering laughter rose behind me, and I didn't have to turn around to know the dead station agent was rising again. But I'd already heard enough words from that thing's mouth, and I didn't want to hear any more.

A rattling shove, and I slid open the warehouse door.

Outside, the air was thick with the stink of gunpowder.

Russell's shotgun boomed in the darkness, but my relief at seeing him alive didn't even last a second.

Bound up in the Winchester's echo was the unearthly baying of a gigantic hound.

The jade statue didn't do the monster justice. Nothing could have. Its clawed feet set coal shards burning as it came down the tracks. But faster than the demon came the darkness, sweeping past the monster like a scalding wave, cascading through the tunnel of pine, filling it, and the demon's eyes boiled in its narrow skull as it was overtaken by a night so black it might have been torn from a patch of universe beyond the farthest star.

Just ahead of the monster, my brother stood his ground. The demon paused only a moment, then reared as it closed on Russell. Its great wings spread, slicing a gap in the nightwave, and its claws drew wide as if ready to tear that piece of earth from the womb of the world along with the man who'd claimed it.

Russ fired the shotgun into the gap between those enormous claws. Again and again, as the monster's talons raked the darkness. Blood sprayed from my brother's chest as he was slammed backward. But the Winchester was still in his grasp, and another blast of oo buckshot splattered the night.

Severed muscles gushed blood. The demon's shoulder was skinned to bone and gory socket, and it howled as the next blast took half its face away. That sound couldn't be described with words, but it didn't defy understanding. Not if you had a something like it locked up in your own guts . . . not if you recognized the doomed tenor of it as my brother did, even with his own life draining away. Russ tossed aside the empty shotgun and struggled to his feet. The demon kept on coming, but blood no longer pulsed from its wounds. Now howls and screams erupted from each buckshot trench, as if every soul the beast had devoured was at long last free of the flesh prison housed within the demon's body.

The sound became a roar . . . a hellish cacophony that shook the earth and blasted glass from the train station windows. And Russ screamed as the demon closed over him . . . screamed those horrible words he'd kept locked inside for so long, the gutter sacrament that had doomed him from the time he first spoke it. But now his words were black taunts meant to challenge his tormentor, and soon those words became a howl of his own, slicing through the night like a scythe.

I ran toward my brother, the .38 in my hand. Russ had drawn the *Nahkampfmesser* from its scabbard and was grappling with the demon, the German knife driving through scaled flesh as the creature's great hands closed around his ribs. I was running fast, faster than I ever had. And then that black wave hit me . . . but it wasn't anything as ephemeral as the night. In a moment I was twisting upward in a flock of gigantic bats, and their wings caught me and raised me into the pines in a boiling whirl, and the howls I'd heard from Russ and the monster and all those tortured souls were lost in the chittering screams of a thousand winged nightmares.

The whole world seemed to spin in that black whirlpool. My hands clawed out, fighting for purchase. As I tumbled through the darkness my fingers brushed the station agent's ravaged face. Pages of the letter whipped by along with the bloodstained box that had held it, and as the demon storm churned on I glimpsed the monster's boiling eye in the distance, much dimmer now. Tattered flesh flapped over it like a broken coffin lid. And Russell was there, too – just for a moment, like dead Ahab riding the whale . . . and then he was gone.

I dropped from the black twister's winged embrace. Pain exploded in my ribs as I slammed down on steel rails. The night spilled past me, twisting into the pine tunnel. I watched it go. Bones cracked against pine boughs as the darkness spun into the forest, and dead wings were carved and torn by swirling eddies of broken window-glass, and gravel waves pounded all until there was nothing left but a final wisp of empty night.

Then came silence. And there I was – down on my knees, shivering against those cold steel railroad tracks. Everything was gone . . .

everything except the thing locked in my grasp. At first I thought I'd managed to hold on to the .38 as I rode the whirlwind, but when I raised my hand I found it wasn't a gun that waited there . . . not at all.

No. The thing that filled my hand was a jade statue.

I threw it into the trees, and I ran.

I must have followed the railroad tracks, because somewhere along the line I jumped a freight and headed east in a livestock car. The train rattled over Emigrant Gap in the dead of night. Nothing in the car but shadows and a howling wind that sliced the low-hanging clouds, whipping white ghosts through wooden slats as the car traveled over snow-capped mountains.

Or so it seemed to me. Except for wind and shadows and those wisps of cloud, the rail car was empty. The railroad didn't ship livestock over the Gap once fall delivered the first heavy snow. Try that, and the company would have ended up with a few tons of frozen meat. And maybe that's how I should have ended up, just a couple hundred pounds of not-so-prime cut ready for God's own butcher shop.

But it didn't work out that way.

I was still alive when the train made it over the mountains.

At least, that's what they told me on the other side.

They sliced off three frostbitten toes at the indigent ward in Reno's main hospital. Stitched up my hand, took care of my other wounds, too. After a few weeks I got around okay. One of the nurses helped me find a job, and I worked in a casino restaurant for a couple months. When I got a little stronger, I landed a gig loading freight for a trucking company. It was a lucky break – the guy who owned the business was a casino regular.

Anyway, the business wasn't always straight up. Some nights the dispatcher would call a bunch of us down to the warehouse and we'd unload a truck of bootleg liquor. The boss must have liked the fact that I didn't nip bottles or run off at the mouth, because it wasn't long before he made me a driver. In those days that was like catching the brass ring. For me, it didn't matter. The way I saw it there was no brass ring. There was just one day, and the next, and the one after that.

But what mattered most were the days that had come before. That's where my mind wandered, and returned. To a leaky migrant tent, where my brother's cough echoed like the spinning tumblers of a locked safe. To a dead man's house, and a broken mirror I stared into morning after morning. To a stolen Nash, where my brother and I found a map with our destination circled in red and a Winchester shotgun that could bring down a demon.

Those memories held plenty of questions, but answers were in short supply. If Russ had any, he didn't share them with me before he died. And now that he was past sharing . . . well, I got to thinking that maybe it had always been that way with Russ.

Even so, I still saw my brother in my dreams. Just in flashes, like a choppy silent movie. *Russ in uniform, digging trenches, a blood-stained spade in his big hands as he unearthed something buried centuries before . . . German flares blooming in the night sky . . . that green idol gleaming in soil that squirmed with gut-colored worms . . . a demon freed from the catacombs of an underground temple, stalking through mustard gas clouds . . . a German soldier's corpse clenched between the monster's teeth, two more dead men locked in its clawed hands . . .*

Those dreams formed a story, but I had no idea if it were true. It hardly mattered. When I woke up in the morning my memories were waiting for me, and they didn't add up nearly so easily. My mind was a haunted house. That black dog of a wind still blew outside its walls, and there was a broken mirror in every sink. A stolen car parked in the driveway would take me exactly where it wanted and nowhere else. But the truth was that I couldn't leave that house. I walked its corridors until I knew every step, even the ones that only led to locked doors.

There were plenty of those, and I didn't have to look very hard to find them. But I did look for answers in other places. We had a pile of maps at the trucking office, and I discovered that there wasn't a town anywhere in California named New Anvik. I checked with the railroad, and there wasn't a train station by that name, either. And that Massachusetts University, the one that had shipped the jade idol to a man in Auburn? A trip to the public library told me there wasn't a university by that name anywhere in the world.

But none of that mattered. A week after my library visit, a package from that university showed up on my doorstep. And yes – it was addressed to me.

I brought the box inside my apartment, but I didn't dare open it. I was supposed to pick up a load of hooch just north of San Francisco that night. Instead, I called in sick. Then I drove into the woods above Donner Lake and heaved the package off a rocky crag. On the way back to Reno I thought about buying a pistol and blowing a hole in my brain. If that box had been waiting on the front porch when I got home, I would have done it. But I never saw it again.

A few months passed. I tried to keep busy. I took every job the trucking company offered, especially the bootleg runs that paid top dollar. When that haunted house started calling, I'd try to distract myself with a stack of novels from the library. If that failed I'd hit the tables at one of the casinos downtown, and I'd keep my mind on the cards.

That's how I ran into the nurse from the indigent ward, the one who'd helped me land that restaurant job. Emma was out with a couple girlfriends playing blackjack, and we started talking across the table. The cards were falling my way. After a while I cashed in my chips for a stack of greenbacks, and I took Emma and her friends out for steak and pre-war champagne at a joint on Douglas Alley that didn't care about Prohibition.

It wasn't the kind of thing I'd ever done. I'm not sure why I did it. But at the end of the night, Emma gave me her phone number. I said I'd call her, but a week passed and I couldn't pick up the phone. I knew why, of course. The short version was that steak and champagne didn't really change anything . . . and the longer version was all the stuff locked up in that haunted house.

But for the first time I thought that maybe I didn't want to look for the key to that house anymore. Maybe what I needed to do was leave it alone. I didn't know if my brother had ever felt that way, but then again I wasn't Russ. What we'd shared we'd always share, alive or dead, just as we'd always be brothers. But maybe the time had come for me to stop being my dead brother's keeper, and the keeper of his ghosts.

I was just about to dial Emma's number when the company dispatcher called and offered me a midnight run to Grass Valley. It was a straight freight deal, no bootleg, but I needed the money after blowing that blackjack bankroll. And I needed time to think, too.

An hour later I was driving through the mountains. Snow was falling. It was quiet. Not like it is when hail or sleet pounds your windshield, and you get the feeling that the universe is firing ball bearings at you from the darkness. No. This was the opposite of that. It was as if nothing was falling through the night . . . as if nothing was filling everything up.

I liked that idea. As I drove west, it seemed as if that white nothing could wipe the whole world away. It felt like starting over . . . or maybe more than that. I pulled over and watched the snow drift down, sipping coffee from my thermos. Then I climbed down from the cab and followed a path that twisted through the pines.

It was cold, but there wasn't a breath of wind. The snow fell through the narrow gap above the trail and between the trees, powdering the ground . . . the branches . . . everything. Even me. I wanted that white silence to stretch behind me and before me like a blank page. I stopped and felt it on my skin, breathed it into my lungs, held it there. And then I closed my eyes and imagined snow falling on the rooftop of that haunted house inside me.

The snow drifted before my mind's eye – heavier, and heavier still – smothering the eaves, burying the whole place in silence . . . burying everything so very deep. And when I opened my eyes it stood before me, waiting there in a clearing. A house dusted in white, with an open door. The house was made of flesh and bone, and the bone gleamed brighter than any snow. The open doorway was a red patch, the door itself like a scarred slab of skin meant to cover an empty eye socket.

My brother stood in that red doorway, a shotgun in his hands. Russell's face was smeared with blood, but he smiled when he saw me.

And then he howled.

Usman T. Malik feels his story, "In the Ruins of Mohenjo-Daro," is "steeped in Lovecraftian influences. Ancient cosmic warfare, blood libations, hints of a world misaligned and warped – even as it surrounds the characters in the story, and irrupts into their puny lives as they struggle to understand it, and through it, perhaps themselves . . . this all strikes me as the essence of Lovecraftian horror. I intentionally stayed away from any of the Cthulhu Mythos to avoid pastiche; there are plenty of myths and legends in Indo-Pakistan that I could explore and subvert."

Malik is a Pakistani writer resident in Florida. He reads Sufi poetry, likes long walks, and occasionally strums naats on the guitar. His fiction has been nominated for the Nebula Award and won a Bram Stoker Award. His work has appeared in *The Year's Best Dark Fantasy & Horror*, *The Year's Best YA Speculative Fiction*, *The Best Science Fiction and Fantasy of the Year*, *Year's Best Weird Fiction*, *Tor.com*, and *The Apex Book of World SF* among other venues.

In the Ruins of Mohenjo-Daro
Usman T. Malik

Look for the ghost trees, memsaab, the college chowkidar had told Noor, grinning from ear to ear, and indeed the road to Mohenjo-Daro was lined with them. Rows of acacia, jand, and Indian lilac stood shrouded in clouds the color of steel filigree. Noor pressed her nose to the window, watching the treetops blur and disappear in the half-breathing ether. The November dawn was clear and without a hint of fog, but the strange gray clouds stretched amebic limbs in either direction mile upon mile as if the Sind riverbank was haunted by a limitless phantom coiling around the foliage. When the school bus sped past one such tree, the wind rush pulsed the specter until it filled with sunrise. Branches red-dark emerged in glistening veins.

Locust swarms, insect hordes, cotton candy – Noor's brain groped for an explanation. Sunlight twitched in one of the cocooned trees and the illusion of giant blood corpuscles recurred. Noor's vision misted; her temple sizzled. For a moment she feared the onset of a cluster headache. The last was two months ago just after she'd joined the cadet college and it had disabled her for two days. Now was not the time.

She stretched her neck from side to side, and flinched when Junaid touched her shoulder. The headache flared. Angrily she turned toward him. His starched white collar jutted into his neck. The striped red tie with the cadet college crest – crossed scimitars underlaid by pine boughs, surrounded by a half moon – looked uncomfortable, but he was beaming, brown eyes sharp and arrogant. He jabbed a stubby finger past her face.

"Spiders," he said and widened his thin lips.

"Don't touch me again," Noor said, voice cold as glass. When he continued to grin, she looked to the roadside. White crab spiders – hundreds of them dangling in the gossamer mass blooming from the trees. Gently they swayed in the wind, milky beads studding the lattice-work – which she now realized was webbing.

"Have you seen any flies or mosquitoes since you came, Miss Hamdani?" Junaid's hand rose crablike to sprawl on the headrest in front of her. "The locals told me this happened after all that flooding last year. Thousands of spiders took refuge in the trees."

Out of the corner of her eye she watched him finger a strip of leather peeling off the seat. His nails were perfectly manicured. He tore off the strip, drew it into his mouth, and spoke around it, "Everyone was worried about malaria outbreaks. Guess the ghost trees took care of that," and when Noor didn't respond, "What? Don't tell me you're still angry."

"I'm not," she said sharply.

"Come now. It's Eid. Let's be festive and forgiving." He was sitting next to her in a row three seats wide and his breath stirred the edge of her hijab. She edged closer to the window. He smiled and began to chew the leather strip. "Kids are watching. Have to be model teachers now, don't we?"

Good point, asshole, she thought and closed her eyes. Another reason, other than his over-inflated ego, she'd spurned his advances since her arrival. Then again, this display of dickhood wasn't limited to him. Many of the faculty – all male except for a quiet burkah-clad part-time lecturer, who disappeared as soon as her classes were over, and Tabinda who now sat left of Junaid in the third seat – took turns leering at her during morning assembly or talking down to her at lunch. Most were graduates of cadet colleges or military academies and had carried the attitude into their professional lives. That she taught English and not history or Islamiat hardened their stance for some reason.

Her students didn't seem to care. Even though they were clearly not used to female teachers, her hijab gained her a bit of respect; something she'd seen frequently in this area. Part of the rural tradition, she supposed. Briefly she wondered how they would react if she whipped out Oxford jeans and long white shirts, her preferred dress back in her high school days in New Hampshire, instead of the plain shalwar kameez and dopatta she wore now.

She glanced at the boys. They'd set out raucous and excited at predawn, but the motion of the bus had lulled them and they were dozing in their seats. Twelve teenage cadets, heads back, eyes closed, athletic arms crossed over their chests or dangling off the armrest. Dara, the tall muscular kid with sharp green Pashtun eyes, was the only one awake and staring at her. She nodded to him. He raised his chin and looked away.

There's another friend I made, Noor thought and covered the smile rising to her face with a hand.

About half past ten they entered Dokri. Junaid pointed out Cadet College Larkana to the boys as they passed it: a pink structure flanked by red brick wings and triangular arches opening onto the first- and second-floor classrooms. A cast iron gate blocked the driveway leading up to the school building.

"This is my alma mater. Hundreds of acres. Large grounds, lots of football and hockey fields," Junaid announced. "We'll stop here on the way back if you like."

They left the town with its streets bustling with cloth merchants, laborers, and food vendors. Noor watched the last of the driver-hotels disappear in the distance and, as always when leaving a town, was filled with loneliness, an incomprehensible nostalgia she couldn't displace no matter how hard she tried.

The feeling lasted until they stopped ten minutes later to fuel up at a small, peeling gas station, and the boys poured out to use the restroom and grab snacks from the mart. While Junaid and the bus driver chatted up the pump attendant, Noor slipped away. She stood behind a row of ghost cypresses and poplars along the riverbank and watched the smoke from her Marlboro Light spiral its way through the spider cocoon swaying above her. Dozens of insects hung dead or twitching in it. Hundreds of eyes glinted. If she reached out with her cigarette, could she set the whole thing ablaze?

"Quite a sight, isn't it," said a familiar voice.

Noor snuffed out the smoke on the bark of the nearest tree before turning. Tabinda leaned against a poplar, gazing thoughtfully at the water shining through gaps in the verdure.

"Cigarette?" Noor said. She'd never seen the professor smoke.

Tabinda smiled. She was a plump woman in her sixties with a bovine face and horn-rimmed glasses. Her teeth were rotten but her smile reached her eyes. "That shit you smoke? Nah." She thrust a chubby hand at Noor as if offering to shake. "Look at my hand. Near the wrist. See where the two tendons join? It used to be easier to find when I was thinner, but can you see the dip in the skin?"

Noor looked at the concavity at the base of the woman's thumb where it met the wrist. The skin was tinged orange, and paler compared to the dark brown surrounding it.

"That's called the anatomical snuffbox." Tabinda lowered her hand. "I used to snort real homegrown tobacco in my younger days, see? Place a pinch in there and snuff it right up. Quit about ten years ago when my doctor found a spot in my mouth. He took it out, biopsied it. Turned out it was pre-cancerous. And that was the end of that." She nodded to herself and turned back to the river.

Noor watched the sun paint the woman's cheek golden. They'd talked a few times before. Shared a few superficialities about families. Noor told her about her mother back in the U.S. and how long it had been since she had seen her; how difficult it was to live a translocated life. Tabinda told her about her marriage to a wife beater in Lahore and how she escaped by moving a thousand miles away to teach Pakistan Studies to this unruly military lot in Petaro. Commiserated about Noor's transfer from Karachi to this "shit-hole town," as she put it. She had a Punjabi accent and a nasal voice. Noor found it easy to like her; she was so jaded and sassy.

"Looking forward to exploring the ruins, Miss Hamadani?" said Tabinda.

"Noor, please."

"Noor. Sorry. At my age it's difficult to discard old habits. I'm used to calling all these men by last name."

"Creates that distance, doesn't it?"

"Yes. Distance can be quite useful in this place," Tabinda said, her eyes invisible from sun glare in her spectacles.

"When did you start working here?"

"Oh, about fifteen years ago."

"The faculty didn't . . . make you feel unwelcome?"

"Of course they did. That's what men do. But I also try not to get in their way."

The rebuke was subtle but unmistakable. Noor stared between the moss-covered trunks at the bus across the road. "What they were doing – it was wrong."

"Bloodshed and sacrifice is a way of life here. Has been for centuries."

"They don't know any better," Noor said. "I can't stand the sight of blood, but that wasn't why I stepped in. Teach kids to enjoy violence and they'll carry that lesson to the grave."

Tabinda laughed. The sound was deep-throated and made her jowls jiggle. "Half these cadets will be dead before they hit thirty. That's the nature of their game. In their hearts they know it and it makes them arrogant." She turned and walked toward the bus. She was agile for her age. Her voice carried back: "This has always been a land of heroes and monsters, Miss Hamdani. Here you pick your battles."

A soft wind soughed through the spider cloud, making the dead shudder. Insect dust pattered down on Noor's shoulders. She brushed it away. You're wrong, she wanted to say. This is exactly how it begins. Hand them a weapon and tell them to man up and that's the way to the mother lode of horror.

But of course she said nothing.

She had come upon them by accident the day before during her morning walk. The boy's name was Abar and he was holding the trussed goat down with his knees digging into its well-fed side. Two other boys Noor didn't know joined him, each squatting to hold the goat's legs firmly. The animal – one of the beautiful tall Rajanpur breed with spotted ears and a milky body – bleated and thwacked its head on the bleached summer grass under the Kikar acacia. The sight made Noor's blood pound and she found herself stomping toward the trio.

"Hey," she called across the football field. "What do you think you're doing?"

The two newcomers flinched as boys will on hearing a teacher's voice and looked up. Abar just smiled and jerked the goat's head back by the ears.

"Sir Junaid's orders," he yelled and positioned the slaughter knife across the animal's throat. The blade glinted silver. It threw a dancing shadow across the green and Noor's vision rippled. For a moment she didn't know where she was, and anger swept over her.

"Put that goddamn knife down. Now!" She was only ten feet away and her voice boomed in the narrow grove of trees dividing the football and hockey grounds. The newcomers dropped the goat's legs and sprinted away, but Abar didn't move. He pressed the animal's head down, an ugly grimace of anger and effort on his face.

"What's the matter, Miss Hamdani?" Junaid had materialized from behind the grove of trees. In his hands he held half a dozen steel skewers, a chopping knife, and a cutting block. Without taking his eyes off Noor, he set these next to the acacia and mopped his brow dramatically. "How can we help you on this fine Eid day?"

"Did you ask the boys to do this?"

"Do what?"

"Slaughter animals on their own?"

He lifted his eyebrows in mock surprise. "Yes."

"Why? Where's the butcher?"

"Sick. Off duty. Does it matter? It's sunnah to slaughter your own animals, isn't it?" He grinned at her. He had what her dad used to call a copstash mustache: a thick wad of hair that bristled at either end. With his crew cut hair it made him look like a thug.

"Tell me again what the Prophet said about teaching mercy."

He pointed at the bleating goat. "That is mutton. You eat it every day—"

"I'm vegan!"

"—and today's Eid. Someone has to slaughter the animal to commemorate Ibraham's gratitude to God for sparing his son's life. It could've been Ismael under that knife. Then we'd all be in a boatload of trouble sacrificing our sons and all, wouldn't we? All I'm doing is teaching our glorious cadets to do it themselves. Very important, learning to steel your heart."

She wanted to punch him. "They're kids! They need to learn kindness before cruelty."

His eyes were chips of hot mica. "Not my cadets. Not in these times. And this is not cruelty." He placed the skewers crisscross on the wooden block. "It's necessity."

Helpless, Noor glanced at Abar. The boy was smiling, a cold twisting sneer that was frighteningly familiar. The feeling of unreality, of red-hot memory, resurged. Noor turned and strode away, blinking away the warmth in her eyes. Behind her rose the chant "In the name of God . . ." and the animal was screaming, a loud gargling sound. If she kept walking, Noor thought, she could outpace the sound. Walk away before steam rises from the animal's throat in the winter air, before the red curtain drops in front of her eyes and the strange staring faces emerge . . . one of which will be Muneer's. Always his.

As she fled, the sound was cut off suddenly.

Then there was chopping.

Through a thicket of trees they trundled into the low-lying areas of Mohenjo-Daro. The Sind River curled a blue finger around the plateau in the distance. Tabinda pointed out dull squat structures that formed the mounds on the ruins' outskirts.

"Pariahs lived in some of these," she said.

The museum at Mohenjo-Daro was a solid red brick building with life-sized bronze replicas of ancient relics flanking its entrance. Two hundred meters away in the desolate sprawl of the ruins the Buddhist stupa rose from the giant mound like a skin-colored tumor. Junaid and Tabinda disembarked to set up a picnic lunch, leaving Noor and the cadets to hurry into the museum.

"Had you come in spring," said the curator, "it would've taken you eight hours to get here from the college. You chose wisely. But, still, *this* late?"

Noor fingered the seated Priest-King statuette the curator had been showing the class, a tiny resin replica with pressed lips, closed eyes, and a gouged nose. A crack ran down its forehead to the left cheek. "Why? What happens in spring?"

The curator glanced at the wall clock. It was quarter past eleven. He scratched the crab-shaped mole on his cheek. "The Sarwar Fair. Hundreds of pilgrims from villages all over the Indus Valley converge on the saint's tomb in the Baluchistan hills. They travel by foot and donkey carts and often clog up the roads all the way from Dadu to Sukkar. The soil of Sind is filled with miracles and magic." His gaze didn't leave the clock.

Noor placed the resin figure back on the counter. "What time does the museum close?"

The man sighed. He was short and swarthy, dressed in a checkered ajrak shirt, white shalwar, and an embroidered Sindi cap. His nametag said *Farooq*. As he looked at the mass of teenage boys loitering about the lobby, distaste crept into his face. "Now."

"It's not even noon."

"It's Eid. We're usually closed for the holidays. I made an exception for the cadet college because I was told we'd be done by ten."

"Oh." She didn't know what to say. They had been delayed at a military checkpoint in Dadu. Apparently a suicide blast had occurred at a small mosque in the outskirts of Khairpur, killing an elderly woman and her two grandchildren. The area was flooded by police and army personnel; checkpoints had been established at various junctures from Larkana all the way to their college at Petaro. The military was worried about a follow-up attack. Junaid said he wasn't surprised. Most terrorist attacks happened in double strikes, a well-known MO used by the Taliban as well as the CIA (where they used drones for warfare).

"Sorry," she said to Farooq who was fingering his mole, "but we traveled a long way for this. Most cadets go home during holidays, but they," she pointed at the boys peering at a representation of the famous bronze Dancing Girl of Mohenjo-Daro and rows of clay urns lining the glass cases, "had no one to take them. Either their families are away or they have no families. So a few of us volunteered—"

"Yes, yes." Farooq waved his hand impatiently. "Spare me heartbreaking accounts of army orphans. I'll give you a quick tour. Is this your entire party? Where's Ms. Tabinda? She's the one who called me."

Noor glanced to the exit. Junaid and Tabinda were setting up lunch. She felt guilty that she couldn't help with such chores; her inability to speak Sindi prevented communication with the bus driver whose Urdu was rudimentary. She wished the older professor could at least take the tour. The Mohenjo-Daro trip was her idea.

"Seems like we're the only ones for now."

Farooq nodded glumly. "This way then. We'll start with the Memories of the Ancients display."

She nudged the cadets and they followed him up the northern corridor.

His voice echoed as they passed through an arched doorway into a long hall flanked by glass cabinets on either side. "Egypt, Mesopotamia, and Indus Valley are the three earliest civilizations of the Old World – China came later – and all, of course, developed along water bodies. We used to believe they evolved and thrived in isolation, but now we know that Indus Valley and Mesopotamia traded with each other for centuries." He pointed left and right at carnelian necklaces, sculptures, gemstone beads, ivory combs, and brass containers with traces of herbal collyrium.

Noor's belly cramped suddenly. Period pains? But she wasn't due for another week. It would explain the headache she had earlier that morning. Wincing, she rubbed her abdomen.

"Discovered in 1922 by an officer of the Archaeological Survey of India, Mohenjo-Daro is thought to have been the most important city of the Indus Valley Civilization. Spread out over two hundred and fifty acres on a series of mounds, its heyday was from 2500 to 1900 BC. It was suddenly abandoned then. No one knows why."

Noor glanced over her shoulder. The kids looked suicidally bored. They drifted behind her, listless, eyes glazed. The Pashtun boy, Dara, had his nose pressed against a cabinet, palms splayed against the glass, but she thought his reflected green stare was fixed on her. His biceps bulged on either side of his head.

"A Buddhist monastery was discovered atop the city's main citadel. You can still see the stupa. We don't know why the builders decided to erect it there hundreds of years after the city was abandoned, but most of Mohenjo-Daro still lies underground. The mounds grew organically over centuries as people built platforms and walls for their houses. The name Mohenjo-Daro means 'Mounds of the Dead' in Sindi."

Farooq waved at a ceiling-high stucco wall covered with black-and-white and sepia photographs. A flicker of interest went through the cadets. They crowded around aerial and ground views of the ruins.

Noor had seen these in slideshows Tabinda put on before the trip. She went to Dara who hadn't moved. He edged left to allow her to lean against the cabinet. This close, he was taller than her. He smelled of sweat and cologne.

"I'm sorry about the other day," she said in a low voice. "I didn't mean to barge in on you two like that."

The tips of Dara's brown ears darkened. She could see the tension in his bunched neck and shoulder muscles.

"And here," boomed the curator's voice, "is the most famous statue found in Mohenjo-Daro. You might have seen the Priest-King's picture in textbooks on Indus Civilization. This is a detailed replica made from a mold of the real thing kept in the National Museum in Karachi."

"It's okay. Really," Noor told Dara. The boy's fingers had closed over the edge of the cabinet. "I won't tell anyone. Some of my friends back in the US were like you. One of them was bullied and ended up struggling with depression for years. I hated that." Her gaze went to the cadets gathered around the pictures. What would they do if they found out about this kid or his friend currently away during winter break? She didn't want to imagine. Seized by instinct, she lifted the corner of her hijab and hissed at him, "We all have secrets. *Look.*"

He didn't turn to face her, but his eyes flicked in her direction. They widened when he saw her left shoulder.

"Some think the Priest-King is neither a king nor a man. Some believe this is in fact a woman of considerable importance to the people of Mohenjo-Daro. A high priestess or maybe a eunuch who led their religious rituals."

"We all have secrets," Noor said again. Dara looked at her with wary eyes. He was a quiet backbencher, rarely said a word. His grades were average. She used to wonder if he was slow.

She dropped her hijab into place.

Dara rapped a knuckle against the glass, and his eyes were green fires. "You don't know anything," he whispered fiercely, turned, and fled down the hall.

She watched him go, then walked back to join the cadets peering at something in a glass case. Farooq glanced up as she approached.

"So glad you could join us." He adjusted the Sindi cap on his head. "I was just telling this young man about seal thirty-four. Dr. Gregory Fossel of University of Pennsylvania believes it represents a sacrifice ritual. Care to listen in?"

She watched him unlock the case and withdraw two artifacts. In one hand he held a reproduction of the tan soapstone seal. The boys murmured and jostled to get closer. A tall angular deity with a horned headdress and bangles on both arms stood atop a fig tree. With a gleeful face it looked down on a kneeling worshipper.

Nearby was a small stool on which lay a human head.

"Seal thirty-four is taken as evidence by some that human sacrifice was practiced as a fertility rite in this region. Similar to such offerings to Kali in certain parts of India."

Noor looked at the seal. Below the kneeling worshipper were a giant ram and seven figures in procession. They wore single-plumed head-dresses, bangles, and long skirts. The sight chilled her; it was so brutal and somber. Her belly cramped again.

"Dr. Fossel, however, has argued that the presence of Pashupati's seal," Farooq held up the stone in his other hand. It showed a naked figure with three grim faces and ram horns seated on a stool surrounded by deer, rhinoceros, and elephants, "means that the people of Indus had the option to proffer animals as substitute for humans."

"Pashupati?" Someone chortled. Noor glanced up. It was Abar, the boy who had slaughtered the goat on Junaid's orders. He had a malicious grin on his face. "What kind of faggot name is that?" He elbowed a friend.

"One of Shiva's names." The curator glared at him. "His incarnation as the Lord of Beasts."

Both boys burst out laughing. A few others smiled uneasily.

"That's enough," Noor told the boys. Giggling, they strolled down the hall. "Sorry about that," she said to Farooq.

His face was pinched and red. "That's the sort of kids we're raising now. Forget it. It's closing time anyway." He muttered something inaudible and led them back to the lobby.

At the exit, Noor flashed a smile and said, "Thank you for the tour. Very educational."

He nodded and began to shut the door.

"Every place has its secret flavor," Noor said through the door opening. "Here's a question I always ask curators and guides." She touched his sleeve and smiled brightly. "Tell us one thing about the site you normally wouldn't tell visitors."

He looked at her with a cocked eyebrow. "Lady, you're not from Sind, are you?"

"Not a difficult observation, I guess, but why do you say that?"

"A local wouldn't ask me that question." His gaze went over her shoulder. Past the verdigris-laced brass statue of the Dancing Girl of Mohenjo-Daro with an emaciated hand on her hip at the entrance, across the rocky slope. He stared at the citadel mound visible from the museum steps. "What does it matter? I'll tell you *two* things," he said, lowering his voice. "First: on the Day of the Goat, no one from Larkana district will stay in these ruins past dusk. Not even the watchman."

"The Day of the Goat?"

"Second—" His eyes gleamed in the doorway. Incessantly he picked at his mole until a drop of blood appeared below its twisted, spidery shape. "Why don't you ask Ms. Tabinda about devil glass? Ask her why she and her crew stopped the restoration dig here in 2001."

"What?" Noor stared at him, but he was already stepping back in, slamming the door, slipping the bolts, and she was left on the doorstep with her cadets milling noisily about her.

They dipped sheermal in chicken-and-lentil soup and chased it down with yogurt lassi. Junaid described the strategic importance of the site's location near a body of water, but no one was interested. The cadets were restless; they wanted to explore. Noor's eyes were riveted on Tabinda who was quietly munching a piece of bread, her gaze never far from the ruins.

A cold wind followed them up the dusty gravel path winding between the citadel mound and lower town. Two miles west of the citadel was lush farmland. Odd that no human dots speckled the furrowed fields. They hadn't seen any ox carts, motor bikes, or bicycles on the road leading into the city either. Noor assumed the laborers and farmhands had taken the day off for Eid. Her belly had settled and she felt more cheerful.

The farmland was separated from the salty sediment of the ruins by a levee. Tabinda said this was reinforced every year to help control the annual flooding.

"Not that it always works. Last year heavy floods topped the levees and brought the white crab spiders out." She smiled. "The locals fear those spider trees, let me tell you. They think them a terrible omen."

"Omen? Of what?"

"Apparently there's a folktale about demon cattle that feed on the leaves of such trees. Some time ago Karachi University published a survey showing that in certain years coinciding with old Sindi lunar calendars, animal sacrifice activity intensifies in this region." Tabinda rubbed her knuckles. "The fact that the floods nearly destroyed the site last year doesn't help ease their minds about evil forewarnings."

She was correct about the damage. By now the city proper had closed around them like a bony fist and the narrow alley they walked was flanked by massive crumbling buildings topped with mud slurry for preservation. Windows gaped in the brick houses laid in a perfect grid. Some houses with exterior staircases that led to the second floor had chipped and eroded steps. The city's smell hit Noor – salinity and dust, floodwater and age – and for a moment she felt as if she were falling, collapsing inside a claustrophobic funnel down into nothing. The feeling passed, leaving her slightly dizzy.

The cadets began to meander. A few headed to the alley leading up to the citadel mound. Noor let Junaid uselessly attempt to herd them together and strode to catch up with the elderly professor walking briskly as ever.

"You didn't tell me you used to be an archaeologist," she said.

Tabinda frowned. She was holding a palm against her mouth, two fingers pinching her nostrils. The edges of her eyelids behind her spectacles were pink. "I hate this weather. Winter brings out all my allergies." She sneezed and rubbed her nose. "I'm not an archaeologist. I assume Farooq told you something. The man couldn't keep his mouth shut if you sealed it with mortar."

She went up a stone staircase and lowered herself onto a platform jutting from the roof. Noor sat down beside her.

"He said you were involved with a dig here."

"Yes. As consultant anthropologist. Greg Fossel and I were working on restoring parts of the site's drainage system. You'd be surprised how extensive it was. One wondered why they went to such lengths for a city this small." She dangled her legs back and forth, her face thoughtful. "Then again, most of it remains underground according to sonar sweeping."

"Why'd you stop?"

Tabinda patted the edge of the platform. "Circumstances."

Together they gazed at the ruins sprawling around them. In the lower part of the city between copses of trees and rocks was more evidence of water damage: caving walls, piles of broken masonry, weathered facades. Here and there the rubble twinkled.

Noor said, "What did Farooq mean about devil glass?"

The professor's black eyes were glazed and inward. "Vitrified pottery of course. Sediment and relics turned to ceramic glass by extreme temperatures."

"I don't understand."

Tabinda laughed. The sound echoed in the alleys, as if it came from within the ruins. "Why would you want to? It's only of interest to old farts like me." She rose and made her way to the staircase.

"Why did he call it devil glass?"

Tabinda stood at the top step, her silhouette dark and bloated against the sun. She seemed to be transfixed by the ruins again. Behind her the stupa and the citadel mound thrust against a desolate winter sky empty of birds.

"When the site was first discovered," she said in a flat voice, "the excavators found piles of glass spherules and silica chunks like those found in Libya and the Sahara. In some places large craters were present. It was assumed that either meteor impact or plasma discharges from lightning had melted the minerals. Fused soil into glass. None of which, of course, explains the hundreds of human skeletons lying bleached in the streets and alleys on top of the glass heaps."

"What?" Noor pushed herself up from the edge. Two streets away one of the cadets was pissing in the shadow of the ancient wall, his shalwar pooled around his ankles. She couldn't tell who. She wanted to yell at him, but the urge was gone as suddenly as it had come. "God. What killed them?"

"Who knows?" Tabinda turned to face her. She shrugged, but did something flicker in the dark of her eyes? Noor couldn't be sure. "Carbon dating approximated it happened around the same time the site was abandoned. The city didn't recover from the catastrophe. Whoever killed those people killed the entire civilization."

A gust of wind swept Noor's hijab back and she stepped away from the platform, chilled and uneasy. Tabinda's fists were clenched by her sides.

She said *whoever*, not *whatever*, Noor thought.

"What happened here in 2001? Come on. You obviously have bad memories."

"We lost three men. All superstitious laborers. One went mad and threw himself off the top of the citadel, smashing his head on the rocks. He was already disturbed, we were told. Another just disappeared. The third tried to kill Fossel and was shot and killed by one of the watchmen." Tabinda shivered. "It was a dark year. And I had such nightmares."

She gave Noor a tired smile. For the first time Noor noticed a mild droop to the left of her face. An old stroke or nerve palsy? The crease of flesh between her nose and lips was flat.

"So I left. Went back to Petaro. Rejoined the cadet college. I haven't looked back since." Tabinda pushed her spectacles up her nose, squinted, then pointed with a pudgy finger. Junaid was walking toward them, waving both hands. His arms looked strange and loose from up here, kameez sleeves ballooning and fluttering like desert birds.

Noor hesitated, then said, "He probably wants us to start gathering the boys. We should leave." Her stomach and flanks tingled. An insistent pressure surged through her lower abdomen. Early, but this was it, no doubt about it now. And she didn't even have pads.

Together they descended the stairs into the lengthening shadows of the city. Noor glanced at her watch. It was three in the afternoon.

Junaid finally caught up with them, panting and shaky. "Why didn't you answer your phone?" he demanded, glaring at Tabinda.

"My purse is in the bus," she said. "Why?"

"We were just about to call the boys," Noor said.

He shook his head. "No. I don't want to create a situation."

"What?"

His face was pale. "Colonel Mahmud just called me. There was a terrorist attack at Cadet College Larkana. At least fifty armed men stormed the premises."

"In Dokri?" Noor's hand went to her mouth. "But we were just there this morning. Oh my God. Are people hurt?"

"Ten dead, and they're holding the surviving cadets and teachers hostage. Two military contingents just left for the town. But that's not the worst of it. Army's got word that a twin attack's been planned on Petaro as well. They're targeting cadet schools for maximum reportage." His manicured fingers rubbed his throat. "Mahmud doesn't want us to return. He wants us to stay here and go to the army base in Sukkar when possible."

"Sukkar?" Tabinda's voice was full of incredulity. "That's a hundred and fifty kilometers away. How will we get past Dokri? The road to Sukkar goes *through* the city!"

"I know that. Don't you think I know that?" His voice was getting louder and a pair of cadets turned their heads.

"Lashkir-e-Jhangvi?" Tabinda said in a low voice.

"No. Pakistani Taliban."

"How far to Sukkar if we go south first and take a detour?" Noor said.

Junaid's nostrils flared. "Four hours by bus."

So at least ten to twelve on foot? She imagined trudging on the cracked, unpaved road under a moonless sky as night fell and surrounded them on all sides. The thought was unpleasant and ridiculous and she pushed it away. They had a bus and a bus driver, and these were cadets, not kindergarten kids.

"Did you talk to the driver?" Tabinda said. "What did he say?"

"He wants to leave. He knows the area well and says he could take back roads, but, look, the problem is the goddamn Taliban." He spat in the dust. "They have spies everywhere. Until it's certain the townsfolk won't snitch on us, Mahmud doesn't want us to leave Mohenjo-Daro. There is an airstrip five kilometers west of here. Worst case: if the hostage situation doesn't clear up, he can call for a large chopper to airlift us out."

Stuck in the ruins. Noor cast a glance at Tabinda. Her face was a mask.

Junaid sounded distracted. "It's cold but there are blankets in the bus, and food, and I can get a fire going. We'll tell the boys it's an Eid bonfire. Dammit," he said through gritted teeth. "I want to be there with the rangers. Larkana's *my* school!"

"Our first responsibility is to the students, don't you think?" Tabinda said. "Besides, you wouldn't leave two women alone with a dozen kids in this place, would you?"

His fingers tugged at his mustache. The ends bristled. "I guess not."

"Good. We need to be calm and think this through."

"Don't tell me to be calm. I am calm."

"Of course you are," Tabinda said speaking each word slowly and Noor looked at her again. The professor had steel in her eyes. Her lips twitched when she smiled at Junaid. "Tell you what, see the citadel mound? It used to be a giant communal bath for the city. There's a rocky grotto right below it. Good place for a fire pit. Why don't you get it going there? I have chickpeas and nuts. We can roast 'em and tell ghost stories and pretend we're on a camping trip."

Junaid's eyes were riveted on Tabinda. The panic had left his face and that mean, arrogant look had returned. "Don't be fucking condescending, you hear me?" He swiveled on his heel and stalked off toward the bus.

Tabinda watched him go, then turned to Noor. Her cheeks were blanched, the facial droop more pronounced. "This is bad."

"Yes."

"This is very bad," Tabinda said and licked her lips. "We shouldn't be here after dusk."

Again that feeling, that sensation of her mind separating from her flesh and eddying down a dusty funnel. Noor's head blazed, pain streaking through her like a dull saw. Dizzy and nauseated, she shot out a hand to clutch a nearby wall.

". . . okay?" Tabinda was saying.

Noor leaned against the wall and closed her eyes. "I think so."

"What happened?"

"I don't know." She tried to control her breathing and it whistled down her throat. "I get cluster headaches sometimes. Maybe it's my period triggering it." She massaged her temples with both hands. Her right eye was beginning to water. "What're we gonna tell the kids?"

"I don't know. We'll think of something. Let's go before they think the city ate us alive."

They trudged between the battered walls, corralling boys along the way. Noor noticed something odd: it felt as if there were more kids dashing, jumping, peering out from behind tall uneven walls and skidding through the dust than a mere dozen. Other tourists? She hadn't seen any vehicles except for the site watchman's Honda bike lolling on a rusty kickstand in the gravel lot. Certainly the two figures – so tall their heads brushed against the doorframe – who goggled at her from one of the houses then danced back into the gloom – were not their boys.

She rubbed her watering eye and continued walking until they reached the bus. Junaid and the bus driver, Hamid, were talking. They fell silent when the cadets approached, but Noor didn't miss the uneasiness in the driver's face and the way he muttered when he thought no one was looking his way.

"Is Hamid from around here?" she asked Tabinda as the kids settled around the heap of firewood.

"The driver? Don't know. Why?"

"Just wondering. He didn't seem too keen on staying here tonight."

"Tell him to join the club," Tabinda said dryly. She was squatting next to the Pashtun boy, Dara, her back to the citadel's eastern wall. The structure towered above them, its shadow pawing the network of alleys that branched and twisted into the city's labyrinthine heart. They were shelling chickpeas and walnuts and tossing the husks inside a metal bowl. Dara had wandered over after Noor and Tabinda cleared broken masonry and stones from the excavated grotto and volunteered to help. He kept his eyes away from Noor's, but she was glad to see him.

She looked across the plateau toward the bus parked by a clump of rocks in the visitor lot and was startled to discover how dusk had whittled the day down to an unsettling purple. The shadows were long and jagged. She could hardly make out the driver carrying stacks of blankets from the bus. He and Junaid had roused the cadets into two wood scavenging teams, and they had piled acacia and poplar twigs crisscross with kindling on top. Noor doubted it would last more than a few hours, but it was better than nothing. Most boys had college sweaters on anyway – navy blue cardigans – and blankets would serve the rest. The remains of the picnic basket had been spread out. Kinnows and apples. Raw peanuts, walnuts, and channa chickpeas all ready to be roasted. Really they were all set to face the cold night.

So why this uneasiness in her body? Her bones felt knobby and sharp against the stony ground, her limbs filled with tar.

Junaid knelt down by them. "Is your phone working?" he said in a low voice.

"What do you mean?" Tabinda said.

"Is your damn phone *working*? I can't reach Mahmud."

Tabinda flicked a peanut shell into the bowl and pulled her Nokia out. She peered at it, raised it high, and frowned. "That's strange. I have no signal bars. "

"Me neither. I can't reach anyone."

"Weather, you think?"

Junaid lifted a hand and rubbed his cheek. "It's not raining and there's no storm."

Tabinda's eyes widened. "No!"

Junaid nodded miserably.

"What?" Noor said.

Junaid looked at Dara, who was quietly peeling nuts, and got up. Noor understood. Rubbing her hands together, she rose and followed him until they were a safe distance away.

"They blew up the signal towers," Junaid said without preamble.

Noor stared at him. "What?"

Junaid bent his knee and placed a boot against the jagged edge of the house behind him. "Cellular base stations. The closest is in Dokri with a network of small booster towers along the way. I'll bet you anything most of them are gone. Which means the fighting is closer than I thought." He sagged a little. "We're stuck here unless they send an air carrier. Or we can drive back."

"You're suggesting it?"

"No! We don't know what's going on out there. This place is safer at the moment."

Noor opened her mouth, closed it. Her gaze went to the vast, empty buildings towering above her. It was quite dark now, the sun just a blood smear on the horizon, and the houses of Mohenjo-Daro pressed together. Broken platforms poked and plunged unevenly; black and formless holes gaped in the walls. Above, an icteric moon sat distorted by a low cloudbank, its light not a promise, but mere possibility.

"We've got to tell the kids now."

"Yes."

Noor shifted her weight; the icy evening wind cut through her kameez and woolen shawl. She shivered. Her abdomen tensed. She hadn't begun bleeding yet, but she would soon.

"Let's get it over with," she said.

They returned to the bonfire. The cadets gathered around and listened to Junaid. Their faces were shocked and delighted by this new excitement. Spend the night in the ruins! Eagerly they asked how long the trouble would last.

"I don't know yet." Junaid shook his head. "We'll just have to be patient."

They left the boys chattering and walked to the bus where Hamid the bus driver was talking with the site watchman, a bald paunchy man with a pockmarked face. The watchman swept a hand toward the mounds and it triggered another round of debate between the two.

"What's going on?" Noor said.

Hamid lifted his head. He was tall and very gangly, features chiseled and filed by many summers spent in this unforgiving land. He wore a khaddar chador around his shoulders in the fashion of northern Pashtuns. He stared at Noor through narrowed, kohl-lined eyes, then turned to Junaid and spoke rapidly in Sindi.

"What's he saying?"

Junaid pressed his hands together. Slowly he began to crack his knuckles. "He says the watchman wants us to leave. He's leaving as well and won't be back for three days."

The museum curator was right. The locals didn't linger here on . . . what had Farooq said? The Day of the Goat. Noor looked at Tabinda who was studying the darkening sky.

"Why?"

"Superstition. They don't like this place at night."

The watchman muttered something and even in the moonlight Noor saw color drain from the bus driver's face. He whispered to Junaid who spoke back angrily. Two cadets who'd followed them here giggled.

"*Chario Hamid. Geedi Hamid,*" they cried.

Noor knew *geedi*. They were calling him a coward. Hamid turned and yelled at them and they laughed and ambled away. Noor didn't like the sound of that laughter; it had a tinge of hysteria about it. Hamid and the watchman stood together, shoulder to shoulder, their faces stubborn and scared.

"*Maryal suyyji waya ahein ayyh raat,*" said the watchman. Hamid flinched and began to murmur what sounded like a prayer.

"Will you please tell me what they're saying?" Noor hissed at Junaid.

"Rubbish." He pulled out his cellphone and looked at the corner of the screen and grimaced. "The dead swell here tonight," he muttered. "What fucking nonsense."

The cold was making Noor's skin tingle. She glanced at Tabinda. She was looking away from the confrontation at the rows of dilapidated buildings ancient and silent on the plateau. Hamid said something and Junaid snapped at him. The driver threw up his hands. The watchman closed his fist and flung all his fingers out at Junaid, a gesture Noor understood without need for translation: *go to hell.* Then he turned and disappeared behind the mounds.

Hamid glared at the three of them, spat something out in Sindi and climbed into the bus. He turned the key and began to rev the accelerator.

"Is he leaving?" Noor said, alarmed.

Junaid's face was furious and helpless. "Yes. He'll leave without us if we don't go now. We've got to gather everyone."

The fire was guttering out when they got back to the boys. Burning wood crackled and orange flames edged with black turned the cadets' faces sly and shadowy when Junaid announced they were leaving.

"We can't go yet," said one in a gruff voice, a freckled rat-faced boy named Tabrez whom Noor recognized as part of Abar's posse. "We need to wait."

"What do you mean?" Junaid said sharply. "Wait for whom?"

The boy popped a handful of roasted chickpeas into his mouth. Crunched them. "They said they had read about a secret room in the ruins. Went treasure hunting . . . Abar and Raheem." Seeing Junaid's aghast expression, he smiled sweetly and added: "Don't worry. They have torches and shovels."

A mile from the city proper, in a narrow ditch between two rocks, Noor undid her nala string, lowered the shalwar, and squatted. She put a hand between her legs, brought it out, and, stared at the viscous stain glisten in the flashlight's glow.

Blood.

The smell was stronger than usual. Fishy. Perhaps it was the air down here. She wiped her hand carefully on the rock, leaving a handprint with beetles squirming in the digits, and let the flow abate. She finished up with paper napkins and bottled water, then rose and stood watching the dot of fire amidst the mounds, one finger scratching beneath her hijab.

She had shown Dara her scars, the raw pink-white ridges coiling serpentine around her collarbone and left shoulder. The thought filled her with amazement at her own daring. She'd never shown them to anyone, not even cheery, gentle Mark with whom she spent one night in Hanover before she left for Pakistan. Her lawyer had appealed for repatriation and to everyone's surprise – most of all, her own – succeeded.

She supposed it made sense. She'd never been charged and couldn't just be guilty by association. Regardless, it was a frightening time, the last of her teenage years.

Mark. God, she hadn't thought about him in a decade, although in the beginning he was all Noor could think about. They had met at rehab soon after they released her. She was required to attend weekly sessions while arrangements were made. Mark was bipolar. Noor was benighted by despair. Terrified of what her past held and what the future might bring. They had made love in darkness, his lips pressed to her neck, the comforting smells of his hair and his body and his seed caustic to her senses; and if he noticed the roughness of her flesh or was dismayed by how she sobbed afterwards, clutched her clothes, and fled never to return, well, he did not call to ask about it.

The night wind gusted, making Noor shiver. She patted her hijab, tucked her kameez into place, and walked back to rejoin the group huddling by the fire.

Junaid crouched on his haunches. He held a lighter in one hand and a newspaper roll in the other. He clicked the wheel and a flame sprouted between his fingers. A red-hot tongue of fire whooshed to life and began to devour the paper.

"Did you find them?" Noor said.

He shook his head. "It's a big place. They could be hiding anywhere. Although, when I do," he gritted his teeth, thrust the burning roll into the dwindling flames, and stirred the cinders with a twig. "I'll beat them to a pulp, I swear." The fire shuddered in his eyes.

They had reached a compromise with Hamid: he would leave the bus behind, in case it turned freezing cold, and hitch a ride with the watchman to Baner, the nearest town. There, he'd try to contact and update Colonel Mahmud on their situation as well as find out details of the confrontation between the military and the militants.

"I really wish you would all come with me," he had told Junaid in Sindi before hopping on the bike, but that was impossible. Abar and Raheem were still missing.

"Mr. Junaid," one of the cadets said. "May we have some more sheer-mal? We're hungry."

"In a bit," he said, then whispered to Tabinda, "How much food is left?"

"Another meal. Maybe two if we're stingy. We didn't prepare for this." She raised her palms to the fire, then shouted, "Who wants to tell ghost stories?"

"Me," called someone, and another muttered, "Dork."

They told stories. Gathered around the flames, ignoring the thrumming black, cold licking their flesh, they gushed out tall tales that became stranger and stranger:

A silent ugly schoolboy bullied by his classmates is wrestled and stripped and thrown to the ground. He turns into a horned beetle, burrows into the earth. Returns night after night as a monstrous insect with a boy's face peering into his tormentors' windows, tapping and chirping, until they go mad from lack of sleep.

A man on a lonely mountain road comes upon a goat, decides to steal it and carry it home – only to find the animal growing heavy on his back, its limbs elongating, cleft hooves dropping until they dangle an inch above the ground. The thief throws the animal off and flees, and monstrous laughter chases him all the way home.

The soot-covered raven man flitting from tree to tree in a Hindu cremation ground.

The pregnant woman in the bushes with snake tresses and backward feet.

A knot of wood exploded in the fire and an ember landed between Noor's legs, startling her. She toed it out with her sneaker, shook the stiffness from her back. She opened her mouth to ask if anyone wanted another blanket. "I know a good one," she said instead, and blinked with surprise.

They turned, fire-lit faces pale and somber. Eyes rheumy from smoke and ash stared at her.

"My mother was a teacher at an Ashkenazi Jewish center in America," she said. Her pulse was pounding in her throat. "She told me the story of the Sent Goat. It scared me witless as a child. Have you heard it?"

They shook their head.

"In the old days, the Israelites performed a rite called the *se'ir mishtale'ach* on the Day of Atonement. Two goats were selected in a ceremony. Healthy, unblemished specimens. Lots were drawn over them: on one was written 'Lord', on the other 'Azazel.' The goat whose lot drew 'Lord' was slaughtered immediately as redemption for the nation's crimes that year. The other . . ." She looked around the campfire, at their reddened, glassy eyes and quivering mouths. "Anyone know what *Azazel* means?"

"Yes," Tabinda murmured. She was sitting next to Noor, her hands knotted together in her lap. "A demon of the wilderness."

"That's correct." Noor nodded. "The second goat was sent into the desert, supposedly laden with the sins of Israel, to Azazel the wild demon, the pagan god, waiting to devour it. Azazel also translates as 'the goat that departs.' The word *scapegoat* in English comes from that." She smiled bitterly. "The animal sacrifice and exile were symbolic of what might happen to an unrepentant tribesman. This was how they made themselves feel better."

The cadets' faces were masks dappled orange and black. They watched Noor with unflinching eyes. The freckled boy, Tabrez, leaned and whispered in his neighbor's ear and they both giggled.

"That's a horrible story," Junaid said. His teeth gleamed in the firelight like a serrated knife. "I didn't know you were so twisted, Miss Hamadani."

He wet his lips and grinned. His hand moved slowly to his lap. Was he turned on? Oddly she didn't feel repulsed, just frigid and tired, and grateful when Dara got up and brought more tinder.

Tabrez whined for dinner and Tabinda handed out four foil-wrapped packets of sheermal. They disappeared quickly. Someone wondered why Abar and Raheem weren't back; perhaps a small group could go look for them in the ruins. Tabinda said "No!" so forcefully it startled them into silence.

Junaid stared at her and said he was sure they'd be back when they got hungry.

The fire whooshed and retreated from the night and Junaid and Dara piled on more wood. A couple of cadets laid out their blankets on the ground near the fire. Before they could start settling in, from beyond the looming citadel came scraping sounds. Pebbles rolled.

Someone was walking the dark near the Buddhist stupa.

They all glanced up. Just a black sky crinkled with a faint yellow moon. In the distance a door swung open on screeching hinges. A shout and a crash.

"Abar," yelled Junaid, springing to his feet. "Is that you?"

One of the cadets screamed and shrank back from a night-thickened alley twenty feet away from which a tall figure jutted its shadowed face. It spasmed briefly, rotating its arms laden with glinting glass bangles above its head, and vanished. The pounding of boots on stony ground. In the ruins someone laughed. The sound was shrill and intermittent, more birdlike than human, and masked the running footsteps until they faded. Junaid shouted the boys' names and plunged into the dark beyond the fire, the halo from his flashlight jittering up and down the streets.

A sound came from beside Noor. She turned. Tabinda's face was doughy, a faint twitch at the left corner of her lips. Her forehead glistened with moisture. Her chubby hand was at her throat, massaging it vigorously.

She's sweating, Noor thought with wonder. In this cold.

An unfamiliar dry smell flooded her nose, triggering memories that disappeared before she could seize them, leaving her breathless and frightened. Her eyes teared up from a sudden raging headache. Tabinda whispered – so softly Noor doubted anyone else heard. The words made the hair stand on the back of her neck. She would remember them later, like a dream song or a grief prayer running in her head again and again while the abandoned city rustled and the river stink of dead fish and reeds and gelatinous old creatures crept into her nostrils.

"He opens his mouth so," said Tabinda. "The Terrible Emperor of the Night."

The cadets held hands, bleary eyes peering in every direction. The ancient houses were entombed in night. Narrow alleys meandered off into the black. So much space devoid of life, yet something *stirred*; somewhere in the ruins Junaid stumbled, crashed, and cursed before falling silent.

Noor's vision pulsed with her heartbeat.

"What's happening, Miss?" cried one of the boys.

"To the bus," she hissed. "Now."

They gaped at her before turning and dashing to the vehicle. Falling over each other, they covered the distance in seconds, piled into the bus, burrowed into their seats. Noor slammed the lock home once Tabinda was aboard. They all stared at the mounds gleaming like gravestones in the moonlight.

"What was that?" said one cadet in a hitching voice.

"Someone turn on the light," said another.

"No!"

"The boys," Noor said. "Probably lost and calling for help."

"By laughing? Are you fucking kidding me?" Tabrez said incredulously.

"Watch your language."

"Screw that. Did you even hear it?" He leaned his brow against the window glass and gazed at the bonfire wavering by the citadel. "That wasn't Abar. Didn't even sound human."

"I shouldn't have returned. I thought, I thought . . . I was *wrong*," Tabinda cried. She had sagged into a back seat. Her hands, like small animals, were hiding beneath her ample thighs.

Noor swallowed. Her lips were parched.

"Maybe an animal. A jackal perhaps," she said.

"Didn't sound like a jackal either," Tabrez said. "Who was that man in the alley?"

The Terrible Emperor of the Night, Noor thought incoherently. She didn't have the energy to grope her way back to question Tabinda. The woman was sunk in her seat, head lolling on her breasts like a rotten fruit.

Noor took note of the remaining water bottles under the bench behind the driver's seat. Two twenty-four packs. She removed one, drank from it, passed it around. Someone made a choking sound then fell silent. Noor raised a fist and knuckled her throbbing right temple.

Tabrez rapped at his window with his knuckles. Someone told him to shut the fuck up. He glared back. Tap tap!

They waited for Junaid. Their breath misted the windshield glass and white sheathed it until their peering faces disappeared.

Tap tap. Tap tap tap.

Some time later sheermaal was handed around again. Noor declined the bread. An odd lethargy had settled on her. The kids chewed, filling the bus with sounds of gnashing teeth and crumpling aluminum. Noor's neck ached as if steel rivets were being driven into it.

She fell into sleep.

She was a teenager – dressed in a black shirt, blue jeans, and leather boots – standing in the middle of Mohenjo-Daro with a bomb vest strapped under her clothes. Her hair whiplashed in the desert breeze. Her gaze was fixed on the citadel – now shaped like the Port Authority Bus Terminal in New York, stripes of neon blue and red racing around its sides. Noor's finger caressed the trigger poking her flat stomach. Her throat was dry.

A finger prodded her in the small of her back. Muneer. He was young and sallow, exactly how she remembered him. Eyes large and white from thyroid proptosis.

"For Dad," he said, voice guttural, toad-like. He pointed a bitten fingernail at hundreds of skeletal men, women, and children twitching their way through sun-baked alleys. They wore business suits, sweatshirts, dresses, and tourist caps. Suitcases and backpacks dangled from bones picked clean by time. They converged at the terminal like pilgrims at the Kaaba, pawing at the steel armature, phalanges digging into bricks, clenched fists thudding on glass.

"For their sins. Go, little sister, go." Muneer looked at her. His bulging eyes made him look shocked and insane. "Soon I will join you."

He shoved her forward. She staggered and began to walk. The people of the city pounded on the walls of the terminal. The half-flesh on a few faces was swollen and distorted, washed by electrified colors blazing from the building's facade. Noor's vest was rough and heavy and it was difficult to breathe. It was summer. She was sweating. Her finger itched.

I can't, she whispered. I don't want to.

But no one was listening, not even God. Faith yanked her forward and she went on a loyal trot, getting closer to point zero. The crowd jittered to the tune of death. An infant drooped from his mother's shoulder and pulled her straggly hair; and in a minute there would be blood, there would be devastation.

Noor turned and bolted. The ground shifted beneath her. Muneer's face was everywhere. "No, you bitch, come back. *Coward!*" he screamed. The world was white noise and it hurt her head. She ran and ran and ran. She would hide somewhere; if she could just reach safety, everything would be all right. No pain, no suffering, no dying, no shame, no guilt. Noor sprinted and the dead sprinted behind her, hundreds of taluses, tarsals, and metatarsals rattling on the ground.

"Pashupati is dead, you miserable slut," her brother shrieked. "He's dead and nothing will do but youthful human blood."

Noor woke, shivering. It was freezing and quiet. The bus was dark, the seats empty. Did Junaid return and take them all elsewhere? Why wouldn't he wake her? Empty bottles, squares of foil, and sheermaal crumbs littered the bus floor. She pulled the shawl tight around her chest and struggled upright. The windows were blinded with white and for a moment she thought they were covered with snow like her bedroom window back in Hanover after a storm. Dad would clear it, his gloved hands patting the glittering frost off.

But Dad was gone. *Extraordinary rendition*, her lawyer called it.

She peered closely and saw the white was fog. Thick smoky layers pressed against the glass, consuming the bus. Sometime during the night it had crept in from the river. She glanced at her watch. It was just past midnight.

She wanted to turn the headlights on but was afraid of what she might see; the dream hadn't left her yet. At least her headache was gone. She made her way to the exit and peered out: white upon pristine white. Wasn't white the sum of all colors? Was it Goethe who said color itself was a degree of darkness? She couldn't even see three feet away. There was a metallic tang in her mouth as if she could taste the vapor.

"Junaid," she yelled. Instantly the fog devoured the cry. "Abar. Tabinda. Anyone."

No answer. Just a susurration of dust and weeds in the wind. No night birds sang. No insects chirped. She was blind and alone. Terror came then on dark wings, engulfing her heart. She shoved it away, even though her stomach and bladder quivered. How could she not have heard them leave? She retreated from the door and clicked on an overhead light. The glow spread like a thin puddle. Her brown eyes were wide and crimson-webbed in the rearview mirror; she looked like she was about to scream. Her hijab had fallen off and lay draped over her shoulder. Noor fixed it with trembling fingers.

Maybe she should drive away. Leave them all here. The thought was so powerful she actually took a couple steps toward the driver's seat before stopping. There was no key in the ignition. Of course, Junaid had it. Movement in the periphery of her vision made her turn.

The bus door had slid open. Tabinda stood in the doorway, a silent rotund silhouette with streams of fog snaking between her ankles. Helplessness had left her eyes, leaving a glassy calm behind. "I came back for you," she said.

Noor wanted to weep for joy. She ran and flung herself at the older woman. Tabinda's arms tightened around her. "Sorry. The kids were cold and you were sleeping."

"Where are they now?"

"In a warm place."

Noor squeezed her one more time and stepped back. "Let's go. Have you seen Junaid?"

Tabinda shook her head. "No." Her face was half-paralyzed now. The corner of her mouth sagged. Her left eye was half-lidded.

"Are you all right?"

Tabinda massaged her cheek. "I had a stroke some years back. This happens once in a great while."

"Were you here in the ruins when you had the stroke?" Noor said. The question came to her familiarly, as if she'd asked this before in a dream.

Tabinda's lips had cracked from cold. They bled a little when she tried to smile.

"How'd you know?" She held the door open. "Shouldn't we get going?"

They strode through air dense as snow. Noor couldn't, for the life of her, understand how Tabinda kept her bearings. Shadows heaved and parted before them. They stepped on twigs, nettles, sharp rocks. The fog sucked its breath in, exhaled and rushed past. When the texture of the ground changed, she knew they were on the city streets. Chips of masonry crunched underfoot; stones, brick shards, gum wrappers, a worker's implement. At least that's what she thought it was. Long and pale, it gleamed in the moonlight. Before she could bend to look at it, her companion took her hand and jerked her in the opposite direction. "This way."

Tabinda scythed the haze with an outstretched arm. They approached a towering structure. The Buddhist stupa. Noor put her hand out and scraped a fingernail across the wall. How cold and brooding and alien it felt with mist clinging to it. She remembered her dream – shiny white phalanges groping the building – and her stomach turned. She pinched her shalwar and rubbed the brick dust off.

"I liked your little history lesson," Tabinda said. "But it has more meaning than the Israelites gave it."

"What?"

"It describes existence accurately. The two goats are life and death, both horrendous conditions. Gods are vindictive, after all. Would you like to hear a similar story? It's from the Mahabharata."

Noor hesitated. Cautiously she said, "Sure."

"In the beginning were three cities that orbited the earth. They weren't happy places."

In the distance vibration rose, faint as insect static. Noor cocked her head. It was coming from beyond the citadel deep in the night.

"What's that?"

"The cities fought each other with iron thunderbolts smelted in a hundred thousand suns. Until one invented a unique weapon."

Tabinda stopped. Before them was a twisted iron door flanked by massive brick colonnades. Rust blanketed it from top to bottom, except for the emblem of the Dancing Girl, hand on her hip, stamped in the middle. Parts of the figure were eroded by age but even through tendrils of fog the dancer's eyes, now open and swollen with madness, were visible. A brass padlock dangled from a moon-shaped hasp. The door was ajar.

"The weapon was wielded with the force of the universe behind it and it annihilated the rival cities. The cost of preparing it was grave, though. The inhabitants of the triumphant city had to use the blood of entire nations on Earth."

Tabinda pushed the door and it screeched inward, trailing the vapor pall draped over it. She stepped back, letting Noor peer in. "After you."

Inside was blackness thick as blood. The noise in the sky was louder now. *Whack whack whack!* It sounded like a piece of meat stuck in the blades of an electric fan.

"Hold on. What *is* that?" Noor said uneasily. Her breath steamed and dissolved in the mist.

The professor stood enshrouded in white, her uneven face still as a deep dark pool. "It's the army chopper come looking for us," she said. "Don't worry. They can't land in this fog."

Noor tried to back out, but Tabinda was quick. A two-handed fist slammed Noor's shoulder blade. Agony shot through her spine, buckling her, sending her flying through the doorway. The black rushed at her. She flailed her arms, trying to grab a handhold but tripped and smashed headlong into something solid. The world exploded into fractals: gray and black and grainy. A buzzing in her ears, something circling her brain, enfolding it like a reptile's maw – and Noor disintegrated.

Someone scraped up her pieces and put her together. She was slithering down steps as cold and unforgiving as faith's hold. Liquid heat simmered in her eyes. Her knees bumped and banged. One shoe jammed in a crack at the edge of the staircase; someone yanked her foot out and continued dragging her.

She was placed on a hard surface. Mist and incense smoke roiled in a vortex around her. Her eyes watered from the fumes. Through the haze she glimpsed figures revolving slowly. Half a dozen, maybe more. They drummed long spear-like objects on their sneakers and boots. She licked her lips. Her tongue was a festering ulcer, her head a beehive of bewilderment.

Pain squeezed her shoulders when Noor raised her head. She moaned. She was lying on her stomach on a narrow ledge inside the citadel, a long rectangular room with a brick ledge running from end to end three feet above the dry communal pool. The great bathhouse. It took her a minute to realize that her wrists were throbbing. They were bound with rope. So were her ankles.

"For a long time I wondered why the inhabitants of Mohenjo-Daro were so particular about the drainage system," said Tabinda. She was standing in the middle of the pool before a brick-lined circular opening about six feet wide. Mist wreathed the hole and Noor couldn't see inside it. Tabinda wore a fan-shaped metallic headdress with its edges dipped to create circular indentations at both ends. Flames flickered in small clay lamps placed inside these hollows. Her face was red with heat and perspiration, the half-paralysis so bad it seemed she was scalded on one side.

"Every house had its own drain connected to a network of brick channels in the streets. The channels ran clever courses and ended here in the bathhouse. I couldn't understand why they'd want to dump sewage here. It didn't make sense."

Tabinda was surrounded by a procession of seven figures: cadets wearing glittering bangles on their arms and circling diya lamps in the dense air. Smoke plumed in rapid spirals, thickening their features, sending sooty entrails across faces shining like glass. Tabrez and Raheem were among them. Tabrez's freckles glistened.

"It wasn't until Fossel and I unearthed the intricate network of brick-lined conduits below the citadel that we understood the purpose of this extensive system."

The seven boys began to gyrate their way across the pool. Their eyes were glassy. The lamps flared and guttered. They disappeared in the murk. Noor's heart beat so fast she could feel her limbs jerk with every pulsation. Terror had driven the pain away.

"To this day the Indus script remains indecipherable to others, but Fossel said he had translated it. The meanings of the symbols came to him in a dream, he said." A grotesque half-smile cracked the right side of her face. "Inscriptions he found on some seals describe the residents' belief in a supreme father. They called this deity the Terrible Emperor of the Night. Said that he ruled the meat-city in the sky with a lightning arm and a thunder fist, and that he had a hungry mouth on earth. Ancients in other cultures knew of this mouth. In their poems they called it the ōs dhwosos."

She was mad. The woman was mad. Noor's blood was ice in her vessels. She strained at the ropes binding her limbs, but it was useless; she was tightly trussed. She arched her back and looked at her captors. Abar had materialized beside the professor. In his hand was a long piece of black glass the size of a child's femur; similar, Noor realized, to what she had glimpsed in the street. Devil glass. Abar's blank gaze was riveted on her. He ran a finger across the jagged edge of the weapon and it came away black with blood.

Abar wiped his finger on his school sweater. There was no cut.

"This wasn't a bathhouse, you see. This was an ablution pool," Tabinda said gently, as if explaining to a child, "filled with the city's libation."

It took Noor a moment to understand what that meant. When she did, her flesh went cold.

"Once a year the omphalos would tauten and the door to His house swing open. At some point in their history, during years of drought and starvation perhaps, the residents turned to their children. Always the oldest offspring lain carefully by the blood gutters. It wasn't until enemy races conquered Mohenjo-Daro that the practice finally came to an end," Tabinda said. She rubbed her throat absently. "The following year, however, in one night the entire city along with its new rulers was destroyed."

The cadets reappeared, dragging a sizable bundle across the dry pool. It left a glistening black trail fading into the mist. A hand dropped from the bundle. Noor began to tremble, her breath hitching.

The fingertips were white, the nails perfectly manicured.

"How could we have known when we began the dig?" said Tabinda. Behind her Abar stood passing the glass knife from one hand to the other. It sparkled in the gloom. "I wanted to flee when the dreams started, but Fossel wouldn't hear of it. He wanted to study the darkness, as he put it. The tablets and seals indicated the secret room was real. And he said he would find it."

They placed the bundle before the brick-lined drain. Tabinda stooped, rummaged, and heaved out a lolling object, which might have been a human head. The oil lamp nearest her winked out. The bundle twitched and began to move. Tabinda tilted her head to the sky. The incense swirled a wreath around her head.

"After the laborers died, after the attempt on his life, Fossel was so shaken he flew out the next day. I left quickly myself. Spent years convincing myself it was a bout of madness. PTSD or some shit like that, but the nightmares just wouldn't stop. Every night the same voices and faces. This fucking room with its heaps of glass. Then I read about exposure therapy. Flood yourself with what you fear most. Sounds like a good idea, I thought. Return to the city on the anniversary of the day the horror began. Pop in, pop out, be done, never go back."

Noor was shaking. Her bladder let go and wetness spread from her thighs to her navel. The cadets had begun to chant. The voices loud and eerily synergistic in the murk rose higher and higher. "Our blood Yours, our meat Yours. On this day gladly we give You our sins . . ."

Tabinda uttered a sudden sob. Her eyes were craters filled with fear and exhilaration. Abar stepped forward. "Don't cry, slut. Don't you dare," he said in a guttural voice that wasn't his. "For this part, we steel our heart." He handed her the knife. It nicked the hollow below her thumb and a drop of blood appeared. Tabinda held the glass knife high like a hammer. The muscles of her shoulders were quivering. The knife blade lashed out. A gurgling sound, and the bundle was thrashing. The perfect fingernails drummed. Tabinda's hand sawed back and forth and glistening dark liquid gushed into the hole.

"He whose house is a-boil, the Adar Anshar. The Croucher in the Mounds. The Terrible Emperor of the Night."

Noor was mute with fear. This wasn't happening. This couldn't be happening. She was at the college in Petaro, there had been an accident, and she was in a coma. She was still in the Burn Center at New York Presbyterian after the blast. Her shoulder burns had become infected and she was delirious, watching her wounds glisten blue-green.

The cadets crooned and gathered around her. The glass spears were thrown away. Between them they hauled her to the edge of the hole, bare feet chaffing on the brick. Tabinda paused, leaned back, wiped her forehead. In the lamp flame the liquid pouring down the hole was ochre. Tabinda murmured. Abar grabbed Noor's head and yanked it back. Fiery bits of glass impaled on metal skewers were jabbed into her nostrils. She struggled but it was futile. The smoke singed her sinuses, parched her tongue, flayed her throat. She gasped for water. A metal chalice was thrust into her hand and she drank eagerly, a grainy hot liquid that could have been molten glass or blood swirled with sand.

In this new state, this moiled clenching, Noor rose. She was twisted upward in a spiral beguiling as the lines on a newborn's palm.

Below her were barren lands stripped by heat, their dwellers evolved into the formless. Towering mammoth structures squelched in magma. Half-buried in this boiling ground were giant hunchbacks whose humps formed the city's mounds. When they stirred, brackish fluid gushed through ciliated maps wavering from their flesh. The maps beat with an unnatural rhythm. Drawn from the hunchbacks' vasculature, they pumped pyroclastic liquid through the land's anatomy. A veined umbilical cord surged from the city center, rising higher and higher, trembling through its singed sky, until it traversed it. The cord shot outward, connecting this world with a blue-green one.

My blood is Yours. My skin is Yours.

Noor splayed her hooves against the throbbing meat tunnel of this omphalos and crawled up-down inside it like a spider. She had three faces, myriad eyes, and a swollen belly. Her brother Muneer hung impaled on a giant claw on the opposite wall. His tongue was rotten, he was covered with running sores. As she watched with her dozen eyes, he swelled suddenly and exploded.

Noor cried out. Her many limbs retracted; suddenly she was falling, tumbling, plummeting until she landed on a hard surface, shattering her extraneous appendages. A dense liquid clogged her airways. She couldn't breathe. She gasped and kicked and someone slapped her back, grabbed her hair, pulled her up.

She sat before the now-bubbling aperture, drenched in hot blood. Clots were already beginning to form in her hair. The citadel was dark except for the intermittent flaring of oil lamps. The mist was thicker, the whirling of the procession speedier. Noor couldn't make out who they were, how many they were. The locus of the dance had shifted away from her toward the other end of the pool. She couldn't see Tabinda anywhere. Her hands and feet were still tied. Sobbing, she slid backward on her buttocks, turned, and began wriggling to the ledge like a worm. Faces glistening with blood protruded from the mist and disappeared. Hundreds of eyes blinked and died.

Someone touched her foot. Noor screamed. Images of that monstrous city swirled in her brain and her eyes bulged until a red curtain slipped over her vision – just like in the early days after Muneer's death. The smell of his flesh, cooked from the blast, on her skin; the sharp iron odor of his blood; the taste of her own misery and terror as she stood shrieking in the summer wind, watching the red-and-white debris that was once her brother – they would come to her months after she left the hospital.

In the end, Muneer had been the only one to die that terrible day. She – she had run to a cop. Had fled her murderous sibling and had been fleeing since. But, afterward, everywhere she looked was a skein of red death wavering like a heat cloud – in the evenings and in the shadowy mornings, until she could hardly leave the house.

Her removal to Pakistan had been a relief.

The Pashtun boy Dara's face loomed above her. It was covered with gashes. He had blood around his mouth. He put a finger to his lips – *sshh!* – slid a glass knife out, and began to hack at the rope around her ankles.

The air thrummed. Voltaic ideograms crackled in the mist. A blue-black diagonal shimmered twenty feet away. A door set low and very wide. The oil lamps were clustered around it, flickering like fireflies.

Dara's hands dripped with sweat. A final swipe, and her feet were free. She couldn't believe it. She could move her legs. Sobbing with relief, she flexed her thighs until she was on her knees. Her period was flowing again, but she hardly noticed. It pooled around her feet and snaked toward the libation hole.

The knife moved to her wrists.

"Goat," Dara said, his eyes dead and crimson. "Depart, goat. Leave before He arrives."

He slashed at the rope on her wrists until it, too, gave. Noor tottered to a stand. The room tilted and her vision turned foggy. She shook her head. A loud noise, like a door banging shut in the wind, came from behind her. Someone screamed in terror or triumph.

Without looking back, Noor broke into a run.

Blackness behind her and darkness in front. She lurched to the stairway and took them three at a time. On the ninth step she slipped and the crack of her butt landed on its edge. Such pain rocketed through her, she thought she'd fractured her spine. Scraping noises in the distance, then galloping. Whatever it was, it moved fast. One hand on her hip, teeth clenched, heart thundering in her ears, Noor glanced back.

Tabinda was at the first step, snorting, pawing at the bricks. She was on all fours. Her face was completely static now, her forehead smooth. Not a fold, not a single crease, as if she were made from polished glass. Drool dangled in corkscrew threads from her chin.

As Noor watched, Tabinda lowered her head, sniffed the bricks stained with Noor's menstrual blood, and began to lap at them.

Noor turned and scuttled up the rest of the stairs. Pain chewed her ribs and back and hips, but she leapt blindly, not caring if she broke every bone in her body. Tabinda's smell behind her was acrid and meaty. It rushed at Noor. Noor vaulted across the last step and sprang toward the iron door.

Outside, the fog was a solid wall. Noor slammed through it, running – blind and barefoot – using the brooding stupa as her only directional marker. Chips of glass and sharp pebbles stung her soles. Branches and what felt like bird bones crunched. Something bellowed behind her. A loud animal grunt, then a pause. Noor clapped a hand over her mouth and kept running. She was wet and cold and trembling. Where was the fucking chopper? The night sky was silent. Her shalwar was soaked. She expected to crash face first into a wall any moment now. Instead, the sounds of the creature faded behind her. Was it licking her blood trail at every step?

Noor fled, weeping. The sharp bites of the alley became hard ground. The fog thinned, showing her the school bus sprawled in the lot like a dead animal. She bounded toward it before remembering she didn't have the keys.

Noor wanted to scream, to slap her breasts, and fall down, crying. She fought the impulse. Behind her the city was wailing. An earsplitting surreal ululation that bounced from wall to wall, door to door, and razored through her head. Lights bobbed in the corner of her eye. She sped past the vehicle, heading toward the road winding out of the ruins, spraying up dirt behind her.

The fog thickened again. Icy air knifed in and out of her lungs. When the sounds of the ruins died, she slowed to a trot. She was shaking all over and crying. Hot tears on frosted cheeks. Her feet were slippery with blood and stung in a hundred places. She had no idea where she was and the moon was dead somewhere. She was plodding through squelching mud now. Another step and her foot sank ankle deep. The wind whistled and picked up. Something rattled. She flinched from the sound. Pattering of feet or clomping of hooves? Terror washed over her. She yanked her foot out, lunged, and landed in gelid water. Something slithered over her foot. A shower of water plumed over her when she struggled upright, tripped, and nearly fell again.

A misshapen root wide as her arm. She was at the riverbank. Had she once thought its smell rotten? It was mossy and sweet. The Sind River gurgled and babbled. Malformed cypress knees poking out of the fog like tombstones. Ghost acacia and lilacs swayed above her, their cocooned branches rustling. Glinting eyes speckled the webs. They undulated and disappeared as she splashed through the tree line. The fog curtain was so dense now she could wrap it around herself and disappear forever.

A figure bobbed ahead in the trees. A flash of light that ignited the mist briefly and was gone. Noor's eyes widened. Her heart lurched and began to thunder in her temples. Part of her wanted to turn and bolt, but what if it was the army come to find them? With utmost care she lifted the cuffs of her shalwar and tiptoed through the water. Curls of dark moss like a woman's hair floated between her legs which gleamed with congealed blood. The cypress knees were more numerous here. They protruded in various geometric shapes.

One was almost like a little stool.

Her sight rippled, but not before she saw the figure crouching in the foliage. It was very tall and angular and seemed to perch on or by a poplar trunk. It wore something around its head, which could have been a headdress or a shawl.

Hamid! The bus driver. It had to be him. Dear God, let it be him. Noor choked back a sob and sloshed through mist and river water toward the silent figure riding the trees.

Silvia Moreno-Garcia wrote "Legacy of Salt" around the time she was reading a lot of philosophy of biology materials and also a Darwin biography as part of her Master's degree studies. "Some of the scientific issues I was exploring collided with this story. I have always found 'The Shadow Over Innsmouth' to be quite fascinating since it seems to dip its toes into the notion of repulsion/attraction. Is it such a bad thing to swim eternally in underwater palaces? I kind of like the idea. The Yucatán peninsula is definitely nothing like New England but the numerous markers for archeological sites somewhat reminded me of the notion of the past creeping upon the present, which occurs in some of Lovecraft's fiction." The story also features a family – as with the Marshes of Innsmouth – who has an odd heritage.

Moreno-Garcia is the author of *Signal to Noise*, a novel about music, magic, and Mexico City. Her first collection, *This Strange Way of Dying* was a finalist for The Sunburst Award for Excellence in Canadian Literature of the Fantastic. Her stories have also been collected in *Love & Other Poisons*. She has edited the anthologies *She Walks in Shadows*, *Dead North*, and *Fractured: Tales of the Canadian Post-Apocalypse*.

Legacy of Salt
Silvia Moreno-Garcia

———

The journey to He'la' was uneventful. He arrived on time, the noon heat greeting him like an old lover. The train platform was filled with vendors hawking their wares. Eduardo ignored them and looked for their chauffeur, but it was a young fellow he did not know who greeted him. The driver had a bit of the Marin look – the hooded eyes, fleshy lips – and Eduardo wondered if he was one of the family's by-blows. It would not be uncommon.

He slid into the car. The Lincoln Phaeton had been a beauty when his uncle had it imported from the States, but that was more than forty years ago, in 1923. Time had chipped its paint, dented it a bit, and now it looked more an oddity than a sensation.

It took an hour to drive from He'la' to the hacienda and with each minute the terrain grew more rugged, the towns smaller, until only old Mayan ruins greeted him from the side of the road, an ancient stone frog, associated with the rain god Chaac, staring blindly at Eduardo as they plunged down a hill. A few minutes later they reached the gates of the white hacienda. Before the Revolution it had produced henequen, but now the machine house lay quiet.

It looked the same since Eduardo had left, when he was twelve, to study at a boy's school in Mexico City. He could glimpse the dirt road that led behind the house, towards the small cenote of perfect blue waters where he swam as a child. There were several waterholes near their home – they dotted all of the peninsula.

A little girl in a faded pink dress sat in front of the house. He wondered if she was a servant or one of his younger cousins, but she scrambled inside before he could introduce himself.

"They told me to bring you to the Blue Room as soon as you arrived," the driver said.

"Very well," he replied, though he had been hoping he could shower and change his clothes before meeting the family.

He followed the driver to the main living room – which still had its blue velvet curtains and heavy wooden furniture, the portrait of grandfather Ludovico with his thick moustache dominating the room. Beneath the portrait was the old armchair that uncle Zacarias preferred. But uncle Zacarias was not in his usual place, smoking his pipe. Instead it was a young woman in a dress of antique lace who rose to meet him.

He did not recognize her, though she was a Marin. She had the heavy-lidded eyes fringed with thick lashes and long black hair that curled past her shoulders. Her neck was long and elegant and her hands, as she extended one towards him in greeting, were delicately formed. Despite her anachronistic dress and hairdo she was very beautiful.

"Cousin, I trust you had a good trip," she said, smiling and with the smile came recognition: Imelda.

She'd been a child of nine when he had left, carrying an antique doll under her arm.

"Very good, thank you," he said.

"You must forgive us. My father wanted to greet you himself but he is indisposed and Aunt Celeste is watching over him. He'll speak to you tomorrow. But today you will have supper with me. You must want to take your nap."

A nap. Yes. He'd forgotten about that. They'd sleep until the midday heat had dissipated.

"I can show you to your old room," she said.

Old was the right word. He recognized the faded wallpaper, the great armoire, the four-poster iron bed with its white sheets. Nothing had changed. The paintings were the same and so were the prints he'd left on the walls. In a corner, forgotten and lonesome, was the rocking horse of his childhood, which was no horse, actually, but a seahorse with a curling tail. The only new element in the room was his suitcase.

He was glad he had not brought Natalia. She would have found the place alien, depressing. He himself could not help the disappointment as he looked around. Everything seem so worn and faded.

"Thank you," he said. "May I use the telephone? I should call my fiancée."

"Have you forgotten?" Imelda said. "There is no telephone."

Eduardo frowned. "But you phoned me."

"Our lawyer phoned you, from his office in He'la'," she said. "If you want to send a telegram you can give the message to Mario and he'll send it for you."

"No, it's fine."

He did not plan to stay for long. In fact, he wanted to leave the next day but first he must speak to his uncle. Zacarias was the head of the house and he had been generous with Eduardo's allowance. Eduardo was aware that this generosity could cease. If his uncle summoned him, he must present himself.

"I'll let you rest," Imelda said. "Mario will fetch you when it's time for supper."

Alone, he explored the room, opening the armoire and running his hands over the hangers. He browsed the dusty books he'd left behind, and even gave the old seahorse a little kick, setting it in motion.

He fell asleep quickly and the warmth of the jungle inspired wild dreams. He dreamt Natalia was in labor and he was attending the delivery of his first child, but what pushed out from between her legs was not a baby. It was a pale, strange thing that had no legs and in place of a face only a maw full of sharp, needle-like teeth. It let out a piercing scream and he woke covered in sweat, his heart hammering in his chest.

Mario – that was the name of the young man who had picked him up at the station – came for him a couple of hours later. He took him to the formal dining room. The dishes were the fine porcelain ones, which were ushered out for special occasions. He sat across from his cousin.

"Is it just the two of us?" he asked.

"Aunt Celeste is still watching over Papa and the young ones have eaten already."

He recalled the girl with the pink dress. Yes, he'd heard Aunt Isabel had married and had children. The little girl might be her daughter.

"Are they the only elders left at La Ceiba? Where is Aunt Isabel?"

"She's left. The change came upon her last summer. Bartolomeo and Patricio changed two years ago. Juana is in He'la', and it seems she will not change, so I imagine she'll remain there. "

"Then it's just Celeste and your father."

"Well, there are the other branches," Imelda said, with a flicker of her hands. "There are plenty of elders in Los Azulejos and others in Principio."

"But this is the main house."

"I know," she said.

The servants brought in the dishes. Pale fish fried with capers and alcaparras, turkey in red-squash seed sauce. There was also toksel and a myriad of other things. An impressive bounty and he knew much thought had been put into it.

"So you are engaged," Imelda said. "I hear she is not of the blood."

"No," Eduardo replied.

"I have not told father. He'll be upset."

"It is 1965, cousin. Our medical issues should not isolate us."

"Our medical issues? Is that what they've taught you in Mexico City?" she said, smiling at him.

"Superstition hangs thick over the family, but I believe we are not the monsters of old legends."

"What do you think we are?" Imelda asked, chuckling with skepticism.

"We have certain genetic issues and I will not argue that heredity has not gifted us with a strange mutation, a degenerative condition, but these tales of gods and—"

"Tales!" Imelda exclaimed.

"It's all it is. We are flesh and blood, like anyone else."

"You have been away from home for far too long."

"I'm a modern man, not some superstitious peasant."

She was upset. He knew she would be. But were there not stranger people than them? Conjoined twins, people missing limbs. Julia Pastrana, born covered in fur, who had toured the world as the Ugliest Woman in the World. Yes, his family had its collection of oddities but also its set of healthy, regular folks. Juana, for one, but also Grandmother Susana who had died at the age of seventy-five, wrinkled and bowed by age, but otherwise perfectly normal. Eduardo's own father had perished in a car accident, handsome as he'd ever been, with no medical issues. And Lucia, Imelda's mother, died giving birth to her, but no abnormalities marred her body.

They ate in silence. Once in a while Mario would walk in, refill their glass, then walk away.

"When our lawyer phoned he said your father needed to discuss an urgent matter with me. Do you know what it is?"

She glanced at him, uncertain.

"Please, tell me."

"Father will not last through the summer. He wants to . . . he'd ask you to be head of the family."

"Head? Me?" Eduardo said with a chuckle.

"Who else?"

"Well, I should expect that would be you, quite frankly," Eduardo said.

"A woman? It'll never do, you know that. The family won't let it be, Tomas will come from El Principio with his lot to set us straight. The minor branches will object, too."

All of a sudden she was on her feet, rounding the table, and she was sitting next to him, clasping his hands between her own.

"You don't need to do anything. I can run this household, I've been running it for the past couple of years and doing quite well at it. All you need to do is marry me."

He recalled when they were children. On one occasion she'd forced him to play the groom and she the bride, they'd been married with her doll officiating the ceremony. It was not an odd thing for cousins to wed, not for the Marins. The blood, after all, mattered very much. But he'd grown out of those peculiar notions long ago. His family was old-fashioned, trapped in the past; he was not.

"I am engaged," he muttered.

"To a stranger."

"To a nice girl."

"You'd have Tomas come here, to handle the affairs of the house? My father sent him away for a reason."

"Imelda, I have a life in Mexico City."

She released his hands and stood up, her eyes cold.

"You did not write. You said you would but you didn't write a single letter."

She left him with that.

His uncle called for him the next morning. Eduardo had seldom been admitted to his room. It felt like a sacrilege to walk past the paintings of long-dead Marins hanging from the walls and approach the bed where Zacarias lay. Even more of a sacrilege to stare down at the pitiful man, old and shrunken, completely bald, drowning in the pillows. He had a rash on his face, his hands were gnarled, stiff with arthritis. How odd and different he seemed now.

"You look just like your father," Zacarias said in a rasping, strained voice. "So handsome. How old are you now?"

"Twenty-three."

"Twenty-three. Such an age. Sit down."

Eduardo sat by the bed.

"I will go away this summer."

"Uncle, has a doctor come to see you?"

"A doctor. It is the change, my boy. Soon I'll go to our cenote."

Yes, the old ways of the family. When the "change" came the Marins threw themselves into the waters of a sacred cenote. Ritual suicide. Eduardo had never been witness to any of these "partings" – children could not witness the rituals – but he'd known of them. They were all instructed in the mysticism of such an experience. When he was small Eduardo had truly believed that the physical changes in some of his family members marked a supernatural change. Now he thought better of it. Disease could cause dramatic changes. A degenerative condition could be the culprit. One need only look at a patient afflicted with syphilis to see the truth of this.

"We should take you to a hospital. The middle of the jungle is no place for you."

"I am going nowhere. Imelda tells me she has spoken to you about the household."

"She did. I am needed back in Mexico City."

"With that woman?"

"My fiancé, Natalia, yes, for one. There's also my job. I'm an architect, uncle, not a family patriarch."

"She's an outsider. Your father married an outsider. You know what happened."

He did. His mother had abandoned him and his father. He'd looked her up after he moved to Mexico City. They spoke over the phone. She had a new family, she told him. Other children. She would not see him. She hung up. He wondered what Natalia would say if he told her they must move to Yucatán. He tried to imagine her in the stifling heat, baking inside the white hacienda. He could not.

"I love her."

"You don't know love," his uncle muttered. "You don't know anything. It was a bad idea to send you to the capital, but your father insisted. He said it would do you good. What has the city taught you? Scorn for your own."

He wanted to protest that he certainly knew love, that he loved Natalia. That he'd learnt how to live a life free of legends and whispers. He held back, knowing what his uncle would think.

"I care about the family."

"Listen to me," his uncle rasped, extending his hand and placing it on Eduardo's knee. It looked more like a claw than a hand. "You will know no happiness outside of La Ceiba. You belong here. The water and the land call for you."

"Uncle . . ."

"I will depart soon. Remain in Yucatán until then. Give me that."

"Very well, Uncle."

"Good," the old man said, closing his eyes.

His father's photographs of Mayan murals depicting Chaac, the rain god – shown with a human body and amphibian scales – spanned from the bottom to the top of the staircase and he paused to examine each one of them. Near the bottom there was one photograph different from the rest, showing his father with a camera around his neck. Eduardo smiled, pressing a hand against the frame.

He was startled by the sound of laughter and saw six children ready to bound down the stairs. Girls and boys in ages ranging from four to about ten. He recognized the girl in the pink dress. These were his little cousins, then. As soon as they caught sight of him they ran off. They seemed afraid. He supposed he would look a bit frightful the way he was dressed. They were still clad in clothes from the Porfiriato, creatures from sepia-toned photographs, while he sported a flamboyant nylon shirt. It was as if time had stopped at La Ceiba. It was a minor miracle they had electricity.

Eduardo wondered what his father would have thought of him if he'd been able to see him now. He'd been different from the rest of the Marins, more outgoing and daring, and he'd had no fear of modernity with his cars and his trips to Mexico City. But he'd loved La Ceiba. Eduardo could not comprehend that love.

He went outside, to the back of the house, and stared at the vegetation bordering the perimeter of the property. Tall, lush trees, the jungle awaiting him at just a few paces. He could hear birds singing, the insects making their music, monkeys rustling in the trees. It was so different from the sounds of Mexico City, so alien.

"I am going to the cenote, are you coming?"

He turned around to see Imelda behind him. She wore another old-fashioned white dress that reached her ankles, her hair was pinned behind in a bun. In the city the girls wore mini-skirts and their hair was cut short.

"I was hoping to find Mario," he said. "I want him to send a telegram."

"It's market day," Imelda said. "Mario left for He'la' already. He'll be back in a couple of hours."

He cursed his luck. Imelda looked at him and smiled.

"You should come with me to the cenote, it will do you good."

He'd loved the cenote. They'd played pirates one whole summer after he read a book about them. He was Francis Drake and she was John Hawkins, and they both attacked San Juan de Ulúa, like the book said. He'd even stolen the sword in father's room – the one that had belonged to an uncle of theirs, the one who had been an officer when Mexico was still called New Spain – and taken it with them for their game.

"I have no swimsuit."

She chuckled. "You can swim in your underwear, which is what I intend to do. I thought you were a modern man," she said mocking him.

It was dreadfully hot. He'd forgotten just how oppressive the weather could be. He'd been looking for a fan the previous night, to no avail. Even the water that flowed from the ancient taps seemed warm.

"Very well," he said.

The trail that snaked behind the house quickly led them to the cenote. The Mayans thought the god Chaac lived in these pools of water. But as a child the cenote behind the house had simply been a place for merriment.

They approached its edge and he peered into its perfect blue waters. Imelda unbuttoned her dress and leapt into the water in her slip. He was a bit more cautious, descending the ancient limestone steps, dipping a foot in the water, then finally jumping in.

"Have you forgotten how to swim?" Imelda asked.

"It's been a while."

She disappeared under the water, re-emerging far from him.

There was a stone carving of a two-tailed mermaid in the old machine house, her face serene and perfect. Imelda looked a bit like the mermaid, enchanting in her loveliness. It was easy to believe, watching Imelda swim, why people might have told those strange stories about the Marins. Her dark eyes pierced him, her laughter was all silver.

He recalled that they used to compete with each other, seeing who could hold their breath the longest under the water, then jumped up, gasping for air and breaking into laughter. And he felt like that in that instant, as though he were gasping for air.

He stretched out a hand to touch her face.

He realized he had been moving closer to her as she swam and they were now facing each other. His hand stilled in the space between their bodies, he pulled it back, pulled himself away.

"I think I've had enough swimming for a day," he said.

He went up the steps and sat next to the edge of the cenote to dry himself. Imelda emerged and sat by his side. Her slip clung to her body. She ran her hands through her hair. He was careful not to look at her, instead focusing on the vegetation.

"I need to see if Mario is back," he muttered and walked toward the house.

Eduardo sent two telegrams. One to the office and another to his fiancée. He hoped he did not have to remain long. But two days turned into four, and four became six. On the seventh day he seriously considered leaving despite his promise to his uncle. The seventh night found him pacing around his room. He could not sleep, the heat allowed him no respite day after day. When he could lie down and close his eyes he had strange dreams he could not fully recall but that followed him like a fog.

There was something else that unsettled him: his cousin Imelda in her white dresses of ancient provenance, her black hair pulled back. She was very beautiful. He was not blind to her charms. In fact, he was very aware of them. When they sat in wicker chairs in the interior garden of the hacienda, sipping cold glasses of tamarind water, he'd turn his head and look at the sweat sliding down her long graceful neck. Or he'd watch her in the library, as she read an old book, her full lips silently mouthing a word. Desire cut deep and he had to remind himself that Natalia waited for him in Mexico City.

Day after day, night after night.

The seventh night he finally stopped pacing and went downstairs in a vain quest for ice (he should have known better). Instead he found Imelda sitting in the Blue Room listening to an ancient gramophone, ghostly music, some melody he had not heard before. All strings and loneliness.

She sat in her father's chair, fanning herself. The fan had belonged to their grandmother, he recognized it. It had one small break at the shoulder of the right guard and the paper lining was split in several spots, but it was still a thing of beauty.

As was Imelda.

She looked up at him as he stood in the doorway hesitating, not knowing if he should step in.

"I didn't wake you with the music, did I?" she asked.

"I was up," he muttered.

She wore a green robe instead of her customary white. It was embroidered with images of leaping frogs, Chaac's messengers.

He felt awkward in her presence, an interloper.

"You hate it here, don't you?"

"It's very different from the city," he offered.

"What is so interesting about the city that you don't want to stay in La Ceiba?"

"I have a life there."

"You had a life here before you left. You were happy."

"Yes."

"You've been happy here the past few days, have you not? Swimming in the cenote, talking to me, dining on your favorite dishes."

"Yes," he said, exasperated. "Imelda, you are dear to me, but I will not do what your father asks of me. I don't belong here anymore in this old house. Christ, nobody does. You should come to the city with me, that's what you should do."

"To the city?"

"Yes! You could go to university, meet people. You are cooped up in this place with only silly legends and stories for company."

"They are not silly legends," she said.

Imelda closed her fan and put it aside. She rose, looking him straight in the eye.

"It is our legacy."

She walked toward Eduardo, shrugging out of her robe. She was naked beneath. She raised her hands, holding her hair up, and turned around, revealing her back to him. A trail of . . . scales, it looked like scales, some skin imperfection, some mark . . . ran down Imelda's spine, a delicate tessellation that ended at her buttocks. She looked at him over her shoulder with disdain.

"Is this some skin condition? Do you know of an ointment that will fix it?"

Eduardo extended a hand, his fingertips brushing her spine. Imelda shivered and he pulled his hand back, as quick as if he'd touched an open flame.

"You were the brave one when we were children," she said casually, letting her hair fall upon her back again, as if she were not nude in front of him. Perfect and nude.

He could not think what to say.

She walked out of the room and he willed himself to remain anchored to that spot, to not follow her.

Mario knocked on his door early the next morning. Zacarias, he said, was going to the cenote. Eduardo knew which one he meant. There could be no other: the old ceremonial one, the place he'd heard about in whispers as a child, where the elders tossed gold and jade into the water once a year. The Mayans thought the cenotes were portals to the realm of the dead, Xibalba, but his family called it by another name, Y'ha-nthlei, and the cenote was Yliah'he. It had no meaning in Mayan, this was an older language, the elders had told them. A language from before the Conquest, before the great pyramids that rose upon the limestone bedrock of Yucatán. Much of the knowledge had been lost through the years, but some true names and words remained. Yliah'he.

Eduardo dressed slowly, dreading the trip. The mirror, weary with age, reflected his tired face. He had barely slept, the image of Imelda seared into his mind.

Mario, Aunt Celeste, and Zacarias rode in the automobile while Eduardo and Imelda went on horse behind them. The car moved very slowly, following an old road that was by some small miracle well kept.

They traveled in silence, Eduardo gripping the reins tightly, wanting to turn back. But he realized this was inevitable, Zacarias would not listen to reason and Eduardo was exhausted, blasted by the heat and the lack of sleep and the sharp pangs of desire. He would not protest.

The car stopped. They had reached Yliah'he.

Mario stood by the car and helped Zacarias out, but he would go no further. He handed Aunt Celeste an antiquated oil lantern to light the way down the steep, wet stairs leading to the cave. Imelda helped Zacarias walk. Eduardo followed last, watching his footing.

They managed to reach a ledge that led down to the water's edge and Eduardo looked up.

A circular opening at the top of the cenote let in the sunlight, illuminating the water. There were very complex cave systems in Yucatán, and he had the feeling Yliah'he's undulating water connected to incredibly deep, long rivers.

"Eduardo, help me," Imelda said.

He took hold of Zacarias left arm and Imelda held the right one. Together they walked into the cool water, heading towards the circle of light. Small white fish, blind from living in darkness for generations, brushed against his feet. The white ladies, they called the fish. He remembered catching them together with Imelda in other cenotes, both of them giggling at the strange creature's broad snout, its translucent dorsal fin.

Once they had reached their destination Imelda took off the heavy golden necklace she had been wearing and placed it in her father's hands. Then she kissed him on the cheek and pulled Eduardo with her, back towards the ledge where Aunt Celeste was waiting.

"Are we going to leave him there, just by himself?" Eduardo whispered.

"Hush," she said.

He did not know what he had expected, but it had not been . . . this. He'd heard the Mayans had sacrificed children to the rain god Chaac, that they wrapped them in ceremonial robes and stabbed them with a flint knife. Somehow the idea of the knife had lingered in his mind, sacrifice. Wrists slit. But was their uncle simply going to stand in the water and starve to death? Would he attempt to drown himself?

What horrid game was this and how had he convinced himself to play it? He ought to have called for a doctor when he first arrived.

They climbed up the ledge and Eduardo turned to Imelda, his voice harsh.

"This is insane."

There was the splash of water as the necklace the old man had been holding slipped from his fingers.

"We need to get him back in the car right this instant," he told her.

"No," she replied, her arms crossed against her chest.

A rumbling distant noise, like the sound of thunder, echoed through the cave. All of a sudden there was a golden light in the water. It did not come from above, but from below. Not the sun's glow. Something else. He blinked and stared and stepped forward to try and get a better, but Imelda grabbed his arm, holding him back.

A curtain of water rose before his astonished eyes, taller than a man. Water that was light . . . or light and water. It was blinding; he was forced to look away. The rumbling grew and grew, like the moaning of some strange beast.

He was afraid and clutched his cousin tight, embracing her. She'd been afraid of the dark, spiders, large dogs. She'd been afraid of so many things when they were children, and now it was he who was terrified.

There came the loud noise of water as it splashed down, the aqueous "wall" crumbling, stray droplets whipping their bodies until the cenote was still and quiet once again.

Eduardo swallowed and looked at the others, looked down at his cousin who was still holding him.

Zacarias was gone.

By the time they exited the cave it had begun to rain.

The night was cool with the refreshing rain, but even though the heat had dissipated he could not sleep. He opened the door to Imelda's room a little after midnight. She was in bed, but her eyes were open. She did not seem surprised to see him there. He made his way slowly towards the bed, sitting at the edge of it and she sat up, her pale nightgown catching the light of the moon.

"Maybe it's this place that makes us so," he said. "Maybe if we went away we might be different."

He tried to picture her in the city, wearing a colorful mini-skirt and high boots, with eyeliner and a martini in her hand. They could be normal. Lead normal lives. He could marry Natalia. Imelda could find some nice boy to care about.

But he thought of the dream he'd had, the horrid pale baby in his arms, and felt his mouth go dry.

"We wouldn't."

"How do you know?" he asked, exasperated. "You've never gone anywhere."

If only she'd give him some reassurance, if only she'd tell him they could escape . . . oh, he'd believe her. He would. He wanted to believe it. If only.

"I can't stay here," he said. "It's like a museum. It's a relic."

"Eduardo, I know the stories, I know the past," she whispered, tossing the covers away and moving toward him upon the bed. "But you understand the present. They sent you to the city for that reason. I can help you and you can help me. Don't you see? We can't have a future without you."

"What future?" he said. "That . . . this . . . is not a future."

She held his face between her hands, forcing him to look at her.

"Do you remember, what grandmother told us? That under the sea there is a phosphorescent palace of many terraces, with gardens of pale corals. There swim those that will never die, in wonder and glory. Forever."

Her fingers touched his brow.

He didn't know if he wanted forever.

"If you won't do it for the family, do it for me. Stay. I've been so lonely."

She kissed his cheek, then the corner of his mouth, before he shook his head and retreated from the bed.

He could feel it, beneath his skin . . . the thread that marked them as the same, that bound them together. But he could not picture it. His life within these walls. His body, deep, deep, within the endless waters.

She pressed a palm against her mouth and her eyes were filled with tears. He didn't want to make her cry.

"Don't say goodbye when you leave," she said.

Her voice cracked at the last word, water breaking against the rocks. He could not bear her grief and rushed out of the room without glancing back.

Eduardo takes a long shower in the morning and shaves slowly, pausing to stare at his face in the cloudy mirror. He packs, then unpacks, sits at the edge of his bed staring at the wallpaper with its blue and green scallops.

He dresses in one of his loud shirts with its bright patterns, and goes in search of Mario. The boy is in the kitchen, drinking his coffee. He looks up at Eduardo and nods his head in greeting.

This is some relative of his, some bastard Marin and Eduardo stares long and hard, trying to detect something else in his features. The covert shadow they both share. But he sees nothing amiss. Perhaps Mario does not carry their old taint, he will not go through the change like the pureblooded Marins do.

It might be the same for Eduardo. This affliction might skip him.

He'll feel better as soon as he boards the train. Once the wheels are turning he'll remember the city, his apartment, Natalia's voice. And the memories will stir him forward, back to a land of concrete and stone where neither water nor salt hold court.

If he boards the train.

"Mario, I need you to prepare the car," he says.

"Where are we going?"

"You're going to He'la', to post a couple of letters for me."

He hands Mario the envelopes and goes outside the house, walking until he is at a good distance, able to observe the whole building. Birds cry in the trees, indifferent to his turmoil, as he slides his hands in his pockets and walks towards the cenote.

He knows she's swimming there even before he glimpses her in the water. It's easy to find her – as if he were looking for treasure upon a map, dashed lines clearly directing pirates to the prize.

He falters only for a moment when he reaches the edge of the cenote, like a man consulting a wind rose, but she raises her head then, sees him, and he takes a deep breath and ventures in.

She's naked and he feels nervous once he reaches her, like a groom on his wedding night, and he supposes maybe that is the right emotion. This is their marriage.

He remembers the tiny, pale fish swimming in the underground pools of water and it scares him. Such depths and darkness.

He lets her fingers run across his skin and she kisses him, wrapping her arms around his neck. His mouth opens under hers.

In Mayan there is no word for "yes," and he's always thought it such a meaningless set of letters, so he spells his answer with his body.

The water is blue and perfect and cool. She pulls him down, into the depths of the cenote and he clasps her hand, follows her, holding his breath like they did when they were children, the jungle whispering secrets to the lovers.

"Much has been said about H. P. Lovecraft's regrettable prejudices," notes **Michael Wehunt**. "I'm not the first to find it rewarding to invert that intolerance by structuring a story around a protagonist with whom Lovecraft would have never engaged – in this case, a black female who learns to be strong in the face of long odds. What would a character with the life Ada has endured do in a cosmic horror scenario, when the stars are right and there is a Door? This story, for me, became all the more Lovecraftian through the very growth of Ada, using HPL's influence in brighter ways, even in the darkness. Naturally, 'The Music of Erich Zann' informed this story, but here the music was to play a different role."

Wehunt spends his time in the lost city of Atlanta. His fiction has appeared in such publications as *Cemetery Dance*, *Shadows & Tall Trees*, *Unlikely Story*, and *Aickman's Heirs*, among others.

I Do Not Count the Hours
Michael Wehunt

—————

—*We've come far.*

　—*Through cracks.*

　—*You could hum the last thread with ours.*

　—*We've looked for you.*

Whispering.

Ada has these thoughts, or they have her, as the window latch closes somewhere to her right. She turns to look but can't see. Coming back to herself in darkness, she feels a crawling dread until she realizes the breath spreading hot across her face is her own, and tugs the sheet off. It puddles on the floor, a grayed moth-eaten black thing that's not hers.

The door to Luke's office is open before her. There's a prickle along her arms, but from what she doesn't know. The sense of a camera, a watcher, a moment it isn't time to have. Or – something. Gone now.

She's had some bad moments. *He has to come back:* this is what she remembers murmuring through the house over and over. She can hardly touch the bow to her viola since he left. The weeping of the strings in all this empty space is just too much.

And now she's Bluebeard's wife holding the word *divorce* in her mouth, the bony shape of it there, its sour ashy taste, but she can't spit it out.

She stands at the entry to hallowed ground: his studio-slash-sanctuary. Just an unused corner room now, two more windows the nights keep peering into. But she needs some sense of him with her. Already she's breathed his smell out of the clothes in his closet. She reaches in and snaps the overhead light on. The room stops breathing and a long shadow shrinks into the far corner.

She steps into the office and she's only Ada, and Luke wasn't quite a Bluebeard until recently. There's a lot left in his office, considering he moved out the day after the Breakup, coming to the house while Ada was sobbing at her friend Regan's place. Four weeks and two days ago.

Empty boxes wait for him just like she does. Two tripods, a dolly, some of his lights are still here. His desk. Only the one bookshelf, half filled with tumbled-over film school textbooks. He was never a big reader until this last, awful year, when his love dried up and he started eating and sleeping in here, collecting piles of books and stacks of pages from his printer. She'd catch glimpses of a huge map with pushpins clustered where the Smoky Mountains rub against the Blue Ridge, papers taped up like detective novel wallpaper. But she never came inside until now.

Gram taught her well, not to go places.

And here, this photo facedown on his desk, is exactly the reason she's still not ready. His whole inner life, separate from their couple-dom, was held in this room, and he's chosen that inner life and left the picture of them behind. She has to gather the courage to turn the frame over. Four summers ago in Raleigh, they're smiling into that piece of future they still have. Luke's reddish straw hair, hazel eyes, his nose orbited by freckles, and Ada's wide dark gaze and a face that always looks so open and sure in photos. Her forever-short hair, her tomboy angles. Their differences are what stand out, because they stood out for him. He loved them, those differences, but she used to hate it when she caught him comparing their skins when they were pressed together in bed. He couldn't get over his fascination of being with a black girl, but she'd welcome it now, to feel him climb onto her.

Stop using the past tense with him, Ada. She positions the picture frame where it would face him if he were sitting in his chair, then starts opening the desk drawers. In the second she finds an empty journal and a sheaf of his photographs. He never let himself get serious with stills. Here's the half-skeleton of a burned house they saw once, out near the beginning of the Blue Ridge Parkway. Luke told her once that some religious group had lived there, probably died there. Ada's sure this is the same house, remembers the day they found it in the woods. That was a fairytale day, but he didn't have a camera with him. She's sure of it. On the back of the photo, in Luke's scrawl: *Still in area? Who owns this land?*

Another picture slowly reveals a shadow of something hanging in the charred doorway of the same ruined house. *STILL THERE* is printed neatly on the back. The next is completely black, but there's the feeling that it's not finished, it hasn't escaped the light all the way. She flips it over and there's a black circle filled in with Sharpie ink. But most of the photos feature trees, the anonymous ground, no art in them, as if he went into the woods and turned in a slow circle. There's no writing on these. In the last two a ring of narrow sticks marks the ground in a clearing.

She rifles through the rest of the drawers, all empty except the last, which is full, inexplicably, of soil. She rakes her fingers through it and stirs up several short twigs, picks one up only to realize it's a dead caterpillar. She jerks her hand away and rubs it on her jeans. There's something else buried there, half-risen, red plastic with a cap on one end and a keyring hole in the other. A USB drive, she thinks, brushes it off, reads the word EMMA scratched into it, penknife etchings.

Emma. He's never said anything of a female subject, or a female friend, but this room feels full of the things he never said. The thought of another woman's been a ghost in Ada's mind for too long now, a ghost she's nearly wished would haunt her. All the bitter energy needs a conduit.

She pulls the cap off and stares into the slit of the device's mouth. Bluebeard's wife again. Her laptop's in the bedroom, but she brings it back into Luke's studio, boots it and tries not to look at the photo of them while she waits. She inserts the drive and clicks its icon when it appears on her desktop.

There's nothing on it except four small mp4 video files in a folder named *found*. They're all dated 16 September, four days before the Breakup. She mouses over the first, *consecrate*, braces herself for a bedroom in low light, writhing movement and Luke cupping breasts much fuller than her own, hungry mouths opening onto each other. A breath, a deeper breath, who are you, Emma? She opens it.

Four figures stand in the middle distance, shin-deep in a creek whose waters in the hazy lens glare run the reddish brown of Georgia clay. They hold hands and stare into the soft current, grouped like a closing parenthesis, water stains creeping up their pants. There's no sound and a vague tracing of video static drifts over the figures. The details of them are hard to grasp. One is taller, stooped, she thinks. Two have short hair, though as she leans closer, dragging the play bar back twice, Ada becomes convinced one of these is something like a mannequin held upright by the others. A thing limp in its clothes, faceless and without clear hands. The clip's all one steady shot, as though from a tripod, a minute and thirty-eight seconds until she notices the blot of shadow coming out of the woods on the other side of the water. It stains a corner of the screen as it spreads toward the creek bank.

Now the shot cuts to black, but still with the grainy digital snow. She lets it play out to be sure, sitting crosslegged on Luke's favorite rug. After nearly three minutes, the audio snaps on, a scrape and the low moan of a cello, a forlorn thing that chills after all the silence. The dark fades bluer and a half-moon suddenly appears, sliding around on the screen. She hears the bow wring one long final note on the cello string that bends in the middle and stops. A click, a lingering hum, then the QuickTime control panel reappears.

She doesn't pause before clicking on the second file, titled *bowl*. Instant movement, the shot traveling through woods in middle-night dark, a flashlight in its dying throes drifting over a carpet of dead leaves. Tree silhouettes, hints of deeper forest. No sound again and none of the snow from the first clip.

The cone of light diffuses, the ground dropping away into a pit of some kind, something dug out of the earth. The view tips forward and Ada can see a long white hump down in the hole, the sprawl of a body, nude or clothed in white. The shot blurs for a moment, whips around to scan the woods behind, silent black cut with wedges of indigo. The camera returns to pan across the pit, and the white body is gone. A flutter, flicker, the flashlight wavers and gives up to the dark.

Again she waits the clip out. It cuts back to life – or the light's batteries are replaced – past the three-minute mark, Ada gasping as she sees two feet in the frame, inches away. The camera is in the pit now, the electric light a degree stronger. White fabric ends at dark knobs of ankles, two dirty feet. For a rattled instant she thinks they are her own feet. Paler than usual in the yellowing light, the shape of one big toe calling to her. Chipped pearl nail polish. But as she peers closer, another figure crawls out of the background, over the body and toward the camera in one lurch. Flat coin eyes gleam and the light spins away, the video ends.

She shoves the laptop across the rug, leans over and snaps it shut. Did Luke shoot these? Are they only found footage, as the folder name might suggest? He loves that stuff. Please, the latter, but there's nothing useful in the file information. She's got the beginnings of a headache, but even after this last horrible video, even after those feet, she has a stubborn, vivid urge to lie down in that hole and pick out the stars caught between branches. The oaks would drop leaves curling in on themselves in death, and she'd watch them spiral briefly toward her. It wouldn't be a grave. Her thoughts are not that lost. It only seems like it might be a closeness she could feel to him.

She won't cry, doesn't know if she can. She has an interview in seven hours, a steady job she needs on top of the unsteady session work, unless she sells the house. But this place is her only lifeline now, and she searches for angry thoughts to keep her here: have the locks changed tomorrow, move her music stuff in here. Get the exorcism underway. She knows better. The third video's filename is *bed*, it sinks in and tugs at her but she has no space for any more. Not the aching panic that would bring, surely, seeing whose bed and what was done on it.

At the window she stares out at the masked trees, outriders of the greater woods that stretch away toward the mountains. Her mountains. She imagines again some part of her approaching the sunken hole, wherever it is. Imagines Luke appearing above her, his face hidden behind the camera. She's learned to look around it.

Ada's heard the word *codependent*, she knows what it means, started reading a book about it. It's under the bed now, the bookmark in chapter two mocking her like a tongue. Gram would tell her she's being a foolish child, didn't she raise her better? But Gram and her impossible love have been gone a long time.

The trouble is, Ada's never been alone. From the moment Ada's parents died when she was three, there was always Gram. There was never any rest from her.

And there was always Luke, after. She'd only taken her first hesitant steps into the world when she met him in a produce aisle. He showed her the world wasn't out to get her. He showed her how, in fact, the world seemed hardly to care. She learned she could be the only one in a room, or by herself in a car, and still be held by the one who loves her. It still surprises her, sometimes, that there are so many little things like these, things wider and deeper than she could understand for a long time, if she even understands them now.

The thought of figuring out how to do this makes her lightheaded. She leans her forehead against the window, sighs an oblong fog onto the glass. The word LEAVE blooms in it, in reverse, and she'd recognize Luke's handwriting anywhere. She breathes all around the word but there's nothing more. One final exhale, then she smears the E and the A into a circle and smiles at LOVE.

"Here's what you do," Regan tells Ada over the noise of the bar, "be an alcoholic until you get this job or you puke the last of your ex up, whichever comes second."

Ada shakes her head. She's never had the stomach for alcohol. "Dangerous when I'm a five-three lightweight," she says.

Regan throws back the last of her second bourbon. She does everything this way, with quick ease. Ada's known her for so long, even though it's only been three years. It's what your first friend feels like. Regan's taller, full of the real world, with hair she can actually style and real cleavage, the jackpot of a white girl's proportions – a long list of needless, absurd comparisons Ada still measures herself against. And now Regan's staring her down. "Have you talked to him?"

Ada hasn't, and she's trying not to talk *about* him, though she's worried sick. Four weeks and three days. She's tried to put everything but her own elusive music out of her mind, but all she's done is listen for that strange cello note in everything, the idling engine of her car, the refrigerator's hum. It reminds her of what music directors have said about her own playing – too intense for us, Mrs. Blount, we're sorry. The interview at Haywood – where she hopes to step foot inside a college for the first time, if only as an admissions clerk – went well, she's letting herself think. Luke's deleted his Facebook and Twitter accounts. She wants to respect his space, hasn't broken down and left him a voicemail in days, and the easiest way to keep that going is to stay away from his things, his office. The rest of those videos.

"No," she says. "Can we just – what is it?"

Regan never bites her lip like this unless it's a new guy or a secret. "Nothing. You've only had the one drink."

"I don't want it, really. Six years, Regan. I met him when I was twenty. I'd never met *any*body." She's doing it, taking her finger out of the dam, watching the cracks spider. "What do you do with six years?"

"You lived them. That's what they were for. They got you closer." Regan laces her fingers through Ada's and squeezes too hard. "Now you file them away on the L shelf and start thinking about yourself. *For* yourself. The A shelf, just Ada, and screw the rest of the alphabet."

"I just—" Ada wonders if the dam will break now and what sad clichés will spill out "—I don't want to be some uneducated musician who has to file papers because violist isn't a real job. Most people don't think it's a real instrument, even." She breathes, she says, "But I don't want any next phase, either. I want last year, and the year before that. There's never been anybody but him. I want him to call. I want him to want a baby. I wish I smoked."

"Well, honey," Regan says, "you live in Asheville. You can busk on the street or you can move to a city with at least four skyscrapers, where they have people who listen to dead-white-guy music. Playing on kids' records every few months is cool, the ASO's nice to shoot for, but I don't see this stuff taking you to great heights."

Regan can't feel the smallness of Ada's world. The thought of leaving her home, the air and the mountains, is terrifying, unthinkable. And her marriage is at least half that idea of home.

She starts to explain, even thinks she'll bring up finding herself under a bed sheet, losing pieces of time, but something drifts close behind her. Ada looks up to see Ms. Hursh, her neighbor from across the street, grinning down at her. "Ms. Hursh?" Ada says. She's a nice enough lady, mid-fifties, but they've shared only waves and maybe a hundred words in Ada's three years on Pinewood Trail. She seems even less a bar type than Ada does. But the woman just stands and grins for several long seconds – Ada has time to glance at Regan, whose face scrunches up, then back – before she winks and shuffles away.

"Okay, that was weird," Regan says, but she's distracted, biting her lip again.

"Never mind that," Ada says, "spill it, what's the big secret?"

"It's nothing. Cheryl saw him the other day, that's all."

"Luke? She saw Luke." And to skip right to it: "Who was he with?"

"Some girl, I don't know. Cheryl only said she was tall, almost freakish tall. And white." She catches the waiter's attention, points down at her glass. "Look, Ada, don't do the 'other woman' hang-up. Think of how long he's been gone. Without so much as a phone call. Think of what he *did* that last night."

"He'd never done that before, not all the way like that. I don't even know *why* he left, Regan. Can you see that? I think he got obsessed with some cult or something. I don't care how long it's been. I'm worried about him."

Regan sighs and looks away. It's clear she doesn't share Ada's concern. "Okay. But don't open that door. Easier said than done, right? But come New Year's, your birthday, tops, you'll start to understand this'll make it easier, that he could be so quick with someone else. I don't want to see you be the woman who defines herself by her man. I can't imagine growing up like you did, hidden from the world until you're twenty, for God's sake. I'd be up to my neck in therapists. But you have to find your own strength sometime." Regan snatches up her bourbon the second the shaggy-haired kid sets it down. "Lecture over. Let's watch movies. Stay over at my place, eat those dollar pizzas I keep buying."

The constant drone of the bar has swelled to a roar. At least she knows Luke's alive, out there in the near world. But Ada imagines her computer screen as though it's open on the table in front of her. The file labeled *bed*. She sees her finger tapping a single time, she sees a woman rising up from cream silk sheets, a long elegant back arched above the grinding hips, Luke's reaching hands, and when she tries to turn her mind from it she sees a different woman's feet sprawled on turned earth in a hole.

"I—" For a moment that single syllable is all she can find. Coming here, it was a mistake.

"Ada, I'm sorry. Let's get you home."

"I can't. No, I mean, I can drive myself. I'll call you. I'm leaving."

That sound of *I* – it's all she is, now – follows her out into the October cold. If Regan doesn't know, if Luke won't know, no one can. She wasn't a person until she met Luke. She had only ever been a granddaughter until she met Luke.

The mountains are turning to russet and fire out there in the dark. She looks above their silhouettes, to the sky, she bites her tongue against tears wanting to brim. The sun, long slipped behind the mountains, the clouds and their shapes, the moon vague as a nickel dropped in water. All of it wavering.

She thinks of the sundial that stood behind Gram's house. There's no such thing as time when the moon's awake and we're all in shadow. She doesn't have to count the hours. From the far edge of the parking lot a black shape watches her. When it stands up she can tell it's not Luke. Her car chirps at her when she presses the key.

—We've looked for you. —You'll happen quickly, now.

Whispering. Ada hears the hall window closing again, the same slide and click as the other night, but when she looks nothing's there. Just the black sheet still pooled on the floor by Luke's office. The thumb drive's on his rug. If she's going to turn away it has to be now, but she scoops it up and goes into the living room, stabs the drive into the laptop's USB port. EMMA, so loud a name, so lightly etched in the plastic. The rush of blood in her head's like the bar noise she left behind.

She almost clicks on the last file, *untitled-1*. Its anonymity feels powerfully safe to her. It could be anything, a beach at sunset, something less haunted by sex or darkness. But it won't be, and even so, she knows she'd watch it with half her mind on the other.

So she taps *bed*. More soundless night, of course, eleven minutes on the timer. It's an incomplete dark, gauzy. As if lost light is nearby. The dark moves – it turns, as if to look elsewhere, and the light grows and concentrates on the left side of the frame. Ada clicks *maximize* and the video window jumps to fill the screen. Nothing happens for more than a minute, only that far light hanging in the black, and the dark shifts again, slow, sliding. It slithers down and off the camera like a solid thing, and she realizes it's a covering. A black sheet, maybe. The light is a small shaded lamp to the left of a bed. A woman is sleeping on the bed. It's not the faceless Emma she's feared. Ada recognizes the lamp at once, because she bought it at a flea market years ago, and only moved it into the bedroom after Luke left. For a long moment she only looks at the lamp. She won't look at the woman on the bed, the woman's short-cropped black hair, the skin a lighter brown than Gram's favorite quilt pulled up to her shoulder. She won't let herself think of the camera, of who is holding it and watching her sleep.

The shot creeps across to the bed, the mattress she and Luke kept planning to replace, toward sleeping Ada, and looks down at her. Ada, too, watches herself. Eight minutes leak away, the camera just there, staring, and the lack of sound is almost the worst part, until the shot dips and the screen goes blank. The picture clicks back right away but she knows that time has passed, doesn't want to think about what might have happened during it. Because something's changed, more than just the steeper angle, the deeper orange of the light.

A shape moves in the back of the room, in the right corner beyond the bed. A face peers through the window, right at her, at *both* of her, somehow. It's too pale to be Ada's face, but it is, her wide eyes and her wider mouth stretching into a grin. And – it's Luke's face, too, his dusting of freckles on her dull cheekbones, his narrower green-flecked eyes. A somehow beautiful amalgam, or a cruel imagining of the child it's never been time to have.

She half-sobs, lowers her hand to the computer. It gets halfway there before reaching for her face instead, checking for a secret grin there, as if to convince herself it's an absurd mirror she's seeing inside the film. But the face in the window just keeps grinning with Ada's mouth. The camera slides back and away from the bed. She sees the insubstantial shape of a white arm to the right. It lifts the dark up and slips it back over the camera.

And in the final seconds, it retreats farther. The same arm – it could be Luke's, she's not sure – reaches outside the dark to grasp the closet door and pull it shut, enclosing itself and extinguishing that sad rumor of lamplight.

The instant the video ends she closes the laptop, shoves the thumb drive in her purse and leaves. She makes it to the bottom of the drive-way, the Volvo's rear wheels in the street, before she stops.

Leave, Ada. Call the police. Call Regan. Make these calls now. She has the video but she knows everyone will think it was Luke. His camera, his storage device, his key to the house. A videographer who dabbles in the experimental genre isn't a stretch to make a creepy movie of his estranged wife. Yes, it has to be Luke. Relief balloons inside her.

Angry confusion flushes much of the fear away as she looks up the sloping driveway at the little brick house, but what remains in the dregs of adrenalin is more a desperate sadness. A shameful ebbing, that she was here, is here, in all of *here*'s meanings.

She digs her phone out of her bag and calls him. It goes to voicemail, as always, a crackle of static over his warm voice. "I need to know you're okay," she says, and hangs up before those words can get their momen-tum going. In the rearview mirror she sees a group of silhouettes scuttle over the roof of Ms. Hursh's house and vanish. "They aren't even there," she whispers. Ms. Hursh is, though, an irrefutable lump of shadow standing across the street next to her fading wisteria.

But what makes Ada go back is the viola. It's her third arm, all she has of her mother, yes, but even so she can't articulate how it pulls at her just now. She stands at the front door for several minutes, listen-ing to the silence, the fall hush of insects dying out in the woods, watching Ms. Hursh watch her. Inside she wanders to the bedroom, deep breaths in front of the closet. Her hand reaches out to the door-knob, then falls away.

She sits down on the bed, expectant and somehow bashful. Once the viola's out of its case and tucked beneath her chin, she plays. For her husband or for something else, she doesn't know. She glides the bow with the old graceful tremble, lento. She plucks, pizzicato. The secret magic comes back to her. The feeling of her skin against the glossed wood feels true as ever, and the Reger suite pours out like something too long corked into a bottle. It was the first thing she ever played for an audience, two years ago. Fourth viola, the least important, feeling sweat trickle down her sides. She wasn't invited back. The memory feels far away.

The Reger loses its form and withers into a sustained note, her concentration holding it in place like a vise. Her precise wrist sways. She plays and sometime later she wakes, muddy light and rain whispering against the house. A plate of dry toast and she starts again, Bach, Berlioz, Bartók, Mansurian. She plays until the works for viola begin to dwindle away, which is always too soon, then wades into the vast pool of music for violin, that movie star of strings. Everything she plays, every movement and measure, threads into that single note, she wanders through variations deep inside it. Soon she abandons all the music she's learned. She opens the first video, clicks past the creek to that moonlit cello note, repeats it and repeats it. Plays on top of it, thinking of her bow as an insect leg, each of its hairs brushing the strings with its own added vibrato.

It's past noon when her wrist seizes on her, a carpal flare that clatters the bow across the floor, and only now does she return completely, blinking out the window at the gray sky that hangs over the day.

She stares at her computer and asks herself if she wants to see what untitled-1 wants to show her. Who is this tall girl, this Emma? It seems clear, by now, that she's being drawn toward something, drawn surely as her bow, and it's time to stop this until she learns what Luke's doing, and why. Or else it's time to follow it to him, blindly. Or else it's time to fend for herself. She doesn't know how to choose.

But when she can't find the thumb drive, frantic and close to tears, throwing cushions and magazines to the floor, the decision seems made. She relaxes, sighs, like a drain unclogged. It's in her purse. The relief is so deep it's exhausting. She gives up to real sleep, falls into a sort of cavern of it.

Night's thickening full around the house when Ada wakes beneath the black bed sheet. There's a missed call from Haywood College and it takes her a moment to remember the job interview. Luke's voicemail is full. She turns on the porch light and movement projects through the quartered half-moon window in the front door. The quality of light shifts and speckles on the inside wall. She needs Luke's height, even on tiptoes she can't see outside, and the angle of the bay window shows her just the empty porch, the still swing.

She opens the door and sees the porch light crawling with moths. They assemble and reassemble themselves, wings pulsing in concert like a gray heart. They must have been worshiping the light before it even came on. She thinks of the drawer full of dirt in Luke's office. The dead worms or larvae there. She thinks of the lamp beside her bed, checks the street for Ms. Hursh or the shapes on her roof. There's nothing.

The last video is the only thing left in the house that seems to have any surety to it. Her wrist still aches, and she's never been a singer. Gram's old forbiddances of her voice still won't let her go. But she senses that for the moment, some moment, at least, silence is necessary. Two laps around the living room. She inserts the thumb drive. A glass of water. She opens the *found* folder, sees yesterday in the Date Modified column, clicks on *untitled-2*, sure that it was a 1 there before.

Dark, again. But now there's sound, two distant violins playing the same coiled notes a quartertone apart. Close, circling the tone the cello played in the first film. Soon there's light, too, a woman's naked back sliding into the frame, and Ada sucks in her breath. A beautiful back, seen from the neck down, the color of rich cream with blond hanks of hair pulled forward over the shoulders. Thin pine trees bunch and crowd the background, insects trailing comet tails through the air in the slow shutter speed. The picture warps, static crumbles vertically. The back flexes, the shoulder blades stretch out like the roots of wings, and the woman bends forward, down out of the shot. A hole looms in the ground, the heads of two figures protruding, hooded or cloaked.

"*Things you see now,*" a voice whispers, and Ada jerks her head around, scanning the room. Outside the half-moon in the door, moths crawl on the glass.

She turns back to the screen and the woman has straightened again, her face still too far above to see, and is turning, full breasts swinging, there's a symbol drawn, tattooed on the swell of the nearer breast. A gorgeous, ungodly squeal fades in from the speakers, a stretched squelch. Ada's eyes swim and her mouth waters, like coins held under her tongue. She grunts at the sudden heat she feels in her cheeks and below, where her legs meet.

"*Things you hear now. The old place, where you told about Gram,*" the voice says, sexless, inflectionless. The film bends in again at the right edge, another image intruding into the frame, the edge of a worn building.

"*Go and see us now. Bring your instrument.*"

A bluer shade of blackness returns, but the sound stays in a swishing of leaves. Once more the dark is brief, the sky lights up like a photo negative, the sky has the texture of hair. The camera pans left and right and picks out suggestions of people passing through the trees. The view straightens and someone is standing in its path. Ada knows at once it's the same woman, Emma, as if an earlier sequence has been spliced onto the first. Then the picture blurs and stutters and snaps off.

She's reaching for the keyboard when it cuts back in, teetering on the lip of the pit. Three figures crouch in its center, in the light of a moon brushing against the Earth. They're draped with black sheets. A fourth lies sprawled and she sees, familiarly, it's a dummy, smooth-faced, black hair scribbled on its head. Its body is stained white cloth.

That squelch goes on. The shot swivels up, for an instant showing the trees full of white faces, and the screen's filled by another, shorter figure, standing above the hole, having just covered itself with its own dark sheet. Ada sees the afterimage of hands fallen, tugging, below the camera's eye. The figure stiffens, staring out of its darkness, out of the screen, then steps quickly toward the camera, spreading its arms.

The tone is severed and the toolbar pops up over the blank video player. She taps the trackpad, sure it's just frozen, this can't be the end. The film starts over and she lets it play again. And again. She loses count. Each time she watches it the sky changes in that moment of anti-light flash, showing her strange shapes filling it through the trees, almost familiar.

In the bedroom, after she's wiped the slick of saliva from her chin, after the shaking has stopped, she crumples the black sheet and throws it at the closet door. She's going mad, that's all. Luke and Ada, both caught in his undertow, like calling to like. He knew Bluebeard's wife would find his films and try to help him.

The old place. Finally, the easy clue she's been waiting for. Three months after they met, they roughed it at a cabin outside of Candler, on the first rises of the Blue Ridge. She remembers the afternoon hike, finding the scorched ruins of a house in the woods, the one that so fascinated Luke. This early in her life after Gram, everything still fascinated her.

And it was the long sweet weekend when Luke took her virginity in his clumsy, quick way. When he told her he loved her. She'd never thought those words could sound like they did, like a chord, something to build a concerto around.

But it wasn't the cabin or the burned house where he said it, it was after that, after they got back on the road home and saw an old severe-roofed church in the distance. Something about its shape, or the way the forest stood guard behind it, made Luke turn down the snaking driveway. The door was not locked. Ada would have followed him into the deepest cave that day. Inside was an air of God abandoning His flock, but the place was clean and still used, no dust on the pews, which were well polished with hymnals in little cubbies along the back of each.

He needed a few minutes in one of those pews before he took her hands. *I love you, Ada.* She can't even remember the name of that church. It was just the old place, when they were new people. But the thrill she has now, what makes her more Ada Blount than she's been in months, is from his choice to mention not the *I love you* but what came after, when she opened up and told him what her life had been.

About how Gram had taken her in when she was three, orphaned in a car accident that had killed her parents instantly without even scratching Ada. How Gram raised a friendless and timid mouse, never let Ada out of sight. Sunday mornings and Wednesday evenings to their tiny church, the grocery store on the fifteenth and the thirtieth, and the rest of it was the house, hiding from a white world in an unlocked cage. They slept side by side in the bedroom off the kitchen. The bathtub was her one privacy, the one place she would sing, always in her softest voice because Gram wouldn't allow song. There was sin in Ada's voice, somehow.

But the viola, Gram almost worshiped that thing, though she knew little of it. Practice after breakfast, before dinner and bed. Even the Bible lessons weren't as strict – Ada's mama, she was supposed to be in a famous symphony some day, but the Lord had told Gram that Ada would do even greater things. For all Ada knew, her mama had only left behind her proud instrument. Ada pretended she could smell her in the wood.

Didn't you go to school? Luke asked, and looked away for a second, just the one second, when she told him no, she'd even learned to tell time with only a sundial. She'd learned to read by the scriptures, made her friends out of her father's records, full of music written by long-buried men. The mountains locked the sky in with her. Gram, always right there, broad and tired and feeling stomachachy, the lines sinking into her face like a sped-up geology. That was her whole world, days strung together into a forever that could have ended sooner than it did. Ada's curiosity was growing right along with her body. But one afternoon, she was seventeen and humming nonsense under her breath in the tub, she heard a soft thunder from the kitchen and there lay Gram on the floor, the oven door open in surprise.

Ada became less a granddaughter than a nurse. The cancer ate Gram's bowels first before spreading its fingers into all her nooks and crannies. She refused chemo, refused hospice, had all she needed with her little Ada.

Gram lasted nearly three years. They called for a hard, dark love but Ada gave it. She sat between their twin beds and played, and Gram talked to Ada's Grampa, who'd passed long before Ada was a dream of a thought. She wailed at that drunken Irish fool who'd killed her daughter and only spent a year in prison. She reached her hands up, her palms white as the pages of her Bible, and clutched at Ada, still trying to protect her.

Ada felt her kinship with the viola deepen in those years. She grew to understand the depth of its androgyny, in its delicate bridging of violin and cello. The notes it wrought were like pheromones.

And the pounds melted from Gram like winter. She died just five months before the day Ada told Luke about her, and it felt like minutes and a lifetime since the brash, vibrant world opened up to a girl of twenty who had only the faintest idea of what to do with it. She'd never been educated. Never known anyone her age. She stood in a doorway with no threshold.

What she didn't tell Luke, though it pounded in her: She couldn't even remember Gram's funeral, or all the strange lonely quiet after. It hadn't gone on long enough, only until she ran out of food and built up her nerve to go to the store. And there had been the answer, smiling, hazel-eyed by the tomatoes.

I love you. The second time he said it was sweeter than the first, more first than the first, somehow. And she loved him back more than he could ever know, because she had never known.

—*We've looked for you.*

Something stirs in the attic, boxes shifting, and her daze breaks apart. When does Luke need her to come? The voice in the film said now. It's late already but the old place can't be more than half an hour south, right inside the cusp of the Blue Ridge.

She picks up her viola. "Is he in trouble?" she asks the ceiling. The shuffling above her stops, waiting, is it breathing at her? Then one long nail of something drags across the inside of the closet door.

"Yes, why don't you go rescue him?" a voice says from the closet, and laughs.

Ada recognizes the voice – her neighbor? "Ms. Hursh?" she says, stepping back until the bed presses into her legs.

"I'm only wearing her, dear. I've watched you. We've come far. And Luke saved you," Ms. Hursh says, only it's started to sound nothing like her. "He gave you a world outside of your grandmother." It's almost Regan's voice now. "Like a birth," now it's Gram, it's someone much, much older, "like a father."

These are Ada's own thoughts, thrown back at her. A challenge, a rite of passage. She takes the wadded sheet from the floor and holds it like a shield.

"I'll show you how we look underneath," that old voice says. There's a wet stretching, a breaking-bone sort of sound from the closet, something growing, and the doorknob begins to turn. She snatches up the viola and runs outside, where the moths are boiling, parting for her like a sea of ash.

It's remarkable, how she's thinking about the end of her marriage from a distance now. Because she's on her way to him, she supposes, but it seems more as though she's just beginning to see Luke clearly, through a truer lens, one that's her own. She can think of arguments they had, how they ran hotter than she told herself when she rewrote them the next day. And she's playing music again, reaching deeper and deeper into her instrument. Her hands feel strong around the steering wheel. Headlights pick out the reds and yellows from the night, the trees leaning over the road, the mountains settling into the changing quilt.

Luke had been under a black cloud for days before the Breakup, and she'd had to beg him to get out of the house and just *be* with her. They sat in a booth in Locke's Pub and Ada tore her napkin into strips. When there was nothing else to do with her hands, she mentioned the books Luke read in his studio, the time he spent on his computer, light bleeding onto his face at two, three most mornings. What was he doing when he hadn't shown her any new work in months? Where did he go when he didn't come home at night?

He got this look to him when she said something bad, it wasn't quite often, but there it was now. "Nothing," he muttered, the naked hanging bulb turning them both into suspects. A glass of something amber and oak-smelling sweated on the table in front of him. "Stay out of that stuff. It's just research on this . . . group I hunted down."

She heard the pause more than the words.

"I thought I was clever, finding them," he said, turning his glass, a thin, circled scrape on the tabletop. "But they let me. They arranged it."

"What kind of group?"

"Just please shut up," he said, and glared across at her. He was almost shaking now. "I look for something. I find out it's what I've been looking for all along, and it turns out I'm not . . . right for the *part*." He swept the glass off the table, and all her hope seemed to follow it to the floor.

The only hard part is which section of 151 the church is set back from in the dark, but she finds it, easily as muscle memory. Or it finds her. There's not a car in sight, but the high-peaked, planked building brims with presence. Every window bleeds light.

The stars tipped across the sky ignore her as she gets out of the car. The earth must cast a small shadow, being in the way of all their old light. The moon's over halfway drawn, she imagines God getting a wrist cramp, like hers, and putting the pencil down on a cloud to massage His hand. She laughs at the image, is aware it's her first real laugh in weeks. She pulls the air in. It still holds the sweetness of the morning's rain.

A woman came over to clean up the broken glass. "What about us?" Ada asked Luke. Making herself look at him, making herself keep it together.

"Yeah, that's the question, what about *you*?" he said, voice lifting toward a shout even with the waitress bending over right there. "The beloveds, people give their lives up for them, it takes years to find the pieces, line them up. They left the door cracked open, but they don't want me."

"The beloveds? Is this for a film you're doing?" Ada asked, scared now by the anguish she heard, the first prickle of something bigger than she understood. "Money for a project?"

"A film, are you kidding? Since when have I ever been this—" He clenched his teeth, his fists. "You know, at first, yes, it's how I got onto their trail, this long-form piece I wanted to do. It was that burned-out house we found, and the vibe in that church. It got me hunting, I traced them back to the nineties when they settled there. But it's grown into . . . I'm not giving up. So I'm done with us."

Luke stood, not looking at her, his face in shadow above the hanging lamp now. "Done with us?" she said. "Done with us?" She kept trying, she kept failing to get past that.

"Done with you, yeah. As in divorce." He threw a $20 bill on the table, and she watched it drink the ring of water where his glass had been. She reached out and took his hand. He looked up at the exposed ceiling and growled something animal. Then she was on him, using her weight to pull him back into his seat, screaming, Don't go, don't go, you can't go.

She stares at the old place as she remembers this last part, the part where he shoved her against the table, drew his arm back like he'd done twice before in their six years, only this time he hit her in the face. Red-black stars bloomed between her eyes. And she remembers coming to, the same waitress holding a bag of ice, she remembers having to breathe through her mouth from the blood, but her memory can't quite finish. It snaps shut on her, even as the sky above is all so clear now.

The bed sheet stays in the car, and the past, too, she tries to hope. Just her viola and a new Ada, crunching gravel under her slippers, the two-thirds moon hanging above her as she walks up the short steps and pulls on the windowed vestibule door. The sound that spills out like it's been held in cupped hands, a secret from the world, is such an unexpected thing, she nearly lets go of the door handle. She smiles. Instruments – strings warming up, muted beyond the set of heavy wooden doors inside.

She passes through the small vestibule and pushes into the wide square room of the church beyond. Fifteen or so people sit scattered in the pews, facing the pulpit. Ada stares where they are staring: Two women and a man sit in small wooden chairs, dressed in white. A fourth chair waits off to the right. She pictures them standing in a creek. The first of the women is strikingly tall, even sitting down, even with the cello clasped between her thighs. The woman's yellow hair hangs over her chest in two thick French braids. She smiles at Ada. A wash of dizziness, this has to be Emma, she pictures her with Luke, imagines her squeezing Luke between those thighs.

At last she can look away, ignoring the red-haired woman beside Emma, the bearded man with hair shorter than her own, almost shaved, each with a violin tipped under the chin. The voice of the empty chair does not even reach her. She's looking for Luke, her attention skimming across the audience for him.

He's not here. She knows he's here.

But the trio has stopped, is ready, the silence swelling to a huge thing, and each head facing them turns on its neck to regard Ada. Ms. Hursh smiles at her from near the front, looking almost exactly like Ms. Hursh. Ada slips into the back row and sits, her forearms covering the viola in her lap, her gaze still darting and searching.

Then the cellist straightens her graceful long back and dips the bow across the strings, sweeps it back, a long mourning rind peels into the room. Ada thinks of the first time she sat here, she thinks of Gram at the end, reaching for her, clutching at her like she always, always did. Such a warmth, a blanket of sound, Ada's lost in its folds. The violins slide in and she recognizes an arrangement of Barber's *Adagio*, such a strange choice for the quality of darkness coming into the tone now, that's been there all along, she realizes. There's dirt in these creases.

The man directly in front of her is swaying his head from side to side. It's a comforting rhythm, an easy metronome, as though this really is church. She lets the motion anchor her, fixating on the weathered skin on the back of his neck. Something peeks out of the man's shirt collar. Small and dark. It wanders out, finally, and she sees it's a moth. It wanders up the neck toward the ear. Another emerges from the man's shirt, and another. Is there a light inside the man's clothes, she wonders, and has to bite her tongue to hold her in the pew. The music and where Luke is, that empty chair and what it means, these things are making her want to get up and do, *be*, though she doesn't know what or where.

A white-yellow cloud catches her eye, drifting into the right of her vision, leaning forward halfway down the pew. Ada turns her head. A plump old woman is smiling at her, showing her teeth. She looks like a white Gram, her hair thin as ground fog, insubstantial. Ada sees moths crawling on her scalp.

She shuts the woman out, those Gram eyes. The music's crawling, too, Ada can't imagine Barber holding so much shadow inside himself. Somehow this trio resonates like a small orchestra, the sound like it's kneeling, in mud and storm and blood, suddenly they abandon the Barber and cut into the middle of Ligeti's first string quartet, the manic depressive *Métamorphoses nocturnes*. Here is a darkness without its cloak.

But this is all a disappointment. Ada has no patience for it, beautiful and almost unprecedented though it is. She wants it to evolve, down into that one unwound, fibrous note she's discovered. If she hears it, she'll know. She'll know this is right, all of it, and she'll stay. But if the endless tone is there, the trio cannot find it. Ada doesn't even hear an awareness of it.

The listeners turn and look back at her. The old woman, mouth smiling too wide, rises from the pew and steps toward the aisle, but Ada's already stumbling into the vestibule and the night outside. Quiet as December, the trees crowding in a semicircle around the church, and the mountains a towering faith out beyond the closeness of the forest.

Ada looks up to the vestibule, sees the old woman staring down at her from the door, like some creature requiring permission to leave. The woman presses a blackened palm against the glass of the door. More than anything Ada wants a needle for this compass, she assumes it's Luke – how couldn't it be? – but what comes will have to come from this center in which she's standing.

She feels the answer pulling at her from the woods. Halfway along the tree line she sees an open notch of deeper shadow. He's watching her from behind the low-hanging branch of a red maple. She goes to him, her true north. He fades back into the trees and she stops, waits. The opening looks natural, as if the forest gave itself an entrance. A sundial stands to the right, long-weathered marble, in a place where it could rarely feel the sun and its purpose. She drags her fingers around every corner, across the carved letters.

"*Horas non numero nisi serenas*," she reads, remembers. And in a voice that sounds cracked to her, like Gram's voice, "I do not count the hours when they are dark." As a girl Ada checked the sundial every morning in the back yard, where the dawn first peeked over the Smoky Mountains at her little world. The slow swing of the blade of shadow, the way it changed its shape to a fan, the way it fell into everything else when night came. Sometimes Gram would whisper those words and Ada would think to herself that time had gone someplace where it could never find its way back to her. She'd be stuck there, forever guarded.

Looking at the inscription now, she senses that Gram might have had the translation a touch wrong, but the sentiment feels true as ever. Has this sundial always been here, or is it another sign given by Luke? She turns back to the church, the windows now filled with watchers. Two shapes crouch on the roof peak, steeples regarding her. Back to the inscrutable trees and their velvet dark, she can't step anywhere but inside charge.

A path opens before her. There's the shush of water somewhere close, and before long she begins to hear movement in the trees on either side of her, the shuffle and crack of leaves.

"We've looked for you," someone says from her right, and overlapping from the left is another voice, a lower register, "Many have come far for you."

Staggering, words stepping on words all around her:

"We settled here for you—"

"The light of stairs—"

"Between stars—"

"Through cracks—"

"Planted our roots for you—"

"You're glad you've found us—"

Ada walks faster, calling Luke's name and getting the same nothing back she's gotten for so long now. But the voices withdraw, or were never there.

A clearing spreads out in the near distance, one she saw lit with flashes not two hours ago on her computer screen. No figure stands in wait and now even the light of the incomplete moon is hidden from her. The obscured mountains give everything an extra weight. And the trees open around her, uncurtaining the hole in the ground, a low and devastating sweep of strings comes from it, two violins again, one cello again. It's nothing and everything like music. It's the most dreadful, pristine thing she's ever heard. The earth falls asleep in its wake, an absence of sound.

She steps forward, one of her shoes gone missing somehow, and peers over the lip of the pit, ten, a dozen feet down. The mouth of it stretches twice as long across. Three figures sit inside, draped in ragged black sheets, placing their instruments aside. The ground is shifting around them, until she realizes the carpet of leaves is alive with moths. They've eaten holes in the sheets. Ada looks for the mannequin, trying to complete the picture, but doesn't see it.

"And she comes," one of them says, the tallest, and all three chuckle. It's a woman's voice, but also the sexless whisper from the film. There's the lightest modulation. "We've looked for you."

"Where's my husband?" Ada says, feeling the air pull at the hairs on her arms, smelling its sharp tang of rain on hot asphalt.

The first draped figure – it's Emma, she thinks, even taller now, and how did she make it through the woods ahead of her? – cocks its head, says, "Ada, your marriage cannot concern us, but I understand. I remember the sentiment. He is close, so don't fear. He's arranged for you to be with us, as bitter as his work has become. But he's been kept safe, as a gift."

"What do you want?" Ada asks, but she finds there are not many questions. None burns in her with a particular heat. She watches the moths rise in brief, spiraling clouds and settle again on the leaves around these – cultists, she supposes that's the word – and catches herself squeezing the neck of her viola, wanting, almost, to play it. "Is your name Emma?"

"It is a name. Emma. And yet we have no name. This we've dug is a bowl, you can see," she says, that flat voice holding the edges of a vibration. The head tilted toward the left shoulder. "This land is a bowl, rimmed by its mountains, and they are old mountains. We are a bowl. So are you, Ada, a bell that's waited long to be struck. It's that tone you will wrap with ours. Bowls are for filling. You've known this, but now you can hear it."

"I don't know any of this. Or any of you. I only saw your name written on something."

"Bowls," the one to her left says, in a deeper but more feminine range, "it's a matter of greater acoustics."

"Resonance," the third whispers.

Ada breathes out. "A door."

"Yes," Emma says, "but not in a way that will open your Earth." She sighs, and there's a thread of static in it. "It's a pretty thought, isn't it, our beloveds dreaming long under these perfect mountains, rising up from the roots of them. But no, they're coming from older doors, through cracks in spectrums you can't imagine. Their light swallows itself, and us into their embrace. The light we're all seeking, even the insects are drawn to it." Her hands creep out from under the sheet and brush across the moths. Dust coats fingers that have too many knuckles. "The three of us were found, like you have been."

"Was that you playing in the church?"

"By some measures, yes. By others, they are our personal acolytes, our skins. A wardrobe for when we want to look, shall we say, nice. You'll have your own very soon. But what you heard them play is very little to do with us. We are mostly silence, as you heard in the footage we made for you. We, and only we, here, have found the right note. The rest is only artifice. No name wears us, but there is a symbol, like a rune, but it's a notation more arcane. We've spent lifetimes learning it. Turning it to sound. We first sequenced its true threads in a machine, in 1968, but it seems to require the intricacies of a human wrist, a human fallacy, perhaps. And since then we've looked for the last thread. Before, only a man named Erich Zann had come close, but he bent his studies to a different resolve. We first heard the true thread, the seed of it, when you were a child crying yourself to sleep, still smelling of your parents' blood. Such a pure frequency, we rejoiced. And when it was cultivated, we rejoiced. You, Ada, you could even hum it over ours."

The other two figures speak a word, a monosyllabic incantation. Their voices are perfect mirror images of one another, coupling, and the sound crusts in Ada's ears, wet and painful.

"The name of the beloveds," Emma says. "The very fact you can hear it means, oh, Ada, such great things. You'll find it interesting that if one could sand off all its burrs and tongues, it might translate, poorly, as 'grandmothers.' Over the river and through the woods."

Grandmothers. Ada feels no surprise, only the old confused warmth. She hears the rustle of leaves, amplified in her pressurized ears, and Luke is here at last, just inside the trees, hiding behind his best camera. It's pointed at her, and she remembers how long he saved up to buy it. Across his shoulder is a black sheet. She recognizes it as hers, somehow, he must have gotten it from her car. Even behind the camera he's still handsome, though he's all sagging skin and bones, he's lost so much weight. His face is ravaged with beard stubble.

"I'm sorry, Ada." He crosses to her, stands there first-date nervous. "I knew you weren't strong enough to come here unless you thought I was in trouble. So they felt you'd respond to film as a way to prepare you." He lowers the camera to smile at her.

"Strong enough? You chose all this over me," she says, and the dam's barely holding now, what's behind it is surprising her. "You chose this over starting a family. This is the past year? Two years, how many years? This is you hitting me? This is what we were?" Shouting – has she ever shouted at anything? – and somewhere the last bird in the forest screams back and bursts into a ruffled flight.

"Please don't – at first I couldn't stand it, that they wanted you. I'm just the glorified cameraman, your – acolyte. I should have accepted it was about you. I should have made our life about you all along." He's crying, she hasn't seen him cry since his father died. "But I'm trying to get it now, it's only you. You have such an honor. And there can still be an us, tell them that."

She's never wanted anything but him, almost from the moment she first found the idea of what wanting could do. Through these trees sits the old place, but she only found him here, in this older place. Gram always said she would do great things, but it's not Gram's voice that's speaking to her now. Gram's voice never let her be. This isn't a voice at all, it's something more atavistic and naked, tipping its head back to where the moon appears in its frame of treetops, waiting for a god to finish it. This is strength, this is what strength is.

"I came here to *help* you," she tells him. In the video, this is the part where she drapes the black sheet over herself like some widow's veil, it's when she goes to him. What is there to mourn, now? "I wanted to be strong for you, to be not like Ada for you. That was stupid. I'll choose what you chose, but for my music. For *me*," she adds, and his eyes get wide, "not for you, and not for *us*." She snatches her sheet from his shoulder, turns away from her name on his lips. She walks over to the hole and drops the sheet on the ground.

Below, the three figures pull theirs off in harmony, revealing thin, over-jointed bodies. Bleached white and hairless, heavily endowed, composed of blunt hominid angles. Their thin tongues are almost translucent. Emma's farthest along in this anthropomorphosis, the shape of her skull in flower, the bones petaling out around the mouth. The black symbol curves up around the heave of her right breast. A beauty that could be appreciated, if given an age. Or by a grandmother, Ada thinks.

From behind comes the sound of Luke's sobs, and another sound, like the interminable ending of a deep kiss, but she doesn't turn. Her eyes crawl over Emma's body, all the ripe firmness.

"You've grown these last days," Emma says, "found your own mettle. We are proud. It gives our gift to you a different flavor, perhaps. Look," and her elongated finger points.

Ada glances back now, reluctantly, to see her husband removing his skin, a costume two sizes too large. Under it there's little blood, little muscle, fewer tendons than seems possible. He's a weak serpent of a thing, young and gasping at the air, folding himself over his arm like a coat.

"He is your own acolyte," Emma says. "A true one. He will be allowed to evolve into a lower form of us."

"He is yours to wear," the second says.

"When we visit here," the third says.

"You always wanted him closer," and Emma laughs.

Ada sees faces appear in the trees, at a discreet distance, most human and lit with expectance, a few sunken and bled white. Ada turns back to the hole. Now the cello is squeezed between Emma's powerful, spindled thighs. The violins are seated under those strange chins. The three of them play, the three tones uncoil, neither major nor minor, cold nor warmth, and the ground absorbs a thick, silent thunder. The sky flashes a negative of itself, it's filled with vast things, endless drifting strands and appendages. Arriving, converging, dwarfing the Appalachians in every direction. Immense limbs like cities, a pulsing architecture, reach down and reduce the Earth's majesty. Ropes of sinew orbited by wan stars. The sky goes moonlit again and they're gone. Ada feels it: that note, the one that has built in her.

The sky burns that non-white a second time, the filaments of gods hanging down from wherever their great eyes blink and gaze. She feels those eyes roll downward, each wet socket a galaxy, tipping toward her, *her*. Dark again, absence again, with them just behind it. They wait for the sky to stay on.

Ada lowers herself to all fours and climbs down into the hole. The finished quartet doesn't commune. The three, waiting for her, begin threading their frequencies into a cord. She realizes she's left the viola above her, the ghost of her mother still in its bones somewhere, and she smiles. She decides to sing instead. She cracks opens her mouth.

The late **Michael Shea** invented a character, "Cannyharme," whose genesis lay in Lovecraft's story "The Hound." "The Hound" involves the exhumation of a ghoul who had lain buried five hundred years in a Dutch churchyard. An amulet – found in surprisingly good condition – is stolen from the skeletal remains as they hear the "baying of some gigantic hound" in the distance. The upper-class grave robbers return to England, but very bad things – accompanied by the hound's baying – happen. It is decided the strange occurrences are connected to the amulet, and the narrator returns to Holland intending to return it to the tomb. The amulet is stolen, but he re-excavates the grave anyway, only to discover the skeleton "not clean and placid as we had seen it [before], but covered with caked blood and shreds of alien flesh and hair, and leering sentiently at me with phosphorescent sockets and sharp ensanguined fangs yawning twistedly in mockery of my inevitable doom. And when it gave from those grinning jaws a deep, sardonic bay as of some gigantic hound, and I saw that it held in its gory, filthy claw the lost and fateful amulet of green jade."

In the short poetic tale here, you can gather much about the nature of Cannyharme, but the fact he is writing to Edgar Allan Poe, dead at least a century before this correspondence is supposedly penned, has another significance. Lovecraft saw Poe as his major influence, his "God of Fiction." "The Hound" is an attempt to emulate Poe, but in retrospect, HPL felt his story was "a piece of junk." Author Lin Carter later agreed, stating it was "slavishly Poe-esque in style" and "a minor little tale. Steven J. Mariconda, although acknowledging HPL's debt to Poe, sees the story as "written in a zestful, almost baroque style which is very entertaining."

Michael Shea first wrote sword-and-sorcery and supernatural/extraterrestrial horror, primarily in the novella form (collected in *Polyphemus* and *The Autopsy and Other Tales*). In the last decade or so he added homages to H. P. Lovecraft to his novella work (as in collection *Copping Squid*.) His novel *Nifft the Lean* won a World Fantasy Award, as did novella "The Growlimb." His most recent novels are dark, satirical thrillers *The Extra* and *Assault on Sunrise*. Shea passed away on 16 February 2014.

An Open Letter to Mister Edgar Allan Poe, from a Fervent Admirer
Michael Shea

——

Optissime! Best of the Best!

It is with reverence and reluctant challenge I unfurl my banner to you herein. Great Poe, of all your peerless poems, it is *The Conqueror Worm* I've cherished most. I have sipped the ichor of its icy truth again and again, amid the dark business of this recent century. The Worm, you see, has long been my *metier*. The Worm has been my very medium, for longer ages than even your great spirit can conceive.

I write, Sir, to apprise you of my apotheosis. For I must, by the law of Majesty, proclaim and present myself a mightier Monarch than King Worm himself. Until I find you, Sir, I produce this document, that you may know Who seeks you. It is with deep regard that I unfold to you this declaration of myself, my Work, my Way.

Ever since your meteoric crossing of the skies – so bright, so brief! – like steeds your melodies, your Stygian rhapsodies have lofted me and borne me worlds away. You must forgive, oh metric Master, the imperfect measures of my fledgling songs. What grace they have, they've learned from you. One of these songs reports my recent rebirth and present course thus:

In Netherlands did old Van Haarme
A vasty boneyard till and farm,
Did plough and plant a funeral field
Where gnarled lich was all his yield,
And parched cadaver all the crop
That e'er the Ghoul did sow or reap.

But it's Carnival Row in latter years
That the canny Hound now scythes and shears.
The boggy graves of his natal feif
He's quit for the Carnival's shadow-strife.
It's Poortown's streets that he seeds now, and tills,
Where the shambling shadow-folk drift without wills.

You who have rendered so well the psychic fecundity of cities will appreciate, I know, the giddy translocation I experienced, from the foggy churchyards of the Lowland, to the human Roil within a maze of pavements. And so, perhaps, you commiserate for what might have been a grave upheaval of my mode of life. But it has not been so! I have blundered upon Powers unforeseen – undreamed! I command a legion here, and have found my own wings in the wills of my *living* prey.

My ancient lust was to enslave the dead
And up the brittle ladders of their bones
To climb to zeniths thick with stars bestrown,
Against vast, cold Eternity to spread
My sinewy wings; to press my taloned tread
Upon the very pinnacle of Time.

But now it is quite otherwise I climb.
For, not long past, my lust did learn to know
Through living flesh a readier way to go
To oversoar the mortal phantomime.

> *Now I empower those who would be mine*
> *To imbibe a deathless vintage, red as wine,*
> *And – ever unentombed – run wild at will,*
> *And breach Time's very walls to make their kill!*

I've passed scarce a century on this continent of yours, *Poetissime*, but the pathway I have found here has long allowed me entry to all Time. Perhaps, back when you lived, as you threaded the human herds (gathering your materials, perhaps, for "The Man in the Crowd"?) – perhaps twice or thrice, on these brooding, watchful peregrinations of yours in a younger New York, you felt the cold touch of my muzzle against your hand. Perhaps you stopped, looked back, looked around, and found no one near enough to have made that contact? And, just perhaps, the chill of that moment sent frosty reverberations through your sense of Time . . . ?

Or whilst sojourning on Brennan Farm – there pondering the ebony bird who quoth "Nevermore!" – mayhap the night wind lofted my unholy baying unto your perceptive ear. Unsure of its existence, perhaps you paused and heard instead the soft susurration of Death whispering of its inevitable approach?

Just where, in the Realm of the Dead you dwell, Sir, is not yet known to me, so vast is that shoreless realm in which you swim. But it *will* be known. And perhaps a soul of your scope can understand this mystery: That from the Dead, the Great can be *retrieved* by those who are themselves above Death's reach. Master, vouchsafe to harken, and to weigh the wonders that I hold in gift.

> *Where the lich in the loam has lain mouldering long*
> *And the maggoty minutes gnaw meat off his bones,*
> *There Time is a monster that mows down the throng*
> *Of once-have-been, gone-again, featureless drones.*
> *And that lich's coffin to me was a door*
> *Through which I went nosing Eternity's spoor.*

> *But the living dead's doorways, once opened, gape wider.*
> *Through these you may go where the galaxies sprawl,*
> *And up through the star-webs dance sprightly as spiders,*
> *And dart quick as rats through Time's ceilings and walls!*
> *There we go feasting and rutting at will,*
> *And Time is a wine we imbibe when we kill!*

While I cannot cease to praise you, Mister Poe, it seems I can't forbear now to *exhort* you. I urge, with every reverence, that you accede to my impassioned suit – for now I must be frank. I wish to crown you as the king among the poets of my retinue. How your silvery lyric will ensorcel them, my legionnaires! In short, I cannot take denial. You must be mine.

Death's whelm is as wide as the starfield, and deep as Old Night, but my eyes are the Lamps of the Tomb, and my nose is keen. The time, Mister Poe, as we two reckon it, will not be long. You will know me when you see me, Bard.

Here, my farewell for now, this Ode and Exhortation I have penned for you alone!

> *Through all the human stockyards you have trod*
> *Where your bestial brothers broil and bleed,*
> *Beseeching brute predominance, their God,*
> *To grant them scope to blunder, bray, and breed—*
>
> *Here you have wandered, haunted by a will*
> *To weave from words a world more rare and bright,*
> *Outreaching death, to shed its radiance still,*
> *When you have sunk to dust and endless night.*
>
> *But I, who lay so long entombed below*
> *That abbatoir by your brutes tenanted*
> *(Oh how their hooves did teach my soul to know*
> *The living deaths by which they're tormented!)*

I who now long have walked among that herd,
I am unroofed by Time. The eons sprawl
Like open fields I plunder undeterred!
My feet o'er leap the centuries' slow crawl!

Know, wordsmith, that it is my wish to shower
This grandeur, this forever, this deathless power
On your rare kind that strive for vaster views—
You hard and hungry one whom the Abyss
Excites to try their wings. You sterner few
I lift up to the plane where I exist!

Faithfully,
Cannyharme

A. C. Wise is the author of numerous short stories, which have appeared in publications such as *Shimmer*, *Apex*, *The Year's Best Dark Fantasy and Horror*, and *Year's Best Weird Fiction*. Her debut collection, *The Ultra Fabulous Glitter Squadron Saves the World Again*, was published by Lethe Press in 2015. In addition to her fiction, she co-edits *Unlikely Story*, and contributes a monthly column – "Women to Read: Where to Start" – to *SF Signal*.

Wise's favorite Lovecraft story has always been "The Color Out of Space." With "I Dress My Lover in Yellow," she pays tribute to "the idea of color itself as a malignant, haunting force. I also wanted to salute the tradition spawned by Lovecraft's works, of authors swapping and mashing-up mythos, and 'playing' in each other's fictional worlds. To that end, I couldn't resist throwing in references to Robert W. Chambers' *The King in Yellow*, another personal favorite that lies on the periphery of Lovecraft."

I Dress My Lover in Yellow
A. C. Wise

———

Enclosed are the documents deemed most pertinent to the ongoing investigation into the disappearances of Rani Alam and Casey Wilton. In addition to one photocopied document are several hand-written copies of original documents from the Special Collections of St. Everild's University Library. These documents have been compared to the originals, and have been found to be faithful and unaltered. The primary handwriting has been confirmed as that of Ms. Wilton. The interstitial and marginal notes on both the photocopy and the hand-written reproductions are confirmed as being written by Ms. Alam.

Excerpted from "The Phantom Masterpiece: Blaine Roderick's Lost Painting", *Great Artists of New England*, A. Jansen and Tucker Cummings, eds, University of St. Everild's Press, 1984.

It is likely Blaine Roderick's career as an artist would be largely unremembered today if it were not for one extraordinary painting or, rather, the lack of a painting.

Little is known about Blaine Roderick. His earliest surviving works date from 1869, just six years before his disappearance. These works consist primarily of commissioned portraits, along with the odd landscape, and are considered largely derivative of his contemporaries while lacking their best qualities. It is known Roderick supplemented his portrait work with irregular teaching stints, the last of which was his position at St. Everild's University.

One painting falls completely outside the pattern established by the artist's early works. This is Roderick's famous (or infamous) lost masterpiece, "Mrs. Aimsbury in a Yellow Dress," known colloquially as "I Dress My Lover in Yellow, I Dress My Lover in Ruin."

By most accounts, "Yellow" is not only Roderick's masterpiece, but far surpasses those contemporaries he is so often accused of imitating, though many claim the painting is elevated solely by the mystery surrounding it. Alas for history, judging the matter is impossible. All that remains of the work is the original frame and a handful of accounts written prior to its disappearance.

Even these primary descriptive sources are considered problematic among scholars, going beyond the subjective and ranging from extreme praise to outright condemnation. Their unreliability, in all cases deemed to be tainted by personal bias, has led many scholars to believe some accounts may be deliberately false.

Regardless, the majority of these accounts focus on the feelings evoked by the work, rather than its content, making them of questionable value to begin with. An example of one such account was penned by Giddeon Parson, one of Roderick's aforementioned contemporaries. Parson calls "Yellow," "a vile piece of filth fit for nothing but the fire, though I suspect even flame would disdain to touch it."

A slightly more tempered account is offered by Vincent Calloway, a frequent contributor to the society pages of the *Tarrysville Herald*, who had occasion to see the work at a fundraiser to benefit the university:

Regardless of what one thinks of Blaine Roderick's skill as a painter, the mastery of his brushwork, his use of light, and the startling effect of his palette cannot be called in to question here. However, one must question his powers of observation. As a personal friend of both Mrs. Aimsbury and her husband, Dean Howard Aimsbury, the portrait struck me as executed by someone who had never laid eyes on its subject. From whence did Roderick draw the wan coloring of Mrs. Aimsbury's cheeks? Never have I known her features to be so sharply sunken. It is most unsettling; one can almost see the skull beneath the flesh.

If the effect is meant to be satirical, it misses the mark, and is furthermore an unwise choice for an unknown artist relying upon the Dean not only for his commission, but his continued employment at the university. The less said about the lewd manner in which Roderick paints the dress slipping from Mrs. Aimsbury's shoulder, the better.

Colorful descriptions aside, a few incontrovertible facts remain. The subject of the painting was Charlotte Aimsbury (nee Whitmore). The portrait, commissioned by Charlotte Aimsbury's husband, Dean Howard Aimsbury, was full-length, oil on canvas, measuring 103¾ by 79 inches. That is where the certainty ends.

The supposed masterpiece either depicts Mrs. Aimsbury clothed in a formal yellow gown, partially clothed in the same, or nude, having just stepped out of the gown pooled at her feet. She either faces the viewer, stands in profile, or looks back over her shoulder. Her expression is one of fear, as though she intends to flee; surprise, as if the viewer has intruded upon her private chambers; or suggestive, as though the viewer is fully expected and welcome.

Most accounts describe the background as largely obscured, as though prematurely stained by a patina of smoke. Those descriptions that purport to be able to make it out chiefly describe indistinct figures, or a city shrouded by fog or blowing sand. However other accounts have the backdrop as nothing but a series of doors receding down a hallway, all closed save for one.

One account – most outlandish and therefore likely false – claims the backdrop depicts an abattoir. This description, as preposterous as it may be, has led some to speculate Roderick reused his canvas, painting Mrs. Aimsbury atop a wholly different scene meant to be a commentary upon the deplorable conditions faced by immigrant workers in America's slaughterhouses.

Beyond its physical appearance, the ultimate fate of "Yellow" is a matter of much debate as well. Later in his life, long after the disappearance and presumed deaths of both Blaine Roderick and Charlotte Aimsbury, Dean Aimsbury admitted to cutting the portrait from its frame and burning it. However, when questioned, the Dean's housekeeper, Mrs. Templeton claimed if evidence of such a burning existed she would have found it. She is further reported to have said the Dean was "poorly" and "prone to confusion and fits of imagination" at the time of this confession.

Amidst this confusion, one thread of commonality does exist across all accounts of the painting: the mention of the artist's use of color, in one form or other. Here again we find equal parts praise and damnation, everything from "brilliant, pure genius" to "having the appearance of a palette mixed by a blind imbecile, producing an effect not unlike physical illness." But every account does mention color, with at least one calling Roderick's use of it "near-supernatural, for good or for ill."

*   *   *

Casey – Before you get pissed at me for writing on your research notes, I submit for your consideration this: You have not taken your nose out of your books in almost three weeks. There's more to life than studying. I am officially kidnapping you for a movie night. No excuses. It's a double-feature: House of Wax and Dementia 13. I promise, you'll love it. I'll even make dinner. Kisses, Rani.

"Toward a New Understanding of Color Theory" by Blaine Roderick (incomplete draft), St. Everild's University, Special Collections, 1877.02.01.17.

> [Appended note from Robert Smythe, Head of Special
> Collections, 1923–47: *The following selection from the papers
> of Blaine Roderick represents an early draft of an unpublished
> treatise on color theory. It is remarkable for the way it mixes
> scholarly writing and personal musings, lending credence to the
> theory Roderick suffered from an undiagnosed mental illness
> at the time of his disappearance and presumed death.*]

If we are to follow slavishly in the footsteps of Isaac Newton, Moses Harris, and Johann Wolfgang von Goethe, we are left with only the primary, secondary, and tertiary colors upon the wheel, leaving no room for the creation of truly transcendent art. While theirs are serviceable models, they admit no space for *otherness*, for the ethereal, the cosmic, that which goes beyond the veil.

What of ecstatic experience? What of true *seeing*, but also in the act of seeing, *being seen*? What is needed from a new theory of color is a way to go between the shades we accept as representing the full spectrum. There are cracks through which we must pass to appreciate the fullness of the universe.

But yellow is problematic. *What* yellow? Not the color of daffodils, sunlight, or the delicacy of a canary's wing. No. The yellow of bruises, aged bone, butter on the cusp of spoiling. There's a taste to it. Slick with rot just starting to creep in. Yellow is joy, hope, life, but its underbelly is cowardice, madness, pestilence. They are not mutually exclusive; they are but two sides of the same skin. Pierce one, and you pierce the other as well.

There are shades between shades, hues that exist on the periphery of common understanding. Purple bleeds if you slice it deeply enough. I have seen such a color, printed on my eyelids. It is an infection, this color, a fever. Hungry. It means to devour me whole.

~~I want~~

Yellow remains problematic.

Why yellow? Because she *must* be dressed so. She is saddled with a husband she cannot possibly love. Too old. The yellow in the pouches under his eyes is common age, weariness. Is the shade I offer any better? Aging slowly toward death would be far kinder. More natural, certainly. But we are not natural creatures, Charlotte and I.

I've seen bones in the desert, scoured by sand. A shadow walks from the horizon, tattered by the wind. His darkness is the space between stars. It is not black. It is a color for which I have not yet discovered a name.

The wheel, were we to rearrange it, swap red for orange, yellow for the lighter shade of blue, would at first seem an affront to the artistic eye. But it brings us closer to what is needed for a *true* understanding of color. One must break to build. See how the meaning of color is changed as it is brought into contact with its opposite and its mate?

It is not simply a color, it is a door. *She* is a door. I know she has dreamed as I have. She has seen the lost city, where we are all hungry. She has seen our king in terrible rags, fluttering like flame in the wind. I tried to speak of it to her, but Charlotte looked so frightened when I touched her shoulder. (Yet I fear she understands far better than I. She will run ahead and I will be left behind.) I only meant to rearrange her into a better angle of light. It left an imprint on her skin, an oval the size and shape of my thumb. I have dreamed the dress in tatters, like the wrappings of the dead.

*   *   *

Casey – I'm sticking with what works. You can be mad at me later. So, movie night take two? I'm sorry I fell asleep last time. I haven't been sleeping well. I wish I could say I was out getting laid, or even being responsible and studying like you. But it's just bad dreams. My dad prescribed me some pills, but they didn't help. Seriously, this shit is supposed to knock you out, put you under so deep you don't dream. But fucking every time I go to sleep I see this fucking city. It's creepy. I don't believe in that reincarnation shit my parents do, but I'm always the same woman and she's me in this city that burns and drowns and is washed in blood. I don't like her. Us. The city. Fuck.

See? I'm so tired I'm not making sense. But I've got my coffee and I'm good to go, so tonight it's your turn to cook. We still have wine from when my parents visited. You can even pick the movies this time. Kisses, Rani

P.S. The sketch you left in the hall? I don't know if you meant me to see it, maybe it just fell out of your bag, but it's really good. Is it supposed to be me?

From the diary of Charlotte Aimsbury, St Everild's University, Special Collections, 1877.02.21.1:

10 August 1874

I met Mr. Roderick today, the artist my husband has commissioned to paint my portrait. First impressions do count for something so I will say this: I do not care for him. The whole time I sat for Mr. Roderick, he never touched charcoal or paper. He simply stared at me in the hideous dress he . . . Well, I cannot imagine where he found it, whether he had it made, or whether he purchased it somewhere. Whatever the case, how is it that the dress fits me so well? Mr. Roderick would not answer my questions. He only insisted I wear it, and that I have always worn it. I could not make sense of him.

He was so insistent, growing flushed and agitated, I finally agreed, though I did not enjoy wearing the dress. There is a weight to it. The feel of it is wrong. It is . . . unearthly. I cannot give it a better word than that. It is compelling and repulsive at once, and yet, for all the madness of Mr. Roderick's words, it is familiar. I do not pretend to understand how such a thing could be possible, but I do believe the dress is mine, and that Mr. Roderick has it in his possession because I must wear it. I have always worn it.

Yet, I feel horrid with it on my person. The silk whispers whenever I move. At times it is like the wind, or sand moving over stone. Other times, I feel there are actual voices inside the dress.

Even if this were not so, Mr. Roderick's gaze alone would be bad enough. I felt like a cut of meat, sitting so still while Mr. Roderick examined me, and he the butcher. I finally asked him if something were wrong, and he snapped at me, commanded (his word, not mine) me not to speak.

I would be tempted to cancel the entire undertaking, but Mr. Aimsbury is set on this idea and it would displease him greatly if I were to protest. As for myself, I have no desire for formal portraiture. Such paintings survive long after one has passed, and all future generations will know of you is the expression you happened to be wearing that day, the way you tilted your head or lifted your hand. Everything *you* were is gone.

14 August 1874

I expressed my aggravation concerning the portrait to Mr. Aimsbury. He convinced me to reconsider.

23 September 1874

It has been weeks of sitting, and I know nothing more of Mr. Roderick than I did the first day. It's as though he's a different person each time we meet. One day he is moody and sullen, the next all charm. Two days ago he kissed my hand and spent the whole sitting contriving excuses to touch me, arranging my chin this way, my hair that. Yesterday he seized my shoulders as if to shake me, then immediately stepped back as though I'd struck him.

Yet my own sensibilities concerning Mr. Roderick are conflicted. I say I do not know him, but there are times I feel I know Blaine very well. But it's not a comforting sort of knowing. Or being known.

Today I asked him about it. "Of course we've met," he said. "The color can only be painted on you. Don't you remember? In the desert? In the city?"

It seemed he would say more, but he stopped as though he'd forgotten how to speak entirely. There was an intensity about him, as though he were in a fever.

He leaned toward me. I thought he meant to kiss me, but he only put his hands on either side of my face and said, "There are colors that hunger, Charlotte. There is a word for them the same shade as hearts heavy with sin."

I hadn't the faintest idea what he meant. Except, I almost did.

13 October 1874

Today, Mr. Roderick spoke barely a word. We sat in silence and I felt I was being crushed to death under the weight of all that horrid silk. It does not breathe. I feel as if I will suffocate. And why yellow? At times, I feel as though the color itself is draining the life from me. Is that possible, for a color to be alive? No, alive is not the correct word. There is nothing of life about it. I am not even certain it *is* yellow. I cannot explain it, but there are moments when the dress gives the distinct impression of being some other color, merely masquerading as yellow. Whatever color it may be in actuality, I do not believe there is a name for it.

14 October 1874

How can I explain the horror of something that seems so simple by daylight? There was nothing monstrous *in* the dream. The dream itself was monstrous.

I dreamt of a hallway going on forever. I was terrified. But of what? A door opening? A door refusing to open?

It is irrational to be afraid of nothing. But in the dream, it was the very nothingness that frightened me. The unknown. The sense of waiting. Wanting. Is it possible fear and desire are only two sides of the same skin? To pierce one with a needle is to pierce both. Then one only needs follow the stitching to find the way through.

30 October 1874

Blaine forbade me from looking at the painting until it is finished. But I caught a glimpse today. It was an accident, only a moment. Perhaps it was my imagination? A trick of my over-tired mind? I haven't been sleeping well, after all.

I saw the hallway. The one full of doors. The one from my dreams. Blaine painted it behind me. I never breathed one word of it to him, but still, there it was.

He means to leave me in that terrible place, a doorway to step through and never think on again.

I will not let him. After dreaming that hallway every night, I know it far better than he ever can. I will learn its tricks and secrets. I will run its length forever, if I must, but he will not catch me and pin me down.

Casey – About last night. Look, you know I like girls. And I like you. I'm just not looking for anything super-serious right now. I thought you knew that. I'm sorry if I gave you the wrong idea. I'm just sorry. Talk to me? Rani.

From the papers of Dean Howard Aimsbury, St. Everild's University, Special Collections, 1879.03.07.1:

18 November 1877

Gentlemen,

It is with a heavy heart that I tender my formal resignation from St. Everild's University. I have had occasion to speak with each of you privately, and I am certain you understand this is in the best interests of all concerned.

I have given over twenty years of my life to this institution, but I cannot—

I cannot.

It is said time heals all wounds, but I have yet to find a thread strong enough to sew mine closed. The past two years since my wife's disappearance have taught me hauntings are all too real. They exist between heart and gut, between skin and bone. No amount of prayer can banish them.

I believed the dismissal of Blaine Roderick would purge any lingering pain. But all it did was limit his access to me and slow the tide of unpleasant – and occasionally quite public – altercations he attempted to instigate.

As I'm sure you know, gentlemen, throughout this ordeal, I have had no care for my personal reputation. I care only for the reputation of St. Everild's. Upon my resignation, I trust you will do your best to repair any damage I have done to the good name of this fine school.

As for myself, what could Blaine Roderick say of me that I have not thought of myself? He made me complicit. He was ever the shadow, the puppet master, steering my hand. I am not blameless, but his will always be the greater share of the blame.

I am not without heart. Nor am I so vain that I cannot sympathize with the notion of a younger woman, married to a man nearly twice her age seeking companionship amongst her peers. If Charlotte . . . I would not blame her. Whatever the truth of their relationships, whatever Blaine Roderick may have felt for Charlotte, I do believe this: He hated her by the end. He feared her. Yet he was ever the coward. He could not bear to do the deed himself, and so he drove me to it.

Gentlemen, you know me. You know I did not, *could* not, commit violence against my wife. I cherished her.

And yet, in the depths of my soul I *know* there might have been a chance for her to, somehow, return. If the painting still existed.

Charlotte's hope for life, for return, is now in ashes. My hand did the deed, but Blaine Roderick bears the blame.

I am weary, gentlemen. If this letter seems improper, I am certain you will forgive me.

Yours, etc.,

Howard Aimsbury

I'm scared, Casey. I can't remember everything that happened that night. I know we both got pretty fucked up. It was a mistake. I'm sorry.

I wanted to tell you . . . I don't think I can stay here. I know I haven't been around the past few days, but it isn't enough. I can't stay in that house with you. When the semester ends, I'm going to call my parents and ask them to take me home.

It's not your fault. We were both . . .

We fooled around. I shouldn't have let it happen, knowing how you feel, and I'm sorry.

But I don't remember everything else that happened. I have bits of it, but there are pieces missing.

All that wine. Everything was so hot, like I had a fever. I remember the color flaking, and falling like ash around me. Then there were colors running down the bathtub drain. I was scrubbing my skin so hard it hurt, and you were pounding on the bathroom door.

There are bruises.

Fuck.

Please don't finish the painting, Casey.

I know it's of me. Even though it isn't done, I can tell. It's fucking with my head, and I'm scared. I'm sorry . . .

I came back to the house just to get my stuff. I looked at the painting again, and it's still wet. I don't remember putting on that dress. Where did you even get it? The way you painted the shadows in the folds of the fabric. They're hungry. Like mouths that have never known kisses, only pain. All those smudges of blue-gray of around my throat. You painted me like I'd been strangled.

I don't even understand some of the colors you used. They're . . . I don't know the names for them. But I can taste them at the back of my throat, slick and just starting to rot. I keep finding paint caked under my nails, like I've been scratching – rust, dirt, bone, a color like the texture of a shadow under an owl's wing, like the sound of things crawling in the earth, like angles that don't match and . . .

I don't know what I did to you. I know. But I'm sorry, Casey. Just take it back, okay?

I can smell the smoke from when the city burned, the tide from when it drowned. It's sand-grit when I close my eyes, rubbing every time I blink. The dress is in tatters, and he is ragged where his shadow is stripped raw from the wind. He is walking from the horizon. I don't want to go. I can't. I have to go.

From the collected papers of Dr. Thaddeus Pilcher (Bequest), St. Everild's University, Special Collections, 1891.06.12.1:

Physician's Report: Patient Charlotte Aimsbury, 1 November 1874
Called to examine Charlotte Aimsbury today. Cause of condition uncertain.

(I have known Charlotte since she was a little girl, and I have never found her to be prone to fits of hysteria like so many of her sex. She has a good head on her shoulders. She is a most remarkable woman.)

Patient claims no memory of collapse. Can only surmise exhaustion the cause.

(I do not blame Charlotte. While I make a point of rising above such things, talk, when persistent enough, often cannot be avoided. Being the subject of so many wagging tongues would be enough to weary even the strongest spirit.

Not that I believe there's any truth to even half of what is said. Having met Mr. Roderick, I cannot imagine Charlotte succumbing to his charms, few as they are. Roderick is brusque, rude, and highly distractible. I see little to draw Charlotte's eye. Yet, I suppose it is no great wonder that many would gossip.

In my own admittedly biased opinion, Charlotte is a very moral and upstanding woman. I refuse to believe her the faithless type.)

Final diagnosis: Exhaustion. Odd pattern of bruising evident on patient's skin determined to be symptom of collapse, not cause. Other physical signs bear out diagnosis – pallor, shading beneath eyes indicating lack of sleep; prominence of bones may indicate a loss of weight. Patient complained of nightmares. Calmative prescribed.

(I pray that will be the end of it.)

Appended Case Note: *The enclosed documents were turned over to authorities by Kyle Walters, a librarian at St. Everild's University, following his report of Ms. Wilton's disappearance in January 2015. The painting described by Ms. Alam in her addition to Ms. Wilton's notes was not among the effects in their shared residence following Ms. Wilton's disappearance, nor was it reported as being present at the time of the initial investigation into Ms. Alam's disappearance in November 2015.*

Mr. Walters admitted to removing the documents from Ms. Wilton's residence, but provided a sworn statement that nothing else had been removed or altered. Mr. Walters is being charged with interference in a police investigation, but at this time is not a suspect in either disappearance. Investigations are ongoing.

"Two elements of Lovecraft's fiction that hold perennial appeal," for **Richard Gavin**, "are his evocations of decayed place and the inconceivably vast machinations of life that churn beneath the crust of civilization. 'Deep Eden' attempts to draw upon both. It speaks of an altogether *other* genesis."

Gavin is a critically acclaimed author who works in horror and the primordial, often illuminating the crossroads where these realms meet. He has authored five books of macabre fiction, including *At Fear's Altar* (Hippocampus Press). His esoteric writings consist of *The Benighted Path* (Theion Publishing), as well as essays in *Starfire* and *Clavis: Journal of Occult Arts, Letters and Experience*.

Deep Eden
Richard Gavin

———

Ash Lake occasionally embodies its name. On November days such as this, when the sunbeams can scarcely press through the leaden clouds, the lake roils gray and ghostly, taking on the appearance of shifting dunes of ash; incinerated remains that somehow survived the crematorium.

How I loved days like this when I was a girl. In those distant autumns I would venture down to the lakefront, with Dad and Rita by my side. Together we would toss stones and spy for any boats daring enough to brave the gales. Those days were buoyed by a feeling, very rare and very delicious, that my sister, father, and I were the only three people left in Evendale.

Of late this same feeling has become a constant, but it has lost its succulence.

Perhaps that was the unconscious source of my desire to make the detour to the beach today: the thin hope that somehow the sight of Ash

Lake in late autumn might uplift me, give me the clarity to make sense of the senselessness that is now the norm in Evendale.

I scooped up a handful of fog-moistened stones, then let them drop un-hurled. As I made my way back to the jeep I listened to the surf whose mist-hidden waves sounded much like mocking asthmatic laughter.

The fuel gauge began to flash "E" as soon as I turned the ignition, so I began to woo the vehicle, coaxing it to carry me far enough to reach the Main Street filling station that still, as of last week, had fuel.

Veering into the narrow lot, I left the engine running and ran out to test the pumps. The first two were bone-dry, but the third valve spat out unleaded. As I filled the jeep I wondered how many tankfuls were left in this town; two, possibly three? The residents of Evendale had, up until recently, kept a routine of sorts, a choreographed pantomime of a sleepy but still functioning town. A certain segment of the locals remained above to man the fueling station, to switch on houselights on a rotating basis, to plow the main roads when the snow accumulated. The concern over keeping up appearances to the outside world has waned now that everyone's below.

My memories of this town, paled as they are, paint Evendale as little more than a tangle of poorly paved roads lined with dreary structures. But neither the years nor the miles that I set between myself and my home could account for its present condition. The houses and shops all have the air of heaped wreckage, of withered husks that no longer sheltered living things.

Most of the spaces advertise themselves as being for lease. A few of them were boarded up with slabs of cheap wood, like coffins bound for pauper's row.

The street entrance to Venus Women's Wear was sheathed in brown butcher paper. A sign in the display window advised potential customers that they were closed for renovation. I made my way to the alley beside the shop and found the side door unlocked.

There was no light inside the shop but I didn't need any. My time below has sharpened my ability to see in the dark. It took me several minutes to find the dress Rita had described to me: purple silk with a dragonfly embroidered in glittering black thread over the left breast. This was the first time she had ever requested anything since going below. How I had hoped that her desire could have lured her up and out, into the light. But Rita never comes above anymore.

I zippered the dress inside a plastic garment bag with the Venus logo and the store's address printed on the back, then I carried it back to the jeep and drove on.

Loath as I am to admit it, I now find being above rather unsettling. The airiness, the brightness, after those first few heaves of revivifying oxygen, sours quickly. More and more I want to be below. But I do not *want* to want that.

I turned onto Apple Road to complete my errand. In addition to the purple dress from Venus, Rita also requested that our late mother's silver-handled mirror and hairbrush set be collected from our house.

Hypocrisy abounds: after robbing Venus I fished out the keys for my childhood home. We keep it locked up snugly, perhaps afraid to lose our past, meager though it may be.

I took the hairbrush and mirror from Rita's dresser. Noting their condition, I rummaged around Father's workroom until I found a can of silver polish and a soft rag. A canvas grocery sack hung from the foyer coat rack. I plucked it from its hook and filled it with a few canned goods, a jar of instant coffee, and some packets of oatmeal. I found five bottles of water left in the back of the pantry then I headed back to the mine.

The Dunford Incorporated coal mine had opened shortly after World War II, and had been Evendale's main employer for nearly forty years before a tragic tunnel collapse took the lives of a dozen miners. Eventually, through resulting lawsuits and legal fees, it also took the life of Dunford Inc. The company declared bankruptcy and shut down the mine in 1983. It stood deserted in the arid field on Evendale's outskirts thereafter.

I escaped Evendale in 1991, moving to the city in search of myself. At that time there were rumblings of a new company purchasing and re-opening the dormant mine, but it was not to be. After Dunford Inc. laid my father off (mercifully, a year before the collapse) he used to tell my sister and me that there was hardly any coal left in those shafts anyway. I'd always thought these words were merely a way for my father to sooth his wounded pride, but given that no one had seen fit to resume clawing at those tunnels perhaps he was speaking the truth.

Either way, the site was left to rot; its towering iron scaffolds bowing like aging men, its subterranean maze resting hushed and hollowed like some vacated netherworld.

As to the origins of the mine's more recent and more rarefied role in the lives of the townspeople, accounts differ depending on whom you ask. That a posse had formed to rescue a child who had climbed down into the shafts on a dare and gotten lost seems to be the most common account. But the age and gender of the strayed child varies from teller to teller. A point that *did* run uniform through this folklore was the discovery of the emerald light.

The search party had apparently bored through one of the walls of the farthest tunnel. Their claim was that the lost child could be heard sobbing and pleading on the far side of that rugged culm barrier. When their picks and shovels and scrabbling hands finally pierced through, they found neither boy nor girl, but instead a luminescence. Were they the beams of some strange fallen sun long-interred in the earth's bowels? A green jewel dislodged from a great crown of one who had fallen from heaven? I can only theorize based on the testimonials that have been whispered to me below, for I have never seen the light myself. Nor has Rita. But unlike me, she is convinced of its existence.

My sister loves to brand me as the eternal skeptic, one unwilling to accept there are things that lurk beyond the reach of our five paltry senses. Honestly, I cannot say I'm even that, for a true skeptic would be eager to disprove the myth of the emerald light, to expose the folly of those below. While I will concede that yes, there may well be a greenish glow in the depths of the mines, I suspect that its presence is some natural anomaly, some phosphorescent property in the carbon, or a trick of the eye when met with absolute darkness.

Still, I am not so convinced of these empirical theories that I am willing to creep down into those far depths to prove or disprove anything.

I was only a few hundred yards from the gate to the mine site when I witnessed the impossible.

At first my brain didn't register what came trundling out of the roadside bracken – a dog – because the sight of a moving thing in Evendale was so rare it actually spooked me. I pressed down hard on the brake pedal and the sack spat out the tinned foods into the jeep's foot-well. The creature plodded onto the road, pausing to turn its dismal face toward me. I put the jeep in park and stepped out, tamping my enthusiasm so as not to startle the animal.

It was a yellow Lab. I crouched down and cooed to it. She came to me without reservation or ardor.

That it had been foraging and roaming for some time was obvious. But I was unaware at just how badly the poor beast had been faring until I ran my hand along its matted coat and felt the fence slats of its ribs pressing against the fur. I raced back to the jeep and retrieved the tin of Spam I'd taken from our pantry, along with one of the bottles of water.

The dog was now reposing as though the littered asphalt road was her bed. I uncapped the bottle, poured some of the water into my cupped hand, and held it out to her. She lapped at it with a pale tongue.

I peeled the label off the Spam, opened the tin and shook the meat out onto the label. This I slid before the dog. She sniffed it, perhaps in distrust or disbelief, and began to lick and gnaw the pinkish cube.

As I sat beside the dog, her tail now beginning to faintly wag, I heard the sound of a helicopter. Shielding my eyes I looked past the rim of the escarpment to see the small chopper coasting in the ashen sky. A TV reporter perhaps, or an airlift ambulance; someone who was merely passing over Evendale. That was what Evendale was now, perhaps what it has always been: a place one passes by or through or over on their way to somewhere else. Is this why the exodus below has been allowed to occur without any outside notice at all? Or is there something other at work here?

"Do you want to come home with me?" I asked. Every inch of me went cold once I realized that I'd referred to those dank and cultish tombs as home. The dog looked at me with her teary, tired eyes. I picked her up and gently piled her onto the passenger seat. Then I drove out to the far end of the road.

Dad was part of that first group that tore the barricades from the mouth of the entrance pipe and breached the mine for the first time in years. I only learned this a few months ago from Rita. She told me that the men were glad to have my father among them, for he was the only one left in Evendale to have worked the tunnels when Dunford Inc. was still in operation. I suspect it was more than his knowledge of the shafts that made Dad a welcome member of the search party. He had always been a calming presence in our home, so I can only imagine what a balm it must have been to have his wise and careful suggestions offered in his sonorous voice, especially once they were down in that stinking darkness.

Just what it was Dad saw in that green radiance I never came to know. I only know it changed him. The fallout of his encounter below was drastic enough for Rita to plead with me to fly home and help her find some means of bringing him back around.

When I returned to Evendale I found a catatonic shell in the shape of my father. He never spoke, scarcely ate, slept nearly eighteen hours a day. I insisted to Rita that a hospital was the only place for him, where he could receive not only medical attention but (perhaps even more importantly) psychiatric care. Rita, despite asking for my help,.

stubbornly refused to admit Dad, stating that this was a family problem and therefore it could be fixed by the family. I suppose I should have protested more passionately, but I didn't. It seems I also inherited the same caginess as Rita. Perhaps it's a symptom of growing up in a small town, but propriety and fear of scandal, however slight, always seemed to trump common sense.

But three weeks ago Rita and I finally agreed that hospitalization could not be put off any longer. Dad had always been a strapping man, so his rapid dissolution was a sobering and painful wake-up call to my sister and me.

Then, the night before we planned to drag Dad off to receive help, he snapped out of his depression. Late that night my sleep was broken by the clanging of pans and the thudding of kitchen cupboards. Rita's bedroom door was shut when I walked past it to investigate.

I found my father preparing a goulash so redolent with spices I felt myself tearing up the moment I entered the kitchen.

"Dad?" I'd said to him.

"Hungry?" was his reply.

I told him no, then watched as he left the ingredients to simmer on the range. He sat down at the kitchen table and asked me to switch off the light. I did and together we sat in the lunar glow from the window, listening to the food bubbling in its pot.

"Can't sleep," he admitted, answering a question I never posed.

"You've probably been sleeping too much."

"Well, I'm awake now."

Something in his choice of words made me queasy.

"Your sister told me that Sadie-Anne next door boarded up her house a couple of days ago."

"Yes, I saw that. Any idea why?"

"Probably to become a pit-canary like the others."

I swallowed what little moisture there was in my mouth. "Why are people running down there, Dad? What are they running to?"

His silhouette shrugged.

"I know about the glow down there, Dad. Rita told me. Is that what the pit-canaries are moving to the mine for? Are they looking for the light?"

If my father was fazed by my outburst he kept it contained, just as he had always done with all things. Dad: even-keeled, stoic, strong, like a lake of still black water.

"I think maybe they're after what's on the other side of that light," he answered.

"What's beyond the light, Dad?" Worry and tears mangled my voice into something thin and reedy. "What did you see down there?"

It seemed like a long span of time passed. We sat in stubborn silence like two monks lost in contemplation. The goulash bubbled over the pot rim and splashed onto the burner, hissing as though maimed.

"Been dreaming a lot lately," he said at last. "Funny thing, that. In my whole life I think I can remember one, maybe two dreams. And those were from when I was a boy. But lately . . .

"There was this one dream. I must've had it three or four nights in a row. I'm in this meadow, real peaceful, real pretty. I'm standing beside an old-fashioned watermill and I'm holding a large bucket with a rope handle. The mill's wheel is turning slowly, but the weird thing is, the only noise I can hear is the creaking of those wooden gears. I can see the brook moving along, I can see it being lathered up by the paddles and I can see the runoff gushing back down into the brook, but the water is absolutely silent. You know how sometimes in dreams you just know things about things? Well, in this dream I knew I had come to this brook to gather water to bring back to my village, which was on the other side of this great stone building that this watermill was attached to. Maybe they were grinding grain or something, I don't know. But I was there for the water because the villagers were all dying of thirst.

"I reached down to scoop up some of that quiet water, when this awful, awful feeling came over me. I stared down into the water and suddenly noticed in the reflection that a figure was now standing above me on the bank. I tried to cover my eyes because I didn't want to see who or what that figure was, but the next thing I knew I was standing face to face with it. It was a woman, a very strange, very thin woman. She was trying to tell me something but she was as mute as that brook, so she traced some symbols in the air with one of her stick-like fingers. She spelled out that the water was poison. I nodded to show her that I understood. Then you know what I did? I filled that rope-handled pail and carried it back to my village and when I got there I took a wooden ladle and I doled out that poisoned water to all those wretched-looking villagers. I poured the last sip into my own palm and drank it myself. Then I woke up."

I wasn't sure how to react to my father's account, but I was desperate to keep him talking, so I asked him what he thought the dream meant. Again he shrugged. Then he rose to tend to his food.

"The light's coming," he announced. At the time I thought he was referring to the sun that was climbing above the hedges beyond our kitchen window. Now I am not so sure.

That was the last time I spoke to my father. The next night, while I slept, he moved below.

The day's organic gloom made it seem much later than it actually was when I edged the jeep off the lane and along the entrance driveway. At one time this passage was truncated by a heavy iron gate bearing a sign that warned of the legal repercussions and physical dangers that trespassers could endure. Today that gate hangs permanently open and the sign has been covered over with spray paint.

The floodlights shone on me, weakly, like potted moons. I gathered up the groceries and the dog that I carried and cooed to as though she were my own flesh and blood. As I crossed the gravel lot toward the mine entrance I tightened my grip on the Lab, for she'd begun to whimper and squirm.

"You're okay, girl," I assured her, "you're okay. What should I name you, hmm? What do I call you?"

But the nearer we drew to that rugged tunnel with its downward pitch, the more the dog began to panic. I knew that my clutching her against her will was purely selfish. How I needed her companionship, her life.

Once I struggled to carry her up the wooden rungs and into the tunnel, the dog began to growl and bark in a sad, effete protest. She could sense the offensiveness of whatever waited beneath. She wriggled free and charged for the tunnel's mouth. I cried out and lunged for her, but she leapt heedless of any risk. I heard her claws scrabbling against the ladder. A moment later I saw the dog tearing across the gravel plain. She neared the road and was soon gone.

I slumped against the cold black wall of the shaft and sobbed. It was the kind of outburst usually reserved for children; the frame-shaking, convulsive weeping that seems to threaten to tear the soul up by its very roots.

The sound of approaching footsteps caused me to fight for composure. How sad is it that even now, under such conditions, we pit-canaries still feel the need for personas.

"Everything alright, miss?" one of the sentinels asked me, the light on his hardhat beaming like a lustrous pearl.

I nodded, picked up the sack of food and brushed past him, negotiating the wooden slats with care as I made the long descent toward the platform where the carts nested.

A family of four sat at one of the platform's picnic tables. They were eating peanut butter and saltines.

The people come to the upper level in shifts. For most of them this is as near to the surface as they're willing to go, despite the dangers to their health. Strategically installed fans spin constantly, both here and deeper below. They do their best to draw the methane out of the tunnels and to coax fresh air down from the surface. But they have been rotting down here since Dunford Inc. shut down production, and I remember Dad saying that even when those fans were new it was always a risk spending too much time "under the crust" as he'd called it.

"One of the drivers will be up shortly," the mother called once she saw me climbing into a cart. I turned back and looked stonily at them, at their wan faces smeared with soot, their clothing hanging loose and grubby from their malnourished frames. They were like a faded photo of some anonymous Dust Bowl family in a history book.

"Never mind," I said, releasing the brake. The ancient wheels squeaked as the cart began to roll toward the greater descent.

Down I went, down, staring numbly at the roughly textured tunnel walls. I began to imagine the juts and groves as being some strange and tedious grammar in Braille, some record of a world that had existed below ours for unknowable years, their entire secret history spelled out here in angled carbon.

These walls are also veined with thick cables that feed power to the vent fans and the garlands of uncovered light bulbs. To my eye those strung lights have all the impact of a lone firefly attempting to illuminate a canyon.

The cart reached the final swoop of the track and I eased up the handbrake to soften the final thud that always came when the track fed into a pent-in platform constructed out of lumber grown soft from too many years in the methane-reeking chambers.

As yet there has been no theft or pillaging down here, but I did my best to conceal the sack of groceries all the same. The converts have commented about how this profound fellowship and egalitarianism is somehow a sign of renewal, of change. Personally I think it is only because things haven't yet gotten desperate enough. They'd start savaging and rending sooner or later. It's all a question of time.

The only proper shelter at this level was the rescue chamber that the miners could use in case of a collapse or other accident, a pod where they could hole up until help arrived. Now, with its oxygen tanks long drained, its food devoured and its water guzzled, the chamber serves as a curious spirit house, a shrine the people have embellished with mementos of those whose spirits they claim have been glimpsed beyond the emerald light, or with fetishes meant to represent things unfamiliar but still experienced.

I sat down at one of the picnic tables where Rita sat knitting a scarf.

I watched her for a spell, watched the way her eyes would habitually move from her needles to the tunnel a few yards away.

"You get my dress?" she asked without looking at me.

"Yes, and the other things you asked for. I also got some food. Not much though. There's water, too."

A young girl, perhaps fifteen, moved past our table and made her way to the decorated tunnel mouth. Rita and I both watched as the girl hunched down and slid her hand into the gap. She seemed to be feeling something in the chute, something that didn't appear to be unpleasant. For a moment it looked as though she was going to enter, but she ultimately lacked the required conviction. She went back to her mattress at the far end of the tract.

"Have there been any changes?" I asked Rita.

"Define *changes*."

"Anyone else gone in . . . or maybe come back out . . . there?"

"Don't be stupid." She put her needles back in her canvas bag along with her yarn. I studied her as she carried the silver hairbrush and the handheld mirror into the pod and added them to the shrine. She wouldn't look at me when she returned. "I'm going to try on my dress," she said, almost daring me to object.

She was on her way to change in one of the old miners' shower stalls – no running water but the remaining plastic curtains offered privacy – when the ground began to quake. This tremor was longer than previous ones, more forceful. Immediately people began to murmur, in prayer or in vexation or simply in fear. The rocking subsided and there was a false sense of relief poured over the area.

Roughly ten minutes later there was another tremor.

Few become true pit-canaries. While the townsfolk dwell below, there is another stage, another extreme that only the most devout have courage or madness enough to explore.

Beyond the tract where the mattresses and bags are strewn there is another tunnel, stiflingly tight and perilously ragged, one bored by something cruder than even the crudest tool. Only those who have dared to squeeze through that aperture earn the stigma of pit-canary because, like their namesake, those birds go beyond.

As to what forged that tunnel, I could add my theory to the hundreds that have been posited before, but what would such a thing prove? The tunnel is somehow connected to the emerald light. I believe this. And I believe that both are the products of something even greater and stranger than both those things combined.

Somehow somebody in Evendale awoke something down there. Now that something is beginning to awaken all of us.

The change is undeniable. Everyone down here feels it, but because it is so indefinable we do not speak of it. We simply accept its presence within us, like a growing contagion.

This is a cold, unwanted revelation, like happening upon a lump in one's breast or testicle; the kind of discovery that makes one yearn for normalcy, tedium, for all those ditchwater-dull afternoons and daily routines that we so foolishly felt needed to be stripped away by novelty and change. Yes, it is that kind of wordless knowledge that there is no going back. Even racing up to the sunlit yards of Evendale would be a small and flimsy defense. And so, we wait.

I'm told that early on some of the men wanted to place bright orange sawhorses before the mouth of that unmapped tunnel as a warning to keep away, but before they could return with their barricade, the mine had produced its own.

The vine sprouted from one carbon wall, drooped across the down-sloping chute, and then poked through the black rock of the opposite wall. Blooming out of this twisting verdant cable were five bellflowers, vibrantly red, as though colored by arterial blood that raced through transparent petals. Deeply fragrant; even the methane fumes were made sweet, so strong was their perfume. The flowers hung inversely. Set against that gaping hole in the mine wall they were positively incandescent, the beginnings of some new garden in paradise. I studied the flowers often, perched upon my plastic lawn chair, coughing into my sooty hands.

I watch the flowers and I wait. Wait for my father. Two weeks ago, much to my shrieking protests, he left the camp here on the tract and he became a pit-canary. He said he'd dreamed my mother had come to him through the emerald light and that she'd encouraged him to see what dwelt on the outer rim of that light. Dad said he believed the light was actually the breath of some living thing, large and ancient and wise. An entity that had been here long before we crawled out of the swamp, just down here sleeping, waiting . . .

He'd also said he thinks this creature, whatever it is, is calling us to descend farther and farther down so it can give us some new kind of fire, the kind that lights up the depths of space.

I'd asked him how he came to know this, but Dad couldn't really say.

Only two pit-canaries have come back in the whole time I've been here, but it seems to be enough to keep people believing, waiting, wondering. The first was an elderly woman who'd owned a cake shop on Main Street. She said she'd heard trumpets and bells in that tunnel, then the green light had welled up to touch her, and for one brief but glorious moment she was able to hold her own heart in her hands. She'd said she tested it for heft and had determined that it wasn't yet light enough, so she'd come back up to fast and pray. She stayed above. I never found out what happened to her.

The other pit-canary who returned only lived for a few seconds. He came crawling out of the tunnel screaming in agony. He screamed and he screamed. He even tore out the vine of bellflowers. When two of the men dragged him out they discovered that he'd been torn open, but the innards that spilled from his jagged and gaping wounds were fossilized; white and smooth and preserved, like the entrails of a marble grotesque.

Only after the commotion ended did someone comment about how the red bellflowers had already grown back across the tunnel mouth.

Another tremor.

And another.

It won't be long now, whatever "it" is.

The bellflowers have begun to ring. Their chiming is open and almost without a source. They swing like their namesakes in a belfry. And like those chapel bells, these seem to rouse the faithful to service.

One by one the people began to crawl through the tunnel. Where they had once given a wide berth to avoid, they now scrambled and fought to penetrate. The emerald glimmer was now visible within the tunnel, cresting upward like a tide of foul sewer water. We both watched as the last resident wriggled toward that ill light.

Rita begged me to let her go, but I held her back. Impulsively, senselessly, she had wrestled that damned dress over her head, tugging it over her filthy T-shirt and jeans.

A short time later we felt the collapse just below us. It shook the ground. The chorus of screams from those below was muffled by the falling black rock but was no less terrible.

Is this what you lured all of them down there for? I wondered.

"Dad!" Rita cried, over and over.

I shrieked for her to follow me into the rescue pod. Eventually she did. I shut the door, praying that the cave-in wouldn't reach this upper level and that it ended swiftly. There was no oxygen in the tank, but we needed shelter from the mushrooms of black smoke that filled the tract. Chunks of coal smacked against the pod like a shower of stones. The light leaked up through the fresh fissures in the ground.

Eventually the thunder waned. I looked through the pod window, expecting to see only blackness. But there was a distinctive glimmer, greenish and persistent, even against the thick filter of coal dust.

I closed my hand over my mouth.

She pushed past me.

I followed her, choking on the fumes and dust.

The emerald light pushed through the collapsed tunnel, shining like a lamp covered with perforated black felt. For a long time we simply stood. Then something pressed through the piled rocks. It rolled near with patient velocity.

I turned to Rita, who was bolted in place. Terror blanched her face and made her jaw hang slack.

I took a step forward.

"No!" I heard my sister scream, seemingly from the far end of the world. "No, goddamn it!"

I reached down, picked up the luminous object, and turned back to Rita.

I rolled the object in my palm before halving it with a forceful twist.

"It's from father," I informed her with a knowledge that had bypassed even my own consciousness.

Rita reached for her half but quickly dropped her hand. She watched in mute but visible agony as I bit into the apple.

Don Webb views his story, "The Future Eats Everything," as a "Lovecraftian intersection of the cosmically strange and impersonal, and the personal and mundane. Lovecraft is seen as the prophet of the former and ungifted as to the latter, but in reality it is he that showed that true fear happens when the cosmic rubs its legs against the sleeping human in the bed of the mundane." Webb's most recent book is collection *Through Dark Angles: Works Inspired by H. P. Lovecraft* (Hippocampus Press). He has had sixteen books and more than four hundred short stories published. He lives in Austin, Texas, and teaches creative writing for the UCLA Extension Writers Program.

The Future Eats Everything
Don Webb

———

It was the day of the flood that Matthew D. Smith discovered the human world faced a menace, always has faced this menace, and will inevitably lose out to it.

Central Texas had been enduring a three-year drought. The weather was so hot and so dry that even the staunchest global warming deniers had begun to doubt. The Catholics had prayed to Mary, the Protestants to God, the Muslims to Allah, the Wiccans to the Goddess, and the Thelemites had practiced sex-magick for rain. Someone or something had heard the call. Matthew pictured God as an old man in a white robe saying, "Me – damn it! I'll give these S.O.B's rain!"

It started with a lightning storm about eight the night before; a heavy rain in less than an hour. Matthew and his wife kept their windows open all night – if you haven't heard rain in many months, it is a sleep-inducing bliss to hear it. Several times during the night Matthew had awakened from vague and uneasy dreams to the sound of the heavy downpour.

At 5:15 a.m. the emergency phone-calling service of Doublesign Data Systems Inc. informed him – in an automated voice – that the work day would start two hours late. "Great I can sleep late." Matthew thought. Then at 5:25 a.m., the Austin Independent School District's automated voice called Kathleen and told her that school would not start until noon. Then at 6:30 a.m. his assistant called him to ask if the message that work was delayed was for real. Finally, at 6:45 a.m. Kathleen's principal called her to see if she had received the 5:25 a.m. message.

Common sense told Matthew he should allow extra time to drive from his south Austin two-story brick home to the one-story white stucco building in Doublesign. But the sweet sound of rain told him to sleep longer. After all, he had driven the same back-road route for nine years and the roads had never been closed. There had been one snowstorm and two other floods in that near-decade, and he'd had no problems.

Matthew took his old black Chevy pickup out at eight and headed south. He noticed no cars were streaming north of Austin on FM 118. Perhaps it was only an early morning traffic problem. The sky glowed with a lovely gray mother-of-pearl color. Matthew always drove to work in the dark; it seemed almost like a luxury to be driving so late in the day.

About a mile out of Austin, two orange sand-filled traffic barrels were set up with a ROAD CLOSED sign between them. But there was space enough to drive around the barricade. He could see a car a quarter of mile ahead where the road twisted through a grove of live oak. If that guy could make it, he could too. He was dammit, a man – even if his big blond wife sometimes disagreed. Matthew drove his truck very slowly between the barrels, its rear panel very gently brushing one of them.

After he'd rounded the bend, he saw a river, which was a surprising sight because there had never been a river there in nine years. There wasn't creek there, or even a dry creek bed. There was scarcely a dip in the road. The cream-colored Lexus he had seen seconds before was making a difficult three-point turn to head back to town. Matthew saw he would have to turn around in the same spot, so he waited for the

Lexus to navigate its turn, then pulled up slowly to the fast-moving river. It was at least waist high in the oaks, and Matthew could see an angry muddy gap in the pavement where the road had once slopped very slightly; chunks of asphalt were falling off into the foaming white water.

This would be a perfect picture to post on Facebook. Matthew pulled a little off the road. No other cars were coming; apparently others were not as foolhardy as he. He left his pickup and made his way to what was now a crumbling shoreline, slipping in the tall wet grass twice. Matthew planted his feet on an exposed limestone ridge and focused his phone at the exposed red earth bank, thinking how it looked like a wound. He was hoping the cloudy morning sky would provide sufficient light for his picture when he saw a really big bug break out of the crack in the earth. At least a foot in length and half as much in width, the pallid segmented creature looked like a cross between a trilobite and a cockroach. It had seven legs on each side of its thorax, and a pair of crablike pinchers glistening with mucus. The thing had tiny mammal-like eyes with light blue irises. As it pushed through the dirt, Matthew saw it had a few brothers or sisters climbing up on the grass – all heading straight toward him at a fast scurry. He broke into a run, fell, got up, and ran some more. He lost his iPhone in the process. Matthew got his pickup turned around in record time and was going down the empty highway at seventy miles per hour, before he could even begin to order his thoughts.

What the hell were they?

Should he go back and get pictures?

Who should he call?

Damn! He'd lost his phone.

Is there any money to be made from this?

Should he keep his trap shut so that he didn't look like a nut?

Matthew thought of Gordon, the school teacher on *Sesame Street*, who never saw any weird phenomena that kids and Muppets saw. So he became the voice of skeptical reason – he was always wrong, of course, but he was supposed to be the smart, credible adult.

Matthew assumed his wife, Kathleen, would be a "Gordon." She taught high school science and would, no doubt, be all practical and skeptical about the bugs.

Instead, she was thrilled. She tossed back her mane of (dyed) blond hair and demanded they drive out to the site immediately.

"Look, the road is still closed," she said. "If you wait until morning, it will be open again and the insects will probably be gone. If we go now, this could be our Discovery."

He definitely heard the big "D."

He called the office and said the road was washed out so he would not be making it in today. Kathleen still had three hours before her school opened – if they opened at all, which was beginning to look doubtful.

It was a scary drive. Rain had continued to fall, albeit much more gently, and the road was slick. There was no oncoming traffic, apparently no one else was foolish enough to risk the drive. Matthew didn't pull his car into the red mud of this morning. He figured it would be way too squishy now and the truck would get stuck. Kathleen practically flew out of the car, carrying the giant flashlight she had bought for emergencies. She found one of the creatures almost instantly. "Matt hold the flashlight while I snap some shots."

The pale-fleshed trilobite (or whatever the fuck it was) didn't seem to like the light. It began pulling itself toward the scar in the earth.

"Matt – grab it."

Matthew made a grab, dropping the flashlight. The bug hissed at him, and he jumped back. It had three rows of sharp-looking teeth – translucent and serrated like some sharks' teeth, but much smaller.

"Okay. Maybe don't grab. Can you get the flashlight back, sweetie?"

Matthew recovered the flashlight and kept the scurrying bug in the center of the beam. It climbed over a gray-green rock as it headed toward the mud. Matthew swung the beam in long gentle arcs across the area. No other creatures were in evidence.

"Move the light back to that rock."

Matthew did so, and he observed what Kathleen was about to comment on.

"Something is written on the rock."

Something was. A rectangular piece of gray plastic – somewhat smaller than a credit card – was embedded in the siltstone. On it, in black letters: XUTHLTAN. Matthew picked up the stone. He tried to knock the plastic tag off, but he could see it was truly and firmly embedded in the rock.

"Hey it's really stuck in there. I mean it's *part* of the rock – like the rock formed *around* it. Why would a rock have a piece of plastic stuck in it?" asked Matthew.

"I don't know. Time travel maybe. Maybe some future person journeyed back to trilobite times and dropped his portable . . . Xuthltan . . . in the muck, probably when one of these little fuckers hissed at him."

Her large brown eyes were shiny with excitement. This was suddenly the sexiest moment of their marriage in the last ten years. Matthew stepped forward, but Kathleen said, "Look!"

They were everywhere. Matthew could see at least twelve of the bugs all headed toward him and Kathleen. Suddenly they all started to whine like summer locusts. Each bug had a slightly different pitch and each seemed to be modulating its tone. As he grabbed Kathleen by the waist, he thought they might be *talking*. He had the presence of mind to shove the rock into his pocket.

The warm Texas sun ruled for the next three days. Floodwater receded. The middle-class neighborhood of Onion Creek dealt with property damage and insurance people; the poor neighborhood of Dove Springs dealt with homelessness and need. The closed streets were opened and Matthew found the strange insectile visitors on his route had vanished. No tiny claw marks in the drying mud. No sign they'd ever been there. All that was left were a few badly lit photos and memories of a night of fear and then lovemaking.

Kathleen pointed out that in an era of Photoshop, bad pictures didn't mean squat.

But there was the rock.

Five years before, when Kathleen was getting her degree at the University of Texas, she had dated a man named Randall Wong. Randall, who worked in the Accelerator Mass Spectrometry Lab, was a careful and thoughtful lover – and was dating three other undergraduates. (These AMS lads were like catnip to the ladies.) All the girls dropped him but Kathleen, who remained his friend (at least on Facebook). He had said to her, jokingly, in an IM just days ago: "If you ever need any carbon-14 dating, just ask me."

Now Kathleen wanted Radall to radiocarbon date the rock.

Matthew wasn't too keen on the idea. In his heart he knew – or was at least 85 per cent sure that Kathleen and Randall had had a little affair last year when he'd worked in Dallas for six weeks. But she seemed so excited by the mystery . . . and seeing the bugs *had* led to them making love for the first time in five years. Besides, he still cherished the hope that "solving" the mystery would mean leaving his dead-end day job.

Dr. Randall Wong was (of course) quite surprised by the rock. It's not that often you see plastic encased in siltstone. In fact, it was impossible. Still, it seemed genuine enough.

Kathleen told Randall she couldn't tell him any details about the artifact, but hinted her uncle in the CIA needed to know and had instructed her to approach her friend on a hush-hush basis. (Kathleen did, actually, have an uncle employed by the Central Intelligence Agency. But as Uncle Fitz only did payroll, any top secret instructions would be unlikely. In fact, impossible.)

Randall didn't like the results.

"Look don't tell anyone the university lab had anything to do with this," Dr. Wong told them after the test. "I could lose my job. This will bring every nutcase out of the woodwork for miles."

Kathleen and Matthew had met him at the Kerbey Lane Café. They looked up from their pancakes and said, "Why?" almost at the same time.

"I'm not giving you the printouts. I'm not giving you anything. The plastic is from now, which shouldn't be a surprise, but the stone matrix was . . . I mean will be . . . laid down about fifty thousand years in the future."

Randall dropped the stone on the café table. Before they could speak, he said, "No. Just no. No, I don't understand it. No, I don't want the publicity. No. Stuff like this ends careers. Investigate if you want, you're a high school science teacher – and you do whatever it is you do, Matthew. But for me? No."

Randall walked out. He had not finished his waffle.

Matthew and Kathleen stared at each other.

Of course the next step was the Internet.

"Xuthltan" was the name of a government official in the Maldives, a word for an evil village in a short story by Texas writer Robert E. Howard, a character in a multi-player online game, and a church in a bad Austin neighborhood.

Austin it was then. The phone number from the website did not work, so Matthew decided to visit the next Saturday. He told his wife to stay home "in case there was any trouble." Matthew didn't know what sort of trouble you could have with people that had artifacts embedded in siltstone formed thousands of years from now; the Internet didn't have any information on the subject.

The Church of Xuthltan was a storefront, part of a cheap-looking row of shops in East Austin. It shared its parking lot with a pawn store, a 7-Eleven, a store that sold knock-offs of famous perfumes, a tattoo parlor, a loan office, and a botánica. Some guys were working on a white car near the church's door.

Matthew peered through the church's grimy glass door. The light was off, but Matthew could see someone inside – an old white guy in faded blue jeans and a dirty white T-shirt. He had a long scruffy white beard and wore a blue baseball cap. He was watching a tiny television. Matthew knocked on the thick glass of the former-shop window. The old man looked up and gave him a wide grin, perhaps one of idiocy. The guy got up and started ambling to the door.

From outside, Matthew could see the church had four rows of

rusty folding chairs facing a pulpit that had seen better days. Behind the pulpit stood what could be a marble baptismal font and a square folding table. A cash register stood on the table. There were bookshelves on two walls. The old guy turned on the overhead fluorescent lights and unlocked the door. He smelled like he had not bathed in a while, but there a cinnamon-y odor coming from the church itself.

"May Xuthltan eat your woes!" said the old man.

"Hello," said Matthew.

"Come in," said the old man, "The Grand Chronopastor is not here, just me. Are you here to buy a book? Light some incense, say a prayer? Or just shoot the shit?"

Matthew saw the pedestal he had guessed was a baptismal font was fake marble; its basin was full of gray plastic rectangles with the word "Xuthltan" printed on each in black letters. These were identical to the one embedded in the stone he was carrying in his left pants pocket. Matthew pointed at the basin as he walked in.

"What are those?"

"Prayer stones." Said the old man. "they're free if you are a member, and a buck (tax included) if you ain't."

"What do you pray to?" asked Matthew.

"Well I ain't much of a theologian," said the old man, "I'd say they was bugs. Hardy bugs of the future, I'd say. Makes more sense than praying to a dead Jewish carpenter, if'n you ask me."

"Why's that?" asked Matthew.

"Well what can a dead carpenter do fer you? Build something in the past? Heck that's over two thousand years ago. Let's say you wanted some bookshelves. You could pray 'Dear Jesus, make me some book-shelves and hide them so I can find them!' Well even if he did make them and hid them real good, you'd have to get on a jet and head off to the Holy Land and try and find them. And if you did find them, they'd be two thousand years old – and what kind of shape do you think they would be in then, I ask ye?"

Matthew wasn't prepared for this line of reasoning. So he asked, "Uh, what can future bugs do?"

"What do reg'lar bugs do? Eat of course. They can eat up your problems if you chant on 'em."

"What do you mean?"

"Well, Praise Xuthltan! I had two no-good sons. Never took care of me. When they was out of jail, they would literally rob me out of house and home. Took my car. Took my tiny savings from the bank. Hell, they tried to steal the silver jar that held their mother's ashes. I used to live over on Chicon Street. One day I walked past this place. Door was open on account of the AC not working. They was all prayin' and chantin' up a storm. Xuthltan! Xuthltan! Xuthltan! And rubbing these little doodads. Then one of them jumped up and said, 'Praise Xuthltan! My husband's gone!' And she showed everybody her ring finger and there was no wedding band on it. I came in and asked just what the holy hell was going on."

"And these bugs had eaten her husband?"

"Of course I didn't believe it at first. But I was hurtin' so bad from the way my no-good kids had done me. I dropped down and started chantin' along with the rest of the morons. I took the talisman home and chanted for three days. Then I looked up. I used to have a picture of my son Ed in his graduation robe in a little frame on the mantel. It was gone! I looked around my house – it ain't very big, so it didn't take me very long. There was nothin' belonging to Ed. There was still some of his brother Mark's stuff, so I went back to chantin', and guess what?"

"Mark's stuff disappeared, too?"

"Well eventually. He called me on his cell phone. All I got is a land-line. He called me and told me his house was full of roaches that were hissin' at him. Could I come over and help him? I told him I could've – had he not stole my car. Said I'd ride over on the bus tomorrow. Told him he could've called his wife – 'cept she was smart enough to leave his ass. Hung up. Unplugged the phone. Chanted for three hours. Next day I took the bus to his neighborhood. Different family livin' in his house. Looked like they been there for a spell. They had a swing hangin' from the sycamore in the front."

"Don't you feel bad?"

"No. That's the beauty of it. The bugs are just tryin' to get here. They're in some crazy war with flyin' octopi or something in the future. When the Reverend Nadis first found them they were a hun'erd million light years away. Now they're maybe a million."

"Closer than that," said Matthew.

"You've received Word?" asked the old man with a look of holy awe, his backwoods craziness suddenly set aside.

"No," said Matthew, "I don't know why I said that."

"They can come through inattention, through synchronicities through certain shapes, as well as the shape waves of the mantra. Their name is not really Xuthltan. That just has the right vibrations. You need to meet The Reverend Nadis."

Matthew felt the hairs on the back of his head stand up. He *didn't* want to meet The Reverend Nadis. He looked over at the books for sale. Most were used paperbacks on the paranormal – *The Truth About Mummies, The Truth About Werewolves, UFOS in Colonial America*, etc. There were a few antique hardbound books with hard-to-read titles in German and French. Money. Money could buy time. Little church like this must need money.

"I would like a couple of the Xuthltan talismans. And let me make a little contribution toward the church."

Matthew took a twenty out of his worn black wallet. Kathleen had given it to him four years ago for Christmas. He never bought wallets for himself, he hoped that she would notice it was time to get him another.

"You don't have to give us anything. We may look like nothing now, but the time will come when this little church in this little strip mall will be the only thing standing."

Matthew could picture what the man was saying. This stupid strip mall on a gray featureless plain surrounded by the bugs. They must have great intelligence to have worked this all out. Somewhere there would be vast insect cities, haunted hives where they fought another incomprehensible race. And they used pure human selfishness as a weapon in their war. Matthew stood there, shocked at the vision – it as though he was really seeing it. He could almost hear their hissing song.

"It gets through to you, doesn't it?" said the old man, his eyes now full of intelligence, his hick accent still gone. Matthew wondered if *this* were The Reverend Nadis. The old man went on, "I see you have a wedding ring, that means you'll be wanting two of the calling cards. Here you go."

The plastic felt slimy in his hands. Almost as if the tokens were alive. He felt – or imagined he felt – the rock twitch in his pocket.

"How long? How long have you known about them?" asked Matthew.

"Now that, sir, is difficult to explain. Working with them plays hell on your time sense. Your mind gets more and more hollow the longer you know them. On the one hand you remember them. But on the other hand you have a great hollowness in your mind. Things echo in hollow spaces, you know."

Matthew turned to leave.

"Come ag'in!" The old man's voice had gone all hillbilly stupid again.

Matthew said, "I won't. I'll throw your plastic prayer stones away, and I'll forget this place."

"Don't matter," the old man said. "Just you comin' starts another cycle in motion. Don't you even want to show me the rock in your pocket, boy?" He laughed a little.

Matthew turned his back and stepped out of the shop.

"Praise Xuthltan!"

On the way back to his house Matthew edited and re-edited the story he would tell Kathleen again and again. He stopped at McDonald's and had a large chocolate shake. He would tell her about the talisman's supposed ability to make people disappear. He would portray the old man as a crazy hick. Overdo the accent when he told his wife – make him sound East Texas, bayou country. He wouldn't mention the vision, and of course nothing about the bugs. The whole thing should be a dead end. He thought about throwing away the talismans, but found he didn't want to handle them. He needed to see Kathleen laugh at them. She was so sensible. She was a science teacher for god's sake. Then after she had destroyed their magic with a good laugh, he could drop them in his document shredder. It was strong enough for credit cards, and these were not much thicker.

By the time he drove home he was all smiles and sheepishness. It had been such a waste of time.

"So he really chanted his sons away?" Kathleen asked.

"He was a crazy old man in a closed-down storefront. He was probably homeless. You should've seen the junk they had for sale."

"But you bought two of the cards?"

"I offered him twenty bucks for them. I figured the guy needed to eat."

"And he turned your money down?"

"I told you he was crazy."

She looked at the cards, shrugged, laid them on the kitchen counter.

She spent longer than usual on her computer that night. He felt sure she was chatting with Randall. He took a long bath, listening for the sound of her going to bed. When he left the tub about midnight, the plastic cards were gone, and she had taken the rock out of his pants pocket.

A day passed, and then a week, and eventually the memory of the strange bugs and the stranger church were obscured by bills and problems at work. WDS lost two technicians, so everyone had to pull an occasional extra shift. Matthew drew Sunday morning. He crept out of the house at 6.45 a.m. and drove into Doublesign. He took great pride in not waking Kathleen, although she got two months off in the summer plus Christmas, fall and spring breaks. He stopped at the Sac-n-Pac store and bought his Diet Dr Pepper and multivitamin packet and let himself in at work. The mainframe was up, the satellite systems were (mainly) up; he checked the night log and the emails. He put coffee on and raided a banana from the boss's fruit bowl. He'd begun file maintenance, when he heard something in the server room. Probably rats. (Rats had given Arjay a huge fright a couple of months ago.) He ignored the sound. Then he heard someone say something. He jumped out of his chair. Should he dial 911 or confront? Probably kids from the Discipline Alternative Program.

He moved to the back and threw open the white painted door. The servers were warm, happy and alone. He stepped in and walked up to them.

Something fell from the ceiling behind him.

He turned.

It was one of the bugs, even larger than before. Two feet long, still the same but bigger sharp legs on each side and pinchers in front. It was bigger now, he knew – somehow – because it had eaten its way closer in time. Two more were crawling along the walls, their blue human-like eyes focused on him. One spoke – not a hiss this time – with his wife's voice, "Xuthltan!" Matthew could see the three rows of glasslike serrated teeth clearly reflecting the yellow, green, and red lights of the servers.

Two scurried out from under the server rack. One spoke with the slightly Chinese accent Dr. Randall Wong affected, "Xuthltan!" Another hissed.

Then they rushed him.

It was quick, but not quick enough.

For *Matthew Carpenter, super-fan*

Nadia Bulkin writes scary stories about the scary world we live in – and sports (metaphorically and in reality) are definitely part of our world. She became a University of Nebraska Cornhusker fan at the age of eleven, but now also cheers for the Washington Nationals (baseball) and Wizards (basketball). When not becoming irrationally angry at sporting events outside of her control, she tends her garden of student debt sowed by two political science degrees. She has written other Lovecraftian stories set in Indonesia (*Lovecraft's Monsters*, *Sword & Mythos*) and Nebraska (*Letters to Lovecraft, She Walks in Shadows*). She apologizes deeply to the athletes who inspired characters in this story.

The genesis of her story lies in "the human cults that worship Lovecraft's monsters, probably for the same reasons that I'm fascinated by real-world suicide cults: why would someone sign up to bring about the end of the world? In this story, I was working on the assumption that some cults are more inviting to the Outer Gods than others. I wanted to chart a history of one such cult that was ripe for the picking: the Church of the Holy Star, obsessed with the idea that absorbing 'superhuman' athletes will enable them to overcome what they see as the fragile weakness of ordinary humanity. Choosing the athletic angle was easy. Saturday in my hometown was the week's true holy day, with eighty thousand people making the pilgrimage to the stadium for three hours of furious communal worship. Even now, just thinking about game day gives me goosebumps."

I Believe That We Will Win
Nadia Bulkin

I. I

When the 1969 Stairway to Paradise Campaign became the Great Famine of 1970, the landlocked city of Jackson's Tomb was hit particularly hard. An estimated 45 per cent of the population of Jackson's Tomb died of starvation and violence before a new population equilibrium was established and the national economy recovered. Riots were suppressed with lethal force until the police force discarded their badges and joined the rioters, at which point only the Tomb's wealthiest citizens could afford to feed or flee. It was in this dark time that Sasha Spell, the "Perfect Ten," star of the 1970 Global Artistic Gymnastic Championships, ignited the dormant passion within her father's Church of the Holy Star.

The Famine brought Sasha Spell home after it forced the nation to withdraw from the 1970 Summer Olympics, and killed her mother. Devout from a young age, Sasha spent up to seven hours a day in solemn prayer. She burned her palms with candles, eating only wax and scar tissue, to show her sleeping god how badly her people were suffering. She finally heard the answer as her father gave a sermon about the holy bread and wine of communion. Unexpectedly struck by the sublime, Sasha approached the altar, declared herself "food for my people," and sacrificed her perfect tiny body with a Swiss Army knife.

And so Sasha Spell became the first athlete to climb that highest rung of divinity and become a true Champion. Her father, Reverend Orrin Spell, was also struck by the sublime: he demanded his congregants accept his daughter's noble sacrifice and began to offer her to them piece by piece. Awestruck by Sasha's purity, the congregants drank of her blood and ate of her flesh, and lo! – they were transformed; rewarded for their piousness and rescued from their human frailty. Raised up by Sasha's well-disciplined muscles and fierce lioness heart, the Church of the Holy Star became stronger and healthier and so survived the Famine. The sole exception was one bookkeeper who doubted the righteousness of St. Sasha's sacrifice and starved in his attic two months later, weak and shriveled like all others in Jackson's Tomb who were unblessed by the Champion, the warrior-angel made flesh.

II. I Believe

As the nation got its feet back underneath it and rediscovered its collective interest in sporting – and resumed sending athletes to the Olympic Games – the Church of the Holy Star dug its way out of the ruins of Jackson's Tomb and entered a world filled with the seedlings of Champions. The Church understood that raw talent needed to be sculpted, funded, positioned. Members became recruiters, elders became boosters, and babies born into the Church were scoured head to toe for talent.

During this period, redheaded Maya Dommel exerted a high degree of influence over the Church of the Holy Star. She was its top recruiter, and had used her unusually persuasive personality to marry an aged industrial baron who loved what he called "sportsball." The Rising Star Foundation was her brainchild, financed by the baron's fortune. It sponsored more athletes at the 1986 Olympics than any other organization; at its heyday, Maya Dommel and the Foundation were even invited to dine with President John Jacob Wilder in honor of their "steadfast commitment to elevating the health and spirit of our youth through sport." The Church launched the careers of a hundred young Champions who returned like boomerangs once glory wore thin and only the long dark slouch into obscurity lay ahead, to give their bodies to splendor while they still could. The Church also propped up the dreams of a thousand others who were not quite *Perfect Tens*, but could still sustain the growing ranks of the congregation.

Most of those attracted to the Church of the Holy Star were the unfortunate, those who sought salvation. They would hear of the Church through friends, neighbors, and family who had joined and grown strong and beautiful. To protect the Church, they were never informed of the community's holy rites until they had signed the paper-work and entered the sanctum. But when they laid eyes on the bronze statue of Saint Sasha the Perfect Ten, almost every newcomer was struck by the sublime, and quickly swallowed their spoonful of Champion blood. The exceptions – weaklings who through some deep fault of their character would rather embrace death than life – were immediately delivered unto the pitiful fate that they had chosen. The Church of the Holy Star provides only what one can handle.

One of Maya Dommel's rising stars was Zola Golding, born to a pair of young alley cats who had found the Church while in need of a firm guiding hand. Their devotion to the Church and its mission was derived from a life spent in hunger. Zola had been reared on the Church diet, weaning off her mother's milk straight to the blood of baseball pitcher Matt Frankberg, whose 120-miles-per-hour fastball might have won him the World Series, if only he were on a better team. Thus Zola showed a gift for speed early, and her parents delighted at the opportunity to repay the Church for its generosity.

Zola Golding received everything that a young runner could need to transcend into a Champion. The best shoes, the best singlets, access to the best training facilities and provision of the best meals – Zola was always among the first to dine on any Champion, and she was served her portion on a porcelain plate, not the great metal trough. She was excused from public schooling and gifted with state-of-the-edge electronics. She was also trained by the best coach available, a man who had spun several gold medals out of impermanent and faulty human flesh.

Early signs of Zola's selfishness were misread by Maya Dommel as ambition. Zola was sure that her new coach could unlock hidden reservoirs of agility, and insisted that her sacrifice be delayed until she was at her physical peak. She wanted to wait for the next Olympics; she wanted to see just how much glory she could attain. This at a time when the congregation, including her parents, was thirsting for the essence of a Champion! But the Founding Father, Reverend Orrin Spell, was reminded of his daughter's indomitable spirit and her own unfairly-aborted Olympic bid, and gave Zola the blessing to train for the 1990 Olympics.

Within two years, she was favored to win the heat that would qualify her for a spot on the national team. Her parents and Maya Dommel watched with bated breath from the bleachers as she lined up alongside her unenlightened competitors, the white and gold shooting star emblem emblazoned across her heart. Her gaze was iron as she crouched on the track, flexing her strong, taut tendons. And yet after the gun was fired and the race begun, Zola showed her frailty: she rolled her ankle before completing her first lap, then lay howling on the clay like a grotesque fallen animal. Afterward in the hospital she thrashed and wept and insisted that she could still heal and glorify Saint Sasha, but the Church had seen clearly from this failure of mind and matter that Zola was not a Champion.

Perhaps they would have only remembered Zola as a misdiagnosed contender if the Church had been an ordinary one; but the extraordinary Church of the Holy Star has eaten the flawless eyes of Champion marksmen and sees all things. In this particular instance the Church's Champion vision moved through Zola's best friend, Julie Chen, who went to the hospital to deliver a care package and overheard Zola laughing fiendishly with her coach, that deviant mortal man. She was laughing, so Julie told the Church, because apparently Zola could not believe she was such a convincing actress. Once aware of this betrayal, the Church of the Holy Star moved quickly to protect itself. The coach was destroyed with no witnesses in his apartment building, but the false champion Zola Golding slithered out of the reach of the Church's justice. It is said that she dwells in a poisoned city across the sea, hiding from the light of the Church and dreading the shame and torture that will befall her on the inevitable Day of Judgment.

Maya Dommel still proclaimed Zola to be an innocent who had been corrupted by her coach, perhaps seduced by his promises of earthly rewards. In dramatic fashion she beat her chest and blamed herself for exposing Zola to the influence of a man who had never been taken into the Church's fold. But a seed had been planted in the congregants' minds: perhaps the willing sacrifice was not a sustainable long-term model for their community.

Zola's good-hearted parents attempted to make amends for their daughter's sins by sacrificing themselves. Yet while their faith was stellar, their bodies were not; in the end they only succeeded in creating more work for the little old woman who cleaned St. Sasha's altar.

III. I Believe That

The treason of Zola Golding shook the foundations of the Church of the Holy Star. The Rising Star Foundation, too, had been embarrassed by her failure to qualify for the Olympics – its mentors and sponsors always stressed to its athletes that they were one enormous family of heroes, and for one of their most-favored sisters to fail so abominably after years of patient, dedicated training cast self-doubt on the entire stable of athletes. The organization did not win a single gold in 1990, and soon a few of its strongest jumped ship to other clubs, citing concerns about Rising Star's strength and conditioning program. The beloved Reverend Orrin Spell died shortly thereafter of a broken heart and a hungry soul, and in this dark and uncertain time several pillars of the Church journeyed out into the wretched world in search of answers.

One of these pilgrims was Professor Richard "Dick" Kettle, who taught Culture and Power in Ancient Societies, The Living Myth, and Advanced Topics in Shamanism at Rosewood College. He took an academic sabbatical to visit the tropical city of Parkidi, which had just begun construction for the 1994 Olympics, and climbed a nearby hill from whose peak he could see into the entrails of the blossoming Olympic Stadium. There he knelt, lit a small candle, opened his mind, and wept for the beauty of the stadium, the purity of the contest, and the failure of the Church to seize upon its potential. He pled with the known and unknown universe to deliver to him, and so to the Church of the Holy Star, the light.

He waited there for two days, and then a man came up the hill from the city shining with the lights of progress. He was tall and slim, wore a jet-black suit and a sympathetic expression, and introduced himself as Hyperon Talta. He said, "I hear that you are in need of help, Professor. I have something to show you." Professor Kettle took his hand, and Hyperon showed him a great many wondrous things about the velocity of blood, and the truth of the sword, and the eternally spinning face of God. Hyperon Talta illuminated a truth that the Church had previously been unprepared to see: sacrifice is noble, but conquest is glorious.

Professor Kettle returned to the Church of the Holy Star and convened an emergency meeting that very night. He brought with him Hyperon, who rose and unfolded like an enormous bat from behind St. Sasha's altar.

"Hold the knife to the throat of weakness."

Hyperon Talta showed them a god that was boundless and limitless: a reveler god whose name was Azathoth the Ultimate. The name itself opened their cells, reconstructed their nerves. For there is nothing larger, nothing stronger, than Azathoth the Ultimate, eater of worlds, absorber of stars, the one and only universe-straddling Champion. Hyperon showed them golden athletes dancing for this god within a stadium of stars. He taught them the games these athletes played: the plucking of the bloodshot eyes, the clack-rattling of the ribs, the drumming of the skin stretched tight and tense. He sang for them the soul-stirring, adrenaline-pumping cacophony of a thousand cymbals and a million trumpets and a billion raw vocal chords strained hard enough to break: a song that he called *The Canticle of the Hunter*.

"Come before God and conquer fear."

Then Hyperon withdrew into his black sleeves and left them to themselves. Nearly all of the Church members threw up their arms in revelation. "Have you ever seen a more perfect vision of victory?" cried Professor Kettle, and the congregants confirmed the answer to be no. Not even those who had witnessed St. Sasha's first, primitive sacrifice could claim not to be moved more violently by this vision.

As always, there were skeptics. Maya Dommel shouted, "There is always another side! He calls it the Canticle of the Hunter. What is that? Who is the Hunter? If we are the Hunters then who are the Hunted?"

Professor Kettle, standing at the pulpit, wisely proclaimed: "If you wish to be one of the Hunted, Maya Dommel, then there is none among here who can help you, and you should never have been taken into St. Sasha's flock. She conquered all there was to conquer. She would never have been Hunted, by anyone."

And so the Church split between those who heeded the guidance of Hyperon Talta, and those who refused to deviate from a tradition that was evidently failing the community. Red-haired Maya Dommel, who proudly took the title Apostle, led the heretics away from the Church of the Holy Star like the Pied Piper stole children – she even lured away the great-nephew of Reverend Orrin Spell, young James "Jimmy" Spell. These shadow-cast stragglers gathered their worldly possessions and drove to the other end of the nation, and in a city of empty factories – near a colossal football stadium that lay gutted to the sky like a dead whale – they established a house of sin and worship that they called the First Church of the Star.

Well into 1993, the First Church of the Star continued to recruit human sacrifices. With their siren songs they encouraged elite-level competitors in basketball, hockey, and baseball to lay down their lives in honor and celebration of the sublime. Eventually, this legion included the starting wide receiver of the team with the wolf herald that played in the dead whale stadium, a passionately religious young man named Henry LaCloak. Henry carried so much finely seeded muscle mass in his gunner's arms that he had to get his dress shirts custom-made. He was also the spiritual leader of his team: it was he who organized pancake and sausage fundraisers, and he who invited the team to join him in mass prayer upon their knees in the traditional Abrahamic style. He had about him an abundance of ritual, including pointing skyward after successful catches and repeated verbal genuflection toward a "Lord" and "Big Man in the Sky."

The First Church of the Star doubted Maya Dommel's decision to make a sacrifice out of Henry. "He is closed to us," they whispered to her. "He is on fire for his god," she replied. "He only needs to be brought to ours."

Ah! You may ask, what god did the First Church of the Star worship, if they refused Azathoth the Ultimate? According to their logs, they worshipped an intangible force that resides within all creatures: the will to improve, strengthen, and prosper – the will, that is, to make one's self a living god, and one's body a beating testament.

Henry LaCloak had tapped into that force at a very young age, when he first won a foot race against his brother. Pursuit of the force had defined his life, just as it had defined the Church. He met Maya Dommel when she asked the team's public relations department if he would co-sponsor a food drive for a local sports team, and Henry LaCloak immersed himself more deeply into the Church than any other recruit ever had.

"All your sacrifice, all your sweat, this is what it was for," Maya Dommel whispered to him as he knelt at the altar of St. Sasha, "This is why you are a winner. This is why you have never been second-string. You are the nectar of the heavens. You are the reason we are alive. This will be your ultimate victory."

"When?" he asked.

"When you have become all that you can be on this mortal plane. Then you ascend."

All threads began to unravel when Henry tried to spread the word of this bastardized First Church of the Star – to his nervous coaches and 'roid-raging teammates, the scandal-hunting reporters who spent nights camped outside their locker room, the little children in the pediatric cancer ward who received chemotherapy in Henry's 9 jersey. Maya Dommel urged him to be silent about his newfound passion but he believed he had found the key to all things and he had only ever wanted to use his athletic prowess to inspire others. When Henry scored touchdowns he now made shooting star gestures. "God was on our side today," he said after a come-from-behind win, "And I just want to thank the First Church of the Star for, uh, showing me why I was made a winner. So I could be the vessel for glory. God bless you, and God bless this city."

None of the unenlightened knew what to make of this, and Henry grew alienated from his team. *Freak*, they called him. *Bible-thumper. Satanist.* A kicker on his team finally agreed to attend a service with him on one rainy Sunday, and despite Maya Dommel's attempts to sanitize her message, the blind cannot be subjected to the light too quickly. The kicker asked Henry, "Why are those crazies so obsessed with you? Aren't you scared of what they want?" Henry said that the Church only wanted the same thing he did: it wanted him to win. Henry was cut from the team after the season was over, citing a disruption to team harmony. It was the first time he had ever failed, as an athlete or a leader, and he came hysterically weeping to the First Church of the Star, where he pulled a switchblade across his throat and sacrificed himself.

Here the full scope of Maya Dommel's error became apparent. The city could not care less for most of its athletes. They were drug addicts, child-beaters, rapists, dog-fighters – criminals who had been lucky to be blessed with phenomenal muscular and skeletal build. In this the city fundamentally misunderstood the Champion spirit – their foolish finger-wagging only served to blind them from the simple, absolute truth of victory, which supersedes all other supposed facts. But the city did love Henry LaCloak, their hero, who reminded them that there was some good left in their vile city. They came a-calling when he vanished. There was no body for them to find, but using their trickery and technology, they were able to show that Henry LaCloak's blood had once dripped upon the gleaming altar that Maya Dommel had erected in her pauper's church, the First Church of the Star.

So it came to be that red-haired Maya Dommel was placed in a human prison whose walls her legion could not penetrate, and sentenced to reside there for the rest of her years. Stories circulated for decades of a cannibal prisoner with a head of flames at Gossling

Penitentiary, but flesh alone would not sustain her – not the flesh of those unclean sinners greased with heroin and greed, and especially not after the eye of Hyperon Talta looked away.

The remnants of the First Church of the Star scattered to the four corners of the known Earth, running like rats into the small, hidden places between buildings whenever they sensed that a triumphant disciple of the Church of the Holy Star was nearby. An attempt was made to recover Jimmy Spell, as he was a blood-relative of St. Sasha, but he had burrowed like a termite into an architectural crevice and moved below ground, leaving behind slanderous warnings in the nation's subterranean train systems – warnings which were, fortunately, too cryptic for the uneducated to understand.

IV. I Believe That We

These had been lean times for the true Church of the Holy Star, which had kept afloat on the unripe, semi-sweet bodies of young athletes who were not yet at their pinnacle but were more easily overpowered. Many had to be kept in cages and bled at length to prolong their usefulness, though the drop-off in the quality of their juices was precipitous. The undernourished Church members gnashed their restless teeth and complained that Maya Dommel's heathen splinter church was feeding just fine on willing sacrifices in the Rust Belt.

"We chase something greater," said Professor Kettle, as Hyperon Talta's long leather-gloved fingers softly clenched both sides of his head. "We must make our break with the past. Sacrifice is over. *Surrender* is over." In the end the flock accepted this; they knew firsthand, now, that sacrificed blood would never taste as rich as spilled blood. It is the difference between an insect trapped in amber and a buzzing fly. There is simply more iron and punch in the latter.

And so, while the false First Church of the Star was hoisted upon its own petard, the Church of the Holy Star continued its holy quest to find its way to Azathoth the Ultimate. Hyperon Talta took up residence in the vestry of the church, counseling the elders and bringing joy to the children through magical binoculars and enchanted gyroscopes. The Church knew it was blessed; Azathoth's emissary could have taken his wisdom anywhere in the world (and perhaps he *was* doing God's work elsewhere, but such is the nature of omnipotence that the Church of the Holy Star never felt his calm eagle-eye waver, not even for a heartbeat), and so committed its best and brightest to Hyperon's makeshift training camp.

All throughout 1993, the Church of the Holy Star perfected its rendition of the Canticle of the Hunter. For those unlucky enough never to have heard it, this is not a song like those children's hymns performed in common ecclesiastical choirs, nor a tearful anthem for a hamstrung nation. It is a calling, closer to the ritual war-chants that human sport clubs have used for decades to support their team and intimidate the enemy: "Rock Chalk Jayhawk," "Glory Glory Man United," "We Are Penn State," "I Believe That We Will Win." The Canticle of the Hunter had no words, only sensations; no gestures, only dreams. To observe a solo performance of the Canticle of the Hunter is to hear nothing but a faint growl emitted from a focused, open mouth. It is also to feel wildly compelled, at a biological level, to join. You may not believe at first that you know how, nor even what the singer is doing. But your mouth will drop before you know it. Because above all else, the Canticle of the Hunter is a demonstration of overbearing and undeniable will. A will that is too great for any individual human to refuse.

At the first public performance of the Canticle, Professor Kettle stood at the back of an underground arena, hot and dark as the womb save for the fluorescent lights that lorded over the boxing ring, and sang to the two heavyweights as they bounced off the ropes in their respective corners. Reginald Peters and Luis Cabron blinked and shook their heads, as if their ears were clogged with water, but neither stopped the fight. They were would-be Champions after all. Professor Kettle did not share the Canticle of the Hunter with the crowd, but their inborn energy still bolstered the song: amplifying its crests, deepening its valleys. The fighters, pre-selected for their ruthlessness, grew bolder and bloodier. In the end it was Luis Cabron who punched his opponent into unconsciousness, and then into death. He tore into the corpse, broke two ribs, and swallowed three mouthfuls of Reginald's deflated lungs. At his murder trial, Luis would claim that voices in his head had forced him to kill Reginald. Due to the cold and clinical nature of human society, there was no consideration of his claim, and Luis was sentenced to death by electric chair.

"Hum, hum," said Hyperon Talta with infinite patience as he sat cross-legged upon the cabinet of vestments. "Azathoth responds to roars, not screams." And so the Church learned that mass action would be needed to please their new God.

In 1994, a small Church mission traveled to Parkidi to pay tribute to the Summer Olympics and perform a second recitation of the Canticle. They chose an early soccer match between two small nations with no love lost between them, thanks to a history of arbitrary and inconvenient colonial boundaries, and from high in the stands unleashed the Canticle of the Hunter. This time, they sang to the crowd as well as the players. For fifteen minutes there was no increase in the number of red cards thrown at players, no unusual noises from the crowd. And then, for what must have been a second but seemed to be an hour, all things aligned for the missionaries, and the ravenous minds of one hundred thousand spectators and athletes were lassoed within one heavenly burning crown.

And then the Church of the Holy Star lost control. To conduct so many souls who had shown so little disposition toward following the weakest of rules was a greater challenge than they had anticipated. The crowd ripped free of the Church's restraints but absorbed the Canticle's rage, and as the noble Canticle splintered into a million shards of petty human anger, the crowd used this psychic bomb to set the stadium and the city on fire. The shock waves from the massive bleeding heart that was the Parkidi Olympic Stadium could be felt hundreds of miles away. Players bludgeoned other players, fans threw their seats at other fans, and the referees, symbols of the dying light of human civilization, ran.

The Canticle of the Hunter is intended to be a missile, not an IED. The Church's missionaries were shoved and beaten in the brawls that followed, and they returned home bruised and ashamed at what they perceived acutely to be their failure. But when they pushed open the doors of their church at midnight, they found Hyperon Talta smiling, cross-legged, at the pulpit.

"I am proud of you," said Hyperon, and the missionaries wept.

V. I Believe That We Will Win

At the midsummer inflection point of the year 1995, Hyperon Talta gathered the members of the Church of the Holy Star around him and made an exciting announcement. "You are finally ready to escort Azathoth into the world," said Hyperon. A few congregants fainted. Just imagine their joy and pride! "But first we must find Azathoth a host."

Azathoth the Ultimate would need the best athlete their little mudball planet had to offer. Several were considered: basketball player T. J. Folger, swimmer Lana Denali, figure skater Choi Ji-Yung. Luis Cabron would have been another strong candidate, with his unworldly ability to withstand assaults upon his person, but he was shackled on death row. Ji-Yung was so very like St. Sasha in her tiny build and steely demeanor that she was nearly chosen, but just as the Church attempted to enter her country, she retired from figure skating – she was getting old, at twenty-two – and shut herself up in her lonely penthouse with no desire for any more quadruple loops nor ice-flowers nor glory. So in the end, the Church elders with Hyperon's approval selected Felix Nordlund, widely regarded as the best tennis player of all-time. Felix not only displayed effortless physical mastery of the court, but an unrivaled intelligence surrounding the game and indeed, motion itself. Other players had beautiful backhands, powerful forehands, unreturnable serves – Felix Nordlund had everything. He had won sixty-three major tournaments since he turned sixteen. He was number one in the world. His dominance was so thorough, and his fashion sense so rococo, that tennis fans were beginning to tire of him – but Azathoth would love him and his command of physics, of this the Church was sure.

Felix was due to play at Mercatilly, the nation's premier tournament. The Church of the Holy Star decided it would meet him there. They waited all the way until the final round, in order to give Azathoth the most impressive entrance: Center Court in the half-light, tucked away in a perfectly-manicured artificial forest, the stadium a perfect serving bowl for Azathoth the Ultimate. It was good weather for a God's landing. At the bottom of the bowl, two lonely gladiators spun their titanium rackets.

Felix was competing for his fifth title at Mercatilly against Drew Stephens, a national. Given the events that followed, we must remember that Drew Stephens, too, was a contender of high athletic caliber, one who had been enrolled in tennis lessons by his fierce mother-coach when he was four years old. Though he had won twelve major tournaments, Drew had never won Mercatilly. In fact it had been seventy years since any national won Mercatilly, much to the ache and angst of the screaming youth in painted flags and the elderly listening on the radio. But as the Church of the Holy Star had always known, patriotism does not assure athletic dominance. Of that there is no guarantor except for talent, labor, and the mystical touch of divine grace. Drew was the best tennis player his nation had spawned in decades, but he was also temperamental, spoiled, lacking in creative game strategy. Yet his greatest failing, the one that prevented him from bringing honor to his homeland, was to have been born a few years after Felix Nordlund. He had been cursed to toil in the shadow of another man's golden era; that was not his fault.

The Canticle of the Hunter was performed at exactly 6.34 in the evening, at the beginning of the third set. Felix had won the first two sets and was calmly eating a banana, staring straight ahead at the scoreboard that clearly reflected his superiority. Drew was muttering to himself, occasionally yelling random words at his mother and coaches who sat biting their knuckles in his player's box. After the players jogged to their respective ends so that Felix could prepare to serve, the members of the Church of the Holy Star stood and began their song. The chair umpire attempted to silence their devotional but could not – for how could this passion, inspired as it was by the height of human greatness, be denied?

It was their finest hour. The crowd was enraptured. With mouths agape, they rose in their seats as one and slipped their necks into the leash of the Church. The few who resisted – Felix's wife, both players' coaches – had their consciousness slammed into a metaphysical wall, and liquefied. The chair umpire made a foolish attempt to call for help through his radio, as if Hyperon Talta would not have blocked all such signals and protected Center Court from outside interference. The two players ran toward each other at the net; the Church assumed they had moved to greet Azathoth, though they looked extremely fragile, and extremely frightened. This is how the Church discovered that even Champions can be overwhelmed. The swarm poured onto the court, threw the chair umpire from his perch and trampled him flat, then took both players in hand. The Church held its breath, anxious to see Felix Nordlund lifted to the sky, to Azathoth.

But the crowd faltered in its mission. Through no fault of the Church, the masses succumbed to the throes of their animalistic and irrational nationalism, and tore Felix Nordlund apart instead. Professor Kettle and his fellow members of the Church of the Holy Star howled. *How thoughtless the human heart, how mad!* Even Drew Stephens seemed to know that the ritual had gone awry, for his cry of lamentation was sadder than all. He screamed Felix's name, as if he knew that Azathoth's first choice in human vessel had been so rashly destroyed. And then he fainted, for there was much blood and gore upon the court.

What could the Church do, but prepare Drew Stephens for the ritual? Only one among the entranced crowd could call Drew Stephens her flesh and blood, but on this day Mrs. Maggie Stephens was joined by ten thousand others who lifted the unconscious body of their little prince over their heads and passed him around, pawing affectionately at his hair. "Quickly!" said Hyperon Talta as the ashen half-light was overcome by the final dark. The Church commanded the crowd to place Drew in the umpire's now-vacant throne, where Hyperon sent a firebolt into Drew's cerebral cortex and awoke him, sweating and afraid.

"Drew Stephens, rejoice!" the Church sang. "For Azathoth wants to live inside you."

Drew Stephens curled like a snail and refused the invitation. Words fail to describe the depth of the humiliation this brought to the Church. To keep Azathoth the Ultimate waiting just one mile overhead was sacrilegious enough, but to deny Azathoth entirely?

"Why are you crying? You are going to become a vessel for a God."

He did not answer, but he did not have to. He wept, the Church realized, because Felix Nordlund was dead. This came as a great surprise to the Church, which having seen all things – dark things, light things, splendid crimson secret things – knew that Drew hated Felix. They had watched Drew smash nine rackets after losing to Felix in the semifinals of the 1994 Gondoi Open. They had heard Drew hiss, drunken and sloppy, that Felix was a "motherfucking fuck." Yet the only recording that played in Drew's head, now at the hour of Azathoth's descent, was an inconsequential blip that had taken place two years ago, when he and Felix had filmed a watch commercial together. It was a dull, flat memory, nothing compared to the spikes of rage that contorted Drew's face every time he lost to Felix and certainly nothing compared to the Church's visions of golden crowns and laurel wreaths. Yet Drew's mind had clenched like a fist around this episode, and as a result he saw nothing but Felix Nordlund juggling the ball and making childish puns, over and over and over again.

When the clouds began to cleave, Drew Stephens jumped from his throne and ran from his fate. He thrashed against the crowd when they tried to feed him little bits of Felix, and screamed for help after he threw open the back doors of Center Court. But all had been put to sleep to allow for Azathoth's successful landing: the groundskeepers, the sponsors, the poor who could not afford tickets to the main event. Hyperon Talta manifested in front of the still-gurgling Fountain of Champions, where all the names of Mercatilly's titleholders had been laid under the water. Azathoth's emissary released the full might of his interstellar strength as he shouted to the restless sinner, "*Drew, why do you run?*"

Hyperon was so overwhelming that Drew could not help but fall to his knees in reverence. "I don't know who you people are," said Drew, his voice muffled by guttural sobs, "but please just let me go."

Was it shame that held Drew Stephens back, the knowledge that he with his 59-20 win-loss record was unworthy of Azathoth? Or was it simply cowardice, the same mental frailty that had prevented him from seizing victory at Falun-Re, at the Parkidi Olympics, at Gondoi? These are questions that the Church continues to debate today. One thing we know for sure, one thing for which there is no doubt, is that Drew Stephens was not a Champion. And when Azathoth the Ultimate descended from the heavens, immediately melting the walls of Center Court, Drew's contemptible eyes and ears began to bleed. Greatness had been thrust upon the boy, and stopped the pitter-patter of his weak little human heart.

And so Azathoth the Ultimate, Lord of All Things, touched down upon planet Earth without a host to contain its splendor. PA systems across the grounds of Mercatilly ripped to life to announce the God's arrival, but their crackly rendition of the Canticle of the Hunter was immediately trumped by the glorious sound emanating from the fires of Azathoth's own eternal furnace – fishermen on trawling boats up to fifty miles away were stunned in their sleep, and altered.

Azathoth tucked Hyperon Talta between its many nests of luminous eyes and galloped northward into the night, leaving brilliant green aurorae burning in its wake.

The Church of the Holy Star wept, for we had been abandoned. But by the grace of St. Sasha we picked ourselves up, and just as she had chased the gold medallion we chased Azathoth the Ultimate, following the trail of skeletonized human wreckage. For glory and grandeur, we will chase forever.

We believe that we will win.

Lois H. Gresh's inspiration for "In the Sacred Cave" came from a museum visit where she saw "thousands of Inca clay pots representing all realms of life, death, and whatever lies beyond death. To the ancients, these realms were intertwined, and one could communicate with and perform actions with beings in these other realms. What came before the ancient Incas? Could they have been unknown Old Ones, and their realms unknown times and spaces? Why would human life matter in such a vast multi-dimensional context? Lois pondered these ideas while in Peru, where she wrote "In the Sacred Cave."

Gresh is the *New York Times* best-selling and *USA Today* best-selling author of twenty-nine books and sixty-five stories. Look for her trilogy of Lovecraftian Sherlock Holmes thrillers coming soon from Titan Books. Her latest book is collection *Cult of the Dead and Other Weird and Lovecraftian Tales* (Hippocompus), and she recently edited *Innsmouth Nightmare* and *Dark Fusions* (both for PS Publishing). She has weird stories in eighteen recently released anthologies, including, *Dreams From the Witch House*, *New Cthulhu 2: More Recent Weird*, *Black Wings III*, *Gothic Lovecraft*, *That is Not Dead*, *Dark Phantastique*, *Mountain Walked*, *Madness of Cthulhu*, *Searchers After Horror*, *Expiration Date*, *Black Wings IV*, *Eldritch Chrome*, *Summer of Lovecraft*, *Mark of the Beast*, and more.

In the Sacred Cave
Lois H. Gresh

Sky so brown, like rusty iron. Tarnished clouds.
   Never anything to do here, just listen to the insects buzz and the world groan.
   Chicya can't spend another day here, she just can't.
   Far below, the river thrashes as if trying to punch its way through the

mountains. Nearby, her alpaca dips its head, and teeth rip the scabby *ichu* from the ground.

Chicya swishes lime around in her mouth, and it mingles with mashed coca leaves. The mountain seems to tremble with her.

The air vibrates slightly. A vehicle rattles.

She scrabbles to the edge of the terrace and cranes her neck over Orq'o Wichay, the sacred mountain of her ancestors. Wriggling down the opposite mountain to the river is the Owambaye pass, known only to the indigenous Inca, never to the Spanish or those of mixed heritage. A pickup truck rumbles around a boulder and totters on the edge of the Owambaye where it hangs a thousand meters over the water.

Chicya blinks to keep colors from swirling before her eyes. What's a truck doing here? They never come this far into the Peruvian mountains.

Should she warn the elders?

No one will believe her. They always say she's loco, born under a dark moon.

The truck vanishes around a bend, *and perhaps she hallucinated the whole thing.* Chicya hangs her head, and the black mood settles over her. *If only I had enough nerve,* she thinks, *I'd throw myself off the mountain and hit bottom, crushed to dust, and let the river heave me downstream.*

If only . . .

The birds cry. The flowers, once drenched in honey, smell stale. The clouds part, only for a moment, and exhale a strand of sunlight before closing again.

Time creeps into the distance.

Suddenly an animal screams, and Chicya's alpaca freezes, head high, drip of vegetation hanging from its mouth. Screams rise and echo and expand in bands of air that puff up to where Chicya slumps on her terrace.

She leaps up, and a wave of dizziness hits. She almost falls but staggers back, careful not to slip off the ledge, *for now is not her time.* She doesn't have enough nerve. Not yet.

The screams are odd. They're not from any mountain creature she knows. Nor are they the shrieks of people, a sound she knows well from childhood. The Shining Path killers are long gone, sequestered in the Amazon now – *and let them have their cocaine trade, for who needs it, not the pure Inca, no, not those of us who still chew the leaf.*

Chicya scrambles up the grass to the plateau and stumbles through the woods. A chinchilla peeks from beneath yellow flowers that spread like stars across the boulders. The blood-colored bark of the paper tree exfoliates, and the twisted limbs grab at her and branches rake her hair. Roots crack through the earth and trip her, and she lurches but regains her footing and scuttles down the trail to the bottom of the mountain. She has to catch her breath, let her heart slow. She leans, hands on knees, and stares at the ground. It's red from clay, red from blood.

The scent of grilled meat floats past, and she lifts her head. She hasn't eaten in two days.

She scoots past the *lapacho* trees to the clearing by the village, then stops. *What good will it do to go there?* This is where she was found as a baby. Shining Path killed her parents, the villagers said. *Sixteen years ago they died.* They rescued her, but the villagers have always hated Chicya. "A drain on our resources," they say, and "you eat our food and live nowhere, and all you do for us is nothing."

Yes, that's what she is, *nothing*, and she knows it. A freak of nature, alone, as adrift as the clouds.

In the clearing, a lopsided van crouches. Its rear lights are bashed, the tires deflated. Dents bruise the back and the side panel, where red letters spell True Sacred Valley. The words look all drippy as if an idiot smeared them on with a brush.

Next to the van is the pickup truck. Up close, it doesn't look so good. Rust scabs the body like a pox. The paint is a color that reminds Chicya of rat skin. Steam rises from three bowls on the open cargo bed. *Stew.* Grilled alpaca with tomato, cilantro, and lime.

Near the vehicles, dozens of villagers huddle in a tight knot. They're all indigenous Inca, just like Chicya, but they've lost their way. They no longer follow the three main Inca laws. They lie and gossip about each other. They're too lazy to rise up and fight the oppressive government. And every one of them would steal from his own mother if given half a chance.

Something squeals, and the villagers scream and pump the air with their fists. Chicya moves closer. Within the knot of villagers, animals scuffle and grunt.

A loud crack rings out, as if metal has cleaved skull, and the crowd goes wild. Another crack, a heavy blow no doubt, and an animal screeches, then whimpers and falls silent.

Chicya elbows her way to the center of the crowd. Those who recognize her scoff and try to shove her away. She retains her footing and glares back.

And then she sees them, the animals that are fighting: two men in loin cloths, squatting close to the ground, their round bodies smashed together. White fur forms patterns on their black skin, making them look faintly like the black-and-white pottery of the ancient Chimus of the Moche Valley. From their shoulders to their waists, blood mats the white fur into pink cotton. Stumps at the bottoms of their legs wobble in the dirt. Nearby is an Incan death club, gold and etched with serpents.

Slowly the men rise, their faces twisted in pain, and Chicya sees that neither man has a neck. They look like men, but there's something *off* about them. Their bodies start sizzling where joined – *and how can this be?* – and the burned flesh crackles.

The villagers shriek and clap their hands.

Chicya turns to run, but her forehead slams against something hard. She reels back, vaguely sees a shovel and a laughing face.

Furry hands grab her. They lift her, and before she knows it, they throw her into the back of the pickup truck. She struggles but can't break free.

Bizarre animals pin down her arms and sit on her legs. She can't kick her legs loose, can't ball her fists and punch the animals.

They might be women, but then again, they might not even be human. Like the fused men, they have no feet. Their bald heads are tattooed with Inca patterns: three stairs, a feline, a deer, a serpent. They wear rags and have no breasts, and in fact, their bodies are as round as urns. Chicya opens her mouth to scream, but several furry fingers jam into her mouth, and she wretches, the fur wet and dirty, the fingers gagging her. She sinks back, willing herself to go limp. Her torso convulses as she gags, and finally, the fingers slide from her mouth.

In the ancient Quechua language, they talk. "An amazing freak and easy to snatch" and "an orphan, nobody will care" and "people will pay a lot for her." They coo at her, they stroke her black hair, and one of them tells her, "Relax. We won't hurt you. You're one of us now."

Fingers peel back her lips and force open her teeth. She tries to bite, but the fingers are too strong. Sweet corn juice, the *chicha*, pours down her throat, and she sputters. But she can't choke, can't let them kill her, *for now is not her time.* She's not ready to die, not yet, not this way.

They help her sit, and they poke alpaca meat into her mouth, and she chews and swallows. They feed her strange corn, each kernel the size of a thumbnail.

She dozes off and on, and is barely aware she's in a truck bouncing down the mountain passages. Wheels grind over rock and dirt. The truck wheezes. Female voices say, "Ollantayambo" and "in the heart of the Sacred Valley." A woodpecker raps a tree, and Chicya pictures its beak and the bobbing of its head. The rapping fades into the crunch of the wheels.

Finally, the truck stops, and the female creatures carry her to a straw pallet, where she sleeps through the night. When she awakens, she's woozy as if drugged.

She slips outside.

The air is heavy again with the scent of alpaca stew. The truck and van are parked by a small roofless building made from stone, where smoke drifts to the sky.

On a rock bench to her left, a large clay pot begins to rattle. Molded in the clay, two girls embrace on the side of the pot, which now clanks across the bench.

Chicya squeezes her eyes shut, then opens them again, but her vision doesn't clear.

The pot spins. The clay girls clench each other more tightly.

Chicya whirls, seeking an escape route. Forest-clad cliffs on three sides. Path snaking down the mountain. And behind the bench, rock stairs thrust into the clouds. How's she going to get out of here?

Her heart raps louder than the woodpecker.

She clenches her fists, wills herself not to cry.

A man saunters from the roofless building. He's short and round with no neck, but what startles her the most is his face: the lidless black eyes, the toothless smile stretching from ear to ear, and the deep creases – *folds really* – that make his forehead look like wet clay. Gold prongs, each the size of Chicya's big toe, skewer his ears, and he wears a gold nosepiece that looks like the spread wings of a condor. His tunic is knit from yarn unlike anything Chicya has ever seen: gold and red, as if spun from a bloody sun, and tufted to make his torso look feathered. Unlike the other monsters, this one holds a gun, and it's aimed right at Chicya.

With his other hand, he shoves a fistful of ground meat into his mouth. The smile doesn't waver, even as he mashes the meat with his gums. As he approaches, she smells *cuy chactado*, fried guinea pig. His pace quickens, and she sees that he has feet. No stumps, but *feet*.

She shrinks back from him.

"Good," he says, "it's good to show respect." His voice is oddly high, and his Quechua syllables end in trills. He pops the gun into a pocket.

"What . . . *who* are you?" she whispers.

"Welcome to the True Sacred Valley. Here, all that matters is the most sacred Inca ceremony. We've never lost it. You'll fit right in."

Her mind reels. What is the most sacred of all Inca ceremonies? She tries to remember. Inca children were sometimes fattened before ritual slaughter. Women drank fermented corn *chicha* before being sacrificed to the gods. Priests wrapped the corpses of royal Inca in beautifully embroidered funerary blankets, and buried them with gold masks, ear plugs, and nostril plates. She stares at the man. He's wearing similar accouterments.

"You have nothing to fear in Wakapathtay," he says.

Surely, he jokes. This can't be Wakapathtay. Nobody's ever seen the village, much less lived in it. According to the ancients, Wakapathtay was the birthplace of those who came before the true Inca. It sat high on a mountain over the Sacred Valley, tucked where only goats and alpaca could climb. Wakapathtay was also home to the Sacred Cave where, in 1544, the leader Manqu Inca – who defeated Hernando Pizarro's forces in the village of Ollantayambo – went to die.

The man takes Chicya's arm, and he gently strokes it. But if he thinks this soothes her in any way, he couldn't be more wrong. Her skin crawls beneath his touch. She wants nothing to do with him or his companions. "You're living proof that Wakapathtay exists, just as we all are," he says. "We remind people of their heritage. You can't get this service anywhere else because, you see, everything springs from Wakapathtay."

"What do you do to these people?" she asks.

"I give their lives meaning." He turns as two creatures hobble on leg stumps from the path that snakes up the mountain. One creature looks like a spotted deer with a rope around his neck. The other has the face of an owl and the body of a cat. Both have spouts on their heads. They carry a stretcher made from the same yarn as the man's tunic. On the stretcher is a bizarre corpse made from two fused men. Although their faces are mangled to pulp, she knows from their black skin and bloodied white fur that these are the "men" she saw fighting before her capture. They had beat the life out of each other with the clubs.

"Come!" The man drags her over to the creatures and their stretcher. He trills wildly, and the deer and owl look relieved. Then he says, "This is an honor and a blessing. Cisco and Luis have done well."

Cisco and Luis, the fused corpse.

The owl creature bobs its head. "We thank you, Maras. You are kindness itself."

The clay pot of the intertwined girls clacks across the bench. The girls writhe, and their mouths open as if they are screaming; and the pot itself seems to wail.

The man, Maras, ignores the commotion on the bench and tells the deer and owl to "bring the new girl to Nayra to feed. She'll make a good replacement for Bachue and Cava." Then he scoops up the clay pot, which writhes and wails more shrilly, and stuffs it into a backpack. "Back to the cave, my lovelies." Unblinking eyes leer at at Chicya, up and down they gaze, as if assessing her value.

The deer grabs one of her arms, the owl grabs the other. She screams and tries to yank her arms free, but these two are strong, like rock, and the struggling bruises her skin. They drag her through the dirt to the roofless building.

Maras clambers up the steep stairs carved into the mountain. His backpack bobs as he hoists himself from stair to stair. Chicya feels sorry for the girls of the clay pot. The pot seemed so alive, the two girls so miserably pathetic and fated to . . . *what?*

As the deer and owl nudge her into the tent, an elderly woman on skinny stumps sways in the breeze. She strums a harp and warbles an old Inca tune.

What might be a girl eases Chicya onto a chair and hands her a platter of food. The stew: alpaca, cilantro, lime, and tomato; and again, the large kernels of corn. The girl: face gnarled like a tree trunk, knobs like giant warts on her neck and arms, hair long and sleek like a black waterfall, body slender like Chicya's; and Chicya dips her eyes, *and yes, the girl has two feet.*

"I'm Nayra." The girl gestures at the platter. "Go ahead. Eat."

Chicya sips from a cup. Fermented corn juice. She sips again and tells the girl her name, then says, "Please, tell me what's going on here. What do they want with me?"

The girl lowers her voice. "If you cook or drive a truck or fix things for Maras, he spares you."

"From what?"

"I cook."

"What does he spare you from, Nayra?"

Nayra quivers. The knobs on her neck shake. "Don't ask me anything else," she says. "Just eat."

And so it goes as time passes. Nayra gives Chicya more food than she can eat, and it's always the same: the corn kernels and fermented juice, the alpaca stew. Nayra refuses to supply any information. Maras checks on Chicya as she rests on her pallet, and he seems pleased. She's too weak to do anything but eat and sleep.

Over time, she changes, and not for the better. Her face feels gnarled, and her skin hurts when she smiles. Her stomach is larger, her waist ill-defined, her toes half the size they were when she first came here. Worse, she feels drugged all the time, and it isn't a good feeling like with the coca and lime. Rather, it dulls her brain and makes her sluggish.

She *could* stumble down the road that winds up the mountain to this place. She *could*, but every time the thought enters her head, she falls back asleep. Besides, her feet have withered and are now mere nubs, so how far would she get? And then, there's that small problem about Maras with his gun . . .

"Did you ever think," Nayra says one day, "that your life would end like this?"

Chicya lies on her pallet. Her arms are heavy, her legs like wood. Nayra sits beside her, stumped legs outstretched, body round now like a ball. She lost her feet weeks ago. Her skin looks jaundiced, or maybe . . . *claylike*.

"Why do you suddenly care about me?" asks Chicya.

"For five years, I've been here and Maras never made me fight. I only had to cook. Now," she blinks back tears, "well, look at me. I'm as good as gone."

"So you let him do this to me out of fear for yourself?"

"I never thought he'd make me fight. He's always favored me. Of course, he had Bachue and Cava to earn money for him, and now they're broken."

Chicya props herself on her elbows. It's hard to keep her head from crashing back to the pallet. She shifts to her side, keeps her left elbow on the bed, then cradles her head in her hand. This keeps her head up.

"What would happen if you stop feeding me the drugged food and drinks?"

"It's not drugged. And the answer is, you would starve. That's all we have."

"Well, if it's not drugged, then what is it?"

Nayra stretches out on the floor and stares at the cloudless sky. She doesn't look at Chicya. "Everyone says our people died because the *conquistadores* brought smallpox, not because their gods were stronger than ours. You remember how the only time the Inca ever defeated the Spanish was at Ollantayambo?"

Chicya doesn't understand. What does this have to do with anything? But she nods. "Yes."

"And how, years later, the Manqu Inca was betrayed and attacked by those under his protection? Barely alive, he came to Wakapathtay to die in the Sacred Cave?"

"Yes."

"Well, what do you think is so special about the cave? About this place?" Nayra asks.

"Look, just tell me. Don't play guessing games. Maybe I can figure out a way to get us out of here."

Nayra scoffs. "This isn't a riddle. I thought you might know more than me. I don't *know* what's in the cave. I never go up there. I don't cross Maras. I prefer to remain *off the shelf.*"

A long pause.

"Besides," Nayra continues, "if you haven't noticed, not many people here have feet or a body shape suitable for walking, much less climbing stairs or mountains." Her voice trails off, and her eyes shut. She fades into the fog of the stew and the corn and the *chicha.*

Maras said that Chicya would make a fine replacement for the Bachue and Cava act. Nayra says that she's turning into a freak because the Bachue and Cava pottery is broken. An image of Cisco and Luis flashes through Chicya's mind, how they clubbed each other to death for the true believers, the Inca of the Sacred Valley.

After Nayra leaves, Chicya plucks a lime slice from a jar of alpaca stew and sucks on it. The tartness revives her, and thinking she might need sustenance, she tucks the jar into the front of her pants, then grasps the pole in the middle of the tent and forces herself to stand. She limps outside, where the forests buzz with insects, twigs crackle, streams slosh, and the alpaca chew the *ichu*. A buzzard whirls overhead. The elderly woman on skinny stumps is a statue by the cook tent, her harp fused to her body.

Chicya isn't sure what's real and what's in her mind. But when she sees Maras hoisting himself up the stairs toward the Sacred Cave, she *knows* that he's real. And this time, she's going up there after him.

His tunic sparkles. The condor wings of his nosepiece shoot light into her eyes. His backpack bobs as he disappears into the brush at the top of the stairs.

Where will she find the strength to follow him?

On the other hand, how many times has Chicya climbed the stairs up Orq'O Wichay? If she can climb her own sacred mountain without eating for days, then she can climb this one, too.

She grasps *ichu* in her fists and hoists herself up to the first stair. She pauses, then hoists herself up two more stairs. A chinchilla darts from the *ichu* to a boulder draped in yellow flowers, scoots across the rock and disappears.

It must be a sign from the true Inca gods. They won't let the false holiness of Maras taint the already warped villagers any longer.

Perhaps Chicya spent her life on Orq'O Wichay for a reason. She kept the ancient ways alive. She was the only one. Perhaps with Chicya's help, the true Inca gods will intervene.

To the left of the yellow flowers, a coca bush displays its leaves like ornaments. Chicya plucks several and chews, mashes the coca with the lime and lets the juice dribble down her throat.

Eventually, she reaches the brush where Maras disappeared. The mountain rises far beyond the top stair, which levels off and joins a rock path cut into the side of the cliff. She ducks beneath the brush, then scoots against the rock wall along the narrow path. Her palms press against the rock, red like clay, red like blood.

She's not afraid. She's been training for this moment her entire life for reasons she only now understands.

The buzzard circles. He's in the right place, *for now is not her time, but it's time for someone else.*

Maras' voice trills happily from the Sacred Cave. "Back on the shelf with you, my lovelies. I need new Inca blood. Perhaps *you* will do. And *you*." Pottery clatters, and an odd keening echoes off the walls of the cave and filters down the cliff.

Chicya slides closer to the cave.

His trilling stops—

and she stops—

and now she inches closer until she finally steps into the mouth of the Sacred Cave. Heat flushes through her body. Her flesh tingles. The ancient air envelops her, and suddenly, *she knows* . . . without a doubt, she knows why she's here.

A candle flickers in the far end of the cave, where Maras tinkers with his pots.

Hundreds of pots.

Thousands of pots.

Shelves reach from the cave floor to the ceiling in all directions, and crammed on every shelf are ancient Incan pots of all sizes, types, and dimensions. Black pots with white paint. Clay pots with red paint. Pots of men fighting. Pots of clay okra, corn, all forms of vegetables and fruits. Pots of doctors performing surgery on a girl's chest, a man's abdomen, a child's head. Pots of women giving birth. Pots of two girls and a dead man having sex. Pots of deer frolicking in the woods. Pots of owl faces with cat bodies.

Next to the broken Bachue and Cava pot – the two girls – is one that looks like the fused Cisco and Luis.

Does Maras plan to turn Chicya and Narya into a pot like Bachue and Cava?

Yes. Maras plans to put Chicya and Narya on the shelf . . .

Chicya gazes at row upon row of the clay figures. Some weep. Some wave their arms at her. Some squirm, some twitch.

The ancients made pots depicting every aspect of life involving humans, animals, vegetables, fruits, and the supernatural dead. In Wakapathtay, the corn is larger than any other Peruvian corn, the alpaca wool is stronger than any other wool, and the alpaca meat tastes the best.

Why doesn't Maras turn into pottery along with everybody else?

The stew jar shifts in her pants, and instinctively, her hand grabs it. Her back knocks against some pots, which rattle on the shelves.

Maras spins, and he whips out his gun. His lidless eyes widen, and candle light flicks across his slick smile. His laughter is shrill. "I knew you were special. I knew you were different. You're feisty, aren't you, little girl?"

He wiggles the gun, breaks into wild laughter, and leaps at her, and his forefinger presses the trigger.

She screams and darts to the side, her back banging against the shelves, as a bullet cracks into a pot of two warriors. They crumble to dust at her feet.

She throws herself at him, tackles him to the ground, and pins his arms down the way the female freaks pinned hers in the pickup truck. The gun skitters across the floor.

He wriggles beneath her, but she's massive now and rock-solid, having consumed so much of the alpaca stew and corn, for now she knows: it is the special alpaca and corn of Wakapathtay that deforms the people and turns the pots into living creatures. It's the only thing that makes sense.

Everyone here eats the stew except Maras, who eats *cuy chactado*. He must have stopped eating the stew shortly after his body began to change. This is why he still has feet, why he doesn't freeze up and turn into a footless freak.

This is why the pots seem so alive, because they *are* alive.

Withhold the stew, the deformed people become pots again. *On the shelf.* Give them stew, the pots transform into mindless fighters.

But how . . . ? Nayda said something about smallpox. This is what she meant: here, in isolation, the virus changed . . . mutated . . . and infected the alpaca . . .

Maras wrenches his arm free, and she cracks it against the ground – it breaks. He howls in pain as she reaches into her pants and removes the jar of stew. His lips burble froth. "No, not that, no!" he shrieks.

What does Maras get out of it, the fighting? she wonders, as she twists open the jar and tilts it over his mouth.

"This is what you've been doing to me all this time, isn't it? Pump me full of alpaca, and I'll become another fighting freak, right? When I'm done fighting, when I'm broken, you'll put me on the shelf with all these other poor people. Well, it's stew time for *you*, Maras, and when you are a neckless monster, I'll withdraw the stew, and then I'll put *you* on the shelf."

He shakes his head. *No no no no no no . . .*

A blob of stew falls between his lips. He chokes, but he must swallow. And now another blob falls.

It was here in the Sacred Cave that Manqu Inca died eight years after defeating the Spanish who spread smallpox throughout Peru. Manqu Inca knew that mutated viruses flourished in the alpaca of Wakapathtay, that the viruses infected the Inca after they ate the meat, and that the Sacred Cave held many of his people – *transformed and on the shelf, but still alive.* Manqu Inca wanted to die among these people, the strangest victims of the Spanish conquest.

"Do the alpaca grazing in Wakapathtay possess something in their meat that gives strength to these pots?" she asks.

Maras shakes his head. *No no no no no no . . .*

She twists her body and sits on his unbroken arm. Her free hand claps the bottom of the jar, and half the stew plops onto his face. She smears it into his wide, wide mouth.

His head slams from one side to the other. The gold ear plugs rattle, and tomatoes drip from the gold condor wings in his nose.

She rips strips from his alpaca tunic, the color of bloody sun. She ties his wrists behind his back and his ankles behind his body. He's face down on the clay-red rock.

She places a huge pot next to Maras's head. His lidless eyes weep. He knows what she's going to do.

The pot is from the time of the people who built the temple Collud, ancestors of Chicya's ancestors, and has a spider's head, a feline's mouth, and a bird's beak. It is the spider god, who fills its webs with decapitated human heads.

She dumps stew on the spider god to revive him, then thrusts the last alpaca chunk into Maras' mouth. She will return and force more meat into Maras. He will be a freak. And then she'll go away from here, far away, and Maras will become pottery with a broken arm –

Unless the spider god takes care of him first.

She imagines the humiliation and torture endured by the spider god time and time again fighting for Maras.

"What did you get out of it?" she demands. "Money? Power? The people thought you provided the true Inca way. They ate your special Wakapathtay stew, thinking it medicine that kept them from turning into monsters. A terrible thought hits her. "They paid you to watch those fights, didn't they? They paid you in hopes you would protect them from becoming freaks. Just like Narya, who cooked your guinea pig so the Inca gods, through you, wouldn't turn her into a monstrosity."

He sputters. She knows that she's right. Money. Greed. Lies. Extortion. The human way.

"You're so common," she spits.

"And you," he manages, "what are you that's so special?"

She knew the answer as soon as she entered the Sacred Cave. It was in the old, old air. Now, she sucks in a deep breath, and heat races through her limbs and into her brain.

"I'm an ancient," she says. "I'm the Inca before there was an Inca. I'm beyond known time. I'm . . ." she pauses. "I'm the Old One." Her words are in the ancient Quechua language but with their original pronunciations. "*Q'ulsi pertaggen cantatro'f'l Cthulhu fh'thagn. Q'ulsi perhagen n'cree'b'f'w'l.*"

"You're nothing! You're an orphan!" he snarls.

"No," she says quietly. "I'm not an orphan. I'm not a *qzwck'l'zhadst.* You see, I never had parents. People found me as a baby. Who were my parents, Maras? Do you know? Does anyone know?"

He's beyond answering. Behind his eyes lurks madness.

She has him on the edge.

"You see, Maras, I never fit in. I never cared about being alive. Death was nothing to me. I've been biding my time, waiting for the right moment. I never understood until now."

A thread slinks from the bottom of the spider god's abdomen. Maras shrinks back, eyes bulging.

Let him think she's brought the spider god back to life. Let him think it's going to devour him or spin him, dead, into a web. What does she care?

These creatures are irrelevant. Maras, Cisco and Luis, Bachue and Cava, Narya, the villagers—

All of them, *irrelevant.*

No more fighting. No more alpaca stew. They will all turn to pots. They're all going on the shelf. Forever.

Her way is the only way. Inca before there was Inca . . . *Old One.*

The sky will hold nothing but tarnished clouds. The world will groan. The Sacred Cave will be hers. The Others will come, and together, they'll spend eternity here.

With "Umbilicus" **Damien Angelica Walters** "wanted to subvert the traditional mythos by writing a Lovecraftian story based on the maiden, mother, and crone archetype instead of an entity like Cthulhu. I asked myself: What if Cthulhu wasn't the only deity who slumbered beneath the waves? What would happen if another, older, deity woke, determined to take her rightful place? What might she unleash upon the world?"

Her work has appeared in various anthologies and magazines, including *The Year's Best Dark Fantasy & Horror*, *Year's Best Weird Fiction*, *Cassilda's Song*, *Nightmare*, *Black Static*, and *Apex*. *Sing Me Your Scars*, a collection of short fiction, was released in 2015 from Apex Publications, and *Paper Tigers*, a novel, in 2016 from Dark House Press.

Umbilicus
Damien Angelica Walters

———

Tess places the last of Emily's clothes in a box, seals it with a strip of packing tape, and brushes her hands on her shorts. Stripped of the profusion of books and games and art supplies, Emily's room is a ghost.

The box goes into a corner in the living room with the other things earmarked for donation. In her own bedroom, she stands before the wall papered with newspaper clippings, notes, torn pages from old books, and turns away just as quickly, pinching the bridge of her nose between her thumb and index finger.

The small air-conditioning unit in the window growls like a cat that swallowed a dozen angry hornets; a similar sound sticks in her throat. Everyone has to say goodbye eventually, her mother said once from a hospital bed, three weeks before her heart failed for the last time.

With her mouth set in a thin line, Tess begins to remove the thumb tacks, letting the paper seesaw to the floor, catching glimpses of the pictures – a school photo with an awkward smile, her own face caught in grief's contortion, a stretch of beach – and the words – *depression in children, somnambulism, unexplained juvenile behavior* – and the head-lines – *Suicide? . . . Not Sleepwalking, Her Mother Says . . . Body Not Found, Presumed Dead . . . Presumed Dead . . . Presumed Dead . . .*

She drops the thumbtacks from her palm onto her dresser and rips the clippings free, tearing them into pieces before she lets them go. When the wall is nothing more than a study of pinprick holes in plaster and the floor a mess of tattered white, she grabs a dustpan and brush and a garbage bag. Sweeps everything in, refusing to pause even when Emily's face appears.

Utter madness to try and find reason in the unexplainable, and Tess knew, without a doubt, she'd never find an answer. Let the doctors claim Emily was depressed – ignoring everything Tess told them to the contrary – and committed suicide, but they weren't there that night. They didn't see what happened, the way the ocean receded—

(the shape in the water)

—the way Emily kept walking, murmuring a word too low for Tess to discern.

She pulls a face. Ties a knot in the bag. Emily was only seven years old; the word *suicide* wasn't even in her vocabulary.

Tess tosses the bag near the front door on her way into the kitchen to wash her hands. On the living room television, a commercial is listing side effects for a medicine to treat high cholesterol, side effects the stuff of nightmares. Background noise, its only purpose to swallow the silence.

"Mommy?"

The voice is muffled, but Tess would know it anywhere. She whirls around, soap bubbles dripping from her fingers, her heart racing madness in the bone-cage of her ribs, and pads into the living room.

"Mommy?"

Now it's coming from behind; Tess races back into the kitchen. "Emily?"

Nothing but the rush of water, then she hears another voice, too low to decipher, speaking under – inside – the water. Her stomach clenches.

Not possible, not possible at all – Emily is gone and all the pennies in the world tossed into a fountain won't bring her back – but Tess grips the edge of the sink hard enough to hurt. "Emily?" she whispers.

Only water splashing on stainless steel answers. Reason kicks in; Tess turns the faucet off and steps back from the sink, wiping her hands on a dishtowel. Through tears, she glares at the boxes piled in the corner – a sandcastle built by sorrow's hands.

From the kitchen window, she can see a small playground just beyond the parking lot. Two children are on the jungle gym, their mothers sitting on a nearby bench. Occam's Razor, Tess thinks. Sound travels in odd ways.

With one hand in her pocket and the other clutching Emily's favorite teddy bear, Tess takes the narrow pathway leading to the beach. Her apartment, the second floor of a converted house, is far away from the tourist trade, and the night is quiet and calm.

The soft whisper of her footsteps in the sand is masked by the susurration of the night waves kissing the shore. Once upon a time she loved the ocean, loved the feel of sand on her skin, loved the sound and smell of the surf – it's the reason she moved to Ocean City the summer after her nineteenth birthday, why she stayed after David took off, leaving her with no warning, no money, and three-month old Emily – but now it's a thing to be tolerated, endured.

She stops well above the waterline, afraid if the sea comes in contact with her skin she'll follow it out, screaming for Emily as she did that night a long year ago. Only this time she won't get knocked back to shore; this time, the waves will pull her in, and she'll let them.

After a time, she lifts the teddy bear to her nose, breathes in, but it no longer smells of Emily, merely terrycloth and fiberfill.

"I'm sorry, punkin. I'm so sorry," she says, her voice hitching. "I love you." She hurls the teddy bear as far as she can; it bobs on the surface for several long moments, and then the waves suck it down.

Clouds scuttle across the moon, turning the ocean black. The weight of the air changes, a pressure Tess senses in her ears. The thunder of the waves striking the shore amplifies, and a stabbing cramp sends Tess doubling over. Her vision blurs, the salt tang of the ocean floods her nose and mouth, and a sensation of swelling fills her abdomen.

She staggers back. Presses both hands to her belly, feels the expected flatness there. The clouds shift again; something dark and impossibly large moves deep in the water, and she flees from the beach without a backward glance.

It's all in your head, she tells herself. All in your head.

When she gets close to the apartment, the bright end of a lit cigarette glows from the shadows of the front porch. Tess waves a still-shaking hand; the orange glow makes a responding arc, but neither she nor her neighbor says a word.

Tess slides a box into the trunk of her car, wipes sweat from her brow, and heads back to the house. Her neighbor is sitting in her usual spot – the battered lawn chair in the corner of the porch – with a lit cigarette in her hand and a glass by her side. Gauging by the bright sheen in Vicky's eyes, the liquid in the glass isn't water.

"What are you up to, lady?" Vicky asks, her smile turning her face into a tissue paper crumple.

"Getting ready to go to the thrift store to drop some stuff off." Tess cups her elbows in her palms, hunches her shoulders. "I finally boxed up some of Em's things."

Vicky nods. Exhales a plume of smoke. "Good on you. It might help, you know?"

"I hope so. I kept putting it off, kept thinking I should leave everything the way it was, just in case, but I guess I'm ready to try and let her go. That's why I went to the beach the other night, to—

(see the shape in the water)

—say goodbye." She touches her stomach. Swallows the unease.

"Grief is a bitch of a monster." Vicky stubs out her cigarette in the over-flowing ashtray. "You think it'll kill you, but it's a hell of a lot more clever than that because it lets you live. Only thing you can do is give it the finger and move on as best you can. Only thing anyone can do." She shakes her glass, rattling the slivers of ice inside. "I need a refill. Want one?"

"How about a rain check for later?"

"Absolutely."

Tess strips off her dusty clothes in front of her full-length mirror. She's all arms and legs and narrow hips and small breasts and her belly has no loose skin, no "pooch" that says a child once sheltered there.

Morning sickness lingering well into her second trimester and a waitressing job kept her from gaining too much weight, but now she wishes she'd gorged on ice cream and chocolate and gained fifty pounds, slashing her skin with stretch marks in the process and turning her breasts to sagging teardrops.

She pushes out her stomach, runs her hand over the curve, remembering the fluttering of butterfly wings and later, the heel of a tiny foot, the point of an elbow.

The air goes heavy and thick with the smell of the ocean. Beneath her palms, her skin ripples, and she yanks her hands away. She feels the tremor again, from the inside, and makes a sound low in her throat, then both the smell and the sensation vanish. Frowning, she pokes her abdomen with her fingertips and doesn't stop until her skin is patterned with tiny red marks like overlapping scales.

When Tess stands, the world swims around her, and she grabs the porch railing with both hands, swaying on her feet.

Vicky laughs in commiseration, not mockery. "Need some help?"

"No," Tess says, cupping one hand to her forehead, although it doesn't stop anything from moving. "I got it."

She takes each step to her apartment with careful measure, ascending one tread at a time the way Emily did as a toddler. Tess can't remember the last time she drank this much; long before she got pregnant, of that much she's sure. Thankfully, she left her door unlocked because sliding a key right-side up in the lock would require a bit more dexterity than she's currently capable of.

Not bothering to remove her clothes, she drops down on her bed, leaving one foot on the floor – she can't remember if that truly prevents a hangover or if it's an old wives' tale – and squeezes her eyes shut. The gray lure of sleep begins to tug.

"Mommy?"

The word cuts blade-sharp through the haze of alcohol, and Tess struggles to sit, her eyelids at war with her intention. Her arms and legs tingle, then her limbs elongate, her fingers and toes deform, her abdomen expands, and a slimy, brackish taste slicks her tongue. She gags, staggers from the bedroom into the bathroom, her body a peculiar, heavy weight to bear, and makes it – barely.

The alcohol and the two slices of pizza she had for dinner come up with a burning rush; she retches again and again until nothing's left but bile, and then again until even that's gone. She runs frantic hands over her arms and legs and torso to find everything the way it's supposed to be and rests her head on the edge of the bathtub, breathing hard.

She flushes the toilet and hears, "Mommy," this time from the chaos of the Coriolis swirl.

"Emily?"

An unintelligible voice – too deep, too *big*, to be Emily's – mumbles something Tess can't grasp; black clouds of octopus ink coalesce in her eyes, and she slips to the floor into darkness.

"Hair of the dog?" Vicky says with a smile.

Tess shudders. "Oh, god, no." She half-sits, half-collapses into a lawn chair and holds her water bottle against her forehead. "How much did we drink?"

Vicky shrugs. "Enough to make you laugh. Hell, you even flirted with the pizza boy."

Tess's cheeks warm. "Ugh, there's a reason I don't drink like that."

"Plenty of reasons why I do," Vicky says, her lips set into a grapefruit twist. "I lost a daughter, too, a long time ago. I was going to bring it up last night, but what's the point? We were having a good time and you seemed happy."

"What happened, if you don't mind my asking?"

"Course I don't mind. I wouldn't have brought it up otherwise. So, what happened to my daughter?" She lights a cigarette, exhales sharply. "Her boyfriend."

Tess gnaws on a cuticle.

"He beat her. She hid the bruises from me, but I knew something was wrong, and when she finally got the gumption up to leave him, he came after her. And I wasn't there to protect her." Vicky takes a long swallow from her glass. "The bastard got his a couple years later. Got jumped in prison after he mouthed off to the wrong guy. Still didn't bring Crystal back, though."

"I'm sorry."

"Me, too. For both of us. And for the record, I don't think you were lying about what you saw that night. Depression, my ass. Anyone who met Emily even once would know that child didn't have a depressed bone in her body. Damn fool doctors don't know what they're talking about most of the time."

"Thank you." Tess touches her water bottle to her forehead again, thinks about what she saw—

(the shape in the water)

—and didn't—

(the shape)

—see.

"Hell, at least your story doesn't make you a cliché or a stereotype. Never sure which one is the right word, but either way, had to be some truth before the word made sense, right?"

Tess can only nod in reply. She closes her eyes; in the shadows there the waves recede, and Emily walks into the space they left behind, and Tess almost remembers what her daughter said.

Tess wakes and she's cold, wet, standing in the shower. Although the faucet is set to hot, the water pouring down is ice, her skin is bright pink, and there's a thickness in her head as though she's been listening to someone speak for hours or for days. Her nightgown is plastered against a protruding belly; she blinks, and it's gone. Her fingers distort, turning too long with jagged fingernails that resemble lobster claws, but the image proves no more real than her stomach; when she reaches for the faucet, her hands are fine.

"Mommy?"

With a grimace, she shuts off the water. Leaves the nightgown dripping on the edge of the tub and curls up in bed, shivering. Disoriented. Scared. She hasn't walked in her sleep since she was a child.

Is this some sort of involuntary penance for thinking Emily was sleepwalking that night, even though she'd never done it before? Tess followed her, remembering how her mother always said waking up a sleepwalker was a bad thing, curious to see where she'd go, and she was only a few paces behind her. More than close enough to keep her safe.

When Emily approached the beach, Tess took her arm, intending to turn her back around, but Emily pulled free and kept walking, heading across the sand toward the water. And then the world changed, became a rubber band stretching Tess into one place and Emily into another with a huge distance between them.

As before a tsunami, the waves pulled back and they kept receding, the sea folding back on itself to reveal an endless stretch of wet sand littered with fish trapped in the throes of death, driftwood, and tangled clumps of seaweed. Tess screamed her throat raw, but Emily kept walking, and no matter how fast Tess ran, Emily remained out of reach. Between her screams, Tess heard Emily say a word (and why the hell can't she remember what Emily said?), and then the waves curled into their rightful place again and Emily was gone. In the space between, did Tess see a shape, an unknowable being, deep inside the water? Her mouth yearns to say no; her mind says an emphatic yes.

Even if the police didn't believe her, she saw *something*. It wasn't an optical illusion, as one police officer suggested, not unkindly. The media shitstorm and the blame from the legions of armchair detectives seems a distant dream now. The press was all too willing to give up when they realized Tess didn't make a good subject; she wouldn't answer their questions, wouldn't get mad and curse them out, wouldn't tear her hair and break down in hysterics. Not in front of them anyway.

Two steaming coffee mugs in hand, Tess pads downstairs, knocks on Vicky's door with her elbow. After she refills their cups a second time, Tess scrubs her face with her hands, clears her throat, and says, "I keep hearing Emily. Every time I turn on the water, I hear her saying *Mommy*." She fiddles with the drawstring on her pants, hating the quiet desperation of her words and wishing she could take them back, inhale them like cigarette smoke.

Vicky takes several sips of her coffee before she answers in a soft voice. "Well . . . You're trying to move on and you're feeling guilty about it, and Emily disappeared in the water so it makes sense you'd hear her like that."

"But it sounds so much like her."

Vicky leans forward. Fixes Tess's gaze with her own. "For a couple years, I used to see Crystal all the time. Once, I even followed a girl nearly a mile because I was convinced it was my baby. And I identified Crystal's body, I knew she was dead, but I knew it up here." She taps her forehead. "I didn't know it here." A second tap, to her chest. "Once my heart caught up, it stopped. You'll get through this part of it, too."

"Right now, I don't feel like I will. Not today or tomorrow or forever."

"But you will. One day you won't hear her, and then a little while later you'll realize you haven't heard her, and then a little while after that, you'll realize you don't need to hear her anywhere but in here." She touches her chest again.

Tess wants to believe her, but her fingers curl in and her fingernails leave half-moon bruises in her palms.

"Mommy?"

Tess's head snaps around, the washcloth falls from her hand. She places her palms on the porcelain, bends over the sink. Takes a shuddering breath. No one there, no one there, she thinks, but another sound emerges from the water, an evocative yet inhuman voice, one she knows she's heard before –*no*. She had too much to drink that night. She heard nothing then and hears nothing now.

Her belly curves, her breasts swell, her limbs are taffy caught in the pull, her mouth is salt tang and bitter.

"No," she snaps. "Do you hear me? No."

Her ears pop, and a dull throb spreads through her abdomen, radiates in a slow spiral to her back. Moaning through clenched teeth, she fumbles for the faucet.

The pain ebbs. Her stomach, her limbs, are perfectly normal, perfectly fine. She rinses away the taste of the ocean with mouthwash, hears only the normal rush of water when she turns the faucet back on.

Tess wakes in the middle of the night with her pulse racing. In her dream, she was on the beach, running toward Emily, and she stopped her before her feet met the water but when Emily turned around, she wasn't Emily but *other*, her skin the white of a deep-sea creature and cold as the Atlantic Ocean in January.

Tess turns on her bedside light and scrubs the sleep from her eyes. The sheets are gritty against her feet, and she throws back the covers – sand coats both cotton and skin. Hands clamped tight over her mouth can't keep in the shout.

*   *   *

Without curtains hanging at the windows, sunlight floods Emily's bedroom. Tess lugs in paint, brushes, and a canvas tarp, and pulls the bed toward the center of the room. From behind the headboard, something thumps to the floor; Tess retrieves the sketchbook with tears shimmering in her eyes.

From the time she could hold a crayon in a chubby fist, Emily loved to draw and while not a prodigy, her passion made up for it in spades. The first picture is her favorite dinosaur, stegosaurus; the pages that follow show more dinosaurs, a picture of Tess wearing a superhero cape, the beach at night, a second sketch of the beach with a scattering of shells, and then the beach with the waves high and arcing and a dark outline in the raised water.

Tess sinks down on the edge of the bed. The shape in the water, done in crude strokes of pencil, is not a whale or a prehistoric shark. It's alien and wrong with too many limbs, too many curves. Tess flips the page. Yet another sketch of the same, the lines more defined, darker, the likeness slightly different, but still improbable. In the next sketch, the shape has altered even more, as if Emily couldn't quite capture on paper what she wanted. Tess's fingers leave indentations in the paper. This can't be real. It can't be right.

"Who are you?" Tess says. "*What* are you?"

What she can't bring herself to say aloud: why did you take my daughter?

Tess stands on the beach, wind tossing sand into her face and twisting her nightgown around her hips. Her mouth opens but nothing escapes. Is she dreaming? Dreaming awake? She turns in a slow circle, spies the steady tracks her feet left behind.

The waves begin to recede, and she freezes in place. A dark silhouette twists beneath the changing water; pain threads through her body, the darkness moves closer, and she sees—

No. It's too much. She closes her eyes, can't bear to look. The agony seizes her tight; when it loosens its hold, Tess runs, kicking sand in wide arcs. Behind her, the waves crash upon the shore, and she hears something else beneath – a moan, a whisper.

(Emily said *Mother*. That's what she said, and Tess knew she wasn't calling out to her, wasn't referring to her in any way.)

By the time she gets to the porch, she's sobbing hard enough that her chest aches, and when Vicky grabs her arm, she shrieks.

"Tess? What's wrong? What's wrong? Talk to me. Are you okay? Are you hurt?"

Words spill from Tess's lips, and she knows they don't make sense, but she can't make them stop.

Vicky shoves a glass in her hand. "Drink."

Tess does, grateful to wash the salt from her tongue.

"Now take a deep breath and talk to me. What happened?"

"I woke up on the beach, and I saw something in the water. I saw, I don't know, I couldn't look, but I know it was there. I felt it. It was there the night Emily went into the water, too. I know it was. I didn't want to believe it, but it was there. I think it wants something from me, but I don't know what it wants. I don't know what to—"

"Shhh, take another drink."

"You don't understand. Emily saw it, too. She drew it in her sketchbook—"

Vicky presses the glass gently to her mouth. Tess drinks, this time wincing at the liquor burn.

"Okay," Vicky says. "I don't know what you thought you saw, or whether you just had a bad dream or what, but maybe you need to get away from here for a while. I know things have been rough, maybe being close to where it happened isn't good for you right now."

Tess pushes the glass back in Vicky's hand. Vicky continues to talk, and Tess responds in the right places with the right phrases while her thoughts drift elsewhere.

She sleeps on the bathroom floor with the water running. Spends the day in the kitchen with the faucet on full blast and the sketchbook in her lap. Ignores Vicky's knocks at the door.

"Why did you want my daughter?" she says over and over, the tone of her voice as foreign as the thing in Emily's sketches. "What more do you want from me?"

After the sunlight bleeds from the sky, she waits until Vicky goes back into her apartment and creeps down the stairs as quickly and quietly as possible. Her hands are shaking when she walks onto the beach, and she steps as close to the water as she dares.

"I'm here," she calls out into the wind.

The waves break and crash, break and crash. Tess steps closer.

"I'm here," she shouts. "Isn't this what you want? Goddammit, isn't this what you fucking want from me?"

The wind tears her words to ribbons. She steps into the waves, hissing at the sudden sting of cold. Like fabric gathered in a hand, the waves recede, and Tess links her fingers together, wills herself to keep still. The water withdraws even more, and a leviathan, the shape from Emily's sketchbook, undulates beneath the darkness. Goosebumps rise on her arms; her nipples go hard and painful; a shiver makes a circuit on the racetrack of her spine. The air thrums with an electric undercurrent.

A distant gaze bores into hers. A distant mind delves, tastes. An image of Emily's face flickers in her peripheral vision, flickers and breaks apart into nothing at all.

"I'll do whatever you want," Tess shrieks. "Just give me back my daughter."

Her mouth is salt and seaweed. Crab claws dig into her stomach, and she falls to her hands and knees. Her abdomen swells; something unfolds inside her, shoving razored points and spiked edges against the confines of her womb. She grips fistfuls of sand and arches her back, lets loose a keening wail.

Muffled by the water, another wail echoes her own, but Tess isn't sure if she's hearing it in her ears or only her mind. She rolls onto her back, supports herself with her elbows, and draws up her knees. The grotesque curve of her belly ripples, and as the claws dig in again, the other cries out as well, a great and terrible groaning cry.

Tess arches her back as an urge to push fills her body. She strains with all her might. And then again. The world melts into shadow and stardust, leaving only the torment inside her and the exertion of her muscles. She screams as something breaks free and falls flat on her back, panting.

Reaching under her nightgown, she expects to find ribbons of torn flesh, and although the contact makes her wince, her vulva is intact, albeit swollen, and there's nothing beneath her but sand. Her stomach is flat, but the skin is loose, elastic.

Emily emerges from the water, walking as though she's forgotten how legs work. Tess climbs to her feet, staggers forward, and then halts, her mouth in a wide O. Beneath a mottled covering of viscous liquid and traces of sand – a nightmarish mockery of lanugo – Emily's skin is sea-pale. Where once she had a navel, she now has a fleshy protuberance resembling an ornate skeleton key emerging from a lock. She blinks once, twice, and nictitating membranes roll back, revealing black eyes – shark eyes – and Tess swallows a scream. This isn't Emily, it can't be.

"Mommy?"

Tess's entire body jolts. The eyes and skin might be wrong, but the voice and smile are all Emily, yet when Tess holds out her arms, Emily steps back, not closer, and lifts her chin. Moonlight reflects in the black of her eyes, and an image comes in view: a still-swollen abdomen, pendulous breasts, vulva concealed by a thick thatch of curls, long tentacular limbs, eel-like fingers ending in claws, a dark eye emerging from tendrils of coiling hair.

Tess backs away, her hands held palm out; Emily stands, face impassive. Her lips don't move, but a deep, mellifluous voice says, "I see you, first mother of my firstborn."

Tess bites back a sob. "What, who, are you?"

"I am the mother of all, she who birthed the world and made it whole. I am all that was, and all that will be."

Emily takes her hand, and Tess hisses in a breath – Emily's skin is cold, so cold – and once again, the world melts away. Tess sees the shape, the mother, sitting atop a throne. Another being emerges from beneath the ocean floor and wrenches the mother from her place. Sand obscures a great battle, then settles to reveal black blood and lifeless limbs, and the mother, battered and bruised, crawling back to her throne. A second beast rears, rends; the mother's mouth opens in a silent scream; battle begins anew. More blood and sand and fury; endless creatures, endless battles.

Tess covers her eyes. No more. She can't bear this. Emily squeezes her hand; she reopens her eyes. Sees Emily walking on the beach and into the waves, into the mother's embrace; sees inhuman hands guiding her between two great thighs, pushing her into a cavernous womb; sees Emily floating, sleeping with her hands clasped together beneath her cheek; sees small creatures crawling from her navel to drift and grow beside her in the amniotic fluid.

Emily withdraws her hand. "Now you see," the voice, not Emily's, says. "The usurper gods are finally dead, and it is time for my children to put the world right. The birthing is over, but your work is not done. You must open the door."

"But why me? Why my daughter?"

"Because you are her first mother and she alone had the strength to answer my call."

Tess swallows hard, pushes defiance in her words. "And what will happen if I don't?"

There is a silence, a profound absence of everything, and stars glitter in the sky. Tess's fingers tremble; in the black pits of Emily's eyes, the mother quivers.

A peal of inhuman laughter slices through the quiet. "Then I will take my children back into my womb, and I will unmake the world."

In Emily's eyes, a face begins to rise to the surface, and every instinct tells Tess to avert her eyes, to run, then the face slips into the depths again. More laughter.

Emily steps forward and touches Tess's cheek. "Everything will be okay." She takes Tess's hand and places it on her belly.

Sobbing, Tess curls her hand around the umbilicus. Its pulsing warmth is unexpected, and she fights the urge to pull away. It changes, softens, wraps around her fingers. The narrow strands dance across her skin, and in the center of it all, Tess's fingertips meet a hardness. Emily's gaze, with its strange, black un-Emily eyes, locks on hers.

Panic courses through her veins. What is she going to set in motion? What if this is the end of everything?

"I love you, Mommy. I've missed you so much."

Tess sobs harder; the panic shatters. "I love you, too, punkin, with all my heart. I've missed you every single day."

Emily smiles. "But now I'm back and everything will be okay, I promise."

Tess sucks in a breath and turns the key. The umbilicus shrivels, turns the shade of an oyster shell, and falls to the sand. The weighted silence returns, hangs, and then the creak of a great doorway opening. From the water emerges a thousand, no, a hundred thousand Emilys, all black eyes and pale skin, but there is something inhuman in their faces, something painful to look upon, as though their Emily skin is nothing more than mimicry and a closer inspection will reveal the truth and send her screaming into madness.

They move with odd, liquid strides and when they pass, each pauses to pat Emily's shoulder and whisper, "Sister." Tess catches sight of jagged teeth, too many teeth, and where navels should be, they have a circular patch of translucent skin that reveals not organs, but a darkness hiding in a shifting sea. As they leave the beach, disappearing into the shadows, Tess whimpers. What are they going to do? What has she unleashed?

And how can such wrongs set anything right?

"Don't worry," Emily says. "They won't hurt you." She blinks and familiar green eyes replace the black, wraps her arms around Tess and the cold is gone, too.

Tears turn Tess's vision to a blur, and she can't speak, can only hold Emily tight, breathing her in, terrified to look too close, to see beneath the camouflage. But she has her daughter back, and that's worth everything and anything at all. No matter what, it has to be.

Some years back, **Veronica Schanoes** was having a drink with Nick Mamatas and John Langan. "They were waxing eloquent about H. P. Lovecraft," she explains. "Though I can't deny that Lovecraft has influenced my work, I couldn't relate to the exalted place he seemed to occupy, and I wondered if the difference could be ascribed to gender. More to the point, I made a sweeping generalization rather off-handedly: 'Lovecraft does nothing for me,' I said. 'That wasn't the horror the girls were passing around in fifth grade. V. C. Andrews is to girls what Lovecraft is to boys.'

"Of course, I was wrong – plenty of women have found Lovecraft very important indeed – but I don't think I was entirely wrong. Lovecraft is the cosmic gothic (how insignificant and futile a thing is man!); Andrews is the domestic gothic (the call is coming from *inside the house!*), and of course the resonance of those categories is highly gendered. So what I have done in my piece is to try to take Lovecraftian themes (monstrous generation, inherited guilt, the horror of the Other) and reconfigure them as domestic gothic, using Lovecraft's own life and predilections. These themes are of course treated by Andrews in the domestic gothic – the monstrosity of one's origin (incest), how one bears the guilt for the sins of one's forbears, and the horror of the Other when the Other is uncomfortably close to being oneself. In this piece, I wonder about Lovecraft's own monstrous generation; about the racist horrors that founded the United States and what they mean to someone who saw himself as an avatar of eighteenth-century America; the horror of the Other that took the form of Lovecraft's anti-Semitism, and what that means to me, as a twenty-first-century Jew in New York City.

"In my book, true horror is already inside the house."

Schanoes is a writer and scholar living in New York City. Her fiction has most recently appeared on *Tor.com* and in *The Doll*

Collection, edited by Ellen Datlow, and *Queen Victoria's Book of Spells*, edited by Ellen Datlow and Terri Windling. She is an Associate Professor in the Department of English at Queens College-CUNY, and her first book, a monograph about feminist revisions of fairy tales called *Fairy Tales, Myth, and Psychoanalytic Theory: Feminism and Retelling the Tale* appeared from Ashgate Publishing in 2014.

Variations on Lovecraftian Themes
Veronica Schanoes

1. Monstrous Generation

By 1898, Winfield Scott Lovecraft had been in the Butler hospital in Providence, Rhode Island, for five years, ever since a delusional breakdown occurring in Chicago during April 1893. His delusions were paranoid in nature, and included the persistent beliefs that men – notably black men – were violating his wife, that his food was being poisoned, and that his belongings were being stolen by hospital attendants, who were understood to be his enemies. (Given the treatment those with persistent mental illness receive all too often in such facilities even today, this last may not have been so far-fetched.)

On his death certificate, his demise was attributed to "general paresis."

General paresis was first identified as a phenomenon in 1822, and was originally believed to be a psychological disorder arising from an innate weakness in the sufferer's character. By 1857, the possibility had been raised that it was in fact an effect of late-stage syphilis, but it was not until 1913 that this hypothesis was confirmed, when Hideyo Noguchi demonstrated the presence of the syphilis spirochete in the brains of the afflicted.

Noguchi himself was diagnosed with syphilis in 1913, after a few years of unethical human experimentation. He died, however, of yellow fever that same year.

Between 1857 and 1913, however, despite the medical community's uncertainty, the specter of syphilis could not be dismissed. We now know syphilis to be caused by the bacterium *Treponema palledum*, a spirochete, and the disease's progression can be divided into four stages. Spirochetes are shaped like microscopic corkscrews, and move by twisting and boring. Syphilis is, the vast majority of the time, sexually transmitted.

I expect you already knew that last part.

Primary syphilis usually occurs around five weeks after exposure to the bacterium, when a chancre – a firm, painless lesion – forms at the point of contact. In men, this is usually the penis.

Secondary syphilis develops a couple of months later and presents as a rash, which can be red or white, and is usually raised. The rash may occur anywhere on the body, but it usually erupts on the palms of the hands and soles of the feet. This stage can also involve fever, sore throat, weight loss, and hair loss. More severe symptoms are also possible.

After this, the disease goes dormant. This may occur early (prior to a year after infection) or late (after a year). During this period, the sufferer is asymptomatic – no doubt a relief.

Latency can last up to thirty years.

A lot can happen in thirty years. A man can marry, father a son. One is less contagious during latency, and one's wife might escape infection, one's son avoid the congenital syphilis that deformed and blinded Gerard de Lairesse, remembered for his painting as well as his theory of art, whose deformities were immortalized by Rembrandt.

A man might die in the course of thirty years.

But Winfield Scott Lovecraft did not die during the latent phase of syphilis.

General paresis is a feature of tertiary stage syphilis, rarely seen in the developed world nowadays, thanks to antibiotics. It involves psychotic delusions that appear quite suddenly and unmistakably. Concentration and short-term memory are affected, and social inhibitions are lost.

In Lovecraft *père*'s case, he was in Chicago when he burst into the common room of the boarding house in which he was staying shouting that "a Negro and two white men" were upstairs violating his wife.

There are physical symptoms as well – pupils that do not respond to light; a loss of the motor control needed to speak; tremors; seizures; and cachexia – a wasting syndrome. By this stage, the progress of the disease can be halted using antibiotics, but the damage already done cannot be reversed. Without antibiotics, death is unavoidable.

In the five years that Lovecraft spent in Butler Hospital, his son was not brought to see him, not once.

Syphilis is caused by spirochetes, bacteria. Once in a host, they replicate until they have consumed all nutrients possible, and then die. A man in the final stages of syphilis is housing multitudes of *Treponema pallidum* in his body, all moving like deadly little corkscrews through his circulatory system, dividing once every thirty hours, colonizing his tissues and fluids, until at last there is nothing left to consume.

You might think that a syphilitically psychotic father dying in a mental hospital could cast a pall over a boy, that the thought of such a parent might prey upon a young man's mind. But, if so, Lovecraft and his biographers have not made much of it, and indeed, the true cause of his father's death may never have been known by the child. Instead, Lovecraft and his chroniclers focus on Winfield's partner in monstrous generation, Sarah Susan Lovecraft, née Phillips.

An indulgent mother, was Susan, indulgent to a fault, purchasing for her son all the books, astronomy and printing equipment any young boy could wish for. Was she monstrously indulgent? Accounts oscillate between blaming her for being "oversolicitous" and castigating her for trying to "mold" young Howard according to her own desires rather than his: dressing him in curls and skirts as a small child (not actually unusual at the time), attempting to make him attend dancing lessons, and, at his initial request, inflicting violin lessons on him. Monstrous, indeed; it is so easy to blame Mother.

Apparently, after two years, the horrific experience of practicing the violin became too much for young Howard's nerves, and, on medical advice, he was allowed to quit.

Poor Mrs. Lovecraft. It seems that almost every aspect of her mothering was lacking. She and her sister danced endless attendance on the grown Howard, who presumably could have stopped it if he had wanted, bringing him milk and ferociously guarding his rest, and in return? They are held responsible for Lovecraft considering himself an invalid, frail in health and nerves. Never mind the doctor who ended the violin lessons.

But Mrs. Lovecraft did undeniably take a very strange turn as young Howard entered adolescence, convincing herself as well as him that he was hideous beyond all compare, so hideous that he should hide his face from the world at large. Strange behavior, and devastating to a growing boy, no doubt. Even stranger is that Howard wore an almost exact copy of his mother's face, and Susan had been considered a beauty.

One wonders if Susan was projecting some self-loathing onto her son.

Poor Mrs. Lovecraft, indeed. In March 1919, she followed in her husband's footsteps, entering Butler Hospital for the Insane, never again to know another home. A family friend reported Susan had spoken to her of "weird and fantastic creatures that rushed out from behind buildings and from corners at dark," and that she gave every evidence of true anxiety and fear during this confidence.

Was she haunted by her son's creations even this early, Cthulhu and his minions casting their shadows before they arrived? Or were these nightmares her own creation, her own monstrous generations, bursting from her brain to dwell in dark corners of the world around her?

She died in 1921, following a gallbladder operation.

Her son was devastated.

I wonder, with both parents breathing their last in the same asylum, with his mother's delusions (presumably) of being haunted by demonic creatures, whether Lovecraft himself ever feared such an end. Certainly enough of his characters lose their faculties as a result of forbidden, dreadful knowledge or hereditary weakness or both to suggest that madness was not beyond the scope of his imagination.

The mind can generate monsters, and then be consumed by its own creations.

Did Lovecraft, like Swift, fear becoming "dead at the top"? Surely a man so concerned with nervous strain, so given to depressive crises, must have considered the possibility.

The true threat is never external – it's not the dreadful non-Aryan immigrants flooding into the United States; it's not the inhuman alien beings, worshipped as gods, who would barely notice humanity as they crushed it. The true threat always comes from the inside, the self rising up beyond all reason, beyond even survival. In the end, the most monstrous growth is always already one's own.

2. Inherited Guilt

"Curse you, Thornton, I'll teach you to faint at what my family do."

– "The Rats in the Walls," H. P. Lovecraft

H. P. Lovecraft was born on 20 August 1890 in Providence, Rhode Island, and he considered himself the very model of a genteel American. Perhaps in this he was correct. On his mother's side, his ancestry can be traced back to John Field, one of the signatories of the Providence Covenant in the first half of the seventeenth century. Field could not actually sign, but made an X.

Like many of his characters, Lovecraft was pre-occupied with his lineage and his ancestors, many times stating his preference for the eighteenth century over the degenerate age in which he found himself.

Ah, eighteenth-century America, what wert thou?

For Lovecraft? The eighteenth century he adored was metered rhyme, neo-classical architecture, Enlightenment values of restraint and balance in all things.

But what if we were to dig more deeply into Providence's eighteenth century, ducking below the surface of self-presentation, of self-professed values?

Rhode Island had been one corner of the Atlantic Triangle trade, perhaps better known as the Atlantic slave trade. Despite a 1652 law banning slavery in the state, apparently never enforced, there were more slaves per capita in Rhode Island than in any other state in New England. Of the 600,000 Africans who were forcibly brought to North America, about 100,000 were carried in Rhode Island ships, and the state was responsible for half of all United States slave voyages.

In Rhode Island's corner of the triangle trade, molasses, produced in the West Indies with slave labor, and transformed into rum, which was then sent to West Africa and used to buy more slaves, who were then taken to the West Indies, where they were bought and forced to grow more sugar cane, which was turned into molasses and sent north to Rhode Island.

West Indies sugar plantations were particularly brutal places, where it was cheaper to work black people to death and then buy new slaves than it was to maintain slaves' lives even in the meager and appalling way done in other contexts.

Rhode Island rum was made from the sweat and lifeblood of black men, women, and children, all being deliberately murdered, faster or slower, but no less certainly. Distillation can effect marvelous transformations indeed.

I am Providence, Lovecraft wrote.

What is Providence, then, but the gothic house, built on the bones of the Wampanoag, the Narragansett, and the Niantic people killed by European disease and European settlers?

So. Consider this fable, then. We can call it "The Horror Beneath Providence."

This house – its occupants liked to speak and act as if it was as old as the bones of the Earth on which it rested, but this was only a charade. True, every surface had been lovingly distressed, genealogies carefully traced, distinctions painstakingly made between old money and new, old families and outsiders. But it was all only a show; nothing was truly old. Even the dust had been lovingly placed, particle by particle, to create the illusion of undisturbed stillness, stultifying tradition, utter respectability. In reality, nothing, not the dust, not the money, not the families, and certainly not the house, could claim a tenure of longer than a couple hundred years.

And no matter how much dust was laid down, how many rooms were constructed, how much furniture distressed, this house could never be older than that.

Into this house was born a child who loved it so much that for most of his life he rarely left it. And he believed even more completely and fervently than most of his generation in the illusion of age that his fore-bears had worked so steadily to cultivate. He felt himself older than his years would grant him and spent his happiest days rummaging in the very "oldest" cellars and basement, caressing the supposed antiquities he found there, studying the manuscript histories of this home, and working back through the plans and blueprints.

It was when he found the recipe used for dyeing the mortar holding the house's bricks in place that the child, now a youth, quirked an eyebrow. For, from what he could read in the self-consciously antique script, the mortar in its natural state was the deep red of spilled blood.

He spent yet further afternoons in the cellars, spelunking in tunnels behind barred doors and chained gates. And during these expeditions, he began to hear sounds, faintly at first, the aural equivalent of a breeze so gentle that it cannot stir even a leaf. Just whispers. Not screams. Not yet.

As he wound his way deeper into the cellars, the sounds got louder. Nasty sounds. Cruel Sounds.

The youth stuffed his ears with cotton and pressed on.

But the cotton served only to keep the sounds inside his head, where they echoed and reverberated, and soon, all that was left in his head were the sounds, suffusing every squamous cell of this brain. And the sounds inhabited every thought he had, even the tears in his eyes, so he saw the world through their haze.

And that world became narrower and narrower, even while the youth believed in the expansiveness of his vision, thought he saw himself as an infinitesimal speck in a cold and infinite cosmos, even while he proclaimed himself lord of all he surveyed, and cast a contemptuous eye over all other models of humanity as weaker, lesser, cruder, worse.

They found him, eventually, the search parties. They were not looking for him in particular, but they found him nonetheless. Their peregrinations were the purposeful journeys of detectives re-examining cold cases, recognizing as murders deaths long dismissed as in the inevitable course of nature.

And they found the youth, now ossified into middle age. He was sitting on a throne built of human bone, his feet propped upon the dying. Blood ran down his face, out of his mouth, and onto his hands as he raved and gibbered, proclaiming himself the pinnacle of humanity and evolution, the society from which he sprang the acme of civilization.

Around him the flies buzzed and maggots crawled.

3. The New York Horror

"As for New York – there is no question but that its overwhelming Semitism has totally removed it from the American stream. Regarding its influence on literary and dramatic expression – it

> is not so much that the country is flooded with Jewish authors, as that Jewish publishers determine just which of our Aryan writers shall achieve print and position . . . Taste is insidiously moulded along non-Aryan lines – so that, no matter how intrinsically good the resulting body of literature may be, it is a special, rootless literature which does not represent us."
>
> – H. P. Lovecraft, 1933

I write and publish about Jews. Most of my protagonists, unless otherwise specified, are Ashkenazi Jews. Well, why should the goyim have all the fantastic, the speculative, the future imperfect? My editors have mostly been Jewish, too.

Are my sensibilities out of touch with those of true Americans?

I suppose so. Certainly John Rocker of the Cleveland Indians thought so when he told *Sports Illustrated*: "Imagine having to take the 7 Train to the ballpark looking like you're riding through Beirut next to some kid with purple hair, next to some queer with AIDS, right next to some dude who just got out of jail for the fourth time, right next to some twenty-year-old mom with four kids. It's depressing . . . The biggest thing I don't like about New York are the foreigners. You can walk an entire block in Times Square and not hear anybody speaking English. Asians and Koreans and Vietnamese and Indians and Russians and Spanish people and everything up there. How the hell did they get in this country?"

I used to live on the 7 line; I used to have purple hair. I don't have AIDS, but I've known plenty of queers who do. And when I used to live in Philly I'd go entire days without hearing anybody speaking anything but English, and I found it depressing.

Whenever a politician starts rabbiting on about "real Americans," I know that whatever they're about to say is going to be completely antithetical to the values I was raised to hold dear.

I love New York City more than I can say, but more and more I wonder if the city I know and love, the city in which I grew up, the city

I am a part of, even exists anymore. Inflation and gentrification – maybe that's the real America.

> "The population [of New York City]is a mongrel herd with repulsive Mongoloid Jews in the visible majority, and the coarse faces and bad manners eventually come to wear on one so unbearably that one feels like punching every god damn bastard in sight."
>
> – H. P. Lovecraft, 1931

> "Although he once said he loved New York and that henceforth it would be his 'adopted state,' I soon learned that he hated it and all its 'alien hordes.' When I protested that I too was one of them, he'd tell me that I 'no longer belonged to those mongrels.' *'You are now Mrs. H. P. Lovecraft!'"*
>
> – Sonia Davis, *The Private Life of H. P. Lovecraft*

Yes, yes, Lovecraft married a Jewish woman. I'm not surprised. I'm sure she wasn't like all those other Jews. Even so, they had a very traditional Ashkenazi marriage, with Lovecraft, hopeless at earning a living, playing the gentleman scholar-writer, while Sonia did the dirty work of trade to keep them both solvent and fed.

So the brilliant princeling shouldn't have to dirty his hands with anything but ink.

There is something very Jewish about Lovecraft's biography, isn't there? The only child, the coddled, cosseted boychik raised by the domineering mother. No surprise at all that he married Sonia Greene. The real question, as far as I'm concerned, is why on Earth she married him.

Internalized anti-Semitism must be a real bitch.

Either way, the marriage dissolved after a few years.

I can't imagine why.

Lovecraft's thoughts on miscegenation and intermarriage are perhaps revealed nowhere more than in "The Dunwich Horror," when the half-human Wilbur Whateley is referred to by the townsfolk of Dunwich as "Lavinny's black brat" and special mention is made of his wide lips and "crinkly hair." This demonic creature grows at a monstrous rate, and reaches full "manhood" at thirteen.

There's a lot to be said about who gets to be an innocent child in the United States, and who is considered grown and dangerous.

Wilbur is not, however, the eponymous Dunwich Horror, an inhuman repulsive monster who shocks onlookers by crying out for help in a human voice, in English, even, as the heroes of the story destroy it.

In the end, Henry Armitage, an "aged scholar" explains that the horror they just dispatched was Wilbur's twin brother, but that "it looked more like the father."

Robert M. Price notes similarities between the portrayal of Wilbur and Lovecraft's own identity, which goes to show the projection essential to racism.

Just as well, I think, that Lovecraft and Sonia had no children.

"My gawd – what a filthy dump! . . . damn me if I ever saw anything like the sprawling sty-atmosphere of N.Y.'s lower East Side. We walked – at my suggestion – in the middle of the street, for contact with the heterogeneous sidewalk denizens, spilled out of their bulging brick kennels as if by a spawning beyond the capacity of the places, was not by any means to be sought. At times, though, we struck peculiarly deserted areas – these swine have instinctive swarming movements, no doubt, which no ordinary biologist can fathom. Gawd knows what they are . . . a bastard mess of stewing mongrel flesh without intellect, repellent to eye, nose, and imagination – would to heaven a kindly gust of cyanogen could asphyxiate the whole gigantic abortion, end the misery, and clean out the place."

– H. P. Lovecraft, 1922

I do not like H. P. Lovecraft, and I doubt he would have liked me.

I am the great-great-granddaughter of four and the great-grand-daughter of two of those Lower East Side denizens he had wished would be gassed (an anti-Semite ahead of his time, was Lovecraft), the fifth generation in my family of the pushy, secular New York City Jews he so despised, and I am currently creating the sixth. Not one of us takes kindly to such statements as the one above.

A friend, a specialist, has recently done genealogical work for me, tracing parts of my family back to the late eighteenth century. One result is that I now know precisely the towns my ancestors came from, and so I know what happened to the Jews who remained in those towns in Eastern Europe.

In Klevan, where my father's mother's family was from, Ukrainian gentiles were all too happy to point out to the SS in 1941 the houses of the Jews. About 28 per cent of the Jews of Klevan – seven hundred people – were murdered during the first days of the invasion and occupation. The corpses were left in the street for dogs and pigs for three days, at which point the surviving Jews were made to take the bodies of their comrades to the local synagogue. Once the bodies were inside, the Germans burned the synagogue to the ground. Later, all Jewish men were ordered to report for work detail to the local castle, where the army murdered 1,160 more. Out of a local population of 2,500 Jews, 1,860 were murdered in 1941. That is about three out of every four. My grandmother's parents had made it safely to Chicago decades earlier, but my grandmother remembered into her final years when letters to cousins stopped receiving answers.

My father's father's family was from Zhitomir, which had been a bustling center of Jewish life and culture. This was where Himmler set up his headquarters during the German invasion of the USSR. In September 1941, at four one morning, Ukrainian militiamen broke down the doors in the recently created ghetto and drove Jewish families out into waiting trucks. The trucks were driven a ways from the city, where POWs had dug giant pits, and 5,145 Jewish men, women, and children were registered, stripped, and shot. Their confiscated belongings were handed over to city officials to be distributed to their gentile neighbors. Again, my grandfather's parents had taken their children (my grandfather not among them – he was the baby of the family and born in the United States) and left decades earlier. They had, however, been there for the 1905 pogrom, when only co-ordinated preparation for self-defense kept Jewish casualties down to twenty-nine dead and 150 wounded.

> "[Hitler's] vision is of course romantic and immature, and colored with a fact-ignoring emotionalism . . . There surely is an actual Hitler peril – yet that cannot blind us to the honest rightness of the man's basic urge . . . I repeat that there is a great and pressing need behind every one of the major planks of Hitlerism . . . The crazy thing is not what Adolf wants, but the way he sees it and starts out to get it. I know he's a clown, but by God, I *like* the boy!"
>
> – H. P. Lovecraft, September 1933

By September 1933, Hitler's policies toward the Jews were clear. Germany had already seen a series of attacks on Jewish businesses, professionals, and synagogues. Hitler had declared a national boycott of Jewish businesses; Jews were legally excluded from a number of professions and forbidden to practice. Those of mixed parentage – or grandparentage – were legally pronounced Jewish, and Jews were attacked economically as well as physically. I'm not sure that "romantic" is the word I would have chosen, but I suppose it's technically accurate insofar as the rise of romantic nationalism in Germany in the early nineteenth century had also resulted in a wave of anti-Semitism.

> "Here [among the Orthodox] exist assorted Jews in the absolutely unassimilated state, with their ancestral beards, skull-caps, and general costumes – which makes them very picturesque, and not nearly so offensive as the strident, pushing

Jews who affect clean shaves and American dress. In this particular section . . . there are far less offensive faces than in the general subways of the town – probably because most of the pushing commercial Jews are from another colony where the blood is less pure."

– H. P. Lovecraft, 1924

There is nothing so offensive as a strident, pushing Jew who affects American dress while taking the subways to and fro, I suppose.

As it turns out, I am the New York horror. I do indeed look a good deal like my father. And I am beautiful.

Acknowledgements

"A Clutch" © 2016 Laird Barron. Original to this volume.

"I Believe That We Will Win" © 2016 Nadia Bulkin. Original to this volume.

"The Sea Inside" © 2016 Amanda Downum. Original to this volume.

"Those Who Watch" © 2016 Ruthanna Emrys. Original to this volume.

"An Open Letter to Mister Edgar Allan Poe, from a Fervent Admirer" © 2016 Estate of Michael Shea. Original to this volume.

"Deep Eden" © 2016 Richard Gavin. Original to this volume.

"In the Sacred Cave" © 2016 Lois H. Gresh. Original to this volume.

"Introduction: Who, What, When, Where, Why . . ." © 2016 Paula Guran. Original to this volume.

"In Syllables of Elder Seas" © 2016 Lisa L. Hannett. Original to this volume.

"It's All the Same Road in the End" © 2016 Brian Hodge. Original to this volume.

"The Peddler's Tale, Or, Isobel's Revenge" © 2014 Caitlín R. Kiernan. A version of this story was privately published in *Sirena's Digest 95*.

"Outside the House, Watching for the Crows" © 2016 John Langan. Original to this volume.